SOVIET MiG. AMERICAN TOMCAT.
BATTLE FOR THE NORTHERN SKY.

0940 hours Zulu
Fulcrum Leader
Northwest of the Faeroe Islands

''Break left! Break left!'' Terekhov screamed the order into the radio. Captain Second Rank Stralbo, commander of the second MiG squadron, was completely outclassed. Luckily the American cowboy had already used up his infrared homing missiles. Two long bursts of gunfire hadn't scored any hits on Stralbo yet, but it was only a matter of time. Terekhov rolled his plane into position above and behind the American, still shouting for Stralbo to break to the left so he could line up his shot.

The targeting diamond centered on the F-14 and turned red. The locking tone sounded in his ear. But Terekhov held his fire because Stralbo couldn't break free. It was as if the American pilot had a charmed life.

Suddenly the Tomcat banked away, aware of the threat. Terekhov stabbed at the firing stud and a missile streaked off . . .

Books in the CARRIER series from Jove

CARRIER

Book Four
FLAME-OUT

Keith Douglass

J

JOVE BOOKS, NEW YORK

CARRIER 4: FLAME-OUT

A Jove Book / published by arrangement with
the author

PRINTING HISTORY
Jove edition / December 1992

ISBN: 0-515-10994-0

Jove Books are published by The Berkley Publishing Group,
200 Madison Avenue, New York, New York 10016.
The name "JOVE" and the "J" logo
are trademarks belonging to Jove Publications, Inc.

PRINTED IN THE UNITED STATES OF AMERICA

10 9 8 7 6 5 4 3 2 1

1827 hours Zulu (1527 hours Zone)
Intruder 507
Over the North Atlantic

Rain spattered the front of the cockpit, loud even against the drone of the A-6E Intruder's two Pratt and Whitney turbojets. Bleed air blasted the rain away from the canopy, but the visibility wasn't good. Not good at all . . .

"Perfect end to a perfect mission," Bannon muttered aloud. It was true. The Intruder squadron off U.S.S. *Thomas Jefferson* had been practicing antiship attacks against the frigate *Gridley* for two hours until worsening weather had finally made further operations impossible. Bannon had made four mock passes against her, but each time the burly man in the Bombardier/Navigator's position beside him had found some fault with the way he handled the plane. And each time Intruder 507 had ended up missing the target. He felt like a newbie aviator back at flight school in Pensacola again.

The weather had clamped down over the carrier deck just in time to screw up their landing approach, of course. That had slowed down the recovery cycle, especially after Lieutenant Commander Anderson had been waved off on two attempts. The delay had kept them circling far longer

1

than he liked, and Bannon had been worrying about the fuel level for the past ten minutes. Ordinarily he would have put in a request to tank up from an orbiting KA-6D tanker, but he didn't want to elicit yet another scathing comment from his companion. Now he was regretting the decision not to ask for a shot at the "Texaco."

"Watch your angle of attack, kid," Commander Isaac Greene growled. He was second in command of the carrier's Air Wing, and he was outspoken, quick-tempered, harsh in his judgment of his subordinates. It didn't help that "Jolly Greene" was a genuine hero, a veritable legend aboard the *Jefferson,* who had earned the right to criticize inexperienced young aviators a dozen times over. As CO of VA-89, the Death Dealers, Greene had led the famous Alpha Strikes of the carrier's Pacific cruise two years back—over North Korea, Thailand, India—before reaching his new post as Deputy CAG. "Save the comments for after we're down on the deck," Greene added.

Now Bannon was part of VA-89 . . . and Greene, with his long-standing proprietary interest in the Death Dealers, was inclined to ride all of the Intruder pilots in his charge. But sometimes it seemed as if the Deputy CAG had a particular wish to make Bannon's life a special slice of Hell.

Bannon felt himself tensing up. He tried to force himself to relax, but it didn't work.

"Aye, aye, sir," Bannon responded. He tried to correct his approach, but it was hard to tell if he had compensated enough. Lashing rain and low clouds and the frustration of the long, fruitless exercise were all combining to sap his confidence.

He glanced across at Greene, but the commander didn't seem to be aware of Bannon's uncertainty. "You're going to need to show me a hell of an improvement before I'm satisfied with your flying, kid," he said inexorably. "The

Intruder's a precision flying machine, but you drive it like a damned truck."

"Intruder Five-oh-seven." The call on the radio was matter-of-fact, almost bored. The Landing Signals Officer had already brought in half a dozen Intruders from the training run, and sounded ready to come in out of the weather. "On line, slightly to the left. Three-quarter mile. Call the ball."

Bannon squinted through the canopy, trying to spot something, *anything,* through the washed-out gray drizzle that made sea and sky look the same. The shape of the carrier was sketchy in the mist. How the hell was he supposed to spot the Fresnel lens that was supposed to help guide his final approach?

But he finally caught sight of it. "Five-oh-seven, Intruder ball," he reported on the radio. "Zero point nine." Nine hundred pounds of fuel left. A bolter now would leave him breathing fumes by the time he was ready for another pass.

"Attitude," the LSO said quietly. The best LSOs in the fleet were the ones who avoided too much instruction when they were bringing a plane in to the deck. Lieutenant George "Hacker" Hackenberg was one of the best.

But Greene, on the other hand, was all too free with advice and criticism. "*Come on,* kid," he amplified. "Your angle's all wrong! Pull up the nose, for God's sake, and line her up!"

Bannon gritted his teeth and corrected more. He was coming down at too steep an angle . . .

"Nose up," the LSO said. "Nose up."

The controls seemed sluggish, slow to respond. Panic gripped him. He pulled back . . . back . . .

Ahead the red lights around the Fresnel lens lit up suddenly, while the LSO screamed in his ear. "Wave off! Wave off!"

He rammed the throttles forward just as the wheels

touched the deck. The Intruder lifted again, but too slow . . . There was something wrong, but he didn't know what, and he couldn't make the airplane respond.

The wheels touched again. Then the Intruder was moving sideways, a sickening, wrenching motion. Bannon fought the skid, but the plane continued its uncontrolled slide across the rain-washed deck. He had a confused impression of a line of parked planes ahead . . .

"Eject! Eject!" he shouted, his hand already closing on the handle. The canopy blasted clear and the ejection seat tried to ram his spine through the top of his head. He was spinning up, up, over the side of the carrier, his chute blossoming above him. It snagged on some projection just as the Intruder slammed into a parked Tomcat and exploded.

The fireball blossoming on the deck lit up the overcast sky, and the roar was deafening. Bannon flinched instinctively from the sound, but the entangling shroud lines held him fast. He shook his head to clear the ringing from his ears, and thought he could hear the klaxons on the flight deck blaring their alarm.

Vaguely, Bannon noticed another chute spread out in the water below him. So Jolly Green had cleared the side of the carrier. Probably, he thought bitterly, the veteran wouldn't allow anything so unheroic as getting caught dangling over the ocean by his chute to happen to him.

Then he passed out.

He didn't know how much time passed before he awakened again, but he was back on deck and being lifted carefully onto a stretcher by a pair of corpsmen. Through waves of dizziness he heard roaring flames and the shouts of Damage Control technicians fighting the fire, and over it all the sound of a Search and Rescue chopper's rotors.

They were strapping him in to the stretcher when Hackenberg's worried face appeared behind the two corpsmen. "What's the word, Doc?" the lieutenant asked.

"Looks like he was just shaken up a little," one of the corpsmen replied, adjusting the strap across Bannon's chest.

"How about Commander Greene? Where's he?" Hackenberg asked.

The other one shook his head. "No joy, Lieutenant. SAR copter couldn't get him. He just sank before they could get to him. Sorry . . ."

Bannon struggled against the straps. It didn't seem possible . . . it wasn't *right*. How had he lived when Jolly Green hadn't?

"Take it easy, sir," one of the corpsmen said. "Easy. Everything's okay."

But Bannon knew better. Commander Greene was dead . . . and it was his fault. All his fault . . .

Darkness claimed him.

CHAPTER 1
Monday, 9 June 1997

2234 hours Zulu (2034 hours Zone)
Tomcat 109, Mercury Flight
Over the North Atlantic

"Mercury Leader, this is Mercury Two. I'm disengaging now."

Commander Matthew Magruder, running name "Tombstone," checked his fuel gauge and eased back on the Tomcat's throttle. "Roger that, Two," he said, trying to keep the anxious edge out of his voice. "Hope you left some for me."

Over the radio he heard Lieutenant Gary "Kos" Koslosky chuckle. "Don't worry, Commander. I'm just a social drinker."

The young pilot's casual tone made Magruder frown. His F-14 was down to less than a thousand pounds of fuel, which would keep him aloft for no more than fifteen minutes. Here in the middle of the North Atlantic, a hundred and fifty miles from the carrier deck that was the only place the Tomcat could land, Tombstone didn't like joking about something so critical.

"Mercury Leader, this is Darkstar," the tanker pilot's voice came over the radio. "Mercury Two is clear. Bring her in."

Tombstone extended the Tomcat's refueling probe and eased the massive jet into position. The KA-6D loomed above and ahead, a silhouette against the starlit night sky. Behind the tanker, the refueling basket trailed along at the end of a fifty-foot hose, almost invisible except for the tiny circular constellation of running lights that showed the mouth of the hose. In the turbulence the basket floated from side to side, making it difficult to line up on the small target.

The Tomcat rose slowly, smoothly, as Tombstone manipulated throttle, stick, and rudder pedals to urge the aircraft closer. It was one of the most demanding maneuvers an aviator had to master, and it had been nearly two years since Magruder had been called upon to attempt a midair refueling. Darkness and fatigue and uncertain winds were all combining to test skills he hadn't practiced for all too long.

It didn't help to realize that his Radar Intercept Officer, Lieutenant (j.g.) Nicholas "Saint" Whitman, wouldn't be much help to him tonight. Whitman was young, inexperienced, a "nugget" Naval Flight Officer fresh from a Reserve Air Group. He hadn't said more than a few words since the Tomcat had first climbed from the runway at Oceana Naval Air Station hours before. Even if he broke his silence now, Tombstone wasn't sure how much he'd be able to rely on the young officer's judgment.

Tombstone bit his lip under his oxygen mask as the probe moved closer to the basket. It looked good . . . good . . .

Then, at the last possible second, the basket shifted upward about a foot and the tip of the Tomcat's probe rimmed it at the nine o'clock position. The basket tilted to one side, then slipped away, lost in the darkness above.

He cut the throttle and started carefully backing down and out from the tanker, all too aware of the dangers posed by that unseen basket. It was deceptive the way it swayed on the end of the long fuel line. Moving at close to three hundred knots, that heavy iron-mesh basket was nothing to be trifled with. If its hundred-pound weight struck the Tomcat's canopy the Plexiglas could shatter, and Magruder had no desire to risk depressurizing the fighter's cockpit at fifteen thousand feet. Flying this close to another aircraft in the dark could only compound the hazards. He'd seen a pilot lose it once during a refueling accident and slam his plane right into the tanker in the first panicked moments after the canopy was breached.

Tombstone let out a sigh as the Tomcat stabilized back where it had started in the approach position. He couldn't see the basket now. It was invisible at night outside of a range of four or five yards, despite the lights around the rim. It took experience and practice to judge an approach, particularly in the dark. He pushed the throttle forward to begin another run.

He picked up the lights of the basket on the left side of the Tomcat, and Tombstone edged over to port to line up his probe. When it was properly positioned to the right of the plane's nose he let the F-14 drift forward slowly. The basket slid along the right side of the canopy and gave a tiny clunk as the probe slipped in. Magruder felt like letting out a triumphant yell, but he didn't break his concentration. The docking process was only the beginning of the refueling operation, and there was still plenty that could go wrong.

The hose was visible outside the cockpit, marked off with yellow stripes every three feet. Proper procedure dictated that he increase his throttle to push the basket forward along the fuel line by two stripes, which would position the nose of the Tomcat about ten feet behind and ten feet below the fat-bellied Intruder tanker. A take-up reel aboard the KA-6D was supposed to reel in the slack automatically until the basket tripped the pump system and fuel began to flow. Tombstone guided the aircraft forward until the two stripes had disappeared.

He looked upward at the basket receptacle in the belly of the tanker above, a circular hole which surrounded the fuel line. On either side of the receptacle lights were mounted, one red, one green. When the green light was lit the pumps were operating, but as Tombstone squinted upward all he saw was the harsh red glare that told him the pumps were off.

"Darkstar, Mercury Leader. Light's still red," he reported.

"I copy, Mercury Leader," the tanker pilot responded. "Try bringing her forward another notch. Maybe that'll do the trick."

"Roger, Darkstar." Tombstone eased the throttle forward a little more. He could feel sweat trickling down his forehead. It took a lot of effort to keep the Tomcat precisely in the groove, and the added strain of the problem with the pumps made it that much worse. The third stripe disappeared, but the red light continued to glow above.

"Still no green, Darkstar," Tombstone said.

"Copy, Mercury One. Back out again and we'll recycle."

Once again the Tomcat dropped aft and down while the tanker crew reeled in the hose and redeployed it again. Tombstone glanced at his instrument panel and felt his throat tighten. Seven hundred pounds of fuel left. If this didn't work there was no way the Tomcat would reach the U.S.S. *Thomas Jefferson* for a safe landing. Without fuel the engines would flame out and they would have to ditch, and Magruder didn't like the thought of a night ejection over the rough waters of the North Atlantic this far from a carrier. It might take hours for an SAR helicopter to find the Tomcat's crew . . . if they were ever found at all.

"What are we going to do if we can't refuel, Mr. Magruder?" Whitman asked suddenly over the Tomcat's ICS intercom. He sounded scared . . . as scared as Tombstone felt.

Before Tombstone could answer, the tanker pilot was back on the radio. "Try it again, Mercury Leader. We're ready."

He glanced at the fuel gauge again as he applied more throttle. Six hundred pounds now. The basket appeared out of the darkness, farther to the right than he'd thought it would be. Tombstone eased the stick over and began to line up.

"Mercury Leader, this is Two," Koslosky called. "Aren't you done tanking yet, Tombstone?"

"Negative," he snapped back, cursing under his breath. The younger pilot's call had made him overcorrect. Now he had to back off or risk brushing the basket . . .

"Help me watch that damned thing, kid," he told Whitman. Even a nugget's eyes would be useful now. When a pilot started paying too much attention to watching his target instead of his controls, it was easy to screw up an approach.

"Aye, aye, sir," Saint replied. "It's looking good . . . real good now . . ." The Tomcat slid forward slowly . . .

A solid clunk signaled a good connection, and the hose rippled in a perfect sine wave from the contact. Tombstone increased power and pushed the basket forward, his eyes on the two lights by the basket receptacle. The red one was still glowing.

"Darkstar, still no green," he said.

"Sorry about that, Mercury Leader," the tanker pilot responded. "Goddamned thing must be Tango Uniform." That was maintenance slang for "tits up"—out of order. "Look, we're pretty far from the Big J. Back her off while I reverse left and we can try again."

"Negative, negative," Tombstone responded angrily. It would take two minutes to turn around, maybe longer, and he was down to less than four hundred pounds of fuel. He wasn't going to waste valuable time waiting for the tanker to get comfortable on a heading for home . . . not when every minute brought him closer to a flameout. "Let's recycle one more time, Darkstar."

"Mercury Leader, Mercury Leader, this is Domino." That was the call sign for Air Ops aboard the *Jefferson*. The voice sounded worried. Had the carrier been listening in on the channel, or had the KA-6 called on higher authority after Tombstone's demand for another try? "Say your fuel state, over."

He answered as the Tomcat backed away from the basket and watched it disappear into the gloom once again. "Point three," he replied tersely. His palms were sweaty now, and he didn't want to be reminded of his fuel state again. The probe reappeared ahead, almost dead on target, and he started forward once again. Tombstone knew this would be his last chance.

"Mercury Leader, Domino. Recommend you back away now. We don't want a flameout that close to the Kilo Alpha. Over."

Tombstone gritted his teeth but didn't answer. He wasn't going to give up yet . . .

The probe hooked up and he pushed the basket forward. It crossed the first line . . . the second . . . still no green light. Magruder muttered a curse against Murphy's Law, gremlins, and careless maintenance men and edged the throttle further forward. Another stripe disappeared . . . and another.

The Tomcat's canopy was only a few feet from the belly of the tanker, and even in the dark Tombstone thought he could see individual rivets in the fuselage.

"Darkstar, I'm pushing her all the way in," he told the pilot. "Stay frosty and keep her level."

"Roger that, Mercury Leader," the pilot replied. "Good luck and may the Force be with you." Behind the banter Tombstone knew the other pilot was as worried as he was.

The Tomcat inched forward . . .

. . . and the green light came on.

"Yes!" Tombstone whooped. He could feel the plane's weight increasing as fuel flowed into the tanks. The Tomcat started to drop back, but Magruder increased the throttle to hold his precarious position. There was no way of knowing if the avgas would continue to pump if he let the plane slip back to the normal position, and he wasn't about to try this maneuver again.

"Mercury Leader, Darkstar. Are you getting anything? Over."

"Affirmative, Darkstar," Tombstone replied. He looked down at the fuel gauge in time to see it rising above the two-hundred-pound mark. It had been a damned close call.

He concentrated on holding the Tomcat steady as the fuel continued to pump into his tanks, easing back after the gauge reported a thousand pounds to a less dangerous distance. The avgas kept flowing steadily, nearly five hundred pounds entering the Tomcat's tanks every minute. Tombstone held the aircraft in position until he had 3500 pounds aboard, then called the tanker again. "Darkstar, Mercury Leader disengaging. And we thank you for your support."

The tanker pilot gave a chuckle on the other end of the line. "Glad to help out. Sorry for the trouble." There was a long pause. "Oh, yeah, almost forgot. Just before we launched the boys in Viper Squadron told me to give you a message, Tombstone. Welcome home!"

2257 hours Zulu (2057 hours Zone)
Air Ops, U.S.S. *Thomas Jefferson*
The North Atlantic

A man-made island far from the nearest dry ground, the U.S.S. *Thomas Jefferson,* CVN-74, plowed through the cold, dark waters of the North Atlantic, her course north-

northeast at a speed of thirty knots. America's newest
nuclear-powered supercarrier, like the other vessels of the
Nimitz class, was one of the most powerful ships of war
ever to sail the world ocean. She measured over a thousand
feet in length, with a flight deck that covered four and a half
acres and ample space to house the 5,500 officers and
enlisted men who called her home. As the core of Carrier
Battle Group 14, comprising seven warships and an Air
Wing of over ninety aircraft, *Jefferson* formed the heart of
a naval fighting force of incredible power and versatility.

But sitting near the back of the glassed-in Air Operations
room, commonly known as Primary Flight Control, or
"Pri-Fly" in carrier slang, Captain Joseph Stramaglia
couldn't help but ponder the limitations of that power.

He had decided to monitor flight operations this evening
from Pri-Fly, and had arrived about the time that the ferry
mission from Oceana NAS had met up with Darkstar, the
KA-6D tanker dispatched from *Jefferson* to top off tanks
that would be running low after a flight of over nineteen
hundred miles. That was about the range limit for an F-14,
and Mercury Flight was still a hundred and fifty miles away
from the safe haven of the carrier. Stramaglia had listened as
the refueling problem had developed, feeling as helpless as
the rest of the men in Air Ops. For blue-water operations
like this there was little margin for error.

When the radio channel finally carried Commander
Magruder's triumphant whoop, a cheer had gone up in
Pri-Fly. Stramaglia had taken a long sip from his coffee mug
to hide the smile on his face. He was a firm believer in
maintaining appearances, and it wouldn't have done to
allow the other men in the crowded little control center to
see just how relieved he was at Mercury Leader's successful
refueling.

Jefferson's Air Boss, Commander Jack Monroe, didn't
bother to hide his feelings. "Hot damn, Stoney Magruder's

back!'' he said. ''That's better'n the time he set down with half his turkey shot away and his RIO bleeding all over the backseat!''

Monroe, Stramaglia knew, had been Assistant Air Boss on *Jefferson*'s last overseas deployment. He was one of the veterans of the carrier's engagements in North Korea and the Indian Ocean, and it was obvious that he shared in the ship-wide adulation for Commander Magruder, who'd become famous for his part in those operations.

Stramaglia huffed into his coffee. He had known Magruder before the youngster had scored his first kill . . . and the enthusiasm of men like Monroe never failed to irritate him. Not that he had anything against Magruder. He just didn't think there was a place for what amounted to outright hero worship aboard the U.S.S. *Thomas Jefferson*.

''CAG?'' A young third class looked up from a console nearby. ''Tango Two-fiver reports they've picked up that Bear. It's still closing on us. Range is five-fifty, speed five hundred knots. Same course and bearing as before.''

Stramaglia nodded and put down the coffee cup. ''Commander Monroe, if the celebrations are over I think we'd better get the Alert planes off. Now, if you please.''

Monroe's grin faded as the Air Boss turned his attention back to the routine of the flight deck. ''You heard the man,'' Monroe said harshly. ''Let's get with it, people!''

Stramaglia turned away, ignoring the rising hubbub of voices as Monroe's white-shirted crew began relaying reports and instructions to and from the flight deck. He knew he was fast earning a reputation for being a tough, heartless bastard, but that was a role he was prepared to fall into if it would guarantee that Air Wing 20 stayed alert and ready for anything. They'd made it through the refueling crisis without having to sacrifice one of Mercury Flight's planes, but there was more than one problem to keep

Jefferson's crew busy tonight. Like the Soviet Tu-20 Bear bomber they'd been tracking for the last several hours.

It was Monroe's job as Air Boss to direct operations on and around *Jefferson*'s flight deck, but Stramaglia had wider duties. His title was CAG—it derived from the obsolete designation of Commander Air Group—and he was the commanding officer of Carrier Air Wing 20, the assortment of ninety-plus aircraft that gave the carrier her teeth. Everything that happened in the air for hundreds of miles around Carrier Battle Group 14 was his responsibility, from refueling problems to Soviet planes to whatever else the fates chose to throw in their path.

And with tensions between the United States and the new Soviet Union higher now than they'd ever been in the bad old days of the Cold War, Joseph Stramaglia was taking his responsibility seriously. That was why he was in Pri-Fly tonight, senior rank and position notwithstanding. When his boys were in the air, he didn't sleep or catch up on paperwork. If he wasn't up there with them, then he was somewhere like Air Ops where he would be on hand to lend his experience and skill to helping them out if they got in trouble.

Despite the outward show of temper, Stramaglia was proud to be a part of this crew, this boat. As the carrier that had seen more combat service than any ship since the heady days of Desert Storm, *Jefferson* had a reputation to live up to. "Big J," they called her.

This cruise, though, was shaping up to be a lot less glamorous, and a lot more dangerous, than her famous tour in the Pacific two years back. Stramaglia had already heard a couple of sailors referring to the carrier as "Big Jinx" after the storm that had wrecked four planes and killed five men, including Stramaglia's Deputy CAG. The trouble Magruder had run into while refueling had seemed to confirm the new epithet. And there was still this Bear to deal with . . .

Stramaglia picked up his coffee mug again, but didn't drink. He stared down into the dark brew as if trying to fathom the future in the tiny ripples there.

CHAPTER 2
Monday, 9 June 1997

2300 hours Zulu (2100 hours Zone)
Tomcat 204, flight deck, U.S.S. *Thomas Jefferson*
The North Atlantic

"Launch the Alert aircraft! Launch the Alert aircraft!" The launch order rang out from the ship's-MC loudspeakers.

"We're on!" Lieutenant Commander Edward Everett Wayne, running name "Batman," set his magazine aside and checked the lacing on his boots carefully before standing up.

Lieutenant Terry Powers was already on his feet, zipping up his heavy flight-survival vest and reaching for his helmet in eager anticipation. "Finally some action!" he said, sounding excited and impatient. Batman thought he detected an underlying current of nervousness as well. Powers hadn't been on carrier duty long, and there was a big difference between training flights with a RAG back in the States and genuine blue-water ops off a carrier deck.

"Whoa there, kid," he warned. "Throttle back and level off."

Powers looked at him uncertainly. "Sir?"

"Alert Fifteen means we launch fast," Wayne continued. "But it doesn't mean we launch dumb. Don't be in such a hurry you forget about safety precautions, kid, or you'll cut

19

off a promising career before you're properly started." He pointed at the lieutenant's feet. "Lace up those boots tighter. If you have to eject, you don't want them catching on something in the cockpit on the way out."

"Aye, aye, sir," Powers said, looking sheepish. He crouched to do as he had been told. "I guess I'm just excited, sir."

"Two things, Tyrone," Batman said. "First off, lay off the 'sirs' for a while. Makes you sound like a midshipmite who can't find his way home. When there's nobody here but us aviators I'm Batman. Got it?"

"Yes, sir . . . uh, Batman."

"Secondly, chill out a little, kid. Take a leaf from Malibu here." He pointed to his Radar Intercept Officer, Lieutenant Commander Kenneth Blake, whose running name of Malibu had been bestowed because of his blond good looks and carefully cultivated California-surfer persona. "He's so cool we use him to keep the beer cold."

Malibu flashed a careless grin. "Maybe so, dude," he said with a deceptively laid-back drawl. "But that just means I always have a supply close by." Despite the banter and the casual tone, Blake was ready to go, helmet under one arm, flight suit zipped up tight.

The fourth man in the ready room of the VF-95 Viper Squadron looked irritated. "Come on, let's get moving." Lieutenant William "Ears" Cavanaugh, who was assigned to fly the RIO position with Powers tonight, could never be described as a patient man. Every word, every motion, was quick and decisive, and the man had trouble dealing with anyone who wasn't in tune with his particular rhythm of life.

The four men left the ready room, not running but moving briskly through the door and toward the flight deck. They emerged on a steel catwalk on the starboard side of the carrier, hanging right out over the angry black sea below.

Batman followed the others up the ladder that led up to the wide expanse of the ship's "roof," the flight deck, thankful for the moonlight that glinted off metal and made it unnecessary to unclip the flashlight hanging from his belt.

As he reached the flight deck he heard Powers enthusing. "Tonight's the night for some action, Ears. We're gonna go out there and get us some Bear!"

He could hear the eagerness in the young voice, and remembered the first time he'd been on one of the flights the Navy called a "Bear hunt." That had been almost three years back now, during the crisis in North Korea. He could still remember his own enthusiasm that day . . . and the chewing out his squadron commander had given him after he had pulled a foolish stunt that had almost resulted in a collision between his Tomcat and the Russian bomber they were investigating.

"Hold on, there, nugget," Batman said. "This isn't a game, Tyrone. You fly this by the book, got it?" He heard Malibu snort, a comment on Batman telling anyone to fly by the book, but ignored it.

But Powers was suitably deflated. "Aye, aye, sir," he said. "By the book."

I'm starting to sound like old Tombstone, Batman thought with a grin. He could still remember Matt Magruder's harsh words after that Bear hunt over the Sea of Japan. *I don't have room on this team for a goddamned hotdog!* the squadron leader had said. *We're already in the middle of one crisis. The last thing we need now is dragging the Russians into it!*

It had been a rough beginning, but he and Magruder had come out of the mess in North Korea as friends. Now Batman was Executive Officer of VF-95, a graduate of the Navy's famous Top Gun school, and for all of his show-manship he had learned the value of caution and teamwork. If he really was starting to sound like Tombstone, he thought, then he really had made something of himself as an aviator after all.

Caution and teamwork . . . that would have to be the watchword tonight. Bear flights over the Atlantic were nothing new. They'd been a familiar routine all through the Cold War and well after the day the Berlin Wall came down. There had been times in the past when American pilots would swap signals with the Russian Bear crews, even talk on the radio. Some old-timers told about incidents where one side or the other would obligingly move their aircraft around so their opponents could take home photographs for their intelligence people.

This time, though, things were liable to be different. For the past five days Soviet troops had been engaged in hostilities against Norway, a one-time NATO ally and still a good friend of the United States.

That first time over the Sea of Japan Batman hadn't really given much thought to the crisis brewing in North Korea or how the Russians might react to it. Like a lot of people he'd gotten out of the habit of thinking of them as the enemy. After those exciting days near the end of 1989 when the Cold War had suddenly come to an end, decades of fear and hate had turned overnight into new feelings of optimism and friendship. Soviet-American cooperation had made the victory in Operation Desert Storm possible, and the failure of the hard-line coup in August 1991 had seemed to mark the end of Communism and the beginning of a brand-new era of world history. Even after the Communists staged a successful military takeover the following year, after harsh winter weather and widespread famine had totally discredited the reform movement, it had seemed that the Soviet Union would never again be able to occupy center stage in world affairs. Communist or not, the new rulers had seemed willing enough to get along with the West. Just a few months after his first Bear hunt Batman had found himself flying alongside Soviet naval aviators of the aircraft carrier *Kreml* during the UN intervention in the war between India and Pakistan.

America had been too wrapped up in domestic affairs to stop the Soviets when they renounced the agreements recognizing the independence of their breakaway republics, and just as slow to react to the invasion of Norway, but now tensions were running high. And Batman now understood the lesson Tombstone Magruder had taught him back on that first cruise. The crisis in Norway had brought Russia and America to the brink of war. Batman Wayne didn't plan to be the man who pushed them over the edge.

He shoved those thoughts to the back of his mind as they reached their planes and started on the serious business of checking the Tomcat over before they entrusted their lives to it. Chief Bergstrom, the brown-shirted plane captain responsible for maintaining and inspecting the aircraft, joined Batman and Malibu as they circled the big interceptor. Bergstrom was a good man, and Batman trusted him, but not to the point of going up without making sure there wasn't some careless mistake by one of the maintenance crewmen just waiting to be overlooked.

Satisfied, they moved to the left side of the Tomcat. Bergstrom folded down the cockpit ladder. "Good hunting, sir!" he shouted over the din of the flight deck.

Batman gave him a quick thumbs-up and climbed into the front of the cockpit. Malibu settled into the backseat a few moments later, while Wayne was still settling his kneeboard into place on his leg.

He went carefully through the pre-flight checklist, suppressing a grin at the thought of how conscientious he'd become in the last three years. It all went back to the tour with Tombstone Magruder, who'd taught him that it didn't always take glitz and glitter to make a first-rate fighter pilot.

The checklist finished, Batman powered up the Tomcat's

two General Electric F110-GE-400 engines, first the right,
then the left. He nodded in satisfaction at their sound and
adjusted the throttle by his left hand to idle. Tradition
maintained that as squadron Exec he should fly Tomcat 202,
but it had been one of the victims the day the A-6E had
crashed on the flight deck. Number 204, this bird, didn't
have his name or Malibu's stenciled below the canopy, but
aviators traded off aircraft assignments often enough. This
Tomcat seemed to be in top shape.

Outside deck crewmen were unhooking parking chains
and clearing away the chocks around the wheels. A deck
crewman whose yellow flashlights identified him as a plane
handler signaled Batman with quick gestures of the wands,
and Wayne followed his instructions and taxied the aircraft
toward catapult number one. A constellation of other
colored lights closed in around the Tomcat. Blue wands
were crewmen checking the control surfaces of the Tomcat,
while ordnance specialists with red wands prepped the
air-to-air missiles, radar-guided Sparrows and heat-seeking
Sidewinders hanging suspended from their launch rails.
Four times a low hum sounded in Batman's headphones as
the ordies passed their flashlights close to the noses of each
Sidewinder. The heat-sensing guidance systems were sensitive enough to detect even a flashlight as a heat source and
alert the pilot that they were locked on a potential target.

A deck crewman appeared to the left of the Tomcat
holding up a lighted board showing the number 65,000, the
takeoff weight of Tomcat 204. It was vital that the steam
catapult be properly set for the weight of the plane to ensure
a safe launch. Behind Batman, Malibu waved a flashlight in
a circular motion to acknowledge the 65,000-pound figure.

Underneath the plan a hookup man connected the launching bar on the F-14's nose gear to the cat shuttle. Once it
was hooked up, Batman knew, another crewman would
check the holdback bar that would keep the Tomcat from

breaking free until the moment of the launch, and the jet-blast deflector would rise into position behind the plane. The dance on the deck was a complex ritual, graceful and intricate, with every move designed to send the plane on its way safely and quickly.

The catapult officer, identified by his green and red flashlights, waved the green light horizontally. Batman obeyed the signal and moved the twin throttles to full military power. He could feel the fighter straining against the holdback bolt, like a wild animal eager to return to its own native element. Batman went through the time-honored ritual to test the control stick between his knees, left, right, forward, back. Then he checked the rudder pedals. All working. All ready.

The catapult officer waved the green light up and down, and Batman shoved the throttle to full afterburner. Light bathed the flight deck from the plumes of flame that twisted and writhed from the two jet engines. "Give 'em the light show, Malibu," Batman ordered. Blake acknowledged the instruction and flicked on the Tomcat's navigation lights, the signal to the deck crew and the Air Boss watching from Pri-Fly that Tomcat 204 was ready to launch. Batman bent his head forward and tensed, anticipating the thrust of the cat shot.

Dropping to his knee, the catapult officer touched the deck with the green wand, the "go" signal to the crewman who controlled the catapult. Acceleration shoved Batman back into his seat as the plane surged forward and rose from the flight deck, leaping skyward.

"Hound Two-oh-four," he said, opening a radio channel to the carrier. "Good shot. Good shot."

"Two-oh-four, good shot," the radio confirmed.

A few moments later the second Tomcat pulled alongside. "Two-one-oh," the pilot announced. "Good shot."

"Hound Two-oh-four, this is Tango Two-fiver," another

voice said, cutting in. "Vector left to zero-three-nine, angels eighteen, and go to buster." That was one of the *Jefferson*'s E2-C Hawkeyes, using its sophisticated suite of detection equipment to track the incoming Russian bomber and direct Hound Flight to intercept it. Batman set his throttles to full military power—"buster" in aviator's lingo—and banked his Tomcat to the left to take up the new heading.

"Roger, Tango Two-fiver," Batman replied. "Coming to zero-three-nine, angels eighteen, buster. You copy, Tyrone?"

"I copy, Two-oh-four," Powers replied crisply. He sounded professional enough now, but Batman glanced across at the other plane through narrowed eyes. He found himself wishing it was Tombstone back in that old, familiar position off his wing.

But it wasn't. This time out, it was Batman Wayne who was the veteran, flying with an eager young hotshot who might not understand just how deadly serious this Bear hunt could be.

He wasn't sure he was fit for his new role.

2310 hours Zulu (2110 hours Zone)
Tomcat 109, Mercury Flight
Over the North Atlantic

Welcome home, Tombstone.

The tanker pilot's words kept coming back as Tombstone guided the Tomcat through the darkness. A layer of low, thick clouds blocked his view of the ocean, but he knew that *Jefferson* and the other ships of CBG-14 awaited him somewhere below. Soon he would see the carrier again, feel the deck beneath his feet once more. . . .

For two long years he had thought of little else. Now Tombstone Magruder was coming home.

What would it be like, he wondered, to be back aboard the *Jeff* again? He'd served in plenty of duty stations over the years, but none of them had been like that last tour aboard the carrier in those exciting days of the confrontation with North Korea and the intervention in the war between India and Pakistan. As squadron leader of VF-95, the Vipers, Tombstone Magruder had flown his Tomcat into action time and time again, earning an unprecedented string of air-to-air kills in the process. His promotion and reassignment to a Pentagon staff post had been inevitable, the accepted next steps in a professional naval career. But that hadn't made the transition any easier.

A glint of pale moonlight on the wing of one of Mercury Flight's two A-6E Intruders caught Tombstone's eye. It was what naval aviators called a ''commander's moon,'' bright enough to help older pilots—the ones who held ranks of commander and higher—compensate for less acute vision in difficult night carrier landings. Commander Matthew Magruder hadn't really thought of himself in that category until tonight, but the difficulty with the tanker had made him all too conscious of the fact that he wasn't the hotshot Top Gun pilot who'd joined the *Jefferson* three years back. Three years could be a lifetime to a fighter pilot.

It also made him realize that this could be his last chance to recapture that old life. And the long ferry mission had made him aware all over again of just how much open skies and thundering jets really meant to him. Coming back to the *Jefferson* again was only part of what was driving him tonight. The carrier was special, of course, but Magruder would probably have jumped at the chance for an assignment anywhere beyond the confines of Washington. Anywhere he could recapture the feeling of freedom this long flight out of sight of land had brought back.

Two years chained to land hadn't dimmed the sheer joy of strapping on an F-14 and reaching for the limitless skies.

Of course he'd flown often enough those last two years, but it hadn't been the same. Getting in enough hours to qualify each week wasn't like the day-to-day cycle of carrier ops. He had always felt tied to the land, bound to that hated Pentagon office that would reclaim him when each flight was done. It had been two years of Hell . . . but it was over now.

Now he was going home to the *Jefferson*. It should have been the happiest day of Tombstone's life . . . would have been, if not for the circumstances that surrounded the new assignment. Seemingly overnight a minor boundary dispute between Norway and the Soviet Union had blossomed into armed conflict. With NATO virtually a dead letter and the United States hesitating over unilateral intervention, the crisis was still a local one confined to Scandinavia. But everything pointed toward a change in the wind, and it looked as if *Jefferson* would once again be sailing into harm's way. Why else would Mercury Flight be ferrying planes out to replace aircraft destroyed in the flight deck accident the carrier had suffered almost a week ago? It wasn't normal practice . . . except when it looked like those planes would be needed.

He supposed the same could be said for himself. That same accident had cost CVW-20 her Deputy CAG. Someone back in Washington must have thought the carrier's air wing would be needing a new second-in-command soon, or they wouldn't have tapped Tombstone for the job. It had been a hurry-up job all around, with no time at all for Magruder to be properly briefed on his new job. It was nice to know that someone thought he could handle the position all the same.

Of course, there was always the chance that this was just another public-relations ploy. The hero of Wonsan and the Indian Ocean crisis was a useful card to play when public support was the goal. And America's new President, the first Democrat to occupy the White House since Jimmy Carter, needed every good card he could lay his hands on now that it looked like the Soviets were bursting back on the world stage with a vengeance.

The thought made Tombstone cringe inwardly. He had never been comfortable with the hero treatment even though he'd come to terms with it after North Korea. But his staff job at the Pentagon had been little more than an excuse to keep him available for public appearances, Congressional testimony, and media events. He had joined the Navy to become an aviator, to fly a fighter like his father and his uncle before him. Boring paperwork and exercises in public relations had never been his goal. A sleek fighter and open sky were all Matthew Magruder wanted or needed.

If his return to active duty on the *Jefferson* was intended or just another piece of PR work, Tombstone thought, then the people who'd ordered it were going to be surprised. He wouldn't allow anyone to saddle him with another rear-echelon role. Never again, he vowed silently.

The moonlight gleamed off the Intruder's wing again. The bomber was drifting right, out of formation. Magruder bit his lip and keyed in his radio. "Mercury Five-one-one, Mercury Leader," he said. "Let's tighten it up, there, Lieutenant."

The reply was a startled "Sorry, sir." Slowly the Intruder nudged back into formation.

It had been a long flight, and all four pilots were tired. This had been the most sustained flying Magruder had done in two years, and he imagined the others weren't much better prepared. They'd been drawn from Reserve Air Groups in the States, and like Tombstone they wouldn't have had much excuse for practicing any of the types of operations that were routine for carrier-based flyers.

Two Tomcats, two Intruders . . . and at that they'd still be short of a full complement by three more planes. That accident on *Jefferson*'s flight deck had been a messy one. It wasn't the best way Tombstone could think of to get the assignment he'd coveted, especially when the Deputy CAG he was replacing had been a friend from the old days. Commander Isaac "Jolly Green" Greene, who'd survived a shoot-down during the Wonsan operation, and had played a key role in the Alpha Strike that had stopped the war between India and Pakistan, hadn't been all that well liked by his comrades on the *Jefferson* back then, but he'd been a first-class Intruder pilot and a fine squadron commander with a reputation for guts and determination. He'd beaten Magruder out for the coveted Deputy CAG post when *Jefferson*'s new deployment had first been announced, and despite his own disappointment Tombstone had been glad that it had been Jolly Greene who took it away from him.

It seemed wrong somehow that the big, sarcastic man had bought it in a flight deck accident. He had survived deadly Triple-A fire over Wonsan and the icy waters off the Korean coast, only to die when the Intruder he was riding in as an observer had skidded while landing on a wet deck. His ejection seat had thrown him clear of the carrier . . . but hours of searching by SAR copters had never found him.

That wasn't how Tombstone would have wanted his homecoming to start . . . but now he'd be stepping into the dead man's shoes whether he liked it or not.

Tombstone buried the thought. At least he was back on carrier duty again, where he belonged. That was what really counted.

CHAPTER 3
Monday, 9 June 1997

2325 hours Zulu (2125 hours Zone)
Tomcat 109, Mercury Flight
Twenty miles abeam of U.S.S. *Thomas Jefferson*

"Mercury One-oh-nine, Charlie now."

Tombstone acknowledged *Jefferson*'s order to break out of the holding pattern and start his final approach. The rest of Mercury Flight had already landed safely, though one of the Intruder pilots had nearly lost it in the last few seconds. Some good coaching from the Landing Signals Officer down on the carrier deck had kept the kid from cracking up, but it had been a close call.

That incident, coming hard on the heels of his own refueling problem, was the sort of thing that would have warned off someone who believed in bad omens. Tombstone had never considered himself superstitious, but this flight was shaking his skepticism.

Now only Darkstar, the KA-6 tanker that had flown back from the rendezvous point with them, remained aloft with the Tomcat. It would keep on circling until the F-14 had landed, in case Tombstone needed to tank up again before landing.

Fat chance, he told himself. The thought of another refueling like the last one was the best inducement he'd ever had for getting his landing right the first time.

He reduced speed to 250 knots, overriding the flight computer's attempts to extend the aircraft's swing wings to their full wing-forward position. The Tomcat's sleek lines wouldn't be visible in the darkness, but Tombstone, like most aviators, made it a point of pride to keep the wings back and the F-14 looking its best all the way down.

The action brought back an old memory of a young RIO who had referred to the forward wing position as "goose mode" because it made the Tomcat look like an awkward goose flaring out as it landed on some still lake.

As the seconds ticked by he checked his airspeed and angle of approach on the Vertical Display Indicator in the center of his control panel, carefully lining up the Instrument Landing System cross-pointers on the glowing cursor that represented the *Jefferson*'s location with built-in corrections for wind direction and speed. He didn't like flying by the ILS, but it was the only way to make a carrier landing approach at night. Except in the brightest moonlight, sea and sky tended to merge into a featureless black cave, and without reference points a pilot could quickly lose his orientation. Vertigo was one of the milder problems associated with trying to fly when it was impossible to judge distance or direction. When traveling at nearly three hundred miles per hour, it only took an instant's confusion to end up a casualty.

At best the carrier itself would be no more than a tiny dot of light set in an otherwise featureless gloom, and that only at comparatively close ranges. That made the ILS essential.

Once the cross hairs were centered Tombstone kept them precisely in position. Luckily, the throttle on a Tomcat adjusted speed automatically, allowing him to concentrate on course corrections and his angle of attack. The F-14 covered ten miles—half the distance between the carrier and the final fix that had been the jump-off point for the approach—in just over two minutes, dropping two thousand feet per minute. Magruder kept his attention focused on the VDI, resisting the temptation to look through the canopy and try to spot the *Jefferson.*

When the range indicator on the display indicated ten miles he "dirtied up" the Tomcat by hitting the switches that dropped landing gear, flaps, and tail hook. He was flying level now, at twelve hundred feet, with airspeed dropping. The ILS cross-pointers were centered near the top of the display, but they crept toward the middle of the screen as the Tomcat continued its approach.

Three miles out he started his descent again, still entirely dependent on instruments. It took experience to handle this part of a night approach, a precise knowledge of just how much to compensate for tiny course deviations. The carrier wasn't a stable, motionless platform, but a moving target plunging through wind and wave at better than twenty knots. And wind was only one of many factors that were making the Tomcat drift off the mark. Correcting for drift was a constant thing, and the closer the fighter got to the carrier the more Tombstone had to anticipate the behavior of the aircraft so his corrections could be applied in time.

His two years away from constant carrier ops had left him rusty, but he found all the old instincts coming back to him. Man and machine worked as the perfect team.

"Two miles out," *Jefferson*'s radio controller said. "Left one, slightly below glide path."

He corrected automatically, almost before the radio call.

As the range indicator showed one mile left, he looked up from the VDI and saw the carrier immediately. It was like a tapering box outlined in white lights, bisected by a centerline that projected out of the bottom edge of the box. Orange lights at the end of the centerline marked the drop line hanging down the stern of the ship, indicating the edge of the flight deck.

He picked out the tiny rectangular shape of the optical

glide-path indicator to the left of the white lights, the "meatball" that helped aviators estimate their height and approach path as they made the final drop to the deck. It was still indistinct at this range, and not very reliable until the range was considerably shorter. But visual acquisition of the meatball meant that Tombstone was ready to bring the Tomcat down.

"Mercury One-oh-nine," he said over the radio. "Tomcat ball. Four point eight." The signal told *Jefferson* who he was, what kind of plane he was flying, and signaled that he had visual sighting of the meatball with 4800 pounds of fuel remaining.

"Roger ball," the Landing Signals Officer said. "Deck's going up. You're looking good."

The meatball was designed to give the approaching pilot a visual indication of his position relative to the deck. If the center of the five Fresnel lenses was illuminated, the approaching aircraft was right on its glide path. It was high if one of the upper lenses was lit, too low if a lens below the midpoint glowed. But at a mile out one notch of the meatball represented thirty-two feet of altitude, so it wasn't the most accurate way to judge the approach. Tombstone kept his descent constant at five hundred feet per minute and relied on the advice of the LSO, a veteran aviator with a much better perspective on the approach than Magruder had himself, to keep him on track.

"Remember, you'll tend to fly low," the LSO went on. The best LSOs were the ones who dropped hints without giving detailed instructions. If Tombstone screwed up the approach enough to become a real danger, the laid-back, friendly tone would change. Right now the LSO was simply a calming voice who worked with the pilot, not against him.

The square of white lights that defined the flight deck was like a hole opening up in front of the Tomcat. There was a tendency for pilots to feel they were too high at this stage of the approach, but it was an illusion. Tombstone eased up on his descent rate, conscious of the other potential hazard, that he would overcorrect and come in too high. It might result in an embarrassing flyby . . . or, if his hook caught a wire even though his landing gear wasn't on the deck, it could end up in a messy crash.

Nearing the half-mile point, Magruder could see the carrier taking on a ghostly shape for the first time. Now he could use the visual clues that simplified carrier landings, including the meatball. There was the usual burst of confidence, and the usual quick realization that there was nothing to be confident about yet. As the last few seconds of the approach ticked away the impression that the deck was really just a square hole came back stronger than ever.

"Come down, Stoney. Down a little," the LSO said urgently. Magruder could picture him getting ready to punch the button on the "pickle switch" in his hands that would signal a wave-off and send the Tomcat back in the air for another run. Tombstone compensated, knowing that too much correction could slam the plane into the ramp.

The landing gear hit hard as the Tomcat touched down, and Tombstone realized instantly that he had overshot the ideal touchdown point. Four arresting wires stretched across the deck, and the optimum landing was one that snagged the number-three wire. The F-14 had been high, and missed that one.

He shoved the throttle full forward, according to standard procedure, so that the Tomcat could get airborne again if it missed the "trap." Even though it was common enough to botch a night landing he felt his face turning red with anger and embarrassment. For Tombstone Magruder, the great naval hero and the new Deputy CAG, to pull a bolter on his first approach . . .

But sudden deceleration caught him by surprise as the tail

hook caught the four wire and the Tomcat jerked to a halt.
"Good trap! Good trap!" he heard in his headphones.

They were down.

"Gotcha! I've got our boy nailed, compadre. Bearing
zero-four-one, range eighty-three miles. He's down on the
deck. A hundred, maybe a hundred fifty feet."

"Nice going, Malibu," Batman replied over the ICS. He
switched to his radio. "You got him, Tyrone?"

"Affirmative," Powers replied tersely. The young pilot
seemed determined to fly the mission strictly by the book.

"Hey, this dude's really trying to catch a bodacious
wave," Malibu interjected. "He gets any lower and they'll
be scraping fish off the front of that thing."

"Trying to duck our radar," Batman said. "And maybe
sucker us into taking a bath if we try to buzz him. Listen up,
Tyrone. The Russkies always get a big laugh when they con
some capitalist nugget like you into hitting water. You
watch your altitude and keep it cool, got it?"

"Roger, Leader," the other pilot replied.

Tyrone's RIO, Lieutenant William "Ears" Cavanaugh,
spoke up. "I've got the bastard too." He gave a dry
chuckle. "Don't worry, Batman, I'll keep the kid out of
trouble." True to standard practice, Cavanaugh was an
experienced hand teamed with one of the squadron's rook-
ies. But Batman had seen the RIO in action during the
intensive air wing training program at NAS Fallon in
Nevada before deploying to the carrier. Ears was a top-
notch RIO, but sometimes he was a little too eager.

"Question is, who'll keep *you* out of trouble, Ears?"

Batman responded. He didn't give the others a chance to answer him. "Tango Two-fiver, Hound Two-oh-four. We've got him on our scopes. Going in to have a look."

"Roger, Two-oh-four," came the reply from the Hawk-eye. There was a pause. "Mind your ROEs, boys. It ain't a shooting war."

"Not yet," Batman muttered. Ever since his first combat experience off North Korea he had mistrusted the limitations set by the Rules of Engagement. They had been designed to keep overeager pilots from precipitating an international incident in the heat of a tense encounter. But they also had the effect of hamstringing those same aviators. Often in modern air combat the first one to lock on and launch was the winner, and when the ROEs said not to fire unless fired upon . . .

Against the sort of opposition the United States had met in the past—the Libyans in the Gulf of Sidra, for example—it didn't matter so much. Technological and doctrinal superiority had allowed American pilots to survive enemy attacks and come back swinging. But against first-class Soviet opposition the same might not be true. If the Russians planned on starting something this flight might be Batman's last.

The dark thoughts flashed through Batman's mind in an instant, but all he said aloud was, "Roger, Tango Two-fiver."

He dropped the Tomcat into a sharp bank and started the descent. The Bear was low, but the Russians had underestimated the accuracy of American radar surveillance. *Thank God for the Hawkeye,* Batman thought. Without the E-2C the Russians might have been able to get much closer before they were spotted.

Bears were archaic by modern standards, but the Bear-D reconnaissance bird was still a deadly threat. That wasn't so much because of the weaponry it could carry, but rather because it could help more sophisticated Badgers or Black-jacks to get a fix on American ships without exposing themselves to detection. And a Badger armed with stand-off missiles could play havoc with the battle group in a matter of minutes.

Each Bear hunt had to be treated as if it was the real thing. And if the reports from Norway were true, tonight the threat was worse than ever before.

He could feel the huge Soviet aircraft long before he saw it. The low, steady rumble of the plane's four Kuznetsov turboprops shook the night sky like distant thunder. He strained to see ahead, looking for some sign.

"Tally-ho!" The old aviator's hunting call came over the radio. Excitement made Tyrone's voice shrill. "Eleven o'clock, Batman, and right down on the deck!"

Batman spotted it then, the constellation of red and green navigation lights that marked the Soviet plane. A red beacon strobed its anticollision warning. At least the Bear wasn't coming in blacked out. That counted for something.

"Tango Two-fiver, Hound Two-oh-four. We have visual on the bandit! Closing now."

"Two-oh-four, this is Domino." That was CAG's voice, relayed by the Hawkeye from *Jefferson*. "Go easy, but let that guy know he's not welcome here."

"Roger, Domino," Batman replied. "Tyrone, hang back and cover me. Stay one mile out."

"Roger," came the laconic reply. Powers was shaping up as a steady hand after all.

Batman turned to port and circled lazily around the Bear, crossing the turbulence of the larger aircraft's slipstream and falling into place alongside. Batman fought to control his heartbeat and breathing. He was in easy range of the Russian's NR-23 cannons, and all it would take was one slip to turn this from a routine encounter to the first shots of World War III.

"Remember the time off Korea," Malibu warned. "They'll probably hit their searchlight."

The reminder came just in time. A blinding lance of light shot out from the searchlight mounting near the tail section, enveloping the Tomcat's cockpit. Batman kept his eyes averted and blinked hard.

Often in night encounters the Russians would illuminate their own plane with the searchlight. It helped avoid misjudged distances and accidental collisions. But within seconds Batman knew that wasn't their intention this time around.

The light held the Tomcat's cockpit, challenging, probing.

"Picking up emissions from Big Bulge," Malibu said. That was the NATO code name for the ship-targeting radar system mounted in the oversized teardrop-shaped housing on the belly of the Bear. It was useless for air-to-air work. The only reason to use Big Bulge was to find surface ships . . . and maybe steer stand-off missiles toward them.

Batman muttered a curse and rolled sideways, increasing speed slightly to clear the searchlight beam. He steadied the Tomcat back on course even closer to the Bear than before, close enough to see dark figures at the windows of the cockpit and the tail section. They could see him as well.

He held up two fingers, then five, eight, and finally a clenched fist, the signal that he wanted to talk on Channel 258.0. That was common enough in a Bear hunt. In times past crews had exchanged comments, questions, even jokes.

But the only response from the Russian was another light show. Were they deliberately trying to blind him, or were they just trying to take pictures? Photographs from encounters like these had helped both sides learn about the planes their opponents flew, but this didn't feel like a photo session to Batman. They were doing their best to make things tough for him.

Batman pulled his stick over sharply to port and shoved his throttle to afterburner zone five. The Tomcat surged up and to the left, crossing in front of and above the Bear's cockpit. He could imagine the Soviet pilot scrambling to avoid the danger.

Somewhere in the back of his mind he remembered Tombstone's admonishment so long ago. He was risking it all. . . .

He cut power and circled again, watching the Bear warily. "Got anything, Malibu?"

"Big Bulge is still on," the RIO replied tautly, all trace of his California-surfer persona gone.

"Right." Batman switched to radio. "Tyrone, give this sucker something to think about. Give him a lock-on."

"R-roger." Powers sounded nervous. He had every right to be. If the Russian decided an attack was imminent there was no telling what he might do.

Batman drifted close alongside again and repeated the 258.0 signal. This time there was a response, a gabble of Russian and broken English over the radio.

"Stoy! Stoy! Nee streelyaee! Not shoot!"

"Okay, Tyrone, cut the lock," Batman instructed on their tactical channel. Then, switching to 258.0, he replied to the Soviet, "Russian aircraft, this is Hound Leader. I am the aircraft just off your port wing. Do you copy, over?"

"Hound leader, is Flight *Varon*. Radar lock is flagrant provocation. I protest this act of aggression. Over."

"Protest all you want," Batman shot back. "You are requested to come to course three-zero-zero and turn off that search radar. In the interests of international good will, you know."

"Nyet! Is not for Americans to order flight plans of Soviet aircraft! Or do you declare exclusion zone?"

Jefferson hadn't taken that step yet. In wartime or a particularly tense crisis an exclusion zone defined an area in which any unauthorized plane would be fired on automatically. That was a much larger escalation of the current tension than anyone had been willing to order so far.

"Negative, Flight *Varon*. But in view of the current situation, don't you think it would be a good idea to avoid . . . unfortunate incidents?"

"Bah! Is blatant interference!"

Batman switched channels again. "Give him another little tweak, Tyrone," he said. "Just to remind him what he's risking."

"Roger, Leader." The younger pilot still sounded tense, but in control. "Got him."

"Flight *Varon,* this is Hound Leader," Batman drawled, back on the common frequency. "Request you comply with our suggestion. My partner has an itchy trigger finger."

There was a long, tense pause. Technically there was nothing Batman could do to stop the Bear unless he was willing to risk a full-blown incident. He was banking on the Russians being as nervous as the Americans.

It was a deadly game of chicken . . . and millions of lives could hang on the outcome.

The rumble of the Bear's engines rose in pitch a little as the aircraft accelerated and started to climb away from the encounter. "Big Bulge is off," Malibu announced.

He watched the Bear turn, not northwest as he'd suggested, but east instead. As it continued to swing slowly around onto a northeasterly heading, Batman rubbed the bridge of his nose. They were on the right heading for a return to Russia. Had the reconnaissance flight been on a routine mission, or had it been especially directed against the battle group?

The answer to that question might tell a lot about Soviet intentions in the unfolding crisis.

CHAPTER 4
Monday, 9 June 1997

2345 hours Zulu (2145 hours Zone)
Admiral's quarters, U.S.S. *Thomas Jefferson*
The North Atlantic

Rear Admiral Douglas F. Tarrant looked up from his computer terminal at the discreet tap on his door. "Come," he said, saving the letter to his wife before shutting off the machine. He glanced at the clock over his desk and raised a surprised eyebrow. There were few people aboard who would knock on that door at this time of night, even if they knew Tarrant was accustomed to working late and snatching short catnaps.

Jefferson's CO, Captain Jeremy Brandt, looked apologetic as he entered. Short, stocky, with close-cut blond hair beginning to go gray, Brandt had a bulldog face and a temperament, so Tarrant had learned, to match. They'd never served together before, but Tarrant had heard nothing but good reports on the captain, and had confirmed them in a month's direct contact. It was Brandt's first cruise commanding a carrier, but he'd put in tours as CO aboard the *Tripoli* and the *Kalamazoo,* with a particularly good record as CAG aboard the *Kennedy* back in '93. The carefully planned career cycle of Navy carrier skippers ensured that the best men made it to the top, but even in that distinguished company Brandt stood out.

"Sorry to disturb you, Admiral," he said. "But Commander Sykes down in CR just processed a Priority Urgent message from CINCLANT." He held up a bundle of teletype printouts.

Tarrant frowned. The bulky ream of paper sent up from the ship's Communications Department had to be detailed situation reports and orders for the battle group from Commander-in-Chief Atlantic Fleet, and the precedence code of "Priority Urgent" meant that it was important enough to require attention within three hours of transmission. That could mean only one thing.

"We're going in," he said aloud. "We must be going in."

Brandt nodded slowly. "That's my guess, sir. Looks like the folks up at NCA finally got off their collective butt and decided to make a move after all."

He took the papers from the captain. "Anything else?"

"Mercury Flight's on the deck, Admiral. Two Tomcats, two Intruders. Not a full replacement, but it's better than nothing."

"Good." Tarrant smiled. "I'll bet CAG's happy at least."

"Yes, sir," Brandt said noncommittally. Everyone on board knew Stramaglia's reputation for never being satisfied. "We also had confirmation from the Hawkeye that the Bear we were tracking changed course after our Tomcats intercepted."

"I'll pretend you didn't tell me," Tarrant said. There was a certain amount of rivalry between Brandt as Captain of the ship and Stramaglia as CO of the Air Wing. In theory they were equals under Tarrant's command, and it might have been considered a breach of protocol for Brandt to report developments that were entirely within the CAG's purview. But Tarrant was more concerned at the moment with information rather than propriety. If the message from

CINCLANT was what he thought it was, he was going to need every scrap of data he could lay his hands on in the next few hours.

"All right, Captain," he went on, adopting a more serious tone. "Pass the word for my staff to meet me in Flag Plot in half an hour. And I want a meeting of the battle group's senior officers on board *Jefferson* tomorrow morning at 0900. Captains and Execs . . . CAG and his staff too."

"Aye, aye, sir," Brandt responded formally. "I doubt Colby or Wolfe can get here for the meeting, though."

They were the skippers of CBG-14's two 688-class attack subs, *Galveston* and *Bangor*. They were ranging far ahead of the surface ships, and it would be awkward to transport officers off the submarines to attend a briefing.

A face-to-face meeting with his ship commanders wasn't absolutely necessary, but it was something Tarrant always tried to arrange when there were important orders to be passed along. It gave him a better measure of the men who had to carry them out. He could see their reactions, hear their opinions. Despite all the myths of modern high-tech warfare it was still the *men* who counted most.

"Don't worry about them," he told Brandt. He'd just have to depend on their skills sight unseen. From what he remembered of them from the short meetings he'd had with the two sub commanders at the beginning of the deployment, he had nothing to worry about from either man. "We'll send them a transcript afterwards. But see to getting the others aboard."

"Aye, aye, sir," the captain repeated, glancing again at the printout with an unreadable expression before turning to leave.

After Brandt was gone Tarrant picked up the printout and began to scan the pages. It was as he had feared. The situation in Norway was no longer to be considered a local problem.

As was so often the case, the crisis had caught everyone, including America's intelligence community, off guard. At the core of the matter lay a long-standing grievance between Norway and the Soviet Union, going back to post-World War II days. The argument over the exact location of territorial water boundaries in the Barents Sea had become a major issue almost overnight. Soviet military maneuvers on the Norwegian border had heightened the tensions without really changing the equation. That was just a routine adjunct to diplomacy as far as the Russians were concerned. The world community had looked on, unable and often unwilling to get involved as the war of words continued. Denunciations of both sides in the United Nations, mediation by the Secretary General—nothing had worked.

But the Soviet President had made his mark on the world stage as a diplomat whose charm and personal style could make things happen where the career negotiators were deadlocked. His well-publicized trip to Oslo on a mission of personal negotiation had been stage-managed with the modern Russian flair for grabbing Western audiences and selling them on the new Soviet Union's dedication to peace and goodwill.

At the time Tarrant had been convinced that the whole dispute with Norway had been engineered just so the President of the Soviet Union could produce another of his famed diplomatic miracles . . . and incidentally counteract the bad press Russia had been getting over the crackdowns on food rioters in Kiev and Smolensk. The Soviets had learned a lot about stage-managing public relations stunts from Gorbachev and Yeltsin.

Then, on the fourth day of June, the unthinkable had happened. In front of tens of millions of television viewers worldwide, a bomb planted in Norway's parliament building had exploded just as the Soviet President had come forward to deliver a speech announcing the settlement of the dispute.

The act had left the world stunned. Not only had the charismatic, reform-minded Soviet President perished in that blast, but along with him numerous high-ranking Norwegian government officials and members of the Storting had died as well. Within a matter of hours there were riots in Oslo and Bergen, and an air of desperation and near-anarchy seemed to dominate Norway.

The Soviet reaction had been both swift and deadly. Declaring the bomb plot and the subsequent disorders in a neighbor country posed a direct threat to the stability of their own nation, Russian leaders announced their intention to restore order before the situation deteriorated further. Russian troops and planes were on their way into Norwegian territory within a day of that fateful assassination.

Tarrant considered himself a student of history, and he couldn't help but draw the parallels between the events the world had just witnessed and another assassination plot years ago in a Balkan city called Sarajevo. But where it had taken over a month for open warfare to break out after the death of Austria's Archduke Ferdinand, this time fighting erupted in a matter of hours.

What other differences would there be . . . and what similarities? Would Norway be another Afghanistan, or the flashpoint for the Third World War?

Tonight the crisis had just escalated one notch higher, and the world had moved one step closer to all-out war between the superpowers.

It was ironic, he thought as he finished the long communiqué and put it aside, the way the crisis had come out of nowhere. Twenty years, even ten years ago, a Soviet attack into Norway would have been unthinkable. Norway was a firm NATO ally, and though foreign troops were not permitted on Norwegian soil in peacetime, the apparatus for getting them there in a hurry was well tested. But the very air of peace and cooperation that had followed the fall of the

Berlin Wall had also undermined the whole fabric of the West's defense plans. NATO was almost a dead letter now, in shambles after fighting had erupted between Greece and Turkey and after Germany's decision to pull out of the alliance and stand alone. The Labor government in Britain had cut back involvement in European affairs as they had cut the British defense budget, and the United States, with liberal Democrats controlling both the Congress and the Executive Branch for the first time in decades, had been just as eager to retreat into a new isolationism. The tireless pursuit of the "peace dividend" had led to closings of most of the major military bases in Europe and massive cuts in personnel and hardware.

America had hesitated when the first tanks rolled across the border. President Connally had been reluctant to make a unilateral commitment of forces, preferring to seek United Nations support for a solution, be it diplomatic or military, to the aggression in Scandinavia. Now, a week into the fighting, he had finally issued the orders to act.

Tarrant tapped the printout absently with the fingers of one hand. The gesture Connally had ordered could easily turn out to be too little, too late. Norway had not been able to put up the stiff resistance everyone had expected the nation to provide in the event of an invasion. Though both sides had been mobilized before the Soviet President's visit to Oslo, the Norwegians had received orders to begin a general stand-down in the wake of the breakthroughs at the conference table. The crippling blow to their government had created massive confusion which the Russians, who had remained on full alert throughout, were quick to exploit. Their advance into Norway had used the kind of AirLand battle techniques demonstrated before by the U.S. in Operation Desert Storm, encircling, cutting off pockets of resistance, using airborne and airmobile capabilities to the fullest. Amphibious operations along the vulnerable coastline had been another key factor in the rapid Russian advance.

It looked now like Norway might fall before American intervention could do anything to save the country . . . and CBG-14 was sailing into the middle of that inferno.

He glanced at the clock again. It was almost time for him to put in his appearance at Flag Plot and set his staff in motion to translate Washington's orders into action. But first, he told himself as he reached for the switch on his computer terminal, he would finish the letter to his wife so it would be ready for the next COD flight.

Admiral Douglas F. Tarrant was all too aware that it might be the last letter he ever sent her.

2356 hours Zulu (2156 hours Zone)
Flight deck, U.S.S. *Thomas Jefferson*
The North Atlantic

Commander Willis E. Grant held on to his cap with one hand and hurried across the deck toward the huddled row of airplanes parked on the flight deck. In the eerie glow of worklights they presented a nightmare appearance, with wings twisted and folded in bizarre shapes to allow them to take up the least possible space. Intruders with wings folded upward at mid-span to meet above the center of the fuselage, S-3 Viking sub-hunters with tails twisted to one side and slender wings laid flat against the top of the aircraft, the weird shape of a Hawkeye with wings tucked close in alongside its body and the huge rotating radar dome on top casting strange shadows, all of them looked like prehistoric beasts lurking in the shadows, waiting to strike.

Around them the steady work of a carrier at sea went on. Grant dodged a pair of green-shirted maintenance men and narrowly avoided being run down by one of the ''mules'' that were used to tow planes from place to place on the deck and were driven by a blue-shirted crewman. Then he saw the newly arrived Tomcat, already tucked neatly into a row of other aircraft, with the familiar tall, spare figure of Tombstone Magruder visible near the front of the plane.

Magruder had his helmet under one arm and was bending over to examine the jet's front landing gear assembly. Grant had seen the hard landing he'd made, and knew what that could do to the wheels. It was typical of Magruder to be concerned for his plane after he was down, a familiar echo of many shared flights.

They went back a long way, Magruder and Grant, all the way back to flight school. Over the years the two of them had been rivals in almost everything, and a lasting friendship had grown up between them along the way. Grant had won their competition for the heart of Julie Wilson, but Tombstone had been best man at their Navy wedding. Then Magruder had won the coveted assignment to Top Gun, narrowly beating out Grant in the squadron competitions for the honor. Tombstone had been a step ahead of Grant when it came to promotions, making lieutenant commander and squadron leader of VF-95 after his graduation from Top Gun. It hadn't changed their friendship, though. Far from begrudging Magruder his advancement, Grant had been delighted for his friend. He had secretly wondered, though, if he himself hadn't been the lucky one of the pair. What he had with Julie was something he wouldn't have given up for all the stripes in the Navy, and by the same token there had always been a restless, questing part of Matt Magruder that was never entirely at ease no matter how much he achieved.

They'd been reunited in the Vipers for *Jefferson*'s Pacific deployment, and it was that cruise that had changed them both forever. While Tombstone was scoring ACM kills over North Korea and starting on the hero's path, Grant had been shot down in the first engagement of the confrontation.

Captured by the enemy, he'd been thrown into a prison camp alongside the crew of the American spy ship that had triggered the crisis. The Marine rescue mission to Wonsan had freed him along with the others, but afterward Grant had come close to turning in his wings. He had come too close to death to ever take anything, especially his happiness with Julie, lightly again.

The one thing that had pulled him through that time of crisis had been Magruder's unyielding faith in him. In the fraternity of naval aviators there was little sympathy for the men who cracked under the strain, who showed even a hint of human weakness. But Tombstone Magruder hadn't turned his back on Grant, and in the end, recovered from his ordeal, Grant had returned to VF-95 in time to fight side by side with Tombstone again in the skies over the Indian Ocean.

It was a debt he would never be able to fully repay. Grant loved flying, and looking back now he knew that he would never have forgiven himself if he'd gone through with that first impulse to quit.

A plane captain clad in a brown shirt had joined Magruder, and was nodding sagely at something Tombstone was pointing out to him. The Tomcat's RIO, looking painfully young and unsure of himself, lingered for a few moments looking uncertainly at Tombstone before he finally started for the carrier's island.

Then Tombstone was finished with his inspection and starting off in the younger officer's wake, heading toward Grant but apparently not aware of him. Grant stepped in front of him, drew up to attention, and tore off a snappy salute. "Deputy CAG, sir!" he said. "VF-95 welcomes you aboard, sir!"

The look on Magruder's face was a joy to behold. Bewilderment, then surprise, then sheer joy spread across his features in quick succession. "Coyote!" he said, using

Grant's well-worn call sign. "God damn, Coyote, what a perfect welcoming committee! I didn't even know you were still on the *Jeff*!"

"There's still a few of us here, Matt," Grant told him, grinning. Despite the best of intentions they'd lost touch over the past two years. Magruder wasn't much of a correspondent at the best of times, and Coyote could imagine how easy it had been for him to put off writing letters in the face of day after day of piled-up paperwork. Though he'd tried to keep up his end, eventually Grant had started letting the contact slide as well. That had been about the time Julie Marie had been born. "Batman and Malibu would've been here too, but they had a Bear hunt tonight. We were afraid we'd lost you to the old five-sided squirrel cage forever!"

Magruder's smile faded. "Biggest mistake I ever made, letting myself get talked into that. I could've had damn near any assignment I asked for after that cruise, but I ended up pushing papers and smiling for the publicity photos." There was a bitterness there that Coyote didn't like. Tombstone had always been a little bit moody, but this was different, grimmer. Like he'd lost a part of himself and wasn't sure he'd ever get it back again. Tombstone shrugged, then said, "How's the baby?"

"Almost three now . . . what they call the 'Terrible Twos.'" Coyote made a face. "Julie claims she'll get over it. I hope the house survives!"

"She must love you bugging out for sea duty again so quick," Magruder commented, chuckling.

"You know Julie. No complaints there." Grant glanced at his friend. "How's Pamela doing?"

"Okay, I guess," Tombstone replied, looking away. "We . . . uh, called it quits a few months back. I haven't seen her in a while, except on the tube."

"I'm sorry," Coyote said, feeling the words were inadequate. "I thought you'd worked out all the . . . problems there."

"I did too. Guess I was wrong." He had that grim look again. Tombstone's romance with Pamela Drake had been the kind of relationship Hollywood screenwriters loved. The red-hot Navy fighter jockey and the beautiful television reporter had seemed perfect together, and Grant had really thought his friend had found something to hold on to at last, something as strong as what Coyote had with Julie. There had been some strains, of course. Pamela had been faced with the problem every service wife or girlfriend had to deal with, the danger of Tombstone's career, and the fact that her Marine brother had died overseas hadn't helped. She'd pleaded with Magruder to give up the Navy, but Tombstone had finally made her see how important his job was to him. "I really thought she understood how much the Navy meant to me, but I guess I was wrong. Even though she gave up on trying to make me a pilot for United or whoever, she kept telling me I should use my reputation to get myself a better job . . . you know, go into politics or on the talk show circuit or something. Can you see me spending all my time making the rounds with Jay or Phil?"

"I'm sorry," Coyote repeated uselessly. "I thought you two had something pretty good going."

"Yeah, me too," Magruder told him. He looked away, then turned back to Coyote with a grin. "Well, if the Batman's on board, maybe he'll teach me how to hold on to women."

They both laughed. Batman Wayne had been as much renowned aboard the *Jefferson* for his conquests in port as for his skill in the sky, but he wasn't good at lasting relationships. Not if "lasting" meant a period of more than a week. But the laughter was strained, and Coyote felt there was a wall between them.

He wanted to change the subject, but after so long he

wasn't sure if there were *any* safe topics left. "How about your uncle?" he said hesitantly. "How's he been doing?"

"Good, good," Magruder said quickly, latching on to the new topic. There had been a time when his relationship to Admiral Thomas Magruder would have been a sore spot as well, but that was one thing that being a hero had helped him come to terms with. The admiral had commanded CBG-14 for a time, and his nephew had taken a lot of flak from people who thought he owed his advancement more to connections than ability. Tombstone had certainly disproved that. "He just got a posting to the Pentagon, in the Joint Operations Staff. A bit of a letdown from Presidential adviser, but after Connally came in it was a pretty good career move. He was moving in about the time I was coming up for reassignment."

"Well, there's one Magruder I'll be glad to have in the Pentagon. The Old Man will show them a thing or two, huh?" They had reached the carrier's island. Ducking through a hatch, they started down one of the seemingly endless corridors en route to the ready room, where Magruder could get out of his flight suit before reporting to Maintenance Control for the usual round of post-flight paperwork. "Oh, yeah, I almost forgot. I took care of your uniforms and your quarters assignment as soon as I heard you were coming aboard. Everything's set."

Magruder looked relieved. "Great. They stuffed us into those planes so fast they didn't even give us time to pack. You're a real buddy, Willie."

Coyote glanced at him. The words were sincere enough, but Grant couldn't help thinking how much they'd grown apart these last two years. It was like he was meeting Matt Magruder for the first time, and there were barriers there that old friendship just couldn't get around.

CHAPTER 5
Tuesday, 10 June 1997

0552 hours Zulu (0552 hours Zone)
Soviet Fulcrum 101, Strike Mission *Letushiy*
Over the Sognefjorden, Sogn Og Fjordane, Norway

"*Letushiy* Leader, *Letushiy* Leader, this is *Khrahneetyehly*. Aircraft activity detected over target. Proceed with caution."

Captain Second Rank Sergei Sergeivich Terekhov checked his radar but saw no trace of the enemy aircraft reported by the An-74 Airborne Early Warning plane circling far to the north of the Norwegian coastline. The lack of radar traces didn't surprise him. The eight MiG-29D ground-attack aircraft in his squadron were less than fifty meters above the quiet gray waters of the fjord. The undulating coastline and rugged mountains masked the MiG's Pulse-Doppler radar system, just as they shielded his planes from detection by the Norwegians.

"Understood, *Khrahneetyehly*," Terekhov replied on the radio channel to the AEW plane. "Request instructions, over."

That was an essential part of every Soviet pilot's training, to work in close conjunction with controllers in the rear. Aboard *Khrahneetyehly*—Guardian—the controllers would be coordinating their information with the other Soviet naval and air units in the area. Their orders would take every aspect of the situation into account.

Terekhov had heard that most Western pilots, especially the Americans, would be expected to make their own decisions at a time like this. He wondered how their commanders expected to maintain control over a battle with so much initiative left in the hands of junior officers who saw only their own tiny portion of the conflict.

"*Letushiy* Leader, engage enemy aircraft at bearing zero-three-five your position with four of your aircraft. Remainder to continue mission as profiled."

"Orders understood." Terekhov switched frequencies and gave the necessary orders. He allowed himself a smile of satisfaction as four of the MiG's climbed sharply away from the rest of the squadron. They would be on the Norwegian air-defense radar screens almost immediately, and distract the patrols the An-74 had detected.

That would leave the way open for Strike Mission Volatile to carry out its attack on the Norwegian defenses.

The high cliffs were narrowing on either side of them now as they raced eastward. Soon they would see the target. . . .

Three targets suddenly appeared on his radar, and mere seconds later he spotted the fast-moving F-16 interceptors flashing overhead. They were gone almost before he could react, and over his radio Terekhov could hear the first warning shouts as the four decoys sighted the Norwegians and engaged. He was tempted to take advantage of the situation and loop back to take them from behind as they fought the rest of the squadron, but he resisted the impulse. For the moment that fight was none of his concern. The mission came first.

Somewhere below a probing radar beam swept over the MiG, and Terekhov felt a rush of adrenaline as the radar-warning receiver on his control panel sounded an urgent alarm. It was always like this for Terekhov when a potential enemy first appeared. Years of training, first with Frontal Aviation and then as part of the expanded Aviatsiya Voenna-Morskovo Flota, had focused on the moment of combat, but so far he had never fired a shot in anger. Nonetheless, each time the probing fingers of an unknown radar brushed his aircraft, he thought about the prospects of combat. Death or glory in the service of Soviet Naval Aviation and the *Rodina*, the Motherland. That was the goal of every fighter pilot.

Today there was no doubt. The moment for action had arrived at last.

Terekhov drew a deep breath and forced himself to stay calm. He was one of the elite, one of the small number of Soviet pilots who had actually passed the difficult carrier landing course at Saki in the Crimea and gone on to become a naval aviator. It would not do for him to allow his excitement to get the better of his judgment today. Giving in to any sort of emotion was an invitation to disaster.

"SAM! SAM!" Captain-Lieutenant Stepan Dmitriyev shouted the warning before Terekhov's radar picked it up. It was locked on to Dmitriyev's aircraft.

"Climb, Stepan! Climb!" Terekhov yelled. The other MiG broke formation and clawed its way toward open sky, but the missile was faster. As if in slow motion, Terekhov saw a puff of chaff ballooning behind Dmitriyev's MiG, but it was too late. An instant later the aircraft was gone, consumed in a flash of flame and debris.

"We have taken SAM fire," he reported, switching to the command channel. "One-oh-six destroyed."

"Continue mission," the controller responded coldly.

As he banked left to line up for the final attack run Terekhov fought to maintain his calm. Bombers were supposed to have softened up the area earlier, but evidently the Norwegians had been smart enough to keep some of their radar and missile assets concealed from that first wave. This wasn't going to be as easy as it had sounded in the briefing room aboard the aircraft carrier *Soyuz.*

The harsh alarm of another threat warning made him scan his instruments. Another SAM was locking on. But this time Terekhov was the target.

Almost instinctively he shoved the throttles forward, igniting the afterburners of the MiG's twin Isotov RD-33 turbofans. Acceleration pressed him back into his seat as he wrenched the stick back and climbed, angling north out toward the line of mountains north of the fjord.

The threat tone went on. He could almost feel the enemy missile closing on the MiG.

With a sudden, violent movement of the stick Terekhov wrenched the aircraft onto a new heading and stabbed at the button that would release his chaff. The cloud of reflective debris would interfere with radar guidance and hopefully confuse the onrushing missile for the critical seconds he needed.

The mountainside rushed past his cockpit as he turned, still climbing fast. Then there was a flash below as the missile, fooled by the chaff, plowed into a cliff wall and detonated.

Letting out a long sigh, Terekhov dropped back into the fjord and reduced his speed. The other two planes were ahead of him now, still flying a tight welded-wing formation.

He spotted the target beyond them by the smoke rising from a fire that burned close by. So the bombers had caused some damage after all. But the Norwegian airfield of Hermansverk was still functional, and so were the coastal defense guns mounted on the cliffs west of the airfield.

"Target in sight," he reported.

"Commence attack run," the controller said. "One-oh-five on the Bofors site. Remaining two aircraft will attack the airfield."

"Message understood," he responded. "Recommend a second strike mission to eliminate further air defenses."

"Noted. Proceed with attack."

He passed the orders on to the others, and watched as Lieutenant Dzhus peeled off to commence his attack on the coastal gun. Then he was too busy to watch the other planes.

The MiG dropped low, sweeping across the arm of the fjord toward the airfield. Terekhov spotted an F-16 speeding down the runway and taking flight. He flipped his selector switch to arm an AA-8 infrared homing missile.

The tone in his ear told him he had a firm lock, and he launched the missile. It streaked away, catching the Norwegian plane before its pilot had a chance to react. That was another Royal Norwegian Air Force interceptor out of the way.

On his left the other MiG released its load of FAB-250 general-purpose bombs and pulled up. Hastily Terekhov nudged the selector switch and found his target, an untouched storage tank in the tank farm on the far end of the airfield. As his MiG stooped low over the RNAF compound he hit the release. The first bomb dropped away and Terekhov pulled up, cutting in his afterburners.

The bomb struck with a satisfying eruption of flame and black smoke. Terekhov banked to port and climbed, scanning the airfield for additional targets. He saw a hardened aircraft shelter which had escaped damage so far.

The second bomb found its mark, but by that time he was too far away and climbing too fast to get a good estimate of the damage. Photo-recon flights could assess that later. Right now his first duty was to rejoin the squadron.

He saw the wreckage of the Bofors gun below as he fell

into formation with the other two planes and turned southwest again. That made a clean sweep for this sortie. It would
look good on the squadron's record, and on Soviet Naval
Aviation's balance sheets. There truly was a place for
carrier-based aircraft in the *Rodina*'s arsenal. Heavy bombers could do a great deal of damage, but strike attacks at
short range were more flexible and better able to obtain
accurate hits. The Sognefjorden, less than a hundred kilometers north of the last major center of Norwegian resistance at Bergen, was one of several potential landing zones
for Soviet amphibious forces, and clearing the air and
artillery defenses was a crucial first step in launching an
assault.

The campaign in Norway would never maintain the speed
it required to achieve total victory unless the Soviets
maintained the rapid pace of their advance down the coast.
The West had been obligingly sluggish reacting to the war
to date . . . but the Soviets couldn't win unless they kept
up the momentum.

Sergei Sergeivich Terekhov smiled again as he led his
planes back toward the continuing battle. With their bombs
unloaded, they would make short work of the outnumbered
Norwegians. Then it would be back to the *Soyuz,* refuel,
rearm, and on to the next mission.

It felt good to know that he and his comrades were
playing an essential role in the rebirth of the *Rodina* as a
superpower.

0915 hours Zulu (0715 hours Zone)
Officers' quarters, U.S.S. *Thomas Jefferson*
The North Atlantic

Tombstone had resisted the temptation to prolong the
reunion with Coyote or even to wait to see Batman and
Malibu return aboard. It had been a long flight from Oceana,

and he was tired. He'd attended to the formalities, the paperwork and a courtesy call to the duty officer in the CAG office to report himself aboard, and within an hour of touching down on the flight deck he had been stretched out in his rack, asleep. After a flight of more than two thousand miles and a late night landing he felt he deserved a chance to rest.

Someone evidently disagreed with that notion.

"Come on, buddy, shake a leg! CAG's on the warpath!"

Through a fog he thought the voice was familiar, but Tombstone wasn't awake enough to place it. The hand shaking his shoulder helped him open his eyes, at least long enough to get rid of the intruder.

"If you want to keep that arm you'd better take it out of here," he growled. "Otherwise I'll tear it out by the roots and beat you with the bloody end."

"That's the Tombstone I remember," the voice said mockingly. "Look, I had late duty, too, but you don't see me threatening my friends!"

Tombstone rolled over to look at his tormentor for the first time. "Wayne? If this is one of your goddamned practical jokes, boyo, I'll personally see to it they reinstate keelhauling just for you."

Batman Wayne grinned. "You would too," he said cheerfully. "But I swear I'm not guilty this time, Stoney. There's some kind of hush-hush staff meeting this morning, and CAG says you're supposed to be there. And he wants to see you in his office first. I heard him chewing out Owens and ducked down here to save your sorry hide."

Tombstone rubbed his eyes and swung his feet to the floor. "The CAG's a tough one, huh?" he asked.

"Don't you *know*?" Batman was looking at him curiously. "It's Stramaglia. The Stinger himself!"

Magruder blinked, slow to react to the name. He hadn't

been given much time to prepare himself for his sudden
assignment. He'd known about his predecessor, Jolly
Greene, because a friend in Personnel at the Pentagon had
told him when he'd lost out on the assignment while
Jefferson was still fitting out. With one or two exceptions he
knew very little about who was aboard the carrier.

But he knew the name Stinger Stramaglia. There were
very few Top Gun graduates these days who didn't.

"You're kidding," he said slowly. "What's the Old Man
doing out here?"

Captain Joseph Stramaglia had been a Top Gun legend,
one of the finest students to pass through the training
program. He'd stayed on as an instructor after graduating,
and worked his way to the top of the team who flew the
aggressor planes students honed their skills against in weeks
of constant aerial duels. Instead of the usual four- or
five-year tour as a Top Gun teacher, Stramaglia had been
there for almost eight. It was said that Stramaglia had never
been beaten in a dogfight in all that time.

Certainly Matthew Magruder had never come close to
beating him in the five weeks he'd been at Miramar.

"It's him, all right," Batman said. "He'd left Miramar
by the time I got my shot, but I saw pictures of him. And I
heard stories I thought couldn't possibly be true . . . not
until I got to meet the man in person."

"Yeah," Magruder said. "Yeah, he's a tough one, all
right."

"Tough! His running name should've been Pit Bull! Next
to him old Jolly Greene was a saint!"

Tombstone didn't answer. He crossed to the locker where
he'd left his meager belongings the night before without
bothering to unpack. While he dressed he thought about
Stramaglia, about the man's reputation as a harsh taskmaster
and the way he had ridden Magruder at Top Gun, in the air
and on the ground alike.

Having the man as his superior officer was going to make this tour on the *Jefferson* . . . what? Difficult? Rewarding? Tombstone didn't know.

But it certainly wouldn't be dull, that much was sure.

Batman went on talking, apparently unaware that Tombstone's mind wasn't on the younger pilot's words. "Hey, Stoney," he said as Magruder made a few hasty passes across his face with an electric razor. Tombstone looked at him, shoving thoughts of Captain Stramaglia aside. "You should see the walls at Fightertown! They got so many plaques up there with your name on them that they ought to open up a new wing just to hold 'em!"

Tombstone laughed. It was an old tradition that the air-to-air kills of Top Gun graduates were commemorated on wall plaques. But on his first tour out of Top Gun Magruder had scored a long string of kills against North Koreans, Chinese renegades, and the Indian Air Force. "Well, how about you? You've had your share, Batman."

Wayne made a face. "That's what I *told* them, man! But I wasn't an alumnus when I nailed 'em!"

They left together, heading down the seemingly endless corridors toward the offices set aside for the Air Wing's staff. As Magruder rounded a corner and stepped high to avoid a "knee-knocker" he heard Coyote's voice intone solemnly, "See, the conquering hero comes!"

Viper Squadron's new commander was sitting at a desk inside one of the offices. Malibu Blake was with him, leaning back in a chair and managing to look like he was on a beach soaking up a few rays.

"Bet you never thought we'd be here, did you, Stoney?" Batman asked.

Magruder laughed. "Hell, no. No way. But I guess they couldn't split up the Three Musketeers for good, huh?"

"Well, thanks a lot, dude," Malibu said. "I guess I know when I'm not wanted!"

"I just figured you'd've ditched this loser by now, that's all," Tombstone said, jerking a thumb at Batman. "I thought you had more sense than that!"

"Hey, that's my main compadre you're talking about," Malibu shot back with a grin. "*And* the squadron XO. So watch the insults, 'kay, dude?"

"If you people are *quite* through," an acid voice cut through their laughter. "Magruder! Get your ass into my office now. And you, Wayne, had better have your report on that Bear hunt finished and on my desk already!"

Tombstone turned and found himself looking straight into Captain Joseph Stramaglia's jet-black eyes. *Jefferson*'s CAG was a small man, but with a presence that could dominate any crowd. He had one of his famous cigars in his mouth, unlit. Stramaglia used those cigars as pointers, and even as improvised model airplanes to demonstrate aerial tactics, but Magruder had never known him to actually smoke them.

"Aye, aye, sir," he and Batman responded almost in unison. He followed Stramaglia to his office a few yards down the corridor from Coyote's.

"Sit," Stramaglia said, gesturing to a chair with the cigar. Magruder sat down uncomfortably, uneasy at the man's manner.

"Well, well," the CAG went on, settling into his own chair behind the desk. "The famous Commander Magruder returns." He regarded Tombstone intently. "I need a deputy who can help me keep this Air Wing at peak efficiency for the next five months. We've had a bad start, planes lost, men killed in a *stupid* accident. And with this mess in Norway brewing there's no telling what we're going to be up against next."

He paused, frowning. "That's what I need. What I've got is a goddamned hero. I don't like heroes, Mr. Magruder. I like good, solid, competent men who get the job done and don't feel the need to keep their reputations all shiny and bright. You read me, Commander?''

"Sir . . . permission to speak freely?''

Stramaglia nodded, a curt, almost angry gesture.

"With all due respect, sir,'' Magruder went on. "I didn't ask for the hero treatment. And I feel it's unfair of you to judge me before I've had a chance to show you how I can perform my duties.''

"Is that all you have to say?''

"Yessir,'' Magruder replied, feeling like a student again.

"Good. Because you're absolutely right.'' Stramaglia allowed himself a faint smile. "I just wanted you to know exactly where things stand. There are a few old shipmates of yours aboard this boat, as you've already discovered, and there a lot of young hotshots who never met you but plan to be just like you given half a chance. You're gonna have to work overtime to get past that hero-worship crap if you're gonna be an effective member of my staff. Understand me?''

"Yes, sir,'' Magruder said again, relaxing a little. Stramaglia hadn't changed much, it seemed. He was still blunt, even harsh . . . but fair enough, in the long run.

"All right, then. I see you having the potential to be a good Deputy CAG, Commander, just as I thought you had potential as an aviator. You didn't disappoint me the last time . . . try not to let me down now.''

"I'll do my best, sir,'' Tombstone said slowly.

"You damned well better believe you'll do your best! When I'm through with you, Commander, you'll know everything there is to know about an air wing. Not just the flashy fighters . . . everything.'' Stramaglia paused. "I'm an old-fashioned kind of officer, and I stick with the old COMNAVAIRLANT policy—air wing commanders fly two types of aircraft off the carrier deck, no more, no less.

My deputies follow the same rules. Your file says you're checked out on most everything we're carrying, right?"

"Fixed wing, yes, sir," Tombstone said. "Not helos, though."

"Good. For now you're cleared for the S-3 and the A-6. Those are the birds your predecessor was assigned to. You can fly them, or you can go up as an NFO, whatever. But unless I tell you otherwise you concentrate on those two birds and nothing else. Got me?"

Inwardly, Tombstone seethed. He'd flown most of the Navy's planes at one time or another, but he had always been a Tomcat driver first and foremost. Stramaglia was cutting him off from the part of the job he really loved.

It was like Washington all over again . . . but with the life he wanted tantalizingly close, hanging just out of reach.

"I understand, sir," he said carefully, trying to keep his voice neutral.

But Stramaglia wasn't fooled. "Not pleased, are you, Magruder? Well, you're not supposed to be. Look, Deputy CAG carries some damned heavy responsibilities. You're my number two. I expect my deputy to know everything there is to know about running the Air Wing, because if I buy it you're the one who has to take over. You need to learn what the rest of the Air Wing does. What you don't need is any more experience in Tomcats, 'cause you've got that down cold already. So you'll concentrate on what you need to learn. Sub-hunting. Executing bombing runs. You're going back to school, son, just like the old days at Miramar."

"Yes, sir," Magruder acknowledged. He could see the older man's point, though it still stung him to be barred from duty with the Tomcat squadrons.

Stramaglia's watch beeped an alarm. He checked it with a frown. "Admiral Tarrant's called a briefing this morning for senior battle group officers. That includes the top CAG staff. So let's get going." He paused, studying Magruder's face. "And for God's sake, stop looking like you're on Death Row. I don't bite, son . . . well, not much, at least."

Magruder forced a smile and rose from the chair, following Stramaglia out of the office.

CHAPTER 6
Tuesday, 10 June 1997

1055 hours Zulu (0855 hours Zone)
CVIC, U.S.S. *Thomas Jefferson*
The North Atlantic

The room was known as "Civic," from the designation
CVIC, the Navy acronym for "Carrier Intelligence Center." It reminded Stramaglia more of a lecture hall than part
of an ultra-modern supercarrier. The grays and off-greens of
the bulkheads were broken up by framed prints along the
side walls showing famous scenes from U.S. naval history,
while the wall behind him was dominated by an oil painting
of the *Jefferson* herself. Behind the podium at the far end of
the room was a projection screen, and folding metal chairs
dominated the center of the room. About half of them were
filled this morning with an impressive collection of senior
officers from Carrier Battle Group 14, and the officers still
milling around were beginning to drift toward their seats.

Stramaglia spotted Lieutenant Commander Arthur Lee,
the Air Wing's Intelligence Officer, coming in by the door
nearest the podium. He waved to attract Lee's attention, and
with a nod the younger officer started toward Stramaglia
and the other two officers representing the CAG staff sitting
with him.

Stramaglia glanced from one to the other. Lieutenant

Commander David Owens, with his fresh face and eager manner, looked too young for his rank. His record said he was qualified, but he didn't have enough experience to suit Stramaglia. With time and seasoning Owens might be all right, but he didn't inspire much confidence. That had been Stramaglia's main reason for requesting an immediate replacement after Greene's death.

The new Deputy CAG, Magruder, certainly had the seasoning Owens lacked. Back in Miramar Stramaglia had marked him out as an officer who might go far. Magruder was thoughtful, not given to the kind of hotdog stunts so many fighter pilots were prone to pull. But he'd also known when to let his instincts take over. His career since Top Gun had gone far beyond Stramaglia's expectations.

All he had to do now was apply himself as well to his new post as he had to flying and Magruder would be a good candidate for his own air wing command some day . . . perhaps even a slot as Exec or Captain on a carrier. That was something Joseph Stramaglia knew he'd never see himself.

The thought still left a bitter taste in his mouth.

For eight years he'd taught the best of the best, the top one percent of the Navy's fighter pilots. It had started as a privilege, an honor bestowed on him for his excellent performance. But each time he'd set out to apply for a new duty station he'd let someone talk him out of it, appealing to pride or duty or vanity to persuade him to put in a little more time as an instructor.

And before he'd realized it eight years were gone, and with them the best chance for a real career. He'd missed out on Desert Storm right off the bat, but the F-14s hadn't seen much action over Iraq anyway. But he'd still been training others while Matthew Magruder was becoming America's latest naval hero.

Now it was too late. He'd finally wangled command of an air wing by pulling every string he could think of. But the chances of rising any higher were slim now. The Navy's program for promoting officers to command slots was getting more and more rigid, and with all the defense cutbacks lately it was getting so there were a dozen or more top candidates for every position. That was especially true with carriers. Fourteen flattops were all there were. Even the chance of commanding a Naval Air Station rated somewhere between slim and none.

Too senior to fly, but without the record to advance any further . . . Stramaglia knew he'd been letting his own bitterness hamper him in dealing with his subordinates, especially Magruder, but sometimes it just didn't seem fair.

Lee sat down next to him. "Looks like this is the big one, doesn't it, sir?" he said. The prospect seemed to excite him. "Did you see the morning news?"

"Yeah," Stramaglia said shortly. Both of *Jefferson*'s television stations carried news programs, a mix of shipboard information and world news picked up by satellite.

"I didn't," Magruder put in. "What happened?"

Lee looked at him. "You must be Commander Magruder," he said, sticking out his hand. "Welcome aboard. I'm Lee . . . Arthur Lee. Staff Intelligence man. I've heard a hell of a lot about you. Some of it was even good." He grinned as they shook hands. "The UN vote finally went down last night. Twelve to two, with China abstaining."

"And it wasn't worth a damned thing because of the Russian veto," Magruder finished for him grimly.

"So much for the 'New World Order,'" Owens put in. "That's what comes of letting the bad guys have veto power."

Stramaglia stayed out of their conversation, but inwardly he knew how they felt. While the Russians cut through Norway's defenses, President Connally had been stalling American reaction until the United Nations could act. It was as if he'd learned all the wrong lessons from the conflict with Iraq, where America had mobilized UN support only *after* guaranteeing assistance for Saudi Arabia. Resolution 782, calling for a peaceful solution to the Scandinavian crisis and condemning the USSR for its aggression, had gone exactly nowhere. And in the interim nearly a week of precious time had been lost. Connally could claim now that he'd exhausted every peaceful means before turning to a military response, but in the process he might just have given the Russians everything they needed to make their attack on Norway stick.

For nearly a decade Stramaglia had been regarded as a bit of a dinosaur where the Russians were concerned. Hotshot youngsters at Miramar had been fond of claiming that future conflicts would follow the pattern set down by Operation Desert Storm: small, outclassed opponents facing the overwhelming air superiority of American technology. But Joseph Stramaglia had never entirely counted the Russians out, not even after Yeltsin had emerged as the leader of the new Russian Commonwealth. There had been too many unknowns, to Stramaglia's way of thinking. Too many factions, like the hard-liners in the military, who hadn't been heard from.

And now it looked like he'd been right after all.

1100 hours Zulu (1000 hours Zone)
CVIC, U.S.S. *Thomas Jefferson*
The North Atlantic

''Attention on deck!'' a junior officer called out as Admiral Tarrant strode into Civic. Every man in the briefing room came to his feet in response.

''As you were,'' he said quickly, strolling purposefully toward the podium at the far end of the long room.

As Tarrant reached the podium he scanned the lines of

seated officers. Brandt was sitting near the front, with his Exec, Commander Parker, and several members of Tarrant's Flag Staff. As he studied their faces, he wondered what they were thinking.

He saw Captain Stramaglia and other officers from *Jefferson*'s Air Wing at the back of the room. Most of the striking power of the battle group was contained in the carrier's air complement, and their role in the next few days would be crucial. Tarrant hoped they would be up to the challenge. Stramaglia had a good reputation, but he hadn't been at sea for over a decade. Did he still have the edge?

And then there was Captain Vic Gates of the *Shiloh*, the battle group's Aegis cruiser. He looked distinctly uncomfortable. His ship, with its powerful radar systems and missile defenses, would be a key player if they faced a major attack. In the Indian Ocean two years back *Jefferson* had come through with minor damage, but her Aegis cruiser escort had been all but crippled. Maybe Gates was thinking about that.

But they'd all have their parts to play, the DDGs *Lawrence Kearny* and *John A. Winslow;* the battle group's three frigates, *Gridley, Esek Hopkins,* and *Stephen Decatur;* and the two 688-class submarines, *Galveston* and *Bangor.* A carrier battle group was more than just the carrier itself. It was a balanced task force in which each ship, each aircraft, each man had a vital role to play.

Tarrant cleared his throat and stepped behind the podium. It was time to let them know the score.

"Gentlemen," he said formally. "You all know what's been going on in Norway. We've been watching the Russians overrun the country for close to a week, and I'm sure most of you have been wondering what the United States plans to do about it. Well, some recent developments have finally shaped our course. We received orders from CINCLANT late last night, and I felt you should all be brought into the picture. Commander Aiken will bring us up to date on the military picture first. Commander?''

Commander Paul Aiken was head of OZ Division, the Intelligence branch of *Jefferson*'s Operations Department. A small, precise man with a dry manner and a face that betrayed no emotion, Aiken was responsible for coordinating all information gathered by a variety of means and making it available to the carrier's command, air, and flag staffs. He advanced to the podium carrying a bundle of papers under one arm. The lights dimmed as one of his officers switched on the projector.

''The situation in Scandinavia has, quite frankly, developed in a totally unexpected manner,'' Aiken began. He gestured to the screen behind him, where a map of the region had appeared. ''During the Cold War it was always assumed that any attack into Norway could be delayed by local forces long enough to allow NATO reinforcement before the Soviets could make significant territorial gains. The entire defensive posture of the country was predicated on this assessment.''

He checked his notes before going on. ''The Norwegians have a long tradition of avoiding European entanglements, and they were somewhat reluctant to get involved in NATO at all. However, the experience of Nazi occupation in World War II showed them that it was necessary to seek protection from stronger powers. Northern Norway guards the main approaches to the bases of Russia's Red Banner Northern Fleet in the White and Barents Sea areas, and this has made the country both a strategic prize for the Russians and a critical strongpoint for the West. Land-based aircraft operating from Norwegian air bases could play havoc with any Soviet fleet sorties, and in addition could protect our own ships making incursions into their waters. Because the Northern Fleet also contains the bulk of the Soviet ballistic missile submarine force, the defense of which takes top priority in Russian naval thinking, the threat of a NATO strike has made it certain that the Russians would seek to neutralize Norway as part of any larger war in Europe.''

Aiken stopped to take a sip from a glass of water on the podium. ''In this case, though, the outbreak of hostilities in Scandinavia does not seem to be part of any larger war effort but rather an end in itself. As a result the Soviets have been able to concentrate far more striking power against the region than had been allowed for in any of our Cold War planning. The scope of operations by Spetsnaz and other covert elements alone is on a scale that has caught us completely by surprise.''

''Does that mean they were planning this all along?'' Commander James Tennyson asked. He was CO of the *Lawrence Kearny,* DDG-59, a big bear of a man whose rough exterior concealed a surprising intellect.

''It certainly suggests it,'' Aiken replied carefully. ''But our intelligence sources haven't been able to confirm that theory. If the Soviets had intended to provoke a conflict there seems little enough reason for their President to negotiate a compromise agreement . . . unless we're seeing an extreme case of the breakdown of cooperation between the political and military sides of their government. There is a temptation to see the assassination as KGB or GRU work designed both to create a pretext for invasion and at the same time to remove the voice of liberal reform which might otherwise have stood in the way, but without more facts at our disposal that must remain an attractive but unconfirmed theory.''

It was a theory, Tarrant thought, that fit the facts damned well. Since the collapse of the Commonwealth and the restoration of the Soviet Union, the struggle between hard-liners in the military and the KGB against liberal reformers and breakaway ethnic, religious, and political groups had been turning Soviet government into a precarious balancing act. The President of the new Union had started out as little more than a front man for the military hard-liners who had reestablished the central authority, but lately he had been striking out on his own, often in direct opposition to military interests. Now that he was gone it looked as if the Soviet Union was speaking with one voice again. And it was the old voice, the voice of Stalin and Khrushchev, the voice of aggression, that was speaking this time.

Tarrant turned his attention back to Aiken, who was continuing from the podium. "Regardless of Soviet intentions, we must accept the realities of the position in Scandinavia. Gentlemen, Russian troops have already overrun most of Finland. The government in Helsinki offered little more than a token protest, and finally capitulated entirely four days ago. And the power brought to bear in Norway will accomplish the same thing there in a very short time unless the Norwegians receive significant support. That support, sadly, is going to be slow to materialize. NATO is barely capable of functioning in its old role now that the EEC countries are more interested in negotiating compromises instead of taking a hard line. There are rumors that the Labor government is going to lose a no-confidence vote in Britain, but even so, it would take time for the Brits to mobilize anything. And you all know how things stand with the United States."

The map on the screen behind him changed. "So much for politics," Aiken said. "What concerns us more at the moment is the military situation in Norway. Soviet troops officially crossed the borders in the early morning hours of June fifth. Bear in mind the presence of the commando forces prior to this, because they've had a significant impact upon the prosecution of the campaign so far. The attack was spearheaded by two front-line motor rifle divisions, the 45th and the 54th. These followed the lines of advance we always assumed they'd use, with the 54th violating Finnish neutrality in order to work its way behind the main lines of defense.''

Aiken took another sip of water as the slide changed to a close-up of northern Norway. ''Front-line defense of Norway was in the hands of the so-called South Varanger Garrison, with a reserve force, the Finnmark Brigade, to provide rapid backup in case of trouble. The paralysis of the Norwegian government in the first few hours of the crisis caused delays in assembling the reserve formations. They had just dispersed after an earlier mobilization order, and the confusion did nothing to improve their situation.''

He jabbed at the map with a pointer. ''Virtually the whole of the South Varanger Garrison and a substantial part of the Finnmark Brigade was surrounded and destroyed by Soviet forces here, at Tana, on the sixth.''

Another map showing the entire country appeared. ''While this was happening, the Soviets were carrying out systematic attacks on other parts of the country as well. There are a few things to note . . . first, the fact that the Red Banner Northern Fleet sortied from the Barents Sea the day *before* the assassination. This could have been coincidence, of course, or a part of ongoing saber-rattling. But it is significant that the fleet was escorting a *very* large contingent of naval infantry and Spetsnaz troops. It hasn't received much notice in the press, but the Soviets have shifted their shipbuilding program over to intensive production of amphibious vessels in the last few years, to go along with their carrier program. A very large portion of that sealift capability is currently in the Northern Fleet. When you add in merchant ships as auxiliary transports you can generate quite a formidable amphibious threat.''

''But do the Russians really have that much capacity for amphibious operations, Commander?'' That was Commander Loren Scanlan, skipper of the *Gridley*. ''I mean, sure, they can put together the ships, but they've never really focused on marines as a major combat arm, have they?''

''More than you might think, though we're not certain of exact numbers,'' Aiken responded with his usual caution. ''Don't forget, gentlemen, that ever since the end of the Cold War it has been common Soviet practice to assign fully functional motor rifle divisions to the navy as a way to get around the provisions of military reduction agreements, since so-called naval troops don't count. And while you can't turn an army division into an instant amphibious force capable of making opposed assaults, you can use them to reinforce strikes delivered by other means. Spetsnaz attacks, for instance, or parachute drops. They grab a likely piece of terrain, and these amphibious troops can come ashore and consolidate too damned fast for the defenders to react.''

The intelligence officer looked around the room as if expecting further comment, but none came. He cleared his throat and went on. ''Air strikes on the first two days of the fighting accounted for well over half of the Norwegian air force. Norway has . . . or rather *had* about a hundred combat aircraft, mostly F-16s. They've put up a good fight, but the odds are just too much. Add the neutralization of several key airfields by commando attacks and runway cratering from missiles and bombs, and you can see the way things are headed. We estimate the Soviets will have virtual air supremacy in Scandinavia within another few days.''

Tarrant scanned the officers for reactions to that. The CAG staff looked particularly grim, as well they might. With most of the Norwegian air force knocked out, carrier-based planes would be seriously outmatched in numbers. Even the vaunted Top Gun ten-to-one kill ratio might not be enough if *Jefferson*'s air wing had to go into battle.

''The final leg of the Soviet attack rested in air transport of sizable combat forces into secured positions in Oslo and

Tromso," Aiken went on. "Here again their commando and desant troops gave them a real edge. The move into Oslo was roughly comparable to the buildup of forces in Kabul during the opening stages of the Afghan war. Combined with amphibious landings at Bodo and Narvik, these operations badly disrupted the entire Norwegian coast. The long, thin nature of the country, with is poor terrain and limited road net, renders Norway vulnerable to this sort of divide-and-conquer technique."

A new map came up, a close-up of central Norway around the city of Trondheim. "This is where the real blow fell, though, in the area called Trondelag. For the past six years it has been the site of a major U.S. Marine Prepositioning center. The equipment and supplies for a specially tasked U.S. Marine Expeditionary Brigade were located here, together with prepared runway facilities at Orland and Vaernes. On June sixth these were attacked by naval Spetsnaz, reinforced by naval infantry and airborne troops. Our best satellite reconnaissance indicates that Trondelag has been all but destroyed . . . and with it virtually every contingency plan the United States had for supporting Norway."

"Christ," someone said from the front row. Tarrant thought it was Commander Don Strachan, CO of the frigate *Esek Hopkins.* "Why don't we just surrender now and be done with it? Or is there some good news buried in all of this mess?"

"The good news, such as it is, came on the seventh," Aiken answered. "On that day a Soviet attempt to take the city of Bergen failed. Bergen was the one area not caught totally off guard by the war. The senior army man there, General Nils Lindstrom, managed to pull his troops into a tight perimeter line. By concentrating air cover and intensive SAM fire and triple-A, Lindstrom knocked out the airborne elements of a major Soviet drive on Bergen. It's located in the southeastern end of the country . . . one of their biggest ports and naval bases, and near some major air bases as well. The city's critical to both sides at this point, gentlemen. As long as it's in friendly hands we have a point of reentry into Norway, and the Soviets know it. Everything boils down now to how long Lindstrom can hold out there.''

''Without effective air?'' Stramaglia snorted. ''The Russkies'll pry them out of there inside a week.''

Aiken nodded. ''That's our estimation, Captain. At the moment they are overextended, but once they've consolidated their position they are sure to muster enough strength to threaten Bergen.''

''Thank you for your rundown, Commander,'' Tarrant said, moving back toward the podium. The lights came up as Aiken took his seat in the front row. ''Gentlemen, that's the situation as it stands now . . . but there is one important addition Commander Aiken didn't mention. Yesterday evening, the White House received a communiqué from the Soviet government reiterating their position that the conflict in Norway is a strictly local matter. In addition, they have declared that all foreign military vessels should stay clear of the Norwegian Sea in an area defined by the Greenland-Iceland-United Kingdom line, extended from the Scottish coast to Jutland. I believe the phrase they used was 'to avoid accidental escalation of the current regional hostilities.' In essence they are saying that any warship entering their exclusion zone is liable to come under attack.''

''But that undermines the whole principal of freedom of the seas,'' the captain of the *John A. Winslow,* Commander Robert Jackson, said incredulously. ''I mean, that was one of the things we were fighting for in the Indian Ocean, wasn't it? Do the Russians really think we'd accept something like that?''

Tarrant spread his hands. ''The Soviets have never understood our theory of seapower, Captain,'' he said. ''I doubt if they realize how critical this issue is to American strategic thinking. In any event, it seems to have hit home in Washington. The new orders I received last night call on us to take the battle group into the Norwegian Sea in direct opposition to the exclusion zone the Russians have laid down.''

"Then we're going in to help Norway, Admiral?'' Commander Bart Thompson of the frigate *Stephen Decatur* asked.

"Not yet, Captain," Tarrant told him. "The Rules of Engagement are very clear. We're to test the Russian determination to keep us out of the Norwegian Sea, but we only fire if fired upon. The decision to actively support Norway hasn't been made yet.''

"Hell, there might not *be* a Norway if we don't do something soon," Captain Brandt said harshly. "Can't they *see* that?''

Tarrant fixed him with a cold look. "We're not talking about Saddam Hussein or the North Koreans this time, Captain," he said in a quiet voice. "No matter how much things have changed since the Wall came down, these are still the Russians we're up against this time around. If we push too hard, too fast, we could end up with nukes flying.''

There was a mutter of agreement around the room. Suddenly the specter of World War III was back among them, closer and more real than it had been since the face-off between Kennedy and Khrushchev. It was sobering to think where this confrontation in Scandinavia might lead.

And Carrier Battle Group 14 was sailing right into the middle of it all.

CHAPTER 7
Tuesday, 10 June 1997

"What's the status on this one, Chief?" Tombstone
Magruder had to shout over the din that echoed through
Jefferson's cavernous hangar deck. Stretching for two thirds
of the carrier's 1,092-foot length and fully two decks high,
the huge chamber was crowded with aircraft and the men
from Department V who were in charge of maintaining and
outfitting them. As always, being down here gave Magruder
a sense of just how small a part the aviators and NFOs really
played in the operation of the carrier Air Wing. From plane
captains down to purple-shirted "grapes" who handled
refueling on the flight deck, these men regarded those
aircraft as their own . . . and quite rightly. Without them,
the aviators couldn't fly.

The brown-shirted plane captain whose name Tombstone
hadn't caught over the noise of the hangar deck gestured at
the wing of the A-6E Intruder in front of them and bellowed
his reply. "I'm not real happy about her, sir! She was on
deck the day of the big cock-up. There was some damage to
the wing . . . here . . . and over here!" His finger
jabbed in emphasis.

Magruder nodded slowly. He didn't pretend to be an expert on aircraft maintenance, but CAG had ordered him to check on the readiness of the wing's Intruder squadron. Now that *Jefferson* was sailing into a potential battle zone it was critical that the attack aircraft be ready for action. "Did you give it a down-check then?" he asked.

The CPO shook his head reluctantly. "Didn't want to, sir. The damage wasn't bad compared to the ones that really got caught in it. But I ain't happy about it."

Rubbing his forehead, Tombstone tried to decide how to respond. Even with the planes he'd brought in the night before *Jefferson* was short of Intruders, and he could understand the chief's reluctance to order another one taken out of service. Intruders were tough birds that could take a lot of punishment and still do the job.

But if the damage was bad enough to weaken the wings, another two-man crew would be facing disaster each time they flew the bomber.

"Give it a down gripe," he said at length. That meant the Intruder's maintenance log would show it as unfit for use until repairs had been made. "But put the sucker at the top of the repair list, okay?"

"Aye, aye, sir," the petty officer replied. He looked happier now. "That's the last of 'em, Commander."

"Good. I want all the maintenance logs on my desk tomorrow morning for review. Got it?"

"Aye, aye," the chief repeated.

Tombstone turned away and started across the wide deck, dodging people, tractors, and parked aircraft constantly. A well-run hangar deck left very little wasted space and still couldn't hold all of a carrier's planes. *Jefferson*'s hangar deck was very well run, and hence very crowded.

He stopped beside the bulky form of an E-2C Hawkeye to get his bearings and pick out the best possible path out of the chaos. Something flapped overhead in the stiff breeze coming through the opening of the number-two elevator, and Magruder looked up. In port, the overhead of the hangar deck would be strung with dozens of flags and banners of states, territories, foreign nations, and so on. When the ship was at sea the flags weren't supposed to be hung, but apparently someone had placed the flag of Norway, a white and blue cross on a red background, in a prominent position dominating the center of the hangar, where everybody could see it. There was little doubt of the crew's feelings, whatever might be coming out of Washington.

Tombstone thought back to the briefing. It was clear enough from the emphasis on the military situation that Admiral Tarrant expected *Jefferson* to be involved in the fighting. Whether the President finally took the plunge and ordered support for the Norwegians, or whether the Soviets chose to enforce their huge exclusion zone, that looked like the most probable outcome. But what could one carrier battle group do to help the beleaguered defenders around Bergen? Land-based air could swamp the carrier's defenses, lurking submarines would be a constant threat . . . and the Soviet Red Banner Fleet was out there somewhere, an awesome assemblage of naval firepower. The Americans didn't even have their old advantage in carriers anymore. There was at least one of the new Russian CVs in the Red Banner Fleet, and even if it was smaller and less dangerous than the *Jefferson,* it was a carrier nonetheless, capable of challenging America's power-projection capability in a way no enemy had been able to try since the Second World War.

It made his new assignment all the more frustrating when he thought about the odds they were up against. While men like Coyote and Batman risked their lives flying cover for the battle group, he'd be condemned to Captain Stramaglia's idea of his proper place.

His proper place, he told himself, was in the cockpit of an F-14.

"Mr. Magruder . . . sir?" The voice came from behind him, loud enough to hear over the hangar deck noise but still somehow tentative and uncertain. Magruder turned to find himself looking at a young, red-haired lieutenant with pilot's wings and an apprehensive look on his freckled face.

"What is it, Lieutenant?" he shouted over the roar of one of the tractors—a "mule" in flight-deck parlance—hauling an F/A-18 Hornet toward one of the elevators.

"Sir, CAG told me to talk with you. Said I should see you before . . . before I turn in my wings . . ."

Inwardly, Magruder groaned. What did CAG expect of him, anyway? Once a pilot decided he'd lost the edge, there wasn't much point in trying to change his mind. In fact it could be dangerous. If this youngster had decided that he wasn't fit to fly but tried to hide it and stay in the air, he could end up making mistakes that would kill people. Including himself.

On the other hand, Magruder remembered the times he'd come close himself to calling it quits. And he'd talked Coyote out of quitting once too. That had turned out for the best, obviously. Coyote Grant was still on his way up.

"Look, Lieutenant, we can't talk here!" he yelled. "Come on with me! We'll find someplace quieter!"

Someplace quieter turned out to be Tombstone's quarters. There weren't many places even on a boat the size of the *Jefferson* where privacy was possible, and if this kid was planning on spilling his guts about his problems Tombstone didn't want a lot of witnesses. Whether he turned in his wings or not, the kid would face a mountain of scorn if he broke the unwritten aviator's law that a good flyer never, ever let the pressure make him lose his cool.

"All right, son," Magruder said at last as he closed the door. "What's your name, first off?"

"Roger Bannon, sir. They call me Banshee." Bannon hesitated. "I'm with VA-89."

Magruder nodded and smiled encouragingly. The wing's single attack squadron, the VA-89 "Death Dealers" flew the A-6E Intruders that Magruder was supposed to be paying special attention to in the days ahead. Perhaps that was why CAG wanted him to deal with Bannon's problem, whatever it was. "It's a damned good outfit," he said aloud.

"Yes, sir." Bannon looked uncomfortable.

"You said you wanted to turn in your wings. Want to tell me about it, son?" He was surprised at how easily he seemed to fall into the role of the father figure.

"I—I was the one who crashed the Intruder last week, Mr. Magruder. I screwed up bad on a landing . . . missed the wires but didn't have enough power to make it a bolter. Skidded . . . God, I couldn't do anything to stop it." Bannon closed his eyes as if reliving the moment in his mind. "The planes . . . the people who died . . . it was all my fault . . ."

"You must've been doing pretty good to eject from that mess," Tombstone said quietly. "Looks like you came through without a scratch."

A spasm of pain crossed the young face. "I was . . . everybody says it was lucky. I wish now I'd never got clear. My chute opened and snagged on something, so I didn't even hit the deck."

Magruder hesitated before probing further. It looked like it wasn't so much fear as guilt that was weighing on Bannon's mind, but he was no expert in psychology. He wasn't sure how to handle the kid. This was really a job for the chaplain.

But chaplains didn't always understand the way another aviator did. Tombstone felt he had to try, at least, to help Bannon. "There must have been an inquiry," he said.

Bannon nodded. "They said . . . they said it was an accident, that I could return to flight status when CAG thought I was ready." He swallowed. "But it doesn't seem right . . ."

"Look, you can't be impartial judging yourself over something like this." Magruder groped for the right words. "You should . . . you should trust what CAG and the Captain had to say about the accident. They've had a hell of a lot more experience than you. When you've seen more carrier duty you'll realize these things happen. Even if you never go into combat you're running a risk when you serve aboard a carrier."

Bannon didn't answer, but he'd fixed a wide-eyed stare on Magruder's face.

"Now the way I see it, son, you've got a couple of choices. If you want to turn in those wings, that's your business. The Navy doesn't want men flying who don't have the confidence to pull it off. But once you do it, there's no second chance. You won't fly for the Navy again. And chances are you'll find out, somewhere down the line, that it was a mistake to run away from the problem. But you'll never be able to face it down, because you quit." He paused. "Your second choice is to try the old 'get back on the horse' philosophy. A lot of people think that's the best way to handle this kind of thing. Me, I'm not so sure."

"What do you mean, Mr. Magruder?"

"Push too hard and you could end up getting into more trouble. Now what I think you need to do is have another little talk with CAG. Keep your wings, but see if you can get assigned as an LSO or something like that. Take it one step at a time. When you're ready, you'll know it . . . and then you'll be able to get back in the cockpit and show yourself and everybody else that it really was an accident. A fluke."

"Do you think Captain Stramaglia would let me do that, sir?" Bannon asked, sounding eager for the first time.

"Give it a try. I've served with him before, and underneath the tough shell there's a tough guy inside . . . but he's fair. And I'll recommend it to him if it's what you decide *you* want.''

"Th-thanks, Mr. Magruder." Bannon started to say more, but Tombstone held up his hand.

"Don't make the decision right now. Think about it. Maybe see one of the chaplains and talk it over with him. When you make any choice, make sure it's one you can live with."

"I will, Mr. Magruder. Thanks again."

When Bannon was gone Magruder let out a long, ragged breath. Had he done the right thing? What if the kid really had been at fault, despite what the inquiry had found?

He decided he'd have to look into the story further before he could make any final decisions himself. That meant research, interviews, the whole wearying round of investigation.

It was hard to believe that it had been less than twenty-four hours since he'd been exalting over his liberation from paperwork and Pentagon bureaucracy, his return to the freedom of carrier life.

1554 hours Zulu (1654 hours Zone)
Flag Plot, Soviet Aircraft Carrier *Soyuz*
Off North Cape, Norway

Like a mother duck surrounded by a gaggle of ducklings, the *Soyuz* led a handful of escort ships through the angry gray waters off the northern coast of Norway, heading southwest into the Norwegian Sea. Displacing sixty-thousand tons and measuring a thousand feet from ski-jump bow to stern, *Soyuz* represented an entirely new concept in the USSR's naval thinking. The multipurpose aircraft carrier of the type employed so successfully by the Americans for over five decades was now an integral part of the Red Banner Fleet.

Admiral Vasili Ivanovich Khenkin winced as an aircraft thundered from the deck, probably one of the navalized MiG-29D fighters that provided aerial patrol and protection for the carrier. Khenkin was still not used to his new kind of ship, part of the legacy of Admiral Gorshkov's bold naval expansion program. *Soyuz* was the second of his class—Soviet ships, unlike American vessels, were always regarded as "he"—and probably the last. Together with his predecessor, *Kreml, Soyuz* had blazed the way, but the latest aircraft carrier, just finishing sea trials in the Black Sea, was larger, the size of the great American supercarriers. The sixty airplanes crowded aboard *Soyuz* would give way to carriers with ninety or a hundred planes before long.

Khenkin looked around the cramped confines of Flag Plot at the staff of officers and seamen who managed the fleet's operations under his command. How many of them realized the significance of this operation? He wondered if any of them realized that they were not merely embarked on the extension of Soviet control in one tiny region, but were actually reestablishing the USSR as a world power once again.

That was what it amounted to, at least. Since the middle of the Eighties Soviet power and Russian pride had taken a beating. Faced with a sagging economy, a hostile West, and a rising tide of discontent, the Motherland had barely survived intact. And at what cost? Retreat from Eastern Europe, and from the vital buffer zone that alone could prevent a repetition of Germany's occupation of Russian soil. Compromise with liberal elements demanding reform in everything from freedom of emigration to private ownership of land and industry to the very organization and function of the government itself. Even the evidence of where it would all lead—the ethnic violence, the riots and strikes, the independence movements in states traditionally part of Russia—had not swayed the reformers from their

headlong rush to virtual anarchy. It had taken the failure of
Gorbachev and Yeltsin and their "new Union" to show the
essential weakness of the reform movements, and just as the
weak-willed Socialist Kerensky had been swept aside by
Lenin and the Bolsheviks, so the democrats had been forced
to return power to the hands of the only people who could
maintain order, the hard-liners of the Soviet military.

Now the damage could all be undone. The death of the
President had been regrettable, of course, but a necessary
first step in the cleansing process. The war with Norway
would end in quick victory, a needed symbol of renewed
Soviet pride. The Americans had gone through the same sort
of process with their short, sharp victory over Iraq, at a time
when the USSR needed Western economic aid more than
the continued existence of a long-time ally. Turnabout was
only fair play, Khenkin thought smugly.

He wondered if General Vorobyev had considered that
particular bit of symbolism while framing the campaign for
Norway's occupation. Symbols could mean a lot. The
carrier, for instance. Starting out as the *Riga,* his name had
been changed to the *Admiral Flota Sovetskogo Soyuza
Gorshkov,* in honor of the Admiral of the Fleet who had
inspired the carrier program in the first place after the
troubles in the Baltics and elsewhere had made the name of
one of the rebellious cities an inappropriate one for a Soviet
warship to bear. Now he was the *Soyuz,* the *Union,* a symbol
of the rebirth of a strong central government that would
carry the USSR into the new century.

"Admiral," an aide said with a crisp salute as he entered
Flag Plot. "We have an updated report on the American
aircraft carrier battle group."

"Ah, excellent. Excellent, Orlov. Proceed." Khenkin
leaned forward in his seat, fixing his eyes on the young
officer. This was a report he had waited a long time for.

"Around midnight last night Greenwich time the battle

group altered course,'' Orlov began. "They are now moving northeast at a speed in excess of thirty knots. Our satellite data is not as complete as we would wish due to increasing cloud cover in the area, but the best estimate is that they are ignoring the warnings regarding the Norwegian Sea." Orlov was sweating, plainly worried at how the admiral would react to the report.

"Is that all? Then you are dismissed, Orlov." Sagging back in his seat, Khenkin closed his eyes. No one had been sure how the Americans would react, but they gave every indication of being too wrapped up in domestic affairs to care what went on in Scandinavia. The planning had relied on the new American isolationism, the call that the United States could not continue as "the world's policeman." In the face of American responses from Iraq to North Korea to the Indian subcontinent, caution had suggested that the plan was foolhardy at best, yet the election of a U.S. President who openly favored massive and unilateral military cutbacks, as well as reductions in all areas of foreign aid, had been encouraging. And his timid reactions, first to the reoccupation of the Baltics, and later to the border dispute between Norway and the Union, had been enough to convince even the doomsayers among the Soviets. Now the Americans were finally beginning to *act*.

Perhaps the declaration of the exclusion zone in the Norwegian Sea had been too much like an ultimatum. Sometimes it seemed as if the Americans believed they owned the oceans.

Khenkin had been against the declaration, but his superiors had overruled his objections. Now it seemed he was being proven correct after all. Instead of backing away from the crisis in Norway, it seemed the Americans were going to challenge the Soviet proclamation directly. But even so, there were still options open. Still a few ways to make the plan work.

"If the Americans are coming, it will risk everything," Captain First Rank Dmitri Yakovlevich Bodansky, Khenkin's Chief of Staff, said quietly. "Success depends upon winning Norway without provoking a wider conflict."

"It is a danger, I agree, Dmitri," the admiral replied slowly. "But it can still be nullified if we are careful. The American President will know that there is little their people can do to assist the Norwegians before our army completes the reduction of the last remaining resistance. He will be seeing this as a gesture of defiance, a symbol to the world that the great superpower does not accept the dictates of a foreign country. We would do the same, would we not? I suspect the carrier battle group is functioning under strict rules of engagement to avoid open confrontation."

"You do not believe they are planning to support their allies, Admiral?" Bodansky sounded incredulous.

"They are in a very awkward position. Soon there will be nothing left in Norway to reinforce, and they cannot wage an effective war so far from home without a friendly nation as a base. Who will help them? The Swedes and the Danes will stay neutral if only because of the threat we pose. In fact they will most likely scramble for the best possible terms. Germany is no friend of America today. There is too much commercial competition there. The English are adhering to socialism better than many of our own republics. When that idiot Hussein invaded Kuwait the biggest mistake he made was in stopping at the Saudi border. Had he gone on the Americans would never have been able to dislodge him. It is a long, long way to America, Dmitri, and only a short way to the *Rodina*."

"So this is a gesture only?"

"Yes. If the only options are backing down or trying to fight a long-range war without effective bases, the Americans will back down. They are too afraid of a nuclear exchange to risk the chance of widening this conflict further. All we need do now is make sure that there is no large-scale engagement between our forces. Let them make their cruise into the Norwegian Sea. We will watch them, remind them of their position, but we will not provoke them far enough to force a response.''

Bodansky rubbed the scar on his chin. ''If the weather down there is getting heavier, satellite tracking will continue to be difficult. We cannot afford to lose them, Admiral. Even if it is only to be sure we stay clear of their ships.''

''I agree,'' Khenkin said. ''We must increase the aerial patrols in that direction.''

''The one we sent yesterday did little enough,'' Bodansky pointed out with a harsh note in his voice. ''They turned and ran as soon as American fighters challenged them.''

''Then we must see to it that the Americans do not challenge any more of our flights. I would say that a pair of escorting fighters would be most useful for these reconnaissance operations. By tomorrow we will be in position to use our own MiGs for this purpose, Dmitri. A chance to remind the generals that the Red Banner Fleet has a major part to play in this, eh?''

Da, Comrade Admiral.'' Bodansky began scribbling notes on to a pad. He stopped and looked straight at Khenkin. ''Of course, Admiral, more escorts will increase the risks as well.''

''They are acceptable risks, Dmitri. As long as we keep careful control over events, we will not be stopped.'' He paused. ''Make arrangements for a reconnaissance flight tomorrow morning. Twice daily until there is a break in the weather.''

He turned away to consider a map of the theater of operations. Yes, the Americans would be kept at arm's length and Norway would fall soon enough. But that was only the beginning. The strategic position and the boost in power and prestige they would gain from this campaign would position the Soviet Union to regain all the lost ground of the past decade and more besides.

American ''experts'' had been fond of saying that they were the only superpower now. Soon those experts would know just how wrong they had been.

CHAPTER 8
Wednesday, 11 June 1997

0848 hours Zulu (0748 hours Zone)
Tomcat 201, Redwing Flight
South of the Faeroe Islands

"Redwing, this is Bravo Six-four. Vector right to oh-one-oh." The voice of the controller flying in the Hawkeye patrol aircraft sounded tense in Coyote Grant's headphones. "Go to buster for intercept with bogie at range two-one-nine November Mikes your position, Angels two."

Grant started banking right as he responded. "Bravo Six-four, Redwing Leader. Roger that. Coming to zero-one-zero, buster. Target at two-one-nine, Angels two."

"Wonder what they're sending us after," Lieutenant John "John-Boy" Nichols said over the ICS.

"Beats me," Coyote replied. "Ours not to reason why . . ."

"Ours just to make 'em fly!" the RIO finished.

Coyote smiled under his oxygen mask. He felt comfortable with Nichols riding the backseat, and picked him as RIO more often than not. Officially there was no such thing as permanent assignments teaming aviators and RIOs, but getting a well-matched pair to work together frequently paid off when things got hot. The Vipers had learned that lesson back when Matt Magruder was still their skipper, in the

97

Pacific, and when he took charge of the squadron Coyote
had encouraged the practice. Just one look at the way
Batman and Malibu flew together, for instance, was proof of
how teamwork could pay off.

He wished he could be more sure of his wingman today.

"Let's get it in gear, Koslosky," he said over the radio
channel to the other Tomcat off his port wing. The new pilot
was one of the replacements who'd flown out with Tombstone, and he was still an unknown element in the squadron.
In fact Coyote had bumped Lieutenant Randy Martin from
patrol duty this morning just to fly with Koslosky and try to
get a feel for how he'd fit in. So far, he wasn't happy with
the nugget. "I've seen jumbo jets fly tighter formation than
that!"

"Sorry, Skipper," Koslosky answered, sounding flus-
tered. The Tomcat drifted closer, its speed increasing
slightly. "Guess I wasn't expecting anything but a routine
patrol this morning."

"CAG's Third Commandment, kid," Coyote said quietly. "'Thou shalt expect the unexpected.' I don't know
what they've been teaching you back home, but out here a
patrol isn't just an excuse to fly the plane and sightsee.
You're up here to *respond* to the unexpected. Got it?"

"Yes, sir," came the subdued reply.

"Redwing. Bravo Six-four. Be advised we have three,
repeat three, bogies bearing oh-one-oh your position. Range
is now one-seven-two, speed three-five-oh."

"Roger, Six-four," Coyote said. He read back the
information. "Any idea what they are?"

"Redwing, wait one," the Hawkeye replied.

"Four to one it's another Bear hunt," Nichols said.

"With those stats? Of course it is. Don't try to take
money from your CO, John-Boy. It isn't healthy, know what
I mean?"

Nichols chuckled over the ICS. "Hey, a guy's got to supplement his income any way he can, right, Skipper?"

"Redwing, this is Dragon's Lair. Do you copy?" That was CAG's voice, patched in from *Jefferson*'s CIC through the orbiting Hawkeye.

"Affirmative," Coyote replied. "Read you five by five."

"Looks like you've got another Bear out of Olenegorsk, Redwing," CAG said. "Main question is whether all three blips are Bears, or if they've got something else coming in too."

"I read you, Dragon's Lair," Coyote said. He understood the edge of concern in CAG's voice, an echo of what he'd heard from the Hawkeye. It wasn't all that uncommon to send up two or three Bears in a single flight. But those other planes could also be escorts . . . or they could be Badgers or Blackjacks carrying antiship missiles depending on a Bear for targeting data.

"Get up close and personal with these jokers, Redwing," CAG told him. "If it's just some sightseers escort them off the premises gently. But eyeball them and keep us appraised."

"Roger that," Grant replied crisply.

"Good. I've got backups on the way. Dragon's Lair out."

Coyote gripped the control stick a little bit tighter. CAG wasn't the sort to get spooked by shadows. If Stramaglia was worried, it was with good reason.

And Willis Grant didn't like to think about what it might take to worry the Air Wing commander.

0855 hours Zulu (0755 hours Zone)
CIC Air Ops module, U.S.S. *Thomas Jefferson*
Northeast of the Outer Hebrides

Jefferson's Combat Information Center, a gloomy, red-lit
cavern buried in the heart of the island on 0-4 level
starboard, was alive with activity as Magruder entered. If
the Bridge was the nerve center and brains of a combat
vessel, CIC was the heart, where the military operations of
the *Jefferson* were monitored and controlled by specialists
of the OI Division of the Operations Department. In a battle
Captain Brandt would fight the ship from CIC, but for
day-to-day operations it was the domain of the Tactical
Action Officer and of CAG, who coordinated combat air
operations in progress.

"Picking up some garbage on the screens now, sir," a
radarman was reporting as Magruder entered the control
center. "I think they're playing with some ECM just to see
how well we can handle it."

"How bad is it, Adams?" Lieutenant Commander Sam-
uel Clayton, the duty TAO, leaned over the radar display to
get a better look.

"Just intermittent so far, sir," Radarman Second Class
Adams replied.

Clayton straightened up and looked across at Stramaglia.
"I don't like this much, CAG. How soon 'til you get some
planes out there to eyeball the bastards?"

"It won't be long now, Commander," Stramaglia replied
gruffly. He jabbed a finger at Lieutenant Bannon, who had
been assigned to the CAG staff for a few days.
"You . . . get on the batphone to Pri-Fly and find out
from the Boss what the hell's taking the backup planes so
long."

"Aye, aye, sir," Bannon responded nervously, hastening to carry out the order. Magruder wondered if putting him here, under CAG's baleful eye, had been the right therapy for his problem. Bannon looked drawn, gaunt, like he hadn't slept for days.

Stramaglia turned his glare on Magruder. "About time you got down here, Commander. I've got a job for you."

"The backup mission, sir?" he responded eagerly. Since the first word of the trio of bogies had started spreading through the ship Magruder had been fighting the urge to call CAG and ask for a shot at them. Surely CAG wouldn't stick to his decision about barring Magruder from fighter missions.

CAG's laugh was a short, barking sound. "Nonsense. Grant and Wayne can handle whatever's out there. No, I'm doubling up on ASW flights for a few hours. It'd be just like the Russians to wait until everybody was focusing all their attention on their radar screens and then try to slip a sub or two into range. You'll fly copilot on Viking 700. Get down to the King Fishers' ready room and start suiting. Launch is in fifteen minutes."

Tombstone tried hard to conceal his disappointment. "Aye, aye, sir," he said crisply.

As Magruder turned to leave, CAG added another comment. "Time to let somebody else share in the glory, Commander. Get your ass in gear!"

0903 hours Zulu (0803 hours Zone)
Tomcat 201
Redwing Flight

"Redwing, Redwing, this is Bravo Six-four," Coyote heard in his headphones. "Backups have launched. Call sign is Ajax. I say again, Ajax."

"Bravo Six-four, Redwing," Coyote responded. "Roger. Backup call sign is Ajax."

"I'm getting something now, Skipper," Nichols reported from the back seat. "Yeah . . . that's our party, all right. Three targets bearing zero-two-five, course one-nine-five, range one hundred three."

"You copy that, Kos?" he asked over the radio.

There was a pause. It was Koslosky's RIO, Lieutenant Ron "Wild Card" Kirshner, who finally replied. "Got 'em, Skipper."

"Change course to intercept," he ordered. "Talk to me, John-Boy. What else've you got back there?"

"Speed is three-four-five," Nichols came back. "They're at angels two . . . no, I think they're dropping. Heading down for the deck, Coyote."

"Just like the other night," he commented. "Those blips tell you anything worth knowing?"

"I read it as one big, two small," John-Boy told him. "Like a B-52 with a couple of Eagles for escort."

"Or a Bear and two large MiGs," Coyote mused. "They're flying with an escort. How sure are you?"

"I'm sure, sir," Nichols said stiffly.

"Don't get huffy with me now, kid," Grant said. "I just want to be damned sure I'm feeding CAG the straight dope. If those are fighters on escort, the chances that the Russkies are just out for the scenery just went down. Okay?"

"Yeah. I get you, Coyote. And I'm sure on the sizes."

Coyote reached for the radio switch again. He hoped Nichols really did know his stuff.

0907 hours Zulu (0807 hours Zone)
Escort Lead, Flight Misha
South of the Faeroe Islands

Captain Second Rank Sergei Sergeivich Terekhov cursed as the radar-threat warning announced the American radar lock. He had been told in the pre-mission briefing that the Americans were likely to try this tactic again, but it still didn't make it any easier to accept. Terekhov preferred strike missions against the Norwegians to the uncertainties of escorting reconnaissance patrols near the American carrier battle group. At least with the Norwegians the situation was clear. Any target that presented itself was fair game.

But out here it was different. The admiral had issued stern rules of engagement aimed at limiting the chances of escalation. It meant that patrols and their escorts had to accept the greater risks that went with giving up the advantages of shooting first. Even maneuvering to break the radar lock could be interpreted as hostile action. And that could be disastrous.

Terekhov forced himself to ignore the icy grip on his bowels. This was just another routine encounter, nothing more. He had engaged in this same kind of game when *Soyuz* first sailed from the Black Sea en route to her new duty station with Red Banner Northern Fleet. Then it had been patrolling aircraft from the carrier *Eisenhower*. This was just more of the same.

If all went as their orders had instructed the flight would not be engaging this morning . . . not unless the Americans decided to play at being cowboys and started something first. Flight Misha was supposed to test the American air defenses, and their resolve, but without provoking an incident. His orders from the commander of *Soyuz*'s air wing had been detailed and specific: push hard, don't back down, but under no circumstances arm or fire weapons unless the Americans did so first.

"Cossack, this is Misha Escort Leader," he said, keying in his radio. Cossack was the call sign for the carrier. A controller there was monitoring every move Flight Misha made. "I have radar-threat warning. Request instructions. Over."

"Misha Leader, Cossack," the radio voice replied. "Fly minimum altitude approach. Keep formation tight and remain on course as instructed. Update as required."

"*Paloochyena,*" he responded. "Message received." Terekhov pushed his stick forward as he switched frequencies. "Misha Flight, drop to minimum altitude and follow me."

Low clouds enveloped the MiG as he descended. He could not help but be conscious of the intense scrutiny that would be focused on this mission. It was rumored the admiral himself had issued the orders to keep the Americans under observation.

Sergei Sergeivich Terekhov was determined to carry out Admiral Khenkin's orders to the letter . . . or die trying.

0910 hours Zulu (0810 hours Zone)
Tomcat 208
Redwing Flight

Lieutenant Gary Koslosky could feel the excitement building inside him. *This* was what he'd joined the Navy for, what he'd become an aviator for . . . the thrill of feeling his Tomcat slicing through the clouds on its way to an encounter with the enemy. It wasn't anything like duty with the RAG back in the States. Nothing was likely to happen on one of those flights. But out here, he could make a difference.

He'd often wondered if he would be afraid the first time he had to fly blue-water ops with the chance of running into a live enemy. But there wasn't any fear, only a sense of purpose, the hope that he'd really get a chance to prove himself.

"Man, it could all happen today," he said aloud over the ICS. "If the goddamned Russkies are really looking for trouble, we'll give it to 'em, right?"

From the backseat Kirshner sounded bored. "Throttle back, rookie," he said scornfully. The RIO was an old hand, but his blasé manner wasn't enough to dampen Koslosky's mood. "It's just another Bear hunt."

Koslosky edged the throttle forward a little. Maybe that's all it was to Kirshner. "Come on, Wild Card, loosen up," he protested. "If the Russkies *do* start something it'll be our big chance. Wouldn't you like to draw first blood for the squadron?"

"Sure. But we won't." He could almost see the RIO's grimace of distaste. "First off, the Commies'll back down, just like they always do. And second, even if something does go down, do you think the Old Man's going to let a nugget get off the first shot? Try reality just for a change, okay, kid?"

Koslosky didn't answer. If things started happening, he thought, he'd be in on it. Nothing was going to keep him from joining the ranks of the select, the fraternity of aviators who'd earned themselves a kill. If Scandinavia was really heating up, he might come out of this war another multiple ace like the Deputy CAG, Magruder.

That thought made him all the more anxious for action.

"Two-oh-eight, ease up your throttle and watch your heading," Coyote snapped into the radio mike. The bogies would be on top of them soon, and he had better things to do than worry about some overeager fighter jockey who wouldn't pay attention.

"Affirmative," Koslosky said.

"They're coming up fast, Coyote!" Nichols said. "Down on the deck and really moving!"

"Right," Coyote said. "Kos, break left and come in over the Bear, parallel and on top of him. Don't push him too much, but keep with him. And stay clear of his tail gun, just in case."

"Yes, *sir*!" the younger flyer replied. The Tomcat started to bank away, turning as it lost altitude and cut back speed. The swing wings flared out, giving it the look of a predatory bird swooping low toward its prey. A moment later Coyote lost Koslosky's plane in the clouds.

He pushed the stick to the right and started a descending turn of his own. "Talk to me, John-Boy. Talk to me . . ."

"Range fifteen, closing . . . closing . . ."

Mist enveloped the cockpit as the Tomcat dropped through the cloud layer. Coyote kept one eye on the altimeter and the other on his radar display. He wanted to close in fast, before the Russians had time to react to his maneuver.

They they were out of the clouds, and the Russian planes were there.

He got a good look at the lead jet, one of the navalized MiG-29Ds known in the NATO F-for-fighter lexicon as

Fulcrum. This model was pretty much identical to the ones that had been flying for years with front-line Soviet air units, with a minimum of conversions to fit it for the carrier fighter/attack role. The Russians had strengthened the undercarriage, added an arrester hook and some avionics that roughly matched the Tomcat's ILS and ACLS gear. Other than that it remained what it had started out as—an extremely effective answer to the very best fighter craft in America's modern arsenal.

The second MiG was close by the leader, not quite in a rigid welded-wing formation, but far tighter than the typical American flight. The Bear trailed them, turboprops thundering. He spotted Koslosky moving into position as he finished his turn and dropped easily into place alongside the Bear.

In the cockpit he could see a Soviet pilot wearing an old-fashioned leather flying helmet. The Russian was gesticulating at him, flashing three fingers repeatedly. So he wasn't going to play coy like Batman's quarry from the other night. This one wanted a chat on 333.3, and from the urgency of the gestures he wanted it in a hurry.

"American fighter, American fighter," Coyote heard as he switched frequencies. "You are about to be violating restricted airspace. You are urged to withdraw for your own safety."

"Redwing Leader to Russian aircraft." Grant gave a thin smile as he made his reply. "You been taking lessons from Khadafy on maritime law, boys?" There was a veiled threat in the bantering words. When Colonel Khadafy had suddenly claimed the entire Gulf of Sidra as Libyan territorial waters back in the early eighties, America had sent in the carriers . . . and the colonel's feeble attempts at enforcement had resulted in some spectacular shoot-downs, all of them of Libyans.

"Ye nye panyemayoo," the reply came back in Russian.

"I not understand . . . Waters of Norwegian Sea declared part of combat zone in police action in Norway. Very dangerous for noncombatants. Very great risk of unfortunate incident. You are urged to withdraw."

"Russian aircraft, Redwing Leader," Coyote said. "Just for the record, are you guys seriously claiming the whole Norwegian Sea as an exclusion zone? Over."

"Redwing Leader, this is Misha Escort Leader," a new voice said, breaking in. "This is not a matter for pilots to debate, *da*? Is for politicians."

"Misha Escort Leader, you will note that we are no longer flying toward the Norwegian Sea," Coyote answered. It was time to change the subject. "We are, however, flying directly toward an American carrier battle group which *has* declared an exclusion zone of two hundred miles radius as of 0500 this morning. Since we're not violating any exclusion zones, isn't it your turn?"

There was a long pause. Coyote suspected the Russians were checking with their home base for instructions. Finally the Escort Leader's voice came back on the channel. "We find exclusion zone around non-involved aircraft carrier most disturbing, Redwing Leader. America and Soviet Union are not enemies. Why do you treat us as such?"

"Now *that's* something for the politicians to talk about, *tovarish*," Grant told him. "I'm just doing my job, which is to see you out of this area. Now . . ."

"Redwing Leader, I have strict orders. I will not deviate. I repeat, I—"

"Heard you the first time, Ivan," Coyote said sharply. He cut the channel off and switched to the link back to the Hawkeye. "Bravo Six-four, Redwing Leader. Got us a stubborn S.O.B. out here who won't turn aside. Do I have permission to give him some encouragement?"

"Redwing, this is Dragon's Lair," CAG's voice answered quickly. "Negative on your request. Negative. Ajax

ETA your position in five minutes. Let's see if four more Tomcats makes them cool off a little.''

''Roger, Dragon's Lair. Redwing Leader clear.''

He switched to the tactical channel and passed the instructions on to Koslosky. The disappointment in the younger man's voice carried over the radio clearly.

Coyote could sympathize with the frustration. He hoped CAG was right and reinforcements would frighten the Russians off. Every second was bringing them closer to the *Jefferson,* and sooner or later the Americans would have to take action. Drastic action, if necessary. They couldn't allow the Russians to overfly the battle group. That would send the wrong signals to too many places, starting with the Kremlin and the White House.

But if they had to resort to force, they could end up with a tiger by the tail.

CHAPTER 9
Wednesday, 11 June 1997

0914 hours Zulu (0814 hours Zone)
Tomcat 204, Ajax Flight
South of the Faeroe Islands

"Still no change in heading. The bandits are still on heading one-nine-five." The tension in Coyote's voice was plain even through the distortion and static of the radio channel.

Batman Wayne didn't like the edge in the squadron leader's voice. The Soviets simply weren't backing off, and Grant was sounding more and more frustrated with the situation. Would the Russians force the Americans to fire the first shots? Did they *want* to start a war?

He keyed in his radio. "Redwing Leader, Redwing Leader, this is Ajax Leader. Don't worry 'bout a thing, Coyote. We're coming up fast."

"One minute thirty," Malibu chimed in from the backseat, all business. "Screen's still empty except for our boys and their guests."

"Keep watching them, Mal," Batman said. He switched frequencies. "Ajax Flight, let's show these gate-crashers what we do when we find unwelcome visitors." He thought back to the intercept he'd done before. "Big D, you and the Loon take the left. Go for weapons locks on the Bear. Make 'em sweat a little. Tyrone, you and me are gonna play tag with the number-two MiG. Got it?"

111

"We're on it, Caped Crusader!" That was Lieutenant Commander Dallas Sheridan, "Big D," flying Tomcat 212. His aircraft peeled off, followed closely by Lieutenant Adam "Loon" Baird in number 205. "We'll be all over that guy like ugly on my mother-in-law!"

"Let's show the Commies what a *real* aviator can do!" Powers added. "They'll never know what hit 'em!"

"Just remember the ROEs, children," Batman said, mostly for the benefit of Powers and Cavanaugh. Even though they'd done a good job in the encounter Monday night he still regarded Powers as a potential troublemaker. The man wanted to score a kill, and Batman was afraid he'd get too eager. He could remember how it had felt when he'd been looking for his first ACM kill. "Do not fire unless fired upon, or until you get the Weapons Free call from the *Jeff*."

"Yes, Mother," Sheridan's RIO, Lieutenant (j.g.) Edward "Fast Eddie" Glazowski, replied. "We'll be good."

Under the lighthearted banter there was an underlying seriousness. These men knew what was at stake today. After years of training for just this kind of confrontation, it was still hard to believe that they were so close to the brink this time.

"One minute, Batman," Malibu announced quietly.

He tightened his grip on the stick and swallowed.

0916 hours Zulu (0816 hours Zone)
Tomcat 208
Redwing Flight

"Damn it, why don't they let us *do* something?" Koslosky muttered. He was maintaining the Tomcat's position above the Bear, but so far there was no sign that the Russians were willing to turn back. By now they would know about the four new fighters from Ajax Flight, and that hadn't seemed to change things either.

"Stay frosty, kid," Kirshner advised him.

Koslosky fumed. It seemed like everyone from the admiral down to his own RIO was letting the Russians get away with murder just because things were hot in Norway. He knew how the Soviets operated . . . hell, everybody knew. They would push as hard and as far as they could just to see how much they could get away with, but the first time they faced *really* determined opposition they caved in. That had been the story of the whole Cold War era. It had led to the end of the Wall and the retreat of the Red Army from Eastern Europe into the Russian heartland.

"The hell with this," he said aloud. With a quick movement he banked the Tomcat right, standing it on one wing and letting the plane lose altitude. He'd give that Bear pilot the fright of his life. Then they'd see how long the Russians ignored the carrier's exclusion zone!

"Jesus!" Kirshner swore. "What the hell're you doing, Kos?"

"Trust me, Wild Card," he said with grin. "I'm just raising them another few dollars."

His hands worked the stick and the throttles deftly, settling the fighter close alongside the huge reconnaissance plane's starboard wing. It was a tricky maneuver, but nothing he couldn't handle. Sliding up to a tanker for a midair refueling was no more hazardous than this. Slowly he edged his speed up so the Tomcat would pull forward alongside of the cockpit. Koslosky grinned again, his mind flashing back to the scene from the movie *Top Gun* where the hero had inverted his Tomcat a few feet over an enemy plane. There was no room for that kind of bravado out here . . . but you could make your point clearly enough just by crowding the opposition a little.

Tomcat and Bear edged closer together.

"New American aircraft have split up," the electronics officer reported nervously. "Comrade Captain-Lieutenant, if they are serious about exclusion zone we will be easy targets."

Captain-Lieutenant Viktor Petrovich Kolibernov had been thinking the same thing. It was easy enough for the *Bolshoi Chirey,* the "Big Boils" who gave the orders, to claim that the Americans would never initiate hostilities. Things looked different from the cockpit of an antiquated Tu-95 with a swarm of American fighters closing in.

He realized he was sweating. Kolibernov wiped his forehead with one gloved hand and then reached up to adjust the large fan positioned above the right side of his seat. He darted a glance at the copilot, but if Lieutenant Adriashenko realized how nervous his commanding officer was he gave no sign of it.

Much as Kolibernov wanted to back off before the Americans got any more persistent, his instructions were specific and allowed him no freedom of action. If he deviated from the reconnaissance mission now, he would have to be ready to face the consequences back at Olenegorsk. Captain-lieutenants were not supposed to take that kind of decision on themselves without a very good reason.

"Weapons lock! Weapons lock!" The electronics officer's voice rose an octave. "They have a lock on us!"

Kolibernov hesitated. In ten years of flying maritime reconnaissance patrols Kolibernov had never felt so close to the edge before. He could finally understand how his father had felt when he served as an officer aboard one of the freighters that had tried to run the American blockade of Cuba back in the tense days of the Missile Crisis. Knowing that if both sides persisted on this course the only result could be war, perhaps the total war of nuclear annihilation. And for all the talk of *glasnost* and *perestroika* and the end of the age of confrontations, history was repeating itself again.

"Fuck it!" he said suddenly, wrenching the steering yoke to starboard. He wasn't going to give the Americans an excuse to start something, no matter what the orders said. Next to him Adriashenko was gaping at him in disbelief.

"Look out! Look out!" someone shouted. Too late Kolibernov saw the American F-14 to starboard.

Too late . . .

0917 hours Zulu (0817 hours Zone)
Tomcat 208
Redwing Flight

Koslosky felt the Bear brush against the Tomcat's wing, a jarring impact that drove the F-14's wingtip downward with a screech of crumpled metal. He cursed and jerked his stick hard over, ramming the throttles full forward to afterburner zone five. The fighter shuddered as it turned, bucking like a wild horse. He fought for control, but the combination of the Bear's impact and the abrupt acceleration he'd applied to get clear made it that much harder to keep from falling into an uncontrolled spin.

"Shit!" Kirshner yelled. "You idiot!"

He ignored the RIO and wrestled with the stick. "Tomcat Two-oh-eight," he announced on the radio. "He hit me! I'm hit!"

The aircraft plunged toward the angry gray sea.

0917 hours Zulu (0817 hours Zone)
Tomcat 211
Ajax Flight

Powers heard Koslosky's shout in his headphones. "I'm
hit!"

"Goddamn!" he yelled. "They've hit Koslosky! The
goddamned Russkies have opened fire!"

Don't fire unless fired upon . . . Though he hadn't seen
the attack, Koslosky's plane had been hit. That scrapped all
the Rules of Engagement. The American aviators were in a
whole new ball game now . . . one where speed and
reaction time counted most. Victory in air-to-air combat
went to the pilots who were quickest to acquire their targets
and get off their shots.

He thumbed the selector switch on the stick to choose a
Sidewinder. On his HUD the target reticule fixed on the
distant bulk of the Bear and flashed red. The hum of a solid
lock-on filled his ears.

"Tone . . . I've got good tone." His thumb jabbed the
firing stud. "Fox two! Fox two!"

The AIM-9M ignited and leapt from under the Tomcat's
wing, streaking toward its target. Mouth dry, Powers
watched the plume of fire racing across the sky.

The heat-seeker struck the Bear squarely in the outermost
engine on the port wing. Powers could see the fireball even
from his position, a distant gleam of flame in the sky.

"Yahoo!" he shouted. "That's a hit!"

He pushed the throttle forward into afterburner, ready to
close in and finish the job.

0917 hours Zulu (0817 hours Zone)
Escort Leader
Misha Flight

Terekhov's head came around as the explosion lit up the overcast sky behind the MiG. He hadn't believed it could happen. But it had . . . the Americans had fired on the Bear.

His orders covered what he was supposed to do in that case.

"Escort Leader to Escort Two," he said grimly. "Weapons are free. Fire at discretion."

They were outnumbered three to one, but the two MiGs of Soviet Naval Aviation would give a good account of themselves regardless of the odds. Senior Lieutenant Nickolaev was one of the squadron's best pilots, despite his reputation for indulging in the kind of cowboy flying the Americans worshipped.

Terekhov cut in the MiG's afterburners, feeling the thrust of the powerful Isotov RD-33 turbofans pressing him into his seat. Pulling back on his stick, he aimed for the clouds.

0917 hours Zulu (0817 hours Zone)
Tomcat 201
Redwing Flight

Coyote watched as flame engulfed the wing of the Tu-95, hardly able to believe what he was seeing. Sheered off by the blast, the wing fell away, and the aircraft spun off out of control, plummeting for the ocean below. As the Bear plunged, Coyote saw Koslosky's Tomcat, its wing visibly damaged, obviously in trouble.

It had all happened too fast . . . so fast that he hadn't been able to stop it. The horror of what had happened dulled his reactions. Viper Squadron had just fired the shots that could lead to outright war.

Then Nichols was shouting over the ICS. "Better look sharp, Skipper. Watch the MiGs!"

He jerked his attention away from the tableau of falling Bear and struggling fighter to see the lead MiG climbing fast ahead. "Batman! We've got a situation here!"

"On our way!"

"Skipper! Skipper! MiG two's on my six! I can't get control to dodge him!" That was Koslosky's voice, sounding panicky.

Coyote banked and turned in time to see the MiG flash past in pursuit of the stricken Tomcat. With a curse Grant tried to bring his plane around, but he seemed to be moving in slow motion compared to the other planes.

The flare he saw under the MiG's port wing was a missile launch, probably an AA-8 Aphid heat-seeker. "Break left! Kos, break left!"

"Can't do it, Skipper!" Koslosky replied. Then his voice rose. "Wild Card! Eject! Ej—"

The missile hit the Tomcat before Koslosky could finish. Coyote turned his head as the explosion ripped the plane apart, feeling sick.

"Oh, God . . ." he heard Nichols say behind him.

"Save it. I want that bastard!" Teeth clenched, Coyote wrenched his stick over and started after the Fulcrum.

0918 hours Zulu (0818 hours Zone)
Tomcat 204
Ajax Flight

"Lead MiG's climbing fast, Batman. Looks like he wants to loop in and nail Coyote."

"Not if we get there first, he won't." Batman shoved the throttles all the way forward and thumbed his selector switch. Sidewinders were their best bet for these conditions.

Behind him he heard Malibu on the radio channel back to the *Jefferson.* "Dragon's Lair, Dragon's Lair, this is Ajax Two-oh-four. We are engaging. Repeat, we are engaging."

Once Batman would have felt satisfaction at those words. Now he knew nothing but a cold gnawing in his guts. They had crossed the line. . . .

0918 hours Zulu (0818 hours Zone)
Tomcat 201
Redwing Flight

"Come on, you bastard," Coyote muttered. "Come on . . ."

The lock-on tone was loud in his ears. "I've got tone!" He hit the firing stud. "Fox two! Fox two!"

"He's jinking!" John-Boy said.

The MiG banked and dropped fast, and the heat-seeker flashed past. "Damn!" Coyote felt his fist tightening around the stick. That MiG driver was good . . . and he himself had been just a little too quick off the mark.

"Easy, Coyote," Nichols told him. "What're you always telling us? Fly with your head . . ."

Grant gave a short nod and forced himself to cool off. There was little room for the aggressive hotdogging so beloved by Hollywood in a real ACM situation. It was the cool hand, the technician who knew precisely what his aircraft could do and was willing to take it to the edge of the envelope, but never beyond, who scored.

Ahead the MiG started a tight turn to the left, the kind of nimble maneuver the smaller Soviet fighters were particularly good at. Coyote pulled back on the stick, bringing the Tomcat's nose up into a steep climb to bleed off airspeed and keep from overshooting the target plane. He rolled left, almost standing the F-14 on its wing so he could keep the MiG in sight, then dropped his nose and started diving. The high yo-yo was one of the classic fighter moves, and this time it went off with textbook precision. The Tomcat settled in squarely on the MiG's six. The reticule centered on the enemy plane.

"Tone! I've got tone!" He fired his second Sidewinder. "Fox two! Fox two!"

It raced toward its target trailing smoke and fire.

0919 hours Zulu (0819 hours Zone)
CIC, U.S.S. *Thomas Jefferson*
Northwest of the Outer Hebrides

"Goddamn them!" CAG Stramaglia exploded. "What the hell is happening up there?"

He had listened to the radio traffic in disbelieving horror as the situation had unfolded. From that first call of "I'm hit!" it had taken almost no time at all for a full-fledged aerial battle to erupt.

"Sir?" A young crewman was looking up from one of the consoles at him. "Sir . . . it's the admiral."

He picked up a handset. "Admiral . . . Stramaglia here."

"What's the situation, CAG?" Tarrant's voice was level but strained.

"We don't know what started it, Admiral," Stramaglia said carefully. "But the Bear and one of our planes are both out of action, and the rest are in a furball."

"Goddamn," the admiral said, echoing Stramaglia's feelings. There was a pause. "All right, CAG. Pull those Tomcats out of there. Fast. There's going to be hell to pay for this one."

"Aye, aye, sir," he answered slowly.

He replaced the handset and reached for the radio microphone.

0919 hours Zulu (0819 hours Zone)
Tomcat 201
Redwing Flight

The Russian tried to evade again, but this time the Sidewinder got a piece of him. Coyote watched as the MiG started coming apart. Somehow the pilot had time to eject.

"Splash one!" John-Boy said.

"Good chute! I've got a good chute from the Soviet!" Coyote added.

His threat warning buzzed. "The other guy's coming down on us," Nichols announced. "He's at five o'clock!"

"Fox two! Fox two!" That was Batman's voice, announcing another Sidewinder attack. Coyote threw his plane into a sharp right turn, hoping that even if the missile didn't tag his opponent it would at least keep the Russian busy enough to allow him to turn the tables.

"No good! Missed the bastard!" That was Malibu, sounding distinctly unlike a laid-back surfer now.

"Where is he, John-Boy?" Coyote asked. He scanned the sky through the canopy, searching for the MiG. "I've lost him."

"One o'clock! One o'clock high!" Nichols shot back.

Coyote spotted the MiG. "All right, Ivan, I'm tired of this game." He pulled back on the stick and went to full afterburner. "Batman, let's nail this sucker so we can go home!"

"Ninety-nine aircraft! Ninety-nine aircraft!" That was CAG's voice giving the code that signaled the message was for all planes. "Break off and RTB. Repeat, return to base!"

"Is he kidding?" Lieutenant Baird asked. "Five to one odds and he wants us to run?"

"I think there was an up gripe about my radio in the last maintenance log," Sheridan added rebelliously. "I'm having a lot of trouble reading them back at home plate . . ."

"All aircraft return to base. Acknowledge." Stramaglia sounded insistent . . . angry. But whether it was at the grumbling or at the orders he was required to give, Coyote couldn't be sure.

"You heard the man," Coyote said. "Break off! Break off! Herd them out of here, Batman! I'll stay on him until you're clear."

"Roger, Two-oh-one." Even Batman, who should have known better, sounded like he was plotting mutiny. But the dots representing Ajax Flight on his VDI were turning away, heading back toward the carrier. That left only the MiG to worry about.

He almost hoped the Russian would give him an excuse to finish the job.

0920 hours Zulu (0820 hours Zone)
Misha Escort Leader
South of the Faeroe Islands

Captain Second Rank Terekhov gaped at his radar display, unable, *unwilling* to believe what it showed. Why were the Americans breaking off? They'd outnumbered him, outgunned him. Yet at the moment when they could have destroyed his aircraft four of them had turned away, and the fifth was doing nothing to close in for a kill.

"Cossack, this is Misha," he said on the carrier control frequency. "Enemy has discontinued action. Request instructions. Over." Part of him was afraid the carrier would order him to attack . . . another part wished that they would. To return home now would be to face punishment . . . disgrace. Better, perhaps, to follow Nickolaev.

"Misha, Cossack," the reply came back quickly. His controller sounded almost as shattered as he felt. Not surprising, in view of what had just happened. For all the smug confidence of the High Command, it seemed the Americans were adopting an aggressive posture after all. "Return to base."

"Acknowledged, Cossack." He glanced at his fuel gauge. "I will need in-flight refueling to reach you."

"Understood. A tanker will rendezvous. Cossack out."

He watched his radar screen carefully as he turned for home, but the lone American fighter continued to circle as before. Terekhov shook his head in wonder. Why hadn't the Americans followed through on their advantage?

Why was he still alive?

CHAPTER 10
Wednesday, 11 June 1997

It was an opulent room, with wood paneling and a thick carpet, heavy brass lamps gleaming with polish, masterpieces hanging on each wall. The inner sanctum of the Kremlin was a place of power, a sharp contrast to the dirty streets and impoverished, hungry people beyond the ancient stone walls.

General Vladimir Nikolaivich Vorobyev wasn't listening to the GRU colonel who was finishing the summary of the situation in Scandinavia and the Norwegian Sea. He had seen the report before the meeting convened. Vorobyev was concerned now not with information but with analysis . . . a quick judgment of how his colleagues might react to the latest news. The coalition of military, KGB, and hard-line party men who had asserted control over the Soviet Union in the wake of the assassination in Oslo was fragile at best. Most of the ten men in the lavish conference room hated most of the others . . . and each one had his own agenda, his own plans for how to isolate the others and consolidate power.

That was neither unusual nor alarming. It was rivalries and hatreds that supplied the checks and balances that had kept the system running for many long years. He knew how they felt about each other, about him. Everything was factored into his plans.

Let them hate me, so long as they fear me. He remembered that the saying was reputed to have been a favorite phrase of the Roman Emperor Tiberius. Inwardly Vorobyev smiled. What would his good Communist ministers think if they knew he was comparing himself to a Caesar?

"Again and again we were assured that the Americans would not become involved!" That was Ubarov, the newly "elected" President, a stolid, unimaginative man who looked and sounded like Khrushchev but had more of the personality of a Chernenko, a compliant mouthpiece who would do as he was told. Ubarov was being surprisingly vocal today. Perhaps he feared the West more than he feared Vorobyev. Or perhaps one of the other power brokers in the room had primed him beforehand.

That was a mistake Comrade President Vasily Fyodorovich Ubarov would make only once.

The GRU man looked unhappy and glanced toward Vorobyev, but the general merely leaned back in his seat and watched the others thoughtfully.

"If the military had played its part properly, they would not have become involved," Aleksandr Dmitrivich Doctorov favored Vorobyev with an oily smile. He was the head of the KGB and thus the closest thing to an ally the general had in this room. The KGB had regained much of the power that had been stripped away from the organization in the wake of the failed coup against Gorbachev by the "Gang of Eight," and Doctorov wielded considerable power. His role in the elimination of Ubarov's late unlamented predecessor had been crucial, but the army and the KGB still needed each other while the new regime was consolidating its power base. Still, old rivalries ran deep, and the alliance would last no longer than absolutely necessary. "Perhaps

we should be concerned with the judgment of our good
Admiral Khenkin?''

Vorobyev toyed for a moment with the idea of following
Doctorov's lead and making Red Banner Northern Fleet's
commander in chief a convenient scapegoat. But the navy
was still too important to Operation Rurik's Hammer to risk
the turmoil Khenkin's disgrace would cause. They needed
Khenkin to make the plan work.

But of course if Vorobyev backed Khenkin now and there
were more failures, Doctorov would have the general neatly
boxed in. That was an accepted part of the game of politics
in the Kremlin, and Doctorov was a master player. The
KGB chief was the sort of man who paid far more attention
to his personal position and security than he did to trifling
issues of victory and defeat. It was that kind of mentality
that had hamstrung the Politburo throughout most of the
Cold War and made the reforms of Gorbachev inevitable.
But the cures embraced by the reformers had been worse
than the disease they were meant to combat, and Vorobyev
was willing to tolerate Doctorov as long as the Union could
be returned to its old status as a superpower.

"I think the admiral can be considered blameless in this
matter," Vorobyev said smoothly. "This looks more like an
accidental escalation. Khenkin's predictions are rarely
wrong, but no one can allow for the tensions of the moment.
The Americans fired . . . but we have no way of knowing
if it was premeditated or simply a tactical miscalculation."

"Surely you are not suggesting we ignore the matter?"
Foreign Minister Anton Ivanovich Boltin looked shocked.
"Whether the cause was an error or some deliberate
Western policy, shots have been fired. The Americans will
not ignore that. Not this time." He paused. "This is not so
much a military failure as one of intelligence, though.
Surely there were signs that the Americans might be pushed
into action."

Vorobyev studied the Foreign Minister thoughtfully. He

had been a reasonably loyal member of the old cabinet, compliant with hard-line policies but apparently close to the President. He was known as a good Party man, but first and foremost as a survivor. Now he seemed to be siding with the military against the KGB, and when a skilled fence-sitter came out clearly on one side or another of a Kremlin power struggle, it was a good indication of where the power lay. There were many lingering resentments between the Party and the KGB. It was hard to forget the days when the KGB had allowed the reformers to consolidate power and outlaw the Party altogether.

"I did not say that we would ignore the situation," Vorobyev said, carefully ignoring the barbed comment about intelligence failures. He was glad to know the military was still on top in the new power structure, but he didn't intend to allow rivalries to come out in the open just yet. "Obviously, with tensions as high as they are now there is no question of trying to smooth this matter over with the Americans. Their neutrality would not have lasted much longer in any event. Norway is an old ally of theirs and we were lucky to get as much time as they have given us."

Boltin nodded thoughtfully. "True enough. In that much, at least, the KGB's predictions were accurate." He favored Doctorov with a venomous look, and there were scattered nods around the table from some of the other politicians.

"Yes, we all owe the Committee for State Security a vote of thanks for their masterful analysis of the West's situation," Vorobyev interjected quickly before the KGB chief could react to Boltin's thinly veiled insult. He needed Doctorov's good will more than the Party's, at least for now, and they couldn't afford to waste time or effort in internal squabbles. The new government's control over the Soviet Union was still tenuous at best, though the mobilization against the "possible spread of Western anarchy" was rapidly allowing the Red Army and the KGB to deploy enough strength to dominate key areas. "We always knew that there were risks involved in Rurik's Hammer, that there were some elements we would not be able to control. Neither the KGB nor Admiral Khenkin can be held responsible for what the Americans choose to do."

"But what do *we* do?" Ubarov demanded. "War with the Americans was never a part of the plan."

"Not an all-out war, no." Vorobyev smiled. "It is in no one's interest for the nuclear missiles to fly. I believe the Americans will feel that as strongly as I do. The important thing now is to hold them at arm's length while we complete the conquest of Scandinavia. At that point they will be in the unenviable position of choosing between an unacceptable escalation or a stalemate. While we, on the other hand, will be poised to dominate Europe from our new flanking positions."

"Hold them at arm's length," Doctorov mused. "Then you mean to strike at the carrier battle group? No other American force is in a position to intervene."

"There is one other that must be cleared in order to isolate the battle group," Vorobyev said. "In fact, a determined strike on this target could well discourage them from further adventures within our exclusion zone." He smiled. "I am recommending that we introduce Plan North Star immediately. At the same time it would be wise to begin harassing the American ships . . . perhaps a few of our attack submarines would be well employed in this. After North Star has been resolved we will evaluate the situation and decide what else needs to be done."

He saw heads nodding across the table, and his smile broadened. They had a tiger by the tail in Scandinavia. Rurik's Hammer had to succeed if the Soviet Union was to regain power in Europe. This time it would be the Germans and the British who would have to come begging to

Moscow for the very right to survive! Every one of those men knew that there was no going back now.

And as long as Rurik's Hammer was in motion, they needed Vorobyev. While Doctorov maneuvered and Ubarov trembled and the rest tried to predict the outcome and make the right political choices, it would be the army that solidified its power base and made sure that the *Rodina* would never again be humbled by the West.

1145 hours Zulu (1045 hours Zone)
Viking 704
West of the Shetland Islands

The S-3B Viking banked left and settled onto a new heading, but as far as Magruder was concerned it might as well have been holding steady on an endless flight to nowhere. Outside was the same monotony of cloud and sea, with little prospect of a break in the routine. It was a common belief among fighter pilots that the men who flew ASW missions slept through their flights and returned home with numb asses, and Tombstone was beginning to believe it.

For a Tomcat pilot, Tombstone told himself, a desk job at the Pentagon was a taste of Hell . . . but the cockpit of an S-3 was Purgatory, pure and simple.

The Viking was an amazing aircraft. That much he was willing to concede. Handsome, high-winged, with fine lines and an aerodynamic design that made it a dream to fly, the S-3 had only one thing in common with the F-14 he knew so well. Both were dedicated weapons platforms, mounting sophisticated equipment and electronics all concentrated on fulfilling one purpose and one purpose only.

In the case of the Viking that purpose was submarine hunting, a job the aircraft performed splendidly. Magruder

couldn't argue with the versatility of the machine or with
the skill and dedication of the three other men aboard, all
experienced sub-hunters from the VS-42 squadron, the King
Fishers.

Tombstone's complaint was with the job itself. The
temperament and skills that made a good fighter pilot were
the antithesis of what made a Viking crewman tick. The
aircraft was designed to remain aloft for long periods of
time, burning fuel at about a sixth the rate of the thirsty
Tomcats. And these extended flights required nothing so
much as patience, a skill few fighter jocks cultivated.

"Want to take her for a while, Commander?" the pilot
asked over the ICS. Commander Max "Hunter" Harrison
was CO of the King Fishers, a soft-spoken black man whose
pride in his squadron was evident in everything he said. He
had elected to come on the mission this morning as the
Viking's pilot as soon as he'd learned that the Deputy CAG
was going out. Tombstone could see that much, at least.
Back when he'd been a squadron leader he had tried to be
on hand anytime CAG or his staff were around.

"What's my course?" Magruder asked. "This game's a
little out of my regular line of work."

"Don't worry about it," Harrison said with a chuckle.
"The computer'll tell you where to steer." He pointed to a
display screen on the instrument panel. "Keep lined up on
this and everything'll be great."

Magruder nodded. His training on the Viking was coming
back slowly. The computer accepted instructions from the
plane's Tactical Coordinator, or TACCO, who designated
where he wished to deploy sonobuoys as part of an overall
search pattern. The computer marked the spot and guided
the pilot there. On reaching the chosen position the number
and type of sonobuoys selected for that location were
ejected automatically from the rack in the belly of the
aircraft.

"Right," he said. He grasped the stick. The Viking was the only jet aboard the carrier which had duel flight controls. That allowed a pilot and copilot to divide up the flying duties on a five-hour patrol. There were other controls at his station in the cockpit besides the regular flight instruments, since the copilot was also expected to assist the TACCO in the sub-hunting part of the plane's work. In fact Magruder was filling the slot of COTAC, although his knowledge of the electronics was limited. "I've got her!"

It felt good to be doing something at least, even if this wasn't the most challenging flying he'd ever been called upon to attempt. The S-3's mission was to range out beyond the screen of frigates and destroyers masking a battle group and crisscross the ocean in search of enemy submarines. The sonobuoys were the key to that. Each one was a floating module containing a sonar transducer and a radio. Once deployed, they sent out pulses of sound which were reflected back by obstacles—the sea bottom, whales, schools of fish, and the occasional submarine. The radios relayed the results of the sonar searches back to the Viking, where a crewman known as the Senso was responsible for translating the arcane data into an approximation of what was in a given stretch of ocean, and where.

The Senso had other tools at his command as well, from magnetic-anomaly detectors to electronic-surveillance gear that monitored radio traffic to FLIR, Forward-Looking Infrared Radar, which could detect the heat emissions of ships and subs lying at or near the surface. But the sonobuoys were the first and most important tool in the ongoing search for enemies lying beneath the waves.

Harrison slumped in his seat, looking completely relaxed. "What d'you think, Spock? Are we going to have anything to show our VIP this time out?"

From the rear compartment of the plane Lieutenant Commander Ralph Meade, the TACCO, gave a cautious answer over the ICS. He was a tall, spare man who bore more than a passing resemblance to the actor Leonard Nimoy, and that together with his precise, measured way of speaking had earned him his running name. "Hard to say, Skipper. SOSUS showed at least five subs filtering out in the past week, but there's no telling if they're still hanging around here or if they've moved on by now."

That, Magruder thought bitterly, was the real problem with the sub-hunting business. The arcane art of ASW work was at least as much an art form as it was a science. Aircraft like the Viking had to fly long, complicated patrol patterns searching for enemy submarines because as yet no one had developed a reliable way to keep tabs on subs from a distance. The first line of defense was SOSUS—for Sonar Surveillance System—a line of permanent underwater microphones strung along the sea floor all the way across the GIUK (Greenland-Iceland-United Kingdom) gap. The technicians in the SOSUS control center back in Norfolk swore they could detect any sub that tried to cross the line, but once a submarine had passed through the network of microphones there was no way to keep further tabs on them except through dedicated ASW ships, planes, and helicopters. Frigates like the *Gridley,* helicopters off *Jefferson* and her escorts, the two submarines attached to the battle group, even P-3C Orion aircraft out of Keflavik in Iceland, all played a part in the ongoing hunt for the weapon most carrier skippers feared above all others. But it was the Viking that was the real backbone of the whole effort.

Yet with everything they could set to hunting they still couldn't cover all the bases. Too much ocean, not enough people. A losing proposition, if viewed strictly from the technical side of things.

But it was possible to improve the odds a little. The ASW coordinator back on the *Jefferson* did his best to think like a sub skipper and deploy sub-hunting assets where they would do the most good. And Meade, the TACCO, was supposed to do the same thing on a smaller scale from his station in the windowless rear cabin of the S-3. Looking for submarines was like a chess game, with a variety of standard moves and gambits, but in the long run it was up to the individual players to make things happen.

ASW work was often regarded as the forgotten stepchild of the carrier air wing, at least by the pilots who flew the more glamorous missions. But the close-knit fraternity who flew the Vikings and the Sea Stallion ASW helicopters regarded themselves as every bit as important as any other element in the Air Wing. From what Magruder had seen so far they were as much masters of their arcane art as any fighter pilot was of the mysteries of air combat maneuvering.

He didn't envy them their jobs. Harrison was a pilot, but nothing like the glamorous men who flew the Tomcats or the Hornets or even the Intruders. The other two were more technicians than aviators, with Meade, as TACCO, trying to outguess veteran sub commanders.

Then there was AW/1 Mike Curtis, the Viking's Senso for this run, and the only enlisted man aboard. It had always surprised Magruder that ratings served in the plane crews of the Vikings and the Hawkeyes. The popular stereotype, which even life in the Navy didn't fully dispel, was of aviation as a game for officers only.

But the special skill it took to handle the electronics aboard a plane as complex as the Viking was a great leveler. The men in the Antisubmarine Warfare military-occupation-specialty category were the high-tech elite of the carrier crew. Though they were often scorned by their own kind, who claimed that the AW stood for ''Aviation Weights''—naval slang referring to someone who didn't carry his load of shipboard duties—they earned their special place in the carrier's hierarchy. Men like Curtis went through two full years of specialty training to get their jobs, while the typical enlisted man learned his specialty in a few short months. Aboard their aircraft, Magruder had heard, there were few distinctions between AW ratings and the officers they flew with, and good AWs had little trouble earning commissions and rising to the TACCO position.

He wondered what sort of a man could fill the demanding job. Curtis had been quiet throughout the flight except for responses given strictly in the line of duty. Was he naturally withdrawn, or overawed by the presence of the Deputy CAG?

"Well, how about it, Curtis?" he asked. "Don't I get a show? Or maybe you at least have some words of wisdom for the rookie?"

"I don't get paid for philosophy, sir," Curtis said over the ICS. "That's for officers to do. Me, I just sit back here and play the most expensive goddamned video game anybody ever saw."

He smiled at that. "And what's the score?"

"I haven't been beaten yet," Curtis said. Then, softly, he went on. "But I've never had to hunt 'em for real, you know, sir? I don't know if that's going to be the same."

Magruder remembered the first time he'd flown in combat, back in Korea. All the flying time, all the Top Gun practice, still hadn't prepared him for the realities of combat.

But the word from the *Jefferson* said Coyote's squadron had already traded shots with the Russians. All too soon Curtis might have his chance to find out what a real sub hunt, a hunt to the death, was really like.

"It isn't the same, Curtis," he said softly. "It's never the same."

CHAPTER 11
Wednesday, 11 June 1997

1445 hours Zulu (1445 hours Zone)
CAG office, U.S.S. *Thomas Jefferson*
Northwest of the Outer Hebrides

"Well, Magruder, how'd you like your first day of sub-hunting?"

Tombstone studied Stramaglia's bland expression carefully before answering. "It wasn't . . . quite what I'd imagined, sir," he said cautiously.

The Viking had set down on the flight deck an hour before, and Magruder's legs were still stiff from too much time sitting in one position. At one point the TACCO, Meade, had offered to swap seats with him for a while, but he'd turned it down. Now he was regretting it.

"Boring as one of my Top Gun lectures, eh, Magruder?" Stramaglia asked with a lopsided smile. "Well, that can't be helped. I want you out on at least one flight a day until I'm sure you know everything there is to know about ASW. Got it?"

"Aye, aye, sir," Magruder replied.

"And knock off the formal little sailor routine." CAG looked down at his desk. His tone changed, losing the mild bantering manner and becoming grim and cold. "You heard about the Bear hunt?"

Tombstone nodded. "Sounds like a real mess. What happened up there, CAG?"

"Goddamn nuggets screwed up, that's what happened," CAG growled. "First one of them wanted to play stunt pilot and got himself in trouble, then his call made another one decide it was time to rock and roll. A right royal cock-up from first to last."

Magruder didn't say anything. He might have been able to do something to keep the situation under control if CAG had let him go up with Ajax Flight as he'd requested, but it didn't seem like the right time to point that out to Stramaglia.

There was a knock on the cabin door. CAG looked up and barked out a quick "Come!" It was Coyote, wearing his khakis now instead of a flight suit and looking just as grim as Stramaglia. "I've got the reports on this morning, sir," he said. He held up a folder in one hand.

"About time, Grant," Stramaglia said harshly. "Park your butt and let's go over exactly what that fine bunch of glory hounds of yours did."

Magruder started to rise. "I'll let you—"

"Stay put, Magruder. If you're going to be my deputy you'd better be in on this."

As Tombstone resumed his seat CAG leaned forward and took the bundle of paperwork from Coyote. Stramaglia deposited the folder unread on the desk and looked Coyote over slowly. "You lost two men and a plane out there this morning, Grant . . . and worse than that, you let your people violate the ROEs and maybe pushed us into a full-fledged war. Does that sum up the situation in your estimation?"

Coyote nodded slowly, his face a mask. "Yes, sir," he said quietly.

"Got anything to say for yourself?"

Hesitating, Grant looked from Stramaglia to Magruder

and back again. "It was a very fluid situation, sir," he replied. "Men can make mistakes . . . especially when the men have limited experience . . ."

"Don't make excuses!" Stramaglia barked. "*You* are the squadron commander, Mr. Grant, and that makes *you* responsible. So don't hide behind your men!"

Coyote didn't answer, but he glanced at Magruder again. There was a long silence before Stramaglia went on. "If we didn't need every experienced aviator in the stable I'd pull you and that kid . . . what's his name? Powers? I'd pull you both off the flight roster. Him for being an irresponsible asshole and you for letting an irresponsible asshole run loose. As it is, I can't afford to do that. But you can be sure I'm going to have some things to say that aren't going to look good in your files, Grant. Do we understand each other?"

"Yes, sir," Coyote said meekly.

"All right. Now on to new business. Odds are our Russian friends aren't going to be too happy with us after this one. Washington hasn't responded with any official word, but the admiral and I are agreed we need to up our readiness in case of a retaliation. *Capish?*"

Grant nodded. "I agree, sir. Best to take the cautious approach."

Stramaglia glared at him. "Glad to hear you approve," he said coldly. "As of now I'm putting one squadron on Alert Fifteen at all times. Javelins will be first up. Owens'll post the rest of the rotation."

"Yes, sir."

CAG's order made good sense, Magruder told himself. It meant that the four fighter squadrons aboard would each pull long hours waiting in the ready rooms each day, suited up and ready to respond to an emergency. But at least they could put eight or ten planes in the air on short notice . . .

although it would give the Air Boss headaches to keep so many aircraft ready for a quick launch.

"That's it for now, Grant," Stramaglia said after a moment. "But make sure you have a little talk with your people about what happened today. Because if Powers or any of those other hotdogs runs wild again, I'll have your hide!"

Coyote left hastily, looking pale. He wouldn't meet Magruder's eyes on his way out.

When he was gone Stramaglia steepled his fingers on his desk and looked at Tombstone through narrowed eyes. "You think I was too hard on him, Magruder?"

"He's a damned good man, sir," Tombstone said. "And he can't nursemaid every nugget up there."

"And he's also your friend." CAG shook his head. "There's no room for friendship in a job like this, Magruder. Think about that. Someday you might have to treat a friend that way."

"But—"

"From where I'm sitting the important thing about what happened this morning is the fact that we just shot up two Russian airplanes. If by some miracle the Russkies don't treat that as an act of war, we've got to make damned sure there aren't any repeats. And if they do come after us I've got to make sure those damned hotdogs are on a short leash. Your buddy Grant's the one who's responsible for the Vipers, so he's the one I have to land on with both feet. If you don't like it, mister, then you'd better not plan on ever sitting in this chair."

Tombstone swallowed and nodded slowly. He didn't like it, but CAG was right . . . as far as he went. But surely there was a better way to handle it. "I understand, sir."

"Good. Lesson over. Now get the hell out of here so I can start figuring out how to save a squadron commander's neck when I file *my* report."

Magruder was halfway out the door before he realized what Stramaglia had said. Perhaps the man really did care about the officers in his outfit after all.

Coyote met him in the passageway.

"Thanks a lot for all the support, *buddy*," he said bitterly, blocking Magruder's path. His face was flushed, and his eyes were angry. "You could've said *something* to get that bastard off my back. Instead you just sat there and let him dish it out!"

"C'mon, Willie . . ."

"Never mind! I guess that's what happens when you get the big promotion, huh? All of a sudden keeping your own nose clean is more important than helping out your friends." Coyote turned away abruptly and started down the corridor.

"Coyote . . ." Magruder began. Then he shrugged and turned away. It was no use arguing with Coyote now anyway. Maybe when he calmed down . . .

How could he think I wouldn't stand by him? Magruder wondered, hurt and angry. He'd gone to bat for Coyote after Grant had left, even knowing that Stramaglia was likely to come down on him just as hard as he had on Viper Squadron's commander. Didn't Coyote realize that he'd never let a friend down that way? Or was the friendship too strained by time and distance now to hold up any longer?

He was beginning to think Stramaglia was right. There was no room for friendship in his job now.

1510 hours Zulu (1010 hours Zone)
Situation Room, the White House
Washington, D.C.

"The President of the United States!"

The men and women gathered in the underground chamber surged to their feet at the announcement from the

Marine guard at the door, but President Frederick Connally waved his hand in a dismissive gesture as he entered, impatient with the ritual. Didn't these people realize there were more important things to worry about than observing the formalities?

He looked around the small room with its walnut paneling and the massive teakwood conference table that dominated everything. The expressions his top advisors wore told him the news wasn't good.

With a sigh he settled into the leather chair at the head of the table. An Air Force officer carrying an innocuous-looking briefcase took up a position nearby.

Connally hated that briefcase and everything it stood for. It was the "football," holding the codes that would grant Presidential authorization for a nuclear weapons release. The football had been much on his mind these last few days.

"All right, gentlemen, let's hear it." The message requesting his presence in the Situation Room had been brief and vague. His Chief of Staff, Gordon West, had framed it carefully to avoid giving away details to any of the senators attending the morning conference in the Cabinet Room. His eyes met West's for a moment, but the former governor of Minnesota looked away.

It was Admiral Brandon Scott who spoke. The Chairman of the Joint Chiefs had a reputation for bluntness and was an outspoken critic of the new Administration's defense policies, but Connally also knew that the man understood his business.

"The Soviets have advanced their front to link up with the amphibious and *desant* forces around Trondheim," Scott said. He touched a button on the table in front of him and the curtains blocking off the rear-projection screen at the end of the room opposite the door rolled back. A map of Norway appeared, showing Soviet positions astride the center of the country in red. A second blob of red marked their bastion around Oslo, so far supplied and reinforced entirely by air.

"How the hell did they move so far, so fast?" Connally asked. "I thought the plans for the defense of Norway were solid. Haven't they been working on them for the past fifty years, for Crissakes?"

"Not quite, Mr. President," Secretary of Defense George Vane responded. "The planning that was put in motion fifty years ago was based on having a strong NATO alliance. Most of them became obsolete the day the Berlin Wall went down and everybody started scrambling to make friends with the Russians."

"I've had about all the anti-Communist bullshit I need for today from the Senate delegation that was just upstairs, George," Connally snapped. "I don't need rhetoric. I need results!"

"It isn't just rhetoric, Mr. President," Vane said quietly. "The simple fact is that the end of the Cold War era left us behind. It's a classic case of being ready to fight the last war when the next one rolls around."

"Just what's that supposed to mean?" the President asked him coldly.

"It means that we didn't evolve new strategies fast enough to keep pace with the new political realities," Scott amplified. "For better than forty years we were all geared for one thing—the big conventional war in Europe, with Russian tanks pouring through the Fulda Gap and the NATO allies rallying to hold them off. The situation changed, but we didn't change with it."

"We counted on a couple of divisions attacking the Norwegian frontier," Vane added. "So far we've identified six divisions on land and the equivalent of another one operating by sea, plus a pair of divisions providing *desant* troops for paradrops and airmobile attacks. There are at least twice as many tactical air units available in Scandinavia as we ever projected. Without the need to support operations in Germany or elsewhere the Soviets can overwhelm Norway without even trying very hard.''

The National Security Advisor, Herbert T. Waring, spoke for the first time. ''There's also the matter of our preparedness. If this had been happening in the seventies or the eighties we would've been on full alert the first day of the crisis, back when it was still just a lot of saber-rattling. We would have been shuttling Marines over there as fast as we could round up the flights to carry them, and the prepositioned supplies we had around Trondheim would've been worth something. Norway could've gone just like the buildup in Saudi before Desert Storm . . . but we let it slip by until it was too late to act.''

''Damn it, Herb, we just can't keep on playing policeman to the world anymore,'' West said harshly. ''The last Administration tried that and ended up screwing around with the budget so much that we may never get the deficit under control again. *And* we came within a gnat's whisker of an all-out war in Korea . . . not to mention the mess in India.''

''And if we hadn't been out there pounding the old beat,'' Scott said quietly, ''India and Pakistan would've bombed each other back to the Stone Age with nukes. The world's too small a place for isolationism to work any more.''

''Gentlemen, this isn't getting us anywhere!'' Connally said loudly. ''I didn't ask for a political debate.''

''You wanted to know why the Russians were able to push so far,'' Vane said. ''You've just heard a few good reasons. Not all of them, by any means. Without the English, supporting Norway is damned near impossible. The nearest air base we've got is Keflavik in Iceland, and that's just not enough to close the GIUK gap, much less help out in Norway.''

''You're still pushing for that, eh, George?'' Connally

said, raising an eyebrow. "If it's such a lost cause, why should we get involved now?"

"Mr. President, we're already involved. The incident this morning—the skirmish between our aircraft and the Russian recon flight—will guarantee that much." Scott looked grim as he spoke. "Unless you're ready to back down publicly in front of the Russians—and I mean the whole nine yards, public apologies, acceptance of their exclusion zone, everything—then we're in this war up to our necks as of today."

"Do the rest of you feel this way?" Connally asked.

Vane and Waring nodded. Vincent DuVall, the Director of the CIA, shrugged. "That's our best estimate, Mr. President," he said.

"Well, I don't agree," West said. "I think all of you are a little too ready to see the old Russian bogeyman lurking in the shadows again. We could stop this crisis right now if we would just give diplomacy time to work."

Secretary of State Robert Heideman looked up. "The Soviet Ambassador was willing to arrange a conference on Norway when I talked to him last night," he said. "Unless this incident with the Tu-95 gets in the way, we still have a foot in the door for some kind of peaceful settlement."

"Sure," Vane said harshly. "And in the two or three weeks it takes to get the conference rolling, Lindstrom's people get the crap kicked out of them and the Russians occupy the rest of Norway. When are you people in State going to wake up and smell the smog? Diplomacy works best when you can back it up with firepower. Just compare the Carter era to the Reagan years. Ronald Reagan put an end to the Cold War, Bob, even if it was Gorby who got the awards."

"I said I didn't want a goddamned debate!" Connally exploded. They had covered this same ground over and over again since the start of the crisis. "Admiral, when you said we needed to show the flag in the Norwegian Sea I went along with it. Now it looks like your precious carrier has landed us in the middle of the war. But before we go any farther I need to know just what you think those men can accomplish. You tell me Lindstrom's not going to hold out, that without British or German help we can't deal with the Russian invasion. So why should I let your people proceed if things are as bleak as you people have been painting them?''

''Let me answer that one, Mr. President,'' Vane said. ''The time has come to quit thinking in terms of incremental jumps. We can't just keep on reacting to each new Russian move. We've got to take the initiative.''

''How?'' West demanded.

''I think our forces should go to DefCon Two immediately,'' Van said. ''Start mobilizing a strike fleet and a Marine Expeditionary Brigade right away, and put the 101st and the 82nd on alert. As soon as possible we need to start putting men into Norway.''

''That's suicide!'' Heideman protested. ''While they have air superiority in Scandinavia we can't possibly get the Army in place.''

''Glad to hear you understand that much,'' Vane commented coldly. ''We'll also need to ferry air units into the Bergen area as quickly as possible so we have a chance to even out the odds a little.''

''Won't all this take time?'' Connally asked.

''Absolutely. Too damned much time. It'll take days just to get the first planes in. There weren't that many serviceable air bases in Norway when all this started . . . it'll be worse now that the Soviets have had a chance to bomb out the runways they've still got. And *that's* why we need the *Jefferson* in those waters now more than ever, Mr. President. Just by *being* there she's a distraction the Soviets will have to deal with. And every day, every hour she delays the advance on Bergen by keeping the Russians occupied out at sea makes our intervention more viable.''

Connally looked around the table. His eyes found the "football" at its place next to him. "So no matter how hard we try, it comes down to all-out war," he said quietly. "Is Norway really worth the risk of a nuclear exchange?"

It was Scott who answered him. "If you're going to ask that question, Mr. President, then you might as well be prepared to resign now and let the Soviets have the entire world. It's easy to argue that a given country isn't really worth all that much. Norway's not that large or that rich. So let it fall. Then what happens? Will you risk a nuclear war over Germany? Or France? What about Great Britain? These days they aren't even our close allies. Will you risk a nuclear confrontation over our right to freedom of the seas? The Russians want to keep us out of the Norwegian Sea now. What if they renew their ties with Havana and try to restrict our access to the Caribbean next?" He pointed to the map. "The only place to draw the line is at the first victim, Mr. President. Whether you're protecting oil in Kuwait or ice and snow in Norway. Because the only alternative is to abdicate our responsibility. Not as world policemen. As a free part of the world community. It's too late to resist a tyrant when he's knocking on your own door.''

Scott fell silent, and no one answered him. Finally Connally stood slowly. "Very well, you've made your point. Order DefCon Two, and begin drawing up a plan to support the Norwegians." He paused. "And God help us all.''

CHAPTER 12
Thursday, 12 June 1997

0545 hours Zulu (0545 hours Zone)
Wing commander's office, Soviet Aircraft Carrier *Soyuz*
The Norwegian Sea

"How could I predict what that fool Terekhov would do, Comrade Admiral?" Captain First Rank Fyodor Arturovich Glushko asked. He was uncomfortably aware of the note of pleading that had crept into his voice. "If he had obeyed his instructions—"

"The transcripts of the radio traffic with Misha show that he *did* obey those orders," Admiral Khenkin said harshly. The heavyset, gray-haired fleet commander leaned across Glushko's desk, his bluff peasant's face flushed. "If you had spent more time reviewing them, or better yet actually listening to the transmissions as they occurred, you would be aware of this."

Glushko stiffened, his face a studied blank that hid the churning emotions within him. It was almost unheard of for an admiral to seek out a subordinate in his own office, especially so early in the morning and with so few minutes left before a major mission briefing. But Khenkin had come to the air wing office today, and Glushko didn't need the flag officer's angry words to tell him that his career, maybe even his life, hung by a thread this morning.

It was not *fair*. For all of his adult life Glushko had played the game of Soviet Navy politics, and played it well. In the late Eighties he had commanded a squadron of Yak-38 V/STOL fighters operating from the *Baku,* but he had seen where the winds of change were leading the Navy and volunteered for training with the first wave of pilots at the flight deck mock-up at Saki airfield in the Crimea. Flying Su-27s off the deck of the fleet's first true carrier back when it was still known as the *Kuznetsov,* he had been in an enviable position as one of the Union's pioneer naval aviators, and that had stood Glushko in good stead.

Now he was commander of the air wing assigned to the *Soyuz,* and well-positioned to advance further. Operation Rurik's Hammer offered him a superb chance to attract favorable notice, though as air wing commander he was relegated more to an administrative role than to the kind of combat duty that might really make his reputation. As a result he had focused his attention on winning over staff and political officers who could make sure that his name would receive prominent notice when the campaign was through. After all, once the Norwegians had been overcome and the conflict was over, there would be plenty of room at the top for deserving officers. General Vorobyev would see to that as he began to consolidate his domination of the new Russia.

Now all of Glushko's efforts were threatened. He had not exactly neglected his responsibilities as air wing commander, but he had delegated much of the responsibility to juniors. Ordinarily it would have been perfectly acceptable . . . except for the horrible set of circumstances the day before that had culminated in the loss of a Tu-95 out of Olenegorsk and one of *Soyuz*'s MiG-29Ds. The other escort plane, flown by Captain Second Rank Terekhov, had broken off the engagement and returned to the carrier unmolested by the Americans.

It had been Terekhov's fault, Glushko told himself again as he concentrated on a spot on the bulkhead above the admiral's head. Surely they did not expect the air wing commander to monitor every routine patrol flight. But Khenkin evidently expected just that, and as a result held Glushko, not Terekhov, responsible for the incident.

The incident that might have drawn the Americans into a direct military involvement in the war in Scandinavia. That was a thought Glushko didn't want to contemplate.

"Admiral," he said slowly, searching for the right words. "I have done my duty to the best of my ability. There was no way to predict what would happen to the patrol mission . . ."

"And you didn't even try," Khenkin finished bluntly. "That is no longer the principal concern. What has happened cannot be changed. What remains for us is to shape the future."

"Yes, Admiral," Glushko said.

"Shut up and let me finish!" Khenkin's voice was loud now in the cramped office. "I have examined all of the plans submitted by your officers for the conduct of North Star. They make very interesting reading." The admiral tapped a stack of file folders on the corner of Glushko's desk. "Tell me, Glushko, what did you think of Captain Terekhov's suggestions?"

"Terekhov?" Glushko almost spat the name. "Too rash. Too daring. He wants to use three full squadrons to escort the bombers . . . too many. It leaves but one squadron to mount CAP over *Soyuz*. You will find the plan I endorsed to be much more balanced in outlook—"

"Bah!" Khenkin exploded. "You would give only token escort to the bombers! This is not a time for half-measures. Why is it so difficult for you to comprehend this?"

"But, Admiral—"

"Spare me the protests." Khenkin rose from his seat and

jabbed a stubby finger at Glushko. "We will proceed on the basis of the plan Captain Terekhov submitted. You will pass orders to have the MiG squadrons readied. The mission briefing will be conducted accordingly. Do you understand?"

Glushko swallowed. "Yes, Admiral. Your orders will be carried out. To the letter."

Inwardly he was caught between fear and anger. Plainly the admiral would be watching him very closely over the next few hours, and any mistakes Glushko made would only fuel Khenkin's ill feelings. He would have to tread carefully.

There was a soft, almost tentative knock on the office door. "Come!" Khenkin barked.

Captain Second Rank Terekhov looked diffident as he entered. "Just a reminder, Admiral . . . Captain. The briefing is due to begin in ten minutes. All squadron commanders and executive officers are assembled as ordered."

Khenkin nodded. "Thank you, Terekhov. We will come."

As the younger officer closed the door Glushko's mind was busy reassessing his prospects. The new orders did offer one bit of hope. At least he could manipulate events to allow Terekhov to hang himself. That would remove one thorn in his side, and he might still be able to use the squadron leader as a convincing scapegoat if he handled the situation skillfully.

The thought made him smile coldly. "I am sure Captain Terekhov's plan will be the best choice at that, Admiral."

0842 hours Zulu (0842 hours Zone)
Soviet Submarine *Tbilsiskiy Komsomolets*
Northeast of the Faeroe Islands

Captain Arkady Stepanovich Emelyanov bent over the radio
operator's shoulder in the cramped communications shack
of the submarine *Tbilsiskiy Komsomolets* and watched the
chattering teletype print out a jumble of letters and numbers.
The submarine, which an American observer would have
referred to as a Victor-class attack sub, was lying at
periscope depth accepting incoming messages bounced off a
communications satellite. The information would be mean-
ingless, of course, until it was decoded, but Emelyanov
liked to study his crewmen in the routine performance of
their duties instead of remaining in isolation like too many
of his fellow captains. It kept the crew on their toes to know
that the commanding officer might come by just to observe
while they were standing watch.

There was a lot of message traffic this morning, he
thought with a twinge of anxiety. Lying so close to the
surface, the submarine could be easily detected, and Emelyanov longed for the safety of the deep. But since the start
of the campaign against Norway there was a lot of information to pass along, and it was vitally important to keep up
to date with the latest unfolding developments. If nothing
else the daily update was necessary because Moscow would
be sending the coded phrase that would indicate the scope of
his current operations. Without that there was no way to
know if he was supposed to initiate hostilities against any
foe other than the Norwegians.

That brought a smile to his lips. Four days ago *Tbilsiskiy
Komsomolets* had scored her first three kills, an Oslo-class
frigate and a Sleipnir-class corvette sailing north from

Bergen, and later on a small, conventionally powered Ula-class submarine that had tried to slip past the Soviet vanguard to interfere with the operations of the Red Banner Northern Fleet. Small victories, perhaps, compared to going up against American or British foes, but still a mark of pride for the attack sub.

Now, though, they were no longer close in to the Norwegian coast. The sub had been ordered to begin patrolling near the Faeroe Islands, along the vaguely defined line of the GIUK gap. It was in some ways more hazardous duty, thanks to the higher chance of detection by the American SOSUS acoustical tracking network, but it had removed the sub from the true war zone, and that was a disappointment.

The radioman made a soft-voiced exclamation that drew Emelyanov out of his reverie.

"What is it, *starshina*?" the captain asked him.

The petty officer looked up at him. "This message is in special code," he said.

Emelyanov took care to control his features. "Very good, *starshina*. Give it to me. Then pass the word for the *zampolit* to meet me in my quarters before you proceed with the decoding of the regular traffic."

He left the communications shack without even waiting for the petty officer's acknowledgment. Special coded messages like this one were almost always concerned with a change in orders, and from its length it had to be more than a mere signal to assume one of the other previously established patrol stations on the list in his cabin safe. Perhaps *Tbilsiskiy Komsomolets* had been picked out for an important new mission.

Inside his cabin, Emelyanov waited impatiently at his desk until the sub's political officer arrived. Mikhail Aleksandrovich Dobrotin was a small, sharp-featured man who never failed to remind Emelyanov of the mongooses he had encountered while serving as a naval attaché in India before the Indo-Pakistani war. Dobrotin took his duties as *zampolit* with the deadly seriousness of a zealot. He was not popular in the submarine's wardroom, but his power was unquestionably respected and feared.

The political officer knocked on the cabin door and entered immediately, without given Emelyanov a chance to invite him inside. "You asked for me, Comrade Captain?"

"I did," Emelyanov replied. "Sit down. There is a message in special code which must be dealt with." That was standard practice. The political officer was required to verify all such messages. It was a safeguard against irresponsible captains who might ignore or exceed Moscow's instructions.

It took only a few minutes to translate the orders into clear copy. When he had finished Emelyanov stared down at the paper on his desk, stunned. Across from him Dobrotin was wearing a smile on his ferret features. "So it happens at last. The chance to engage the Americans." There was nothing but triumph in the *zampolit*'s tone.

Emelyanov looked at the man. He had been chosen for his political reliability rather than any technical knowledge, but surely Dobrotin knew how difficult these orders would be to carry out. Or did he? The Americans were second to none when it came to ASW operations . . . but with the true faith of a fanatic whose religion was the State, the political officer probably did not or would not believe that anyone could defeat a Soviet vessel in time of war.

War . . . It had finally come to war then.

Stiff-featured, Emelyanov reached across to switch on the intercom on his desk. "Bridge. Captain."

"Bridge here," the duty officer's voice responded with commendable promptness.

The captain scanned the transcript once again, noting the latest intelligence information on the carrier battle group which was their new target. It was a daunting prospect, but he would carry out his orders . . . or die in the attempt.

"Take us below the thermal layer we charted this morning. And come about to course one-seven-five, ahead two thirds."

"Yes, Captain."

He swallowed and continued, aware of the narrowed eyes regarding him across the desk. "And send the crew to battle stations. This will not be a drill, Comrade Lieutenant."

"Yes, Captain," the officer repeated.

Emelyanov cut off the intercom and met Dobrotin's eyes. He hoped the *zampolit*'s faith in their invincibility was not misplaced.

0852 hours Zulu (0852 hours Zone)
E-2C Hawkeye Tango 65
Over the southern Norwegian Sea

"So what'd'ya think, Brownie?" Lieutenant Kevin Wheeler glanced up from his radar station to look at the Hawkeye's Air Control Officer. "Do you think we're gonna fight the Russkies?"

Lieutenant Brown shrugged. "Beats the hell out of me, man," he said. "For ten years they keep telling us the Commies are really our buddies now . . . then wham! All of a sudden they're making good old Saddam Hussein look tame."

The Hawkeye was on station slightly ahead of the *Jefferson* battle group, circling slowly at an altitude of thirty thousand feet above the Norwegian Sea. From that height the AN/APS-139 radar system could detect and identify airborne threats to a range of up to three hundred miles. From its current position Tango 65 could track aircraft as far away as the coasts of Norway and Iceland. The passive electronic-surveillance system could pick up enemy emissions twice as far away.

At least one Hawkeye had been kept in the air at all times since the beginning of the crisis in Scandinavia. The range and versatility of the Airborne Warning and Control System concept had been demonstrated time and again in recent years, and was absolutely essential to all other aspects of carrier ops. Wheeler had taken plenty of ribbing from the "real aviators" who flew the Tomcats, Hornets, and Intruders in combat, but they all knew as well as he did that without the Hawkeyes they would never carry out their jobs.

"You see that profile on the tube last night?" Wheeler asked, yawning. They were near the end of their patrol period, and he was ready for a few hours' sack time.

Brown laughed. "You mean that ACN thing? There's a joke for you." *Jefferson*'s five thousand-man community was served by two on-board television stations that showed a mix of canned programs and movies together with shows picked up off satellite feeds. The documentary from the American Cable Network covering the crisis in Norway had been one of the featured programs on Channel Eight the night before.

" 'Nine Soviet aircraft carriers ready to challenge America's control of the seas,' " Wheeler quoted with a grin. "What the hell are those people playing at anyway? You'd think they'd learn the background before they went on the air with that shit, y'know? At least enough to tell a helicopter cruiser from a carrier!"

It had been greeted with laughs aboard the carrier, but Wheeler couldn't help but be indignant at the thought of the message the documentary had delivered back in the World. He could imagine his mother and father seeing that broadcast and worrying unnecessarily at the media's claim that the Soviets had nearly as many aircraft carriers as the

United States, and most of them much newer and more modern than the American boats.

Apparently ACN didn't realize—or hadn't bothered to report—the truth. Most of the so-called "carriers" in the Soviet Navy were ships of the Kiev and Moskva classes, strange hybrids between cruiser and carrier designs that carried helicopters or V/STOL fighters and served primarily in an ASW role. Of the three true carriers in Soviet service, only one was nuclear powered, and it was still undergoing sea trials in the Black Sea. Unless the Russians were really desperate it was unlikely that she would leave friendly waters. Only the two conventional carriers, *Soyuz* and *Kreml,* were anything like the *Jefferson.* At that they were smaller and much less capable than any of the Nimitz-class ships.

And the Soviets had been using carriers for less than a decade. They still had a long way to go before they would evolve the expertise and experience of their American counterparts. The Russians could be dangerous foes, but it was foolish to believe that they could seriously challenge the United States Navy in a stand-up carrier-to-carrier engagement.

Brown laughed again. "Maybe we should surrender now so we don't disappoint the newsmen, huh?"

"All right, you guys, let's can the chatter and concentrate on the job." That was Lieutenant Commander Jake Braxton, the CIC officer. Despite his words he sounded amused. "Let's save the battle of the airwaves for when we're back on the *Jeff* and stick with watching for Russkies while we're up here, okay?"

"Aye, aye, oh, lord and master," Brown responded. As with most aircraft crews the men on Tango 65 were easy about rank, at least in the privacy imposed at thirty thousand feet.

Wheeler noted a threat light and checked his instruments.

"The ALR's picking up electronic emissions. Bearing zero-five-zero, range four hundred."

"Any idea what?" Braxton asked.

Pursing his lips, Wheeler studied his readouts. "Down Beat," he said at last, giving the NATO code name for the Russian radar system.

"That's either a Blinder or a Backfire," Brown said. "Bombers."

"You getting anything on radar yet, Wheeler?" Braxton asked.

Wheeler shook his head. "Still out of range." He paused and looked down at his radar screen. It was beginning to show an irregular pattern of streaks and clutter. "Getting some jamming now. Probably an EW bird out there with them."

"Great," Braxton said sarcastically. He turned back to his own station and checked the Link-11 data-transmission system that was supposed to relay information back to *Jefferson* and the rest of the battle group. The CIC officer picked up a radio mike. "Camelot, Camelot, this is Tango Six-fiver. Come in, Camelot. Over."

Wheeler watched the radar screen and tapped his fingers on the console nervously. It was possible they were picking up a Russian raid against the Norwegian forces around Bergen . . . but a twisting in his guts told him that this was something else, something bigger.

And *Jefferson* was likely to be right in the middle of whatever the Soviets were pulling.

CHAPTER 13
Thursday, 12 June 1997

0855 hours Zulu (0855 hours Zone)
Dirty Shirt Wardroom, U.S.S. *Thomas Jefferson*
Southeast of the Faeroe Islands

They called it the "Dirty Shirt Wardroom" because it was the officers' mess hall set aside for informal meals, where an officer could eat without changing from his work clothes into the regular uniform of the day. Lieutenant Roger Bannon felt conspicuous in his neatly pressed khakis as he hunted for a place to sit with his breakfast tray. His neat uniform was an unhappy reminder of his new duties, and he felt as if every eye was on him and every tongue was wagging with the story of the crash and his decision to give up flying.

An aviator who lost it, who couldn't go back up again, became a pariah among his peers, and the center of gossip for half the carrier. Bannon suppressed a shudder as he found a chair. It was hard to face the crowded corridors aboard *Jefferson* with the specter of failure forever before him.

Probably the crash was forgotten, and outside of his own squadron no one had even noted Bannon's decision. The half-dozen officers from the Air Department at the next table, still wearing their motley array of colored jerseys that

161

identified their individual duties and roles on the flight deck, were no doubt entirely preoccupied with the increased tempo of operations that had kept them busy ever since CAG had ordered the higher state of readiness for *Jefferson*'s fighter contingent. They looked too tired from extra duty to be interested in Roger Bannon's sins.

But that thought wasn't even comforting. It only intensified his feelings of guilt. When he had taken Commander Magruder's advice and asked for some time off flight status, CAG had posted him to duty as an aide in the Air Wing office, a job that consisted of little more than running errands and pouring coffee for the regular staff officers. So now, while the rest of the carrier was bracing for the confrontation everyone knew was coming with the Soviets, it was as if he was taking a vacation from his duty.

Yet the thought of climbing back into the cockpit of his Intruder still gave him the shakes. He wasn't sure he'd ever be able to fly again without reliving the horrors of the crash and the guilt of losing Commander Greene.

He took a sip of coffee and tried to consider his future objectively. If he turned in his wings and walked away he would have to live with the knowledge of failure for the rest of his life. They probably wouldn't even let him stay on board *Jefferson* longer than they absolutely had to. It was never considered wise to keep a failed aviator on his old ship. Short of resigning his commission and looking for a civilian pilot's job, he might never fly again.

And yet flying was all he had ever wanted to do. As a boy he'd hoped to earn his wings and then look for a shot at astronaut training, but once he'd been in the cockpit it was enough just to be in the air, in control, free of the restrictions of an earthbound existence. Until he'd run up against the Deputy CAG and lost his confidence, Bannon had been in love with flying, and even Jolly Green's criticism hadn't been enough to dampen his enthusiasm for his chosen life.

That had only come after the criticism had stopped forever. After Greene's death.

He shook his head slowly and stared down at his cup. He would have to face his fears again if he was ever going to be whole . . . but he didn't know if he had that kind of courage inside him.

Then the blare of the klaxon jerked him out of his reverie. "Now hear this! Now hear this! Battle stations! Battle stations! All hands to battle stations. That is, battle stations! This is not a drill!"

His battle station was in the Air Ops module of CIC, with CAG. Bannon pushed back his chair and stood, gulping the rest of his coffee. Then he was caught in the swirling mob of men rushing from the wardroom.

Thoughts of the future would have to wait.

0857 hours Zulu (0857 hours Zone)
CIC ASW module, U.S.S. *Thomas Jefferson*
Southeast of the Faeroe Islands

"We just got an update in from SOSUS Control, sir. Feeding in the new info now." The AW/2 looked too young to be in the Navy, but he knew his job. Lieutenant Eric Nelson leaned forward to study the electronic display map as new contacts appeared.

"I don't like the looks of these," he said softly. "Rodriguez, what've you got on this contact?" He used his keyboard to highlight one of the symbols.

AW/2 Carlos Rodriguez checked his own terminal before replying. "Victor III," he said. "The SOSUS trace reported it was probably diving and increasing speed as it was picked up." He paused. "The triangulation isn't real accurate, sir. That could mean more than one contact, or it could just be bad conditions."

"Could be . . ." Nelson shook his head. " 'Could be' could get us killed. This guy's not that far away. How'd the sub-hunters miss him?"

The Hispanic sailor shrugged. "He's probably been laying low, sir. Running on minimal power and waiting."

"Well, he's not waiting now." Nelson picked up a handset. "Get me the Air Ops module." He masked the phone with one hand. "Rodriguez, make sure this gets passed on to the rest of the battle group pronto. Especially *Gridley*. She's closest."

"Aye, aye, sir."

0859 hours Zulu (0859 hours Zone)
CIC Air Ops module, U.S.S. *Thomas Jefferson*
Southeast of the Faeroe Islands

"Air Ops," Stramaglia growled into the batphone. "CAG speaking."

"This is Nelson in ASW. I've got at least one SOSUS sub contact two hundred thirty miles north-northwest. Possibly multiple contacts. I think you'd better check it out."

"All right. I'll get on it as soon as I can. We've got some other problems to get to first." He slammed down the handset and turned to study the map. "Any change, Howard?"

Radarman Second Class David Howard shook his head. "No, sir. Still reading twenty aircraft. Same course and speed as before."

That was the other problem, and right now it loomed higher on Stramaglia's list of concerns than the sub contact Nelson had reported. They had appeared on Tango Six-five's radar screens a few minutes earlier, flying at low altitude and on a course that could only have brought them from one of the Soviet air bases in the Kola Peninsula.

Launching during a window when there were no U.S. spy satellites overhead, they had very nearly taken the battle group by surprise.

But their course, so far, wasn't bringing them directly toward the carrier. They had been curving west and south, parallel to the Norwegian coast. That could mean they were going after a target in Norway.

Or it might be that the Russians weren't sure of the exact location of the *Jefferson*. Stramaglia couldn't be sure . . . but he wasn't planning on taking any chances.

At that moment the screen came alive with new symbols, three-letter ID codes next to each of the dots representing an enemy plane. BKF . . . that meant Tu-22Ms, Backfires in NATO's B-for-bomber code. They were a powerful threat to the *Jefferson*.

Stramaglia drummed his fingers on the console, frowning as he stared at the moving symbols on the screen. Viper Squadron was on Alert Fifteen this morning, and he'd ordered them to start launching as soon as the bombers had first appeared. The Tomcats were ideal for this situation. Their Phoenix missiles were designed to knock out Soviet cruise missiles as well as the bombers themselves, and if those Badgers really were searching for the *Jefferson* Viper Squadron might just turn the tide.

He found himself wishing the other Tomcat squadron, the War Eagles of VF-97, had drawn this watch. Stramaglia wasn't sure how much he trusted some of those hotheads in Grant's outfit.

Probably the War Eagles were no better. They needed a tight rein to keep them in check, though, and with Magruder already out on a Viking sub hunt, that left Stramaglia with very few options. It went against the grain to leave CIC at a time like this, but he might just be able to show the youngsters what a real Tomcat pilot could do.

"What's the word on the flight deck?" he asked Bannon, who was hovering nearby.

The Intruder pilot looked up, holding a hand over the batphone to answer him. "Three planes are up, CAG, and already starting to refuel. The Boss says he'll have four more up in the next five minutes if he has to go out there and throw them off the deck himself!"

That brought laughs to the men in the Air Ops module, but Stramaglia didn't even smile. This was the kind of situation every carrier officer dreaded, with the battle group sitting exposed to a massive strike by Russian bombers armed with stand-off weapons.

On the screen the lines showing the Backfire flight paths were altering. The bombers were changing course, driving west now away from the Norwegian coast. They were still well to the north of the carrier battle group, but if they turned again they would be in range in no time.

"Tell the Boss to ready the double-nuts bird too," he ordered. "And find me an RIO. I'm going up with them!" He stood up, looking across at Bannon. "Call Owens to relieve me here, Mr. Bannon. And pass on the SOSUS info to Magruder in 704. Let's get moving, people!"

He looked down at the screen again and prayed they wouldn't be too late.

0905 hours Zulu (0805 hours Zone)
Air Operations Center
Keflavik, Iceland

"Snowman, Snowman, this is Watchdog. Snowman, this is Watchdog. Respond, please. Over." The radio voice was heavily spiked with static, but even through the distortion Major Peter Kelso could hear a note of desperation.

"Watchdog, Snowman. Can you boost your signal,

over?'' Kelso replied. Watchdog was an orbiting E-3A AWACS Cape Straumnes on the northern coast of Iceland. There shouldn't have been that much static.

''Snowman, this is Watchdog. We're already on maximum. Heavy jamming on radar and radio. Repeat, heavy jamming on radar and radio. Do you copy, Snowman?''

''Roger, Watchdog,'' Kelso told him. ''Do you have any radar contacts? Over.''

''Cannot confirm . . . Wait one! Wait one!'' There was a long pause before the message resumed. ''Snowman, Watchdog. Flash priority, Warning Red. We have multiple contacts. Multiple contacts! Zombies are inbound, repeat zombies inbound bearing between zero-zero-zero and zero-one-zero. Range is two-five-zero November Mikes. Angels two. Speed is four-five-zero.'' The E-3 crewman paused again. ''Snowman, we now make at least twenty-four zombies inbound, maybe more. Radar interference makes count unreliable. Over.''

Kelso read back the figures for confirmation even as his hand moved to hit the button that sounded the alert. Klaxons began to blare around him.

This was the situation Keflavik had rehearsed for thousands of times in the past. But this time it was real.

Through the windows overlooking the base Kelso could see men in motion on the field, pilots racing for their F-15 interceptors and ground crewmen hastening through their paces in an effort to get the planes aloft. Activity inside Air Ops had intensified as well, as controllers took their positions and started trying to find order in the middle of chaos.

''Watchdog, do you have an India Delta on the zombies? Over.''

''Snowman, our best estimate is Badgers, repeat best estimate is Tango Uniform One-sixers.'' Kelso nodded at the words. The Tu-16 family of Soviet aircraft, ''Badger'' in the NATO lexicon, dated back to the same era as the ubiquitous Bears. The turbojet bomber had been adapted to a wide variety of functions, from missile carrier to ECM platform, recon aircraft to tanker.

Recon planes and tankers didn't travel in packs of twenty or more. Each one of those Badgers could carry a pair of air-to-surface missiles and a conventional bomb load as well, more than enough to ruin all four of Keflavik's runways.

Outside an F-15 screamed past the windows as it took off. The 57th Fighter Interceptor Squadron, the "Black Knights," was the only line of defense for the base. There were six Eagles already airborne, and twelve more in reserve. If they couldn't stop the Badgers . . .

At least they hadn't used Backfires. The Tu-22 was a supersonic bomber, far more capable than the antiquated Badger.

"Major!" An enlisted communications man looked up from his console. "Message from CBG-14. They are tracking twenty Backfires over the Norwegian Sea. Target uncertain. Could be the battle group . . ."

"Or us," Kelso finished. His mouth was dry. The Russians weren't fooling around. He raised his voice. "Radio CINCLANT that we're under attack. And get every bird airborne . . . the Orions and those two transports too. I don't want anything on the ground when those bastards start shooting!"

0908 hours Zulu (0808 hours Zone)
Badger 101, Strike Mission *Gremyashchiy*
Over the Greenland Sea

"We have been detected, Comrade Lieutenant."

Lieutenant Stanislav Dzhiorovich Meretskov gave a curt acknowledgment to the report from the commander of the

reconnaissance aircraft. The planes of Strike Mission
Thunderous—*Gremyashchiy*—had flown in low to avoid
detection for as long as possible, but it had been certain
from the start that the American AWACS would spot them
far out in the waters north of Iceland. Even the jamming
from the Tu-16J accompanying the strike mission had only
bought them a few extra minutes.

But it was all part of the mission profile. Now that the
enemy was tracking them, it was time to press home the
attack.

"*Gremyashchiy* Leader to all aircraft," Meretskov announced. "Proceed with attack run."

He pulled back on the yoke and increased speed, and the
bomber began to climb. A low altitude was best for dodging
enemy radars, but the optimum altitude for a missile launch
was eleven thousand meters. The Tu-16G angled sharply
upward, clawing for altitude.

"An American plane approaching from the southeast,
Comrade Lieutenant," his copilot reported. "F-15 interceptor at Mach two point five, altitude eight thousand meters,
range thirty kilometers, closing."

"Ready countermeasures," Meretskov ordered. He
checked his instrument panel. They were still climbing, past
nine thousand meters . . . 9500 . . .

"Radar lock! They have radar lock!" someone shouted.
"They are firing!"

"Chaff!"

"Chaff released, Comrade Lieutenant," the copilot replied. The cloud of metallic strips would distort the American radar lock, and hopefully carry the enemy missile off
course.

Ten thousand meters . . .

"Weapons officer," Meretskov said. "Stand by . . ."

"Second F-15 coming into range," the copilot warned.

"Fire missiles!"

The aircraft shuddered as the first AS-6 missile dropped from the left wing pylon. Flame leapt from the rocket motor and the missile streaked ahead. A moment later the second missile followed. As Meretskov started a banking turn he saw both missiles rising according to their flight profile. They would reach eighteen thousand meters and a cruise speed of Mach three before locking on to radar emissions from the enemy base and diving toward their targets. More missile raced south as the rest of the bombers released their loads.

Their mission was accomplished. In minutes the defenses at Keflavik would be overwhelmed by the onslaught of forty radar-homing missiles. The enemy would be blind . . . and at the mercy of the follow-up strike already on the way.

He enjoyed his satisfied smile for less than thirty seconds before the first American missile slammed into the Tu-16G.

0915 hours Zulu (0815 hours Zone)
Echo Leader
Over the Greenland Sea

"Fox one! Fox one!" The voice on the radio was wild with excitement. "Whoo-ee! Talk about a target-rich environment!"

Captain Frank Gates pulled the trigger to launch another Sparrow as he replied. "Never mind the commentary, Tarzan. Just nail the bastards while they're in range."

He checked his fuel and shook his head slowly. Gates and his wingman, Lieutenant John Burroughs, had been on station with the AWACS over northern Iceland, and they had been near the end of their patrol when the enemy bombers had first appeared. They had been the two best-placed Eagles to mount an intercept, but their fuel state wouldn't allow them to engage for long. Pursuit was out of the question . . . and by the time the rest of the Black Knights made it to the threatened sector this batch of enemies would be long gone.

But the Russians had left a calling card Keflavik couldn't ignore.

He switched frequencies on the radio. "Snowman, Snowman, this is Echo Leader. We are engaging. Badgers have released missiles. Repeat, missiles released by Badgers. Estimate thirty-five-plus Kingfish inbound to you."

"Roger that, Echo Leader," a controller back at Keflavik replied. He sounded remarkably calm for a man who was about to be on the receiving end of that much Soviet ordnance. Each AS-6 Kingfish missile carried a thousand kilograms of conventional explosives . . . or a 350-kiloton nuclear warhead.

He didn't think the Russians would be using nukes . . . not yet. But conventional warheads would be bad enough.

He checked his fuel again and switched back to the tactical channel. "Tarzan, I'm on bingo fuel now. We've got to break it off and look for a gas station, man."

"Fox one! Fox one!" Burroughs said as he fired again. "That was my last Sparrow anyway, Crasher. Damn! We could've taught those Commies a real lesson if we'd had some more avgas."

"Never mind, son," Gates said. "They'll be back. I guarantee!"

The Russians would be back . . . if there was anything left of the American air base after this attack.

CHAPTER 14
Thursday, 12 June 1997

0917 hours Zulu (0917 hours Zone)
Viking 704
Northeast of the Faeroe Islands

"Sonobuoy away. Come right to three-five-zero."

Magruder banked the Viking in response to Lieutenant Commander Meade's order, trying to get the feel of the aircraft's controls. The S-3B's handling was entirely unlike a Tomcat's. Both were responsive and graceful in flight, but where the F-14 was a sleek racehorse the Viking was more of a predatory bird, swooping low over the water on outstretched wings. Today Tombstone was having less trouble with the technical end of flying the plane—he knew the layout of the controls now, and was less awkward in making the aircraft do what he wanted—but he was still finding it hard to adjust to the difference in style and pace. In a Tomcat slow loitering and circling were anathema. Aboard the Viking everything went at a slower pace.

"Contact! Contact!" Curtis chanted. "Jezebel five is hot."

"I'll take her, Commander," Harrison announced from the pilot's seat. He put his hands on the yoke. "I have control, sir," he added formally, but with a sidelong grin at Magruder.

His reply was just as formal. "I relinquish control, sir,"
he said, feeling relieved. For a moment he'd been afraid the
ASW men would require him to handle the Viking all the
way through. Right now he preferred the job of observer.

"Punching in new coordinates now," Meade said. "Jezebel five is at bearing one-two-four, range twenty-five."

"One-two-four, range twenty-five," Harrison echoed.
He looked at Magruder. "Always best to know the target
even if the computer is supposed to steer you," he said.

Tombstone nodded. "So is this an attack run?"

Over the ICS, Meade laughed. "Hell, no. Jezebel five is
one of the omni-directional sonobuoys we've been laying.
An SSQ-41. They use passive sonar sensors to pick up
underwater noise." He chuckled again. "Nope, the fun is
just getting started, Commander. We know about where the
bad guys might be, but now we've gotta find the bastards."

"And of course while we're closing in they're still
moving," Harrison added. "That means the area we have to
cover as we hunt gets larger as time passes. We've got a
nice long time to go before we start shooting at anything."

Magruder settled back into his seat, trying not to betray
his disappointment. It looked like it would be a long, boring
morning.

0918 hours Zulu (0818 hours Zone)
Air Operations Center
Keflavik, Iceland

"Vampires! Vampires! Missiles inbound!"

Major Peter Kelso could feel the tension thick within the
command center. "What's the status on the runways?"

"Four Eagles to go, sir," someone said. "Then the
Orions."

"Damn," he muttered to himself. "Not fast enough.

Damn!'' Each passing second brought a wave of missiles closer and closer to the air base. Outside, klaxons continued to blare warning, but everyone he could see on the field below was staying at his post, trying to get those last few airplanes off the ground.

"Christ Almighty, will you look at that!" someone yelled. "Captain Blackwell just nailed two of the vampires with Sparrows!" That raised a cheer in the room, though everyone, from Kelso down to the greenest enlisted man, knew that taking out only two missiles from that swarm was about as effective as trying to bail out a sinking battleship with a spoon. "He's closing in . . . what the hell?" The controller paused. "Blackwell got another one . . . I think he rammed it . . ."

The room grew quiet for a moment before someone else broke the stillness. "They're tipping over."

Far above Keflavik the missiles were reaching their maximum altitude and starting their descent toward their targets. "Kill the radars," Kelso ordered. "Now!"

It was a long shot, but it might confuse the missiles enough to keep a few of Keflavik's radar installations intact. If they were radar-homers . . .

The first missile hit at that moment, striking near the far end of runway two with a flash of light and an upwelling cloud of smoke and debris. The sound didn't come for several more seconds. By then more missiles were hitting, and the popping, rumbling, tearing sounds of successive blasts merged into a single cacophony of sound.

Kelso felt rather than saw the blast that struck to the south of the building. It was a close hit, and sound and pressure rolled through Air Ops like a giant hand sweeping aside all it encountered. The force of the explosion knocked him off his feet.

An unknown amount of time later—seconds? minutes?—Kelso realized he was lying facedown on the hard floor.

There were shards of glass everywhere like a shimmering blanket. A radio was squawking a request from one of the Eagles, but no one answered. The rumble of missile hits went on.

Kelso struggled to rise, but his body wouldn't obey his will. Something warm and sticky soaked the front of his uniform.

Slowly it dawned on him that it was blood, but by then it was too late for Major Peter Kelso.

0920 hours Zulu (0920 hours Zone)
Flight deck, U.S.S. *Thomas Jefferson*
Southeast of the Faeroe Islands

The catapult officer dropped to one knee and a tremendous force pressed Stramaglia back into his seat as the F-14 roared off the deck. As the Tomcat clawed its way skyward he hit the radio switch. "Good shot! Good shot! Tomcat Two-zero-zero, Good shot!"

"Squadron's formed up at Point Bravo, sir," his RIO said. Lieutenant Dennis Russell was Viper Squadron's apprentice Landing Signals Officer, but he'd been pressed into service in his old calling as an RIO to fly with Stramaglia. His running name, true to his new job, was "Paddles."

"Lancelot Two-zero-zero, this is Camelot," a voice said over the radio. He recognized Owens, the Junior Deputy CAG who had relieved him in CIC. "Be advised, Keflavik has been attacked by Soviet Badgers carrying Alpha Sierra Six radar-homing missiles. Red Raid One still heading course two-eight-zero."

"Copy, Camelot," he replied curtly.

Keflavik . . .

The course of the Russian Backfires, designated Red Raid

One on *Jefferson*'s plotting boards, suggested that they were also heading for Iceland. That would make sense if they were designed to be the second half of a one-two punch, with the Badgers delivering antiradar missiles designed to neutralize the defenses and the Backfires coming in to clean up what was left. Backfires could carry either missiles or bomb racks, and were capable of delivering enough ordnance, including specialized loads like the five-hundred-pound BETAB retarded antirunway bomb, the Russian equivalent to NATO's Durandal, to wipe out the main American base in Iceland beyond all possibility of quick repair. That could have devastating effects. Iceland was the only possible staging point for reinforcements while England remained on the fence, and the P-3C sub-hunting patrols out of Keflavik were vital in sealing off those parts of the GIUK gap out of range of the carrier-based S-3s.

It had taken balls for the Russian commander to order the Backfires to swing so far south before striking out for Iceland, Stramaglia told himself with a grim smile. They'd kept the American forces off balance by threatening multiple targets—Bergen, the battle group, and Keflavik all at once—but they had also exposed those Backfires to a quick stroke that could blunt their attack . . . if the Tomcats could get there in time.

"Camelot, Lancelot Leader," he transmitted. "I want both Hornet squadrons prepped for air-to-air ASAP. Get 'em up and feed 'em in as quick as you can, boys. We're going to bite those Russkies right on the ass!"

"Roger, Leader," Owens replied. Stramaglia could hear the excitement in his young voice and felt his resolve waver. After everything he had said to Magruder he had still elected to join the interceptors in the air. Had it been the right decision? Or had he just let the years of frustration and bitterness get to him at last?

No. They needed a firm hand up here, and Commander

Grant still hadn't shown Stramaglia that he knew how to apply that firm hand.

And he was Stinger Stramaglia, who had never been defeated at Top Gun, finally doing for real what he'd practiced for over the course of nearly a decade.

"All right, Paddles," he said to the RIO. "Talk to me, son. Where's the party?"

The Tomcat streaked northward through the cold gray sky.

0925 hours Zulu (0925 hours Zone)
Viking 704
Northeast of the Faeroe Islands

"So what happens now?" Magruder asked as a thud from the rear of the plane announced the deployment of another sonobuoy.

From his position in the right rear seat, Meade answered in a distracted tone. "Now we hunt. We just dropped a DICASS, an SSQ-62. Instead of the Jezebel's passive sonar the DICASS will send out active pings on command. We've got to lay several of the suckers so we can triangulate range and bearing data and locate our underwater friend." He paused. "The Skipper has the next set of coordinates locked into the flight computer now, and Curtis is busy working on the acoustic data from the Jezebel."

"Anything I can do?" Tombstone asked.

"Now that you mention it, yeah. Keep an eye on the nonacoustic sensors. We ran over them yesterday, remember?"

"Yeah." Magruder found the panel and nodded even though the TACCO couldn't see him. "Yeah, I've got 'em."

"Good. Keep a close watch on the MAD. It'll pick up a

sub by detecting the metal in its hull . . . if we get close enough, and if it isn't one of those new titanium hulls the Russkies have been playing with. Anything registers on the MAD and you sing out, Commander. Okay?"

"I think I can handle it," Tombstone said.

Curtis spoke up from the left rear Senso position. "I make the contact a Victor III. Number five, I think, but I'm not positive. The signal's a little bit confused."

"Confused?" Meade asked.

"Yeah . . . I don't know, sir, there might be more than one engine making the noise down there, but it's intermittent. I thought I heard two boats for a while, then only one."

"SOSUS reported possible multiples," Harrison reminded them. "But you're sure about the ID, Curtis?"

"Wouldn't swear to the specific boat, sir, but the sounds I heard were a Victor III all right."

"I'm tagging it on the tactical plot," Meade said. "Curtis, pass the data back to the *Jeff* over the Link-11."

"Aye, aye, sir," the enlisted man replied.

Magruder was still unfamiliar with many of the more arcane aspects of sub-hunting, but he remembered that the Link-11 was the on-board Navy Tactical Data System which kept track of the ships, aircraft, buoys, and submarines in a given area. It could be monitored by the ships of the battle group. The Senso and TACCO shared the responsibility of keeping the NTDS data current and sending it off to the ASW module in *Jefferson*'s CIC.

"What's the nearest help we can tap, Spock?" Harrison asked.

Meade didn't answer immediately. "Hmmm . . . *Gridley*'s closest," he said at last.

Harrison glanced across the cockpit at Magruder. "Commander, get on the horn to the *Jeff* and ask ASW if we can get a little help from the *Gridley*. A LAMPS helo would be a big help tracking down that sucker."

"And the frigate's towed array'll spot anything trying to break out to the southeast," Meade added. "That'll keep the bastards from getting any closer to the battle group."

Magruder keyed in the radio and passed the request to the *Jefferson.*

"Viking Seven-oh-four, this is Guenevere," Lieutenant Nelson's voice came back. "Request acknowledged. Wait one."

Seconds ticked by as the Viking continued its low-level flight barely two hundred feet above the ocean. Magruder heard another sonobuoy launch, and the S-3B banked left to take up a new heading.

"Viking Seven-oh-four thanks you, Guenevere," the radio announced. "Switch to Channel Five. Call sign is Jericho, repeat Jericho."

"Guenevere, Seven-oh-four thanks you," Magruder said. He switched frequencies to establish contact with the *Gridley.* "Jericho, Jericho, this is Viking Seven-oh-four."

"Seven-oh-four, Jericho. Copy you five by five. We're readying you a helo now. Call sign will be Trumpet. ETA your position is thirty Mikes, repeat thirty Mikes."

"Roger that, Jericho," Tombstone responded. He was disappointed at the long delay, still reacting with the instincts of a fighter pilot to whom thirty seconds, not thirty minutes, was considered a long time. But Harrison didn't look concerned. "We'll be in touch. Seven-oh-four is clear."

"Got something on DICASS two, sir," Curtis announced. "Same signature . . . bearing from buoy is one-eight-one . . ."

"Range?" Meade demanded.

"Close . . . damned close . . ."

Magruder saw the MAD indicator register a contact. "MAD is active!" he said sharply. "MAD active!"

"Christ!" Harrison said. "We're right on top of the guy!"

"Got a line from buoy one now," Curtis said.

"That's our boy!" Meade said. "Triangulating now."

"Course is one-seven-five degrees, speed ten, depth two-one-five," Curtis reported.

"Range is eight hundred yards," Meade added a second later. "Man, what a break!"

"We've hooked him," Harrison said. "But we've still gotta nail him. I'll circle in for an attack run."

"Better hurry, Skipper," Curtis said. "The pings've spooked him. I'm getting changes in speed, target aspect . . . sounds like he's diving, too. Updating . . ."

"Dropping a fish," Harrison announced. "Bay doors opening."

Magruder felt rather than heard the grinding sound of the bomb bay opening to expose its lethal cargo. The S-3's internal bay held four Mark 50 lightweight torpedoes, specifically designed for the Navy's ASW aircraft. As he heard the sound of the release mechanism dropping one of the torpedoes Magruder could imagine it falling, its parachute deploying to slow the weapon's fall. When it hit the water the torpedo would start its own hunt with an on-board sonar system.

"Torpedo running," Meade announced. "I think we have acquisition . . ."

Magruder closed his eyes. The detached air of the Viking's crew seemed unreal to him. Down below the aircraft the torpedo was closing on the Soviet submarine at a speed of over fifty knots, yet the matter-of-fact voices in the S-3 cabin might have been discussing sports scores for all the emotion they expressed. This was a new kind of war for Tombstone Magruder.

A war he wasn't sure he'd ever really understand.

0926 hours Zulu (0926 hours Zone)
Tomcat 201
Northwest of the Faeroe Islands

"Help me out, John-Boy," Coyote said, trying to keep the edge of tension out of his voice. "Come on, man, you've got to have something for me!"

Viper Squadron was spread out in a loose formation, angling north and west at fifteen thousand feet. The carrier was far behind them now, the Russian bombers somewhere ahead and down on the deck. It was clear now that they were heading for the coast of Iceland and not the *Jefferson*'s battle group, but that didn't diminish the threat they posed. They could still double back.

And right now spotting the enemy was no easy task.

"This jamming's just too damned thick, Coyote," Nichols complained. "All I'm getting is fuzz."

"Well, keep on it," Coyote snapped.

He regretted his tone at once. He was letting things get to him again, losing control of his temper. That, he thought bitterly, was a sure way to get shot out of the sky. All other things being equal, it was the aviator who kept his cool and made the fewest mistakes who got home in one piece.

But today he couldn't seem to keep a tight rein on his feelings. There was no one cause, no one solution, and that was the real problem. Too many emotions were distracting him.

There was fear, of course. No carrier pilot left the flight deck without knowing fear, no matter what sort of facade they presented to the outside world. In a combat situation, as in a night landing, the "pucker factor" was that much worse, but it was something an aviator learned to handle. Coyote had probably come closer to death than anyone in the squadron. He'd been shot down in the Sea of Japan, and had cradled his dead RIO in his arms as he awaited the SAR helo that never showed up. The North Koreans had threatened him with execution, and wounded him in the leg during an escape attempt. And there had been plenty of tight moments in the skies over the Indian Ocean as well.

Coyote could have dealt with the fear alone. But today there were other things on his mind. The confrontation with Magruder, for instance . . . and the close scrutiny he felt from CAG. The captain seemed determined to find fault with Viper Squadron and its commanding officer, and the extra pressure to perform was the last thing Coyote needed right now. And on top of that Stramaglia was flying as his wingman, and that worried him. The man was a brilliant instructor and a natural fighter jock, but he'd never heard a shot fired in anger in his entire Navy career. Two years behind a Pentagon desk had changed Matt Magruder. What had nearly a decade ashore done to Stramaglia?

Too many worries . . . too many distractions. Coyote knew what that could do to a pilot. He remembered his first time back up in a Tomcat after the North Korean incident, when the memory of being shot down and captured, the fear of losing Julie, had been overwhelming. The same kind of uncertainty gripped him now.

"Hey, dudes, I got something!" Malibu's cheerful voice roused him from his reverie. "Bearing three-four-five . . . multiple targets! Multiple targets!"

"Three-four-five . . ." he heard Nichols muttering over the ICS. "Where . . . ? Yeah! I got 'em, Skipper! Got 'em! It's faint with all this clutter, but I got bogies on the screen!"

Over the radio Coyote heard Stramaglia's growl. "Tighten up and go to afterburner. This is the real thing!"

"Range is one-for-oh, closing," Nichols reported. "Angels one . . ."

"What's the count?" Coyote asked as he shoved the throttles forward.

"Can't tell . . . damn this shit!"

"Easy, John-Boy," he said with a steady voice that belied his own inner turmoil. Everyone was on edge, not just him. This time there was none of the uncertainty they had felt the day of the Bear hunt, but knowing the score didn't necessarily make things any easier. The Soviets were far more capable opponents than Libyans or Iraqis or North Koreans.

"Range one-twenty," someone said on the radio.

"All right, weapons are free," Stramaglia said. "Let's get some use out of the Phoenix today."

Coyote already had his selector switch set to launch the AIM-54 Phoenix. It was the Navy's longest-ranged air-to-air missile, capable of reaching out and knocking down a target over a hundred nautical miles away. The Tomcat had been specifically designed to carry Phoenix, using the sophisticated AWG-9 radar/fire-control system. Each aircraft in Viper squadron carried four of the deadly missiles plus two Sidewinders for close-in attacks. Given the high success rate of the Phoenix—eighty-five-percent accuracy was the usual figure—the squadron stood a good chance of knocking out most, even all of the Soviet bombers they had detected earlier.

If only they could be sure of the enemy numbers now. The intense jamming could have covered a group breaking off from the main body.

"All right, boys, show 'em what you've got!" Stramaglia said over the radio. "Fight's on!" That was the traditional call to Top Gun students announcing the beginning of an exercise.

"Got a lock!" Nichols said. "Got a lock!"

Coyote's finger tightened on the fire control, and a Phoenix leapt from the Tomcat's wing with a roar of flame and thunder.

0927 hours Zulu (0927 hours Zone)
Soviet Attack Submarine *Komsomolets Tbilsiskiy*
Northeast of the Faeroe Islands

"Torpedo! Torpedo in the water!"

Emelyanov looked up at the call from the sonar operator. The atmosphere in the cramped, red-lit control room had been thick with tension ever since the passive towed sonar array had first detected the passing American aircraft above them. It hadn't taken the enemy long to begin the hunt, using sonobuoys to send out pings of sound that had echoed through the sub's steel hull. Nonetheless the captain had counted on more time before the hunters triangulated on the *Komsomolets Tbilsiskiy*. Whoever the American was, he'd been incredibly lucky to spot the boat before Emelyanov's evasive maneuvers had taken him out of harm's way.

Too late now to dwell on the question of luck. "Take him to three hundred feet," Emelyanov snapped. "Fire control, ready decoys."

"Fifteen degrees down angle on planes." That was Captain-Lieutenant Yuri Borisovich Shvachko, the submarine's *starpom*. The Exec picked up a PA microphone and pressed the switch. "Dive! Dive!"

As the deck began to angle downward Emelyanov swallowed and looked across the control room toward the sonar repeater station. "Sonar, report."

"Range eight hundred meters, closing," the sailor at the repeater answered promptly. "Bearing one-one-six. Speed fifty knots . . ."

The Americans had dropped the torpedo almost on top of the sub. Emelyanov didn't waste time cursing. "Helm, come to course one-one-six. Flank speed!"

"Left full rudder. Increase to flank speed." The Exec's voice was cold, level, giving away no hint of emotion or concern. Emelyanov felt a flash of admiration for the way the young officer carried himself. Shvachko knew as well as anyone just how risky the maneuver his captain had just ordered really was. It was a testament to the way he had trained all of his crew, officers and seamen alike.

In theory turning into the enemy torpedo was the most effective defense they had. In the best-case scenario, the torp would hit the sub before it had time to arm. At least they might hope to get past it, buy a few more minutes of safety before it could turn around and use its sonar to reacquire and home in on the sub. But it was still incredibly risky.

"Decoys ready, Captain!" the fire-control officer announced.

"Range five hundred, closing," the sonar operator added.

Emelyanov's hands gripped the edge of the chart table of their own accord. He could feel the sweat trickling down his face. He had been through countless exercises in preparation for a moment like this, but the reality was nothing like the simulations or the practice runs against Soviet hunters.

"Four hundred . . . three-fifty . . . three hundred . . ."

"Depth now two-twenty-five meters," the planesman reported.

There was an inversion layer somewhere around 250

meters beneath the surface, a layer of water where the temperature rose sharply. Thermal variations could distort or block sonar signals, providing a narrow pocket of safety where a sub could disappear from its pursuers for a time. If they could get there, they might be able to break contact. If . . .

"Range two-fifty . . . two hundred . . ." The ping of the torpedo's active sonar was growing steadily louder and faster as the range closed.

"Fire decoy!" Emelyanov ordered. "Helm, come to course one-two-five!" Silently, he uttered an old prayer his Ukrainian mother had taught him.

His eyes met Dobrotin's. He wondered for an instant what the *zampolit* would think if he knew the captain was seeking solace in the religion still officially rejected by the Communist Party despite all the efforts of the liberal reformers.

Then the torpedo struck.

0929 hours Zulu (0929 hours Zone)
Viking 704
Northeast of the Faeroe Islands

Tombstone Magruder found it hard to believe that they were involved in a battle. There was none of the excitement, the adrenaline, the feeling of life and death hanging on every move they made that characterized the combats he was used to. The Viking crew was cool, professional, almost matter-of-fact as they waited to see the results of their first attack.

"Torpedo running," Curtis reported. "Running . . . sub's put out a decoy now . . . Hit!" His voice rose suddenly, cracking with sudden emotion for the first time. "That's got to be a hit, by God!"

"Get on those sonars, Curtis," Harrison ordered. "Confirm the kill."

The S-3B started a long, banking turn, skimming low over the ocean. Magruder scanned the angry waters, looking for some outward sign of the battle. There was something unreal about a fight where you couldn't even be sure you'd scored a hit. Even when a Phoenix knocked out an enemy plane at a hundred miles' range, the bogie would disappear from the radar screen. But ASW warfare remained a matter of guesswork, surmise, assumption, from first contact to the very end of the engagement.

He cut his reverie short and pointed. "Down there, Commander," he said.

Harrison grunted acknowledgment. A froth of bubbles was rising to the surface, along with a few unidentifiable bits of debris. "Not much junk," the pilot said. "Curtis, what are you getting?"

"Decoy's obscuring it," Curtis replied. "But I don't think the bastard's out of action yet."

Submarines customarily carried decoys that simulated a sub's engine noises to confuse enemy sonars. The decoy dropped by the enemy Victor was still emitting its signal, which made it hard for Curtis to interpret the other noises his passive sonar receivers were picking up. But if he was right, the Russian was still down there, status unknown.

"Don't worry, Commander," Harrison said. He seemed to sense Magruder's train of thought. He gave a wolfish grin. "Down there's the deep blue sea. We're the devil. I wouldn't want to be in that Russkie's shoes right now!"

0930 hours Zulu (0930 hours Zone)
Backfire 101, Strike Mission *Burlivyy*
Northwest of the Faeroe Islands

Captain First Rank Porfiri Grigorevich Margelov pushed the throttles forward and listened to the roar of the twin Kuznetsov NK-144 turbofan engines with a tiny smile of satisfaction. The Tu-22M's variable-geometry wings slid further back as the bomber gathered speed. He pulled back on the steering yoke, and the bomber angled upward, clawing for altitude.

"Missile launch! Missile launch!" the copilot shouted in warning. "American air-to-air missiles . . . AIM-54 type . . . Reading eight . . . ten . . . twelve!"

"Range?" Margelov asked sharply.

"One hundred fifty kilometers."

Margelov frowned. The American Phoenix was a lethal weapon, capable of striking at targets far from their launch platforms. But it was a mixed blessing for the Americans to be able to open fire from such a long range. The bombers of Strike Mission *Burlivyy*—Tempestuous—would have plenty of time to react to the launch and get off their own missiles . . . and the Americans would face a significant time lag before they could engage at closer range with more conventional air-to-air missiles. The Phoenixes might cause heavy damage to the Tu-22Ms, but they weren't going to stop the attack.

"Range to target?" he asked.

The weapons officer responded quickly. "Four-two-five kilometers, Comrade Captain."

That put them within range of the American base in Iceland, but only barely. They could afford to wait a few minutes longer.

Margelov switched his radio to the strike mission tactical frequency. "*Burlivyy* Leader to all aircraft. Prepare for missile launch on my signal."

The other bombers acknowledged the signal in rigid order as the bombers gained speed and altitude. The copilot called off the range of the approaching Phoenixes in a voice edged with worry. The reputation of the American missiles was enough to shake even the steadiest hand.

"Range six-zero kilometers, closing. Fourteen missiles."

Over the radio Margelov heard a low-voiced exclamation. "*Bojemoi!* Picking up another missile launch from American aircraft!"

"Confirmed! Confirmed!" someone else added. "Six missiles incoming . . . nine . . . twelve . . ."

"I have them on our screens," the copilot agreed. "It looks like two waves of fourteen missiles each. Enough to take all of our planes out of action."

"Relax, Mikhail Mikhailovich," Margelov said quietly. "The Americans have good weapons, but they are not infallible." He checked his altitude and activated the radio again. "*Burlivyy* Leader to all strike aircraft. Commence missile launches . . . now!"

He listened to the babble of acknowledgments as the Tu-22M shuddered with the release of one of the two AS-4 air-to-surface missiles. The Badger strike on Keflavik had concentrated on crippling the air defense systems of the base, especially radar installations. This wave of missiles would be directed at more general targets, while each of the missile-equipped Tu-22Ms would hold back one AS-4 to use at closer range . . . if they could run the gauntlet of the American Phoenixes and whatever aircraft had survived the first attacks over Iceland.

Even more important than delivering another wave of missiles, though, was the protection of the four Tu-22M bombers armed with BETAB antirunway loads. Those were conventional iron bombs slung on racks mounted under the air intakes on each wing. Those weapons would complete the destruction of Keflavik as a functional air base.

Getting those four planes over the target was the crucial thing now, Margelov thought. He reached for the radio, switching channels. "*Svirepyy* Leader, this is *Burlivyy* Leader. Commence Operation Kutuzov. Repeating, commence Operation Kutuzov."

Margelov smiled grimly. It was time the complacent

American attitude with regard to their naval air superiority was shattered once and for all. And Operation Kutuzov was designed to do exactly that.

They would soon be entirely too busy to interfere with the bombers.

0931 hours Zulu (0931 hours Zone)
Fulcrum Lead, Escort Mission *Svirepyy*
Northwest of the Faeroe Islands

"*Burlivyy* Leader, *Svirepyy* Leader," Captain Second Rank Sergei Sergeivich Terekhov responded to the call from the Backfire flight. "Orders acknowledged. Commencing breakaway maneuver . . . now!"

He banked sharply to the left to get the MiG-29D clear of the bombers and turned toward the oncoming American interceptors. Thirteen other MiGs and eight Su-27D fighters followed the plane in a tight formation, skimming less than two hundred meters above the wave tops.

Escort Mission *Svirepyy*—Ferocious—consisted of attack aircraft from the carrier *Soyuz*. They had shadowed the bombers for nearly an hour now, flying right down on the deck. The mission planners believed that they might escape detection by the Americans, who would naturally tend to focus on the bombers. If so, the MiG-29s and Su-27s might just take the enemy by surprise.

He hoped so. The plan he had submitted for North Star had involved a considerable risk in this mission, dispatching three of the four available fighter squadrons to escort the Backfires and, with luck, to ambush the Americans. That left only one squadron of Su-27s to provide CAP over *Soyuz*. With both Royal Norwegian Air Force fighters and planes from the American carrier battle group in range of *Soyuz*, it must have taken iron nerves for Admiral Khenkin to order the air wing to leave his flagship exposed.

But of course the Norwegians were having enough trouble contesting air superiority against land-based Soviet fighters, and as for the Americans . . . well, if everything had gone according to plan the Americans would only now be realizing that there were Soviet fighters over the Norwegian Sea. By the time they could hope to organize a strike mission the opportunity would be gone. That had been his reasoning in writing up the operation, but he had never expected Khenkin or Glushko to go along with it.

"Cossack, Cossack, this is *Svirepyy* Leader," Terekhov said, switching to the carrier control frequency. "Beginning Operation Kutuzov. Request situation update and instructions."

"*Svirepyy* Leader, wait one," came the reply. The voice belonged to Captain First Rank Glushko. If anything pointed up the critical nature of this operation, it was the air wing commander's close personal supervision. Normally Glushko didn't dirty his hands with ordinary day-to-day operations. Terekhov remembered the angry words he had heard in Glushko's office before the mission briefing. The air wing commander had a lot riding on today's operation.

"*Svirepyy* Leader, Cossack," Glushko's voice said at last. "Reports from the An-74 indicate additional launches under way from American aircraft carrier. Intentions not yet clear. Be prepared to withdraw on my orders if the enemy is launching a strike on *Soyuz*. Otherwise proceed with attack as planned."

"Message understood, Cossack," Terekhov replied, trying not to betray the uncertainties Glushko's message had unleashed. If Glushko really was looking for a scapegoat of his own . . . "Proceeding with attack according to mission profile."

The possibility of a threat to the carrier could ruin the entire plan. If Terekhov was too deeply involved in the air battle he might not disengage in time to support *Soyuz*. But if he held back from the fighting here he could be accused of disobedience or even cowardice. It was the kind of dilemma that had scuttled any number of careers before his.

But he couldn't let doubts about the future keep him from doing his duty now. He pulled back on his stick as he rammed the throttles forward. The MiG-29D streaked skyward, the G-force slamming Terekhov back into his seat. The need for secrecy was past. It was time to let the Americans see what they were up against.

All he could do now was hit hard and hope for the best. The Soviets would have the advantage of striking from ambush and, at least for the moment, superior numbers. He could imagine the surprise the Americans would feel as the sleek fighters appeared on their radar.

That would have to be enough.

0932 hours Zulu (0932 hours Zone)
Tomcat 200
Northwest of the Faeroe Islands

"Lancelot, Lancelot, this is Tango Two-five. Tracking additional targets. New aircraft on same bearing as Red Raid One, range from your position four-zero November Mikes, angels one point five and climbing. Course is one-five-zero degrees. Designating new targets as Red Raid Two."

"Shit!" Stramaglia cursed. "You see anything, Paddles?"

The RIO was slow replying. "I don't . . . Good God! There they are! They just popped onto my screen!"

"That's a hell of a reception committee," Batman Wayne commented on the radio. "They must've been down on the deck to stay off our radars. Hiding in close to the bombers too."

"I make it twenty . . . no, twenty-two aircraft, sir," Russell reported from the backseat position. "They're going supersonic."

"Too small to be more bombers," another voice chimed in. Stramaglia thought it was Wayne's RIO, Lieutenant Commander Blake. "Looks like we got us one awesome batch of fighters to play with, compadres."

"Cut the chatter," Stramaglia snapped. He was having trouble concentrating with all the talk. "Paddles, what's the status on the Phoenixes?"

"Still on target, CAG," Russell answered. "First wave is twenty-five miles from Red Raid One."

Frowning, Stramaglia knew a moment's indecision, something he'd never felt in years of Top Gun dogfights. With all of the squadron's Phoenixes already expended on the Backfires, the American planes would be short of ammunition to meet the new threat. Eight planes with two Sidewinders apiece couldn't take out all the enemy aircraft, even assuming every missile found its intended target. And dueling with guns, up close and personal, was always chancy . . . especially against an enemy with plenty of missiles to throw away.

The prudent course would be to call off the pursuit of the Backfires and retire to the vicinity of the battle group, where they could link up with the Hornet squadrons and *Jefferson*'s Combat Air Patrol planes before risking an engagement.

But there was still a chance those Backfires could turn back and strike the carrier with the missiles they hadn't fired already. And Soviet Fulcrums, like the American F/A-18 Hornets, were designed as dual-role fighter/attack planes. They couldn't mount any of the larger Soviet antiship missiles, but they could carry bombs and rockets. Letting them get in close to the battle group was an open invitation to disaster.

Which should he choose? Stramaglia closed his eyes, trying to focus, trying to decide. He had never realized before now just how different life on the front lines was from the simulations at Top Gun. Technically, the experience a pilot racked up at Miramar was superb, and the aviators who came out of the course, the best of the best, really were equipped to squeeze every last ounce of performance out of their machines. But all the technical skill in the world couldn't prepare a man to make decisions like the one that faced Stramaglia now.

0933 hours Zulu (0933 hours Zone)
Tomcat 201
Northwest of the Faeroe Islands

''CAG? CAG, do you copy?'' Coyote fought down a queasy feeling in his stomach when Stramaglia didn't respond to the radio call. ''Stinger, this is Coyote. How do you want to take these little red buggers?''

There was a long pause before Stramaglia replied. ''Two-oh-one . . . engage. Engage at will. Hold 'em 'til the Hornets get here.'' CAG's voice sounded ragged, like he was nervous . . . or confused.

Coyote bit his lip. He had been afraid CAG might not be up to this. Now it looked as if his fears had been well-grounded. There was no room for indecision in the fast-paced action of air-to-air combat.

''Roger that, Stinger,'' he responded, trying to maintain an outward air of calm. ''All right, Vipers, time to earn our pay. Batman, Trapper, you guys go left. Big D, Loon, go right. Tyrone, you stick with me. We'll go in right up the middle.'' He hesitated. ''CAG, may I suggest you back us up here . . . unless you have another idea?''

''No . . . I'm with you and Tyrone.'' Stramaglia's

voice sounded a little stronger, a little surer. Maybe he was snapping out of it.

Coyote knew the odds were against them . . . but he'd seen Viper Squadron tackle tough odds before and come out on top. With a little bit of luck they could dish out more punishment than the Soviets were willing to take.

"All right, John-boy, give me the straight dope," he said over the ICS. "What've you got?"

As the RIO started to talk, Coyote thumbed his selector switch to ready a Sidewinder.

The outnumbered American fighters streaked toward the Soviets, ready for battle.

0932 hours Zulu (0932 hours Zone)
Soviet Attack Submarine *Komsomolets Tbilsiskiy*
Northeast of the Faeroe Islands

"Damage control!" Emelyanov gripped the intercom mike like a lifeline. Around him the bridge crew was slowly stirring again. The lights flickered a few times before the backup generators came on line. "Report!"

"He is damaged in the engine room. Stern compartments flooded." The damage-control officer was shouting the report over a confused hubbub of background noise. "We have lost the screw and the towed array. Flooding is contained, but we must get him to the surface."

The torpedo must have hit just as the sub began to turn away, Emelyanov thought. Had it hit forward, it might have taken the torpedo room. The secondary explosions would probably have finished the sub then and there.

Not that they were in much better shape this way. Staying submerged was a certain death sentence . . . but surfacing now, with an American sub hunter still in the area, was just as bad.

But if even a few of the men would get off before the Americans destroyed the boat, it would be worth it. Perhaps they would even accept a surrender. In any event Emelyanov was not going to throw lives away in a useless gesture of defiance when there was a chance some of the hands might survive.

"Emergency surface," he said harshly.

"Surface! Surface!" Captain-Lieutenant Shvachko repeated slowly. The *starpom* looked dazed but otherwise unhurt. His beefy hand gripped a steel support that had come loose from the chart table, and he was looking at it with a startled expression, as if he didn't recognize what it was. But his experience and professionalism were still unshaken despite his obvious confusion. "Blow all tanks! Surface!"

"You don't mean to surrender, Captain?" Dobrotin broke in, sounding groggy. He had hit his head on the chart table in the instant of the torpedo's impact, and there was a smear of blood on his forehead. The blow hadn't dimmed the fanatic light in his eyes. "We must fight!"

Emelyanov shrugged. "I invite your suggestions, Comrade *Zampolit*," he said reasonably. "Our opponent is an American aircraft, and we cannot reach him. Our propeller is ruined. We cannot escape. And remaining submerged will put an unbearable strain on the hull, which is already weakened. How do you propose that we fight? With Marxist rhetoric perhaps?"

"We are officers of the Red Banner Fleet. Surrender is a betrayal of the *Rodina*!" Dobrotin took an unsteady step toward him. "You are relieved, Captain."

"Perhaps the blow to your head has hurt you more than we first thought," Emelyanov said in the same reasonable tones. He gave a single sharp nod.

Shvachko took a step forward, raising the hand that still gripped the metal support. It slammed down across the back of the *zampolit*'s head. Dobrotin sagged to the deck. Unconscious or dead, it didn't really matter. At least he was silent now.

"Idiot," Emelyanov said. He spat. "Come on, you landsmen, look alive! Surface!" He looked toward the communications shack. "Can you broadcast a surrender, *starshina*?"

The radioman was the one who had been on duty when the orders came in. Emelyanov remembered his excitement. He shoved the thought from his mind and concentrated on the man's reply. "Radio is out, Comrade Captain! I cannot trace the fault!"

That meant they would not be able to call off the Americans if they were waiting for the attack boat to surface. The Soviets would have to abandon ship and hope the enemy didn't attack until the life rafts were clear.

Emelyanov looked across at Shvachko. "Make preparations to abandon ship, Comrade *Starpom*." They were the most difficult words he had ever spoken.

The stricken submarine rose through the dark waters slowly, awkwardly. Now he had two enemies to fear . . . the unseen Americans, and time.

0934 hours Zulu (0934 hours Zone)
Viking 704
Northeast of the Faeroe Islands

"There she is!" It was the pilot who was pointing this time, and Magruder squinted into the morning sunlight. The submarine broke the surface slowly. Even Tombstone's untrained eye could pick out the clues to her state—the decks almost awash, the stern lower in the water than the bow, the plume of smoke that poured from a hatch aft of the low, narrow conning tower as someone threw it open and staggered out on the exposed hull. The twisted remnants of a pod mounted on top of the sub's tail were all that showed of the sub's stern.

More figures emerged, some carrying bundles. In a matter of seconds the first life rafts were inflating on the deck.

"They're abandoning!" Magruder said.

"Yeah." Harrison looked grim. "But we still have to finish the bastard off. No way to tell how bad the damage is . . ."

"And we can't afford to leave a Victor III in any state to come after the battle group," Meade added. "I concur, Skipper."

The pilot glanced across at Magruder. "You're the head honcho, Commander."

Magruder nodded reluctantly. "Do it," he said. It was hard to give the order. The sub was helpless out there . . .

But this was war.

"Do it," he repeated. "Take her out."

"Torps?" Meade asked.

"Negative," Harrison told him. "Save 'em for the ones we can't get at. Let's make it a Harpoon this time."

Though designed primarily for ASW work, the S-3B also mounted Harpoon antiship missiles on pylons below each wing. The AGM-84A antiship missile had proved its mettle in combat from the waters of the Libyan coast to the narrow confines of the Persian Gulf and beyond. Though it was now considered one of America's most versatile weapons systems, Magruder had only recently learned from his fellow sub-hunters that the Harpoon had originally been conceived as a means of knocking out Soviet Echo-class cruise-missile submarines on the surface. It was ironic that the Harpoon was reverting to that old role again today, though the target was an attack sub this time.

The pilot banked left and began to climb away from the surfaced submarine. Magruder watched the ocean surface recede below them, and thought again of the Russians who would lose their lives. In an air-to-air duel it was a test of skill, courage, and training. Each pilot had a chance to win the victory. This was more like shooting fish in a barrel . . . the Soviets couldn't even shoot back.

Next to him Harrison pulled up the cover that shielded the missile firing button. "Harpoon ready," he said quietly, his voice almost drowned out by the sound of the Viking's engine. The pilot started another turn, and in seconds the wallowing submarine was visible ahead once more, surrounded by the tiny dots of life rafts attempting to get clear of the vessel.

"Firing!" Harrison said. "Missile away!"

The Harpoon dropped from the right wing pylon, flames kindling from the missile's tail. It streaked toward the target.

As if in slow motion Magruder saw the missile strike just below the low hump of the conning tower, tearing into the hull with a gout of fire, smoke, and debris. The whole submarine shuddered at the impact. It began to settle into the water.

The Viking skimmed low over the stricken hulk as Meade, Curtis, and Harrison let out whoops of triumph. "One for the King Fishers!" Harrison said with a grin.

"Good shooting, Commander," Magruder told him. "A nice morning's hunting!"

Harrison laughed. "The hunt's only starting, Commander. We've got a patrol to finish."

Over the ICS Meade added, "I'm still not happy about those signals we got at the beginning. The Russkies like to send their attack subs out in teams, Mr. Magruder, and I'm afraid there might be more lurking out here somewhere."

Tombstone shrugged. "Well, back to the old grind then, I guess," he said. "I hope the next one's that easy."

"That was beginner's luck, Commander," Harrison said with a wry smile. "You still haven't seen a *real* sub hunt."

With a sigh, Magruder looked down at his instruments.

"What do you want me to do?" he said resignedly. The momentary thrill of the hunt had faded.

He wished, just for a moment, that he could be flying with a Tomcat strapped on and a hot dogfight around him.

0935 hours Zulu (0935 hours Zone)
Tomcat 201
Northwest of the Faeroe Islands

"Tyrone, you take the eyeball," Coyote ordered.

"Two-one-one, eyeball. Roger." Powers sounded tense as he acknowledged the command, but his Tomcat accelerated smoothly as he maneuvered to take up his assigned position. The "loose deuce" formation preferred by American aviators deployed each pair of F-14s into an "eyeball" and a "shooter." Powers would move a mile above and a mile and a half ahead of Coyote's Tomcat, where he would act as a spotter during the critical opening moments of the engagement.

He hoped the kid was up to it. If Powers made another mistake like the one in the Bear encounter, he could land his wingman in serious trouble. And Grant still wasn't sure if Stramaglia, whose Tomcat was now falling behind 201, could be relied on. CAG's sluggish reactions were worrying him.

"Two-eight miles to the closest bogie," John-Boy reported. "They're still maintaining course and speed. Angels eight now."

"Launch! Launch! Two-one-one has visual on Flanker launch!" Powers was shouting. He sounded on the ragged edge of panic.

"Confirmed! Confirm two missiles launched!" Cavanaugh, his RIO, was calmer. "Two-one-one, two-five miles."

"Let's get in there and mix it up, Vipers!" Coyote said. He pushed the throttles up to Zone-Five afterburner and felt the G-forces pressing him back into his seat.

The American planes had been loaded out for long-range interception, with four Phoenix and two Sidewinder missiles apiece. Now that the Phoenixes were gone, they no longer had a long-range attack option to match the Soviet AA-10 Alamo, a radar-guided missile similar in performance to the U.S. Sparrow. That meant that the Americans would have to press to close range if they were to put up any kind of fight at all.

Meanwhile they'd be running the gauntlet. . . .

0936 hours Zulu (0936 hours Zone)
Fulcrum Lead, Escort Mission *Svirepyy*
Northwest of the Faeroe Islands

"Hold launches! Hold launches!" Terekhov shouted into the radio. "Make your missiles count, you stupid peasant!"

He hadn't realized how much on edge he was until the words were out. The pilot of the lead Su-27 had let loose two long-range radar-guided missiles, probably without even attempting to get a lock on any of the Americans. Even among the carrier-based elite of Soviet Naval Aviation there was a tendency to let sheer volume of fire replace accuracy.

Terekhov wasn't going to tolerate that today. They would make every shot count. . . .

"*Svirepyy* aircraft, spread out and prepare to engage," he ordered, keeping tighter control over his voice this time. "Pick your targets and *bring them down*! For the *Rodina*!"

He was gratified to hear the answering calls of "The *Rodina*!" from the rest of his command. With this force, he would sweep the skies clear of the American flyers.

0937 hours Zulu (0937 hours Zone)
Tomcat 211
Northwest of the Faeroe Islands

The threat light on his instrument panel blazed, and Powers felt his blood run cold. ''They got lock on me!'' he shouted. ''Coyote! They're locking on!''

It was as if all his training and practice counted for nothing. All he could do was stare at the threat indicator. He was going to die.

''Missile launch! Missile launch!'' Cavanaugh reported from the backseat. ''Multiple launches. Looks like there's one . . . two . . . no, four headed our way. Better run for it, kid.''

He heard the words, but they didn't mean anything. Powers tried to focus on the voice, tried to figure out what the RIO was trying to tell him.

''Come on, kid!'' he heard Cavanaugh's voice, loud and angry, over the ICS, but it sounded distant, remote. ''Damn it, Tyrone, do something! Do something!''

Powers shook his head, trying to get a grip on himself. All at once he was able to react again. He pulled back on the stick and rammed the throttles forward. The sudden acceleration was like a giant fist against his chest. ''Hit the chaff, Ears,'' he gasped, but Cavanaugh was silent now. The RIO had passed out from the G-force.

One sluggish hand groped for the chaff-dispenser switch, found it. The launcher rattled once, twice as the Tomcat continued its high-speed climb. Blood pounded in his ears, and a red haze obscured his vision.

0938 hours Zulu (0938 hours Zone)
Tomcat 201
Northwest of the Faeroe Islands

"Hold on, kid," Coyote grated. "Hold on . . ."

The panicky voice of the young Tomcat pilot seemed to echo in his ears, but there wasn't much he could do to help Powers yet. The nearest Russians were still almost twenty miles away, beyond the range of Coyote's two AIM-9M Sidewinders. His fighter was already pushing the edge of the performance envelope. No amount of prayer, cursing, or wishful thinking would close the range any faster.

"Tyrone's climbing," John-Boy reported. "He's got two missiles on his tail. Whoa! One's gone! Still got one on his tail . . . climbing . . . climbing . . . Second one just went off! The kid's clear!"

"Good dodging, Tyrone!" Coyote called on the radio. "Good dodge! Now get the hell out of there!"

There was no answer for several long seconds, then only a dull "Aye, aye" from Powers. Grant bit his lip. The kid was finding out that a real air battle was a lot different from shooting down a helpless Bear.

The question now was whether the strain of learning that lesson would be too much for him.

"Fifteen miles to nearest bogie," Nichols reported from the backseat. "Still closing."

"Target! Target!" That sounded like Batman, flying eyeball on the left side. "Where's the damned tone?" There was a pause. "Tone! I've go tone! I'm taking the shot! Fox two! Fox two!"

"Look out, Batman!" Trapper Martin shouted. "You've got a bunch of shit coming your way!"

"Got one!" Batman called, ignoring Martin's warning.

Excited, eager, he sounded ready to take on all of Soviet Naval Aviation by himself. "That's another kill for the Batman!"

Coyote's HUD display came alive with targeting symbols "Two-oh-one, in range," he said. He banked sharply to the left, trying to line up a shot, but with the two forces closing so fast it was hard to get a target lock.

"Two coming at us," John-Boy warned.

Coyote nodded. Two planes, no more than dots in the distance, were streaking toward the Tomcat, weaving from side to side, too slippery to nail down. "I'm going to take them down the right side," he said. "CAG, you copy?"

"Copy," Stramaglia's voice answered.

The tiny dots swelled suddenly and flashed past the right side of the fighter. In the instant he could see them clearly he identified them as Su-27 Flankers, long, lean birds with a characteristic goose-necked fuselage that made them look like birds of prey stooping in on their victims. Then they were gone.

Coyote heeled the Tomcat over in a tight righthand turn that stood the fighter on its wing. In seconds he had settled in behind the second Flanker. The Russian bucked and jinked, but Grant clung to him doggedly. "Come on, you bastard, hold still," he grated. "Come on . . ."

The lock-on tone sounded loud in his ear and Coyote's finger tightened on the firing stud almost instinctively. "Fox two!" he shouted. "Fox two!"

The Sidewinder streaked from its launch rail, trailing fire and smoke. Moments later it found its target, slamming into the Su-27's port engine. Flame engulfed the Flanker.

"Two-oh-one, splash one!" Coyote called.

"Just one?" Batman asked. "Hell, boy, I just got my second. Going to guns now! This might be my chance to finally even up with old Tombstone!"

"Keep on 'em, Batman," Coyote said, searching for the

second Flanker. He was glad to hear that Wayne was still in the fight, still sounding the same. Batman was older and wiser than he'd been back in the Indian Ocean, but down deep he hadn't changed that much. Dogfighting was like a game to him, a game he played very, very well.

"Two o'clock, Coyote! Look to your two!" Nichols shouted.

That was the second Sukhoi, climbing fast and trying a tight turn to get behind the Tomcat. Coyote answered with the high yo-yo, matching the Flanker's turn and pulling back sharply on his stick to lose airspeed and keep from overshooting. An instant later the targeting tone sounded again and he fired his second Sidewinder. The missile struck the Soviet plane's left wing, sending the Flanker spinning out of control. Coyote caught a glimpse of a blossoming parachute. "Splash two," he announced. "Two-oh-one, splash two. Come on, John-Boy, find me somebody else to play with!"

0940 hours Zulu (0940 hours Zone)
Fulcrum Leader
Northwest of the Faeroe Islands

"Break left! Break left!" Terekhov screamed the order into the radio. Captain Second Rank Stralbo, commander of the second MiG squadron, had been dodging a team of aggressive American fighters, but somehow one of them had still wound up on Stralbo's tail. Luckily the American cowboy had already used up his infrared homing missiles. Two long bursts of gunfire hadn't scored any hits on Stralbo's MiG as yet, but it was only a matter of time. It was clear that Stralbo was completely outclassed.

Terekhov rolled his plane into position above and behind the American, still shouting for Stralbo to break to the left so he could line up his shot. The targeting diamond centered on the F-14 and turned red, the locking tone sounded in his ear, but Terekhov held his fire. "Roll left, Stralbo!" he bellowed again.

It was as if the American pilot had a charmed life. Just as Stralbo started his turn the Tomcat banked in the opposite direction, as if suddenly aware of the threat. Terekhov stabbed at the firing stud, but too late. He had lost the target, and the missile streaked off into the distance, harmless.

Then his threat indicator lit up.

Turning his head back and forth, he spotted the second F-16 angling in from his aft port quarter. He had forgotten the American fighting style, the "loose deuce" that allowed wingmen to cover each other flexibly. Soviet fliers rarely used anything but a tight "welded wing" formation, and it was easy to forget that not all adversaries followed the tactics he had become used to in half a lifetime in the cockpit.

He caught sight of a plume of flame below the Tomcat's wing. This one still had missiles.

Terekhov wrenched his stick back and shoved his throttles full forward. Acceleration pressed him into his seat as he climbed. Fighting to retain consciousness, he watched his radar through a red haze, saw the blip that was the heat-seeker closing . . . closing . . .

In a smooth motion he cut his power with a swift jerk of the throttles and triggered a pair of flares. It was a risky move that could lead to a flameout or an uncontrolled spin, but by suddenly killing his hot afterburners and throwing out the flares he stood a good chance of defeating the American A-9M.

The missile went off a good hundred meters behind and below him, and he instantly shoved the throttles into the highest afterburner zone and turned sharply toward the American plane.

0942 hours Zulu (0942 hours Zone)
Tomcat 204
Northwest of the Faeroe Islands

"It's getting too damned thick here, Mal," Batman said. "There's too many of the bastards!"

The RIO's reply was all business. "That MiG's coming down on Trapper! Three o'clock!"

Batman cursed and accelerated into a turn. "This guy's starting to piss me off," he commented. The same MiG had spoiled his chances of taking out another Russian a few moments before. The Russkie was good, that much was certain. The guy had dodged Martin's Sidewinder and then turned to carry the attack back to the Americans.

"Watch him, Trap!" he warned. "I'm on the way!"

"He's all over me!" the lieutenant responded, sounding worried. "Hurry up, Batman! Hurry up!"

He spotted the two planes, Martin climbing sharply, the Russian matching him move for move. "Lead him this way! Come left! Left!"

Then a missile leapt from the MiG's wing. Martin's Tomcat was turning, climbing . . .

And then there was nothing left but a fireball.

CHAPTER 17
Thursday, 12 June 1997

0942 hours Zulu (0942 hours Zone)
Tomcat 201
Northwest of the Faeroe Islands

"They got Trapper! Trapper's hit!"

Coyote heard the edge in Batman's voice. Wayne had already fired both Sidewinders, so he was down to nothing but guns . . . and now his wingman had been hit. "Get the hell out of there, Batman!" he called. "Disengage! Disengage!"

"No can do, man," Batman replied, sounding calmer now, grim and determined. "They'd be all over me if I tried."

"We'll get you some support." Grant cursed under his breath. Powers was still clear of the fighting after his first brush with Russian missiles, but he hadn't made much of an effort to get back into the game, and Coyote wasn't about to depend on him for anything. That left it to Grant . . . or to Stramaglia. "CAG . . . can you give Batman some backup?"

There was a moment's pause. "On my way," Stramaglia said at last, sounding more animated than before. On the radar monitor the blip that represented the double-nuts bird was already angling to the left.

Coyote let out a sigh and hoped he'd done the right thing. But he couldn't waste time on the might-have-beens. For good or ill the choice was made, and he had a battle to fight.

0943 hours Zulu (0943 hours Zone)
Fulcrum Leader
Northwest of the Faeroe Islands

Terekhov heard exultant shouts over his radio and smiled. It was strictly against regulations for pilots to clutter up the communications channels with useless noise, but he wasn't about to reprimand anyone. The sight of the American fighter engulfed by his missile's fireball had given him the same feeling of elation. The plan was working. The Americans had fallen into the trap and this time they would be defeated.

"*Svirepyy* Leader, this is Cossack," Captain First Rank Glushko's voice grated over the radio. "The An-74 now reports ten more American planes in the air. We cannot afford to continue to leave *Soyuz* uncovered. Cancel Operation Kutuzov and return to base. Repeat, return to base!"

"*Nyet!*" Terekhov muttered under his breath. They were so close to making this work. One enemy plane destroyed . . . six to go. And not all of them were flying aggressively enough to press in close and use the short-range firepower that was all any of them had left. To turn back now when they had the opportunity to defeat these Americans in detail was worse than foolish. It was suicide. The best way to guarantee that the Americans would keep their distance from the fighting in Norway was to cripple their combat power here and now. With the bombers taking out Keflavik and a large chunk of their carrier air wing crippled, they would be stymied for the critical weeks it would take to finish off the Norwegian resistance. Then the

Rodina could consolidate her gains with little hope of a Western counterattack.

Didn't Glushko realize that the Americans couldn't possibly be planning an attack on the carrier? It took time to plan a strike mission, arm attack aircraft, brief pilots . . . such an effort couldn't be mounted in the short time since the first strike on Keflavik. Even if the Americans had been foolish enough to keep fully armed strike aircraft ready on the flight line just in case they might be needed—and there was no way anyone would do something that dangerous except in the direst emergency—the reaction time was just too short. These were fighters, kept on a high state of alert, being dispatched to shore up the weak squadron facing Terekhov now. That was the only possible explanation.

He reached for the radio mike. "Cossack, Cossack, this is *Svirepyy* Leader. We cannot break off now! The enemy is running low on ammunition. We can sweep the sky if you just give us a few more minutes!"

There was a long pause on the other end. Terekhov could imagine Glushko's dilemma. It was easy enough to say that those couldn't be attack planes on their way to hit *Soyuz* . . . but suppose they were? If Glushko abandoned the operation entirely he would be throwing away the best hope of victory. But if he gambled with the survival of the carrier and lost it would be a disaster. Would the air wing's commander pass the decision to higher authority, or would he make the choice himself in hopes of restoring his sagging credit with the admiral?

At last Glushko replied. "Detach the Sukhoi squadron," he ordered. "They will return to cover the carrier. Your MiGs may remain and do what further damage you can."

It was a compromise . . . and like most compromises it was a poor one. Even without the Sukhois Terekhov could probably defeat these Americans easily enough, but if those planes really were reinforcements they would catch his squadron in the same relative state as he had caught the Tomcats—low on ammo, perhaps on fuel, and unable to risk a prolonged engagement.

But he knew it was the best Glushko was likely to offer. Best to continue the fight with whatever the air wing commander would leave him rather than risk an unequivocal recall order. "Acknowledged, Cossack," he said. As he switched frequencies he allowed himself a grim smile. His own enthusiasm for continuing the battle would fit in nicely with Glushko's private agenda. Leaving Terekhov with reduced numbers to finish the dogfight was the best way to get rid of a troublesome subordinate.

He switched frequencies and passed the word to the other planes, encouraging his MiG pilots to redouble their attack and cover the withdrawal. Then Terekhov checked his instruments and scanned the horizon, seeking out a foe of his own.

The American pilot with the charmed life was making an impossibly tight turn off to the left, trying to launch another attack on Terekhov. That one, at least, wasn't shy about joining battle, even though he had no missiles showing below his wings and must be running low on cannon rounds by now. It was almost a shame to think of shooting the man down. He was a warrior, a modern knight, like one of the Order of the Round Table that had followed King Vladimir.

Terekhov pushed the thought from his mind. There was no room for mercy today.

In a sudden decision Terekhov jerked his stick hard over and swung the MiG around in pursuit of the American. His enemy weaved from side to side, like a fish on the hook, but Terekhov clung to his prey with grim determination.

Then the reticule centered on the Tomcat and flashed red. The tone sounded in his ear as the heat-seeker locked on.

"Now I have you," Terekhov said aloud, finger tightening on the trigger. This time his prey would not escape him.

0944 hours Zulu (0944 hours Zone)
Tomcat 204
Northwest of the Faeroe Islands

Batman knew something was wrong even before Malibu's shout came over the ICS. "Incoming! One missile . . . two! They're coming right up the tail pipe!"

"Hold tight, buddy!" Batman shouted, ramming the throttles forward and pulling back on his stick. "Nap time!"

Acceleration pressed against his chest, and a red haze obscured the HUD in front of him. Batman could hardly move against the powerful G-force, but somehow his hand groped its way to the flare-dispenser panel.

With a grunt, he cut the throttles back and released three flares in quick succession, rolling left at the same time. For an instant the Tomcat hung inverted at the top of its climb, with the cold gray waters of the Atlantic spread out far below.

The two missiles went off in rapid succession behind and below the F-14, decoyed by the hot-burning flares. "Not this time, you bastard," Batman said, letting gravity help the fighter complete its loop and advancing the throttles back to the zone-five afterburner setting. The Tomcat's engines growled at the punishment, but responded.

"Ho, Malibu," he said, still gasping from the effects of the hard climb. "Let's go, man! Reveille! The taxpayers ain't paying for you to sleep through the battle!"

Even though they were outnumbered, the Americans had to keep the initiative, and that meant attacking whenever they could. That would break the rhythm of the battle, throw the Russians off their stride. Once they could control the tempo of the fighting, the battle would be over.

Wayne's Tomcat stooped down into the aerial battlefield once more, seeking out a new victim.

0944 hours Zulu (0944 hours Zone)
Tomcat 211
Northwest of the Faeroe Islands

"Some of the Russkies are breaking off! Some of them are *running,* fer Chrissakes!"

Terry Powers didn't know who had called out the news, but he could see the Russian planes breaking away on his radar screen. The sight of those blips turning away helped steady his shattered nerves, and he slowly became aware of Cavanaugh's voice raging at him over the ICS. His hand was locked in a painfully tight grip around the joystick, but as he forced himself to relax it started to shake uncontrollably.

"Come on, you bastard! Get in the game! What the hell do you think you're doing? Snap out of it, kid, and get in there before any more of my buddies buy it!"

In his daze he had been flying blind, running without even realizing it, and the Tomcat had left the fight a long way behind. Shaking his head from side to side to try to clear it, Powers gritted his teeth and banked left.

He had allowed himself to give in to panic, and that was something he could never atone for. But Cavanaugh was right. They had to get back into the battle. Even if he had to die today, Powers would die fighting. The alternative— living with the knowledge of having turned his back on the others when they needed him—was unthinkable.

"All right, all right, Ears," he said, his voice quavering. "I'm taking us back in! Now shut up and find us a target!"

He pushed the throttle all the way forward, and his hand only shook a little bit.

0945 hours Zulu (0945 hours Zone)
Tomcat 201
Northwest of the Faeroe Islands

"Two bogies, three o'clock! Watch 'em, Coyote, they're closing fast."

Grant glanced to the right at John-Boy's warning and saw the two MiGs streaking toward them, flying wing-to-wing. He stiffened as the threat receiver shrilled a warning.

"They're locking on!" John-Boy called unnecessarily.

"Tell me something I don't know!" Coyote shot back, jerking the stick hard to the right to turn into the two attackers.

The enemy planes crossed behind the Tomcat at a sharp angle, the radar lock momentarily broken. Coyote looked back again over his left shoulder in time to see the lead MiG starting to match his right bank. The second Russian aircraft was slipping to the outside of the turn, reacting slowly to the change or more concerned with guarding his wingman's tail than he was with maintaining the tight formation.

The tone sounded a second time as the lead MiG lined up again, and this time Coyote swung sharply back to the left. His finger tightened on the trigger on his joystick as the Tomcat's nose swept past the trailing MiG, but there was no apparent effect. Guns were chancy at best except at very close range, despite their popularity with Hollywood film-makers. But with both his Sidewinders expended the M61A1 20-mm cannon was the only firepower he had to work with.

"Goddamn!" Lieutenant Commander Sheridan swore. "They got Loon and the Saint! No chutes . . . I don't see any chutes . . ."

Another Tomcat gone. Lieutenant Adam Baird, "Loon,"

had been planning to marry his girl after this cruise was
over. Now he never would. Coyote hadn't seen much of
Whitman, who'd only come aboard with Magruder's flight.
Was it only three days ago? It seemed like an eternity.

He couldn't let himself think about it. Instead he cut back
across the two MiGs again in another right-hand turn. The
trailing plane was trying to cut back toward him now, its
role reversed by the new situation. Coyote squeezed the
trigger again in a series of short, fast bursts as he lined up.
In a defensive situation like this there wasn't time to wait
for a sure target. All a flyer could do was take his best shot
and trust to luck.

And this time luck was with him. As he flashed past the
MiG Coyote saw the port-side wing coming apart, ripped
loose by his cannon fire. Over his shoulder he saw the
canopy pop and the Russian pilot hurtle clear of the
disintegrating aircraft. His chute opened a moment later.

This far from the Russian fleet, though, there wasn't
much chance the man would live long enough to be picked
up alive.

"Beautiful!" John-Boy exalted from the backseat. Then,
serious again, the RIO went on. "Watch your six, Coyote.
His buddy's coming in mad!"

He glanced at the radar display and cut back on his
throttle just as the threat indicator shrieked its warning once
more. The MiG shot past to the left of the Tomcat, and for
an instant Coyote considered pursuing. But right now he
couldn't afford to keep up this running battle. By his best
count there were still at least ten MiGs in the air, and with
Baird gone and Powers still out of the battle there were only
four American planes still in action. They had to tighten up
and try to support one another if they were going to hold out
long enough for the reinforcing Hornets from the carrier to
join them.

"Two-one-two, this is Leader. Close in around Batman and CAG," he ordered.

"Copy," Dallas Sheridan responded laconically.

He turned away from the MiG and kicked in his afterburners again, trying to put as much distance as possible between his plane and the opposition.

This one didn't press the pursuit . . . but there were plenty of other Russians out there who were still fighting hard. The withdrawal of the Sukhoi squadron had given the Vipers a fighting chance to hold out. But the odds were still against them, and at this point it still looked like the Hornets would come in time to avenge the Tomcats, but too late to rescue them.

0945 hours Zulu (0945 hours Zone)
Tomcat 211
Northwest of the Faeroe Islands

"Break right! Break right!"

Batman responded to the urgency in Malibu's voice and banked to port. Most of the MiGs seemed to be swarming around his plane now, presumably because they'd spotted CAG's bird moving in to support him. As the F-14 turned he spotted a MiG matching his maneuver and cursed. The fight was starting to remind him of a Top Gun exercise where the instructors just kept pressing, never letting up until all the students had been pronounced eliminated.

This time, though, defeat wasn't just a radar lock and a lecture back on the ground. The Russians were pulling out all the stops. It was worse than Korea . . . even worse than the desperate fighting over the Indian Ocean.

"Damn it," he said aloud. "There's just too many of them!"

Stramaglia's gruff voice broke in. "What's the matter,

Wayne? Aren't the bad buys playing fair?" The CAG bird
had appeared as if by magic on Batman's radar display, and
even as he watched he saw a Sidewinder streak toward the
MiG that had been maneuvering after him. "Fox two! Fox
two!" CAG continued smoothly. A moment later the
heat-seeker struck, breaking off the Russian's tail in a
spectacular blast.

"Thanks, CAG," Batman said, letting out a shuddering
breath. He hadn't been counting on Stramaglia. The captain
had seemed so disoriented at the beginning of the fight. But
now CAG was in the battle, and even though his one
remaining Sidewinder wasn't much, it was better than any
of the other Tomcats had.

"Save it," Stramaglia growled. "Now let's get in there
and show these bastards what a Top Gun really is! You take
the lead, and I'll cover your tail . . . compadre."

Behind him, Malibu chuckled, and Batman gave a wolfish grin. "On my way, CAG!"

"Up here it's Stinger. Stop talking and start shooting!"

The two Tomcats streaked toward the nearest MiGs,
carrying the fight to the enemy.

0946 hours Zulu (0946 hours Zone)
Fulcrum Leader
Northwest of the Faeroe Islands

Terekhov saw the newly arrived American hit one of his
MiGs with a heat-seeker and cursed. He'd thought that the
Americans would have fired off all their missiles by this
time, but some of the pilots had held back. Some of his
planes were out of missiles already, even though they'd
started with full loads. If only more of his men would be as
disciplined as the Americans! The *Rodina* would have
nothing to fear if fewer Russian pilots substituted firepower
for tactics.

It was frustrating to watch the battle unfold, to know that the Americans were outflying and outfighting his elite Naval Aviation men at every turn. The kill ratio was running close to four-to-one despite the numerical superiority of the MiGs. Even though the enemy could ill afford any losses, they kept on coming, *attacking* against the odds and somehow, by sheer nerve apparently, getting away with it.

He wished now that he hadn't consented to giving up the Sukhoi squadron to Glushko's overcaution. The object of the ambush was to crush this American force quickly and completely, and those extra aircraft might have allowed him to finish off the enemy with fewer losses to his own planes.

No matter. The Americans were still outnumbered and would soon be eliminated, even if it did cost more MiGs to destroy them.

He spotted the two Americans driving toward Lieutenant Oganov, who had impressed Terekhov as one of the finest pilots in his squadron. Oganov's wingman had been shot down in the first exchange with the talented American who kept cheating Terekhov. He was just the man to call on now, cool and cautious, the kind of aviator who could time a maneuver right down to the second.

"Oganov," he called. "Draw out the Americans. Let them think they have you. I will support you."

He increased his speed and double-checked his missile load. He only had two more radar-homers.

That would be enough.

0946 hours Zulu (0946 hours Zone)
Tomcat 204
Northwest of the Faeroe Islands

"He's running! I'm on him!" Batman could feel the adrenaline surging through his veins. Drugs had never tempted him, because no drug could substitute for the thrill of combat. "I'm gonna nail this bastard, Malibu!"

"Watch out for company," the RIO warned. "Stay frosty, man."

Batman grinned under his oxygen mask. Despite the odds he felt like nothing in the skies could beat him today.

The MiG ahead was running flat out, hardly even jinking. It would take time to get close enough to hit him with guns, but as long as he kept this up it would be an easy kill. With Stramaglia back there covering his six, he didn't have anything to worry about now.

"Two-oh-four! Two-oh-four!" It was Stramaglia. His voice was flat, but Batman thought he could detect a note of concern. "Break off your attack, Batman! I've got company back here, and I need some help."

He broke to the left in a tight turn and spotted Stramaglia almost immediately. CAG had understated the situation. A quartet of MiGs were harrying the Tomcat, keeping him on the defensive. Stramaglia dodged and twisted with all the skill of the best of Top Gun, but the MiGs clung to him with bulldog tenacity.

"On my way, Stinger!" he called. He cursed under his breath. One of those Russians would have been a sitting duck for a Sidewinder . . . but Batman didn't have one.

He could only watch and wait, praying he could get in range before it was too late for Stinger Stramaglia.

0947 hours Zulu (0947 hours Zone)
Tomcat 200
Northwest of the Faeroe Islands

Stramaglia turned hard to port and started a dive, fighting his controls and trying to keep track of the MiGs swarming around him. It was a situation he'd never envisioned himself in, a dogfight where he couldn't instantly see the solution to the tactical problem.

"Talk to me, Paddles," he said. "Stay on top of them."

"Four o'clock! Closing in fast! Turn right! Right!" The RIO's voice was on the ragged edge of panic, but somehow that just helped Stramaglia throw off the last of the lassitude that had gripped him before.

When the fight had begun the *reality* of it all had overwhelmed him. Even the toughest situation was easy enough when it was an exercise, but with real lives at stake it had simply been too much. In those critical opening minutes of the battle Grant had stepped in and taken charge, and it gratified Stramaglia to know that the squadron leader had been there. After the Bear incident he'd been worried about how Coyote would handle his next encounter, but it had been Stramaglia himself who couldn't deal with the problem of leading men into battle. The irony would have been funny . . . but no one was laughing.

He'd finally found his combat rhythm again, but even as he struggled to stay a step ahead of his opponents the differences between real life and simulated combat gnawed at him. Instinct and training told him what to do, but there was a part of him, a scared part, that knew all too well the price of a single mistake or miscalculation.

A tone sounded in his headphones as his last Sidewinder locked onto one of the other planes. That would narrow the

odds a little . . . and when Batman joined the game they'd
crack these Russians wide open.

His finger clamped down on the firing stud, and the
Sidewinder *whooshed* from the launching rail. "Fox two!"

0947 hours Zulu (0947 hours Zone)
Fulcrum Leader
Northwest of the Faeroe Islands

Terekhov saw the heat-seeker leap from the Tomcat's wing
and streak toward his wingman's plane. "Right! Break
right!" he shouted, but it was too late. A moment later the
MiG was consumed in flame and thunder.

He tried to match the American's weaving course, but it
wasn't easy. This was one of the best pilots he had ever
encountered. The other Tomcat's pilot had guts combined
with luck, a potent combination, but he couldn't approach
the skill this one showed.

Then the tone of a radar lock sounded in his ear, and
Terekhov fired both his missiles in rapid succession.

0947 hours Zulu (0947 hours Zone)
Tomcat 201
Northwest of the Faeroe Islands

"Cavalry's on the way, Batman," Coyote called. He could
see the desperate fight unfolding on his radar screen, but he
couldn't do much about it yet. But Stramaglia was teaching
the Russians the same tough lesson he'd been teaching to
Top Gun students for years, and if he could just hold on for
a little while longer . . .

A MiG vanished in an expanding fireball, and Coyote
heard Malibu giving a cheer.

"Two-double-oh, splash another one," he said. "Good shot, CAG!"

"It's just like a bicycle, Grant," CAG responded. "You never forget how to do it . . . you just don't want to fall off at Mach two!"

"Missiles! Missiles incoming!" Paddles shouted suddenly. "Two missiles—"

Then another fireball lit the sky.

And the CAG bird was gone, a cloud of debris raining onto the hungry sea below.

CHAPTER 18
Thursday, 12 June 1997

0947 hours Zulu (0947 hours Zone)
Tomcat 204
Northwest of the Faeroe Islands

Batman stared at the shattered Tomcat, breaking apart as it started to spin in toward the ocean, seeing the action as if it were playing in slow motion. It could only have taken a few moments, but it seemed like an eternity.

"Two-one-two, splash a MiG," he heard Dallas Sheridan saying over the radio. For an instant he thought Big D was talking about CAG's plane. Then he realized that Sheridan still hadn't hooked up with the rest of the fast-shrinking command, and must be reporting an engagement of his own.

No one responded, and a long moment later Sheridan went on. "Hey, come on guys, talk to me! What's going on?"

Coyote's voice replied, choking on the words. "CAG's bought it." Then he seemed to gather his wits again. "Batman, form on me. Big D, get your ass back here now! Let's do it!"

"Two-oh-four, roger," Batman responded slowly. He banked left and gained altitude, looking for Coyote.

Behind him, Malibu seemed to share in the shock. Over the ICS his voice was bleak, a far cry from his usual

227

bantering tone. "We're not going to get out of this one, are
we?"

Batman didn't answer.

0948 hours Zulu (0948 hours Zone)
Fulcrum Leader
Northwest of the Faeroe Islands

"Stralbo! Oganov! Form on me!" Terekhov couldn't keep
his voice from betraying his excitement now that total
victory was almost in his grasp. "All planes, press the
attack!"

"Comrade Captain," another pilot broke in. "I have
multiple targets on my radar, closing on us at high speed!"

Terekhov bit back a curse. The American reinforcements!
Why hadn't Glushko or the crew of the An-74 warned him?
Were they still so concerned with organizing the defense of
Soyuz that they were ignoring the possible danger to the
attack squadron?

He had often wondered if the Soviet carriers would be
able to stand up to the tests of combat conditions. For fifty
years the Soviet Union had ignored the whole question of
carrier aviation, and when they'd finally decided to deploy
modern carriers they had been forced to learn the entire
science virtually overnight. Measured against the Americans, who had been developing their carrier doctrine and
technology gradually ever since the great carrier battles of
the Forties, the Russians still looked like amateurs. The fact
that officers like Glushko could hold key commands was
only one of many symptoms of what was wrong with Soviet
carrier aviation.

"Cossack, Cossack, this is *Svirepyy* Leader," he said,
switching to the command frequency. "Respond, please."

"*Svirepyy,* this is Cossack," Glushko replied.

"The second American force is nearly here," Terekhov said slowly, trying to maintain his calm. "Request you send the other squadron back to support us. They outnumber my surviving planes and are fresh."

"Nyet, nyet," Glushko replied harshly. "This is only a feint. They want to draw off our defense so they can strike the carrier. Those planes will not be armed for air-to-air. Break off your current engagement and attack them!"

"That isn't the plan!" he shot back. "We have *these* Americans in our sights!"

"That is a direct order, Captain Terekhov," Glushko told him. "Are you disobeying me?"

"Negative, Cossack," he said hastily. "We will begin a disengagement here and attack the new wave . . . but if they are armed as interceptors we will have to receive support or withdraw. We cannot fight another extended battle without rearming."

"Just *do* it!" Glushko said.

Terekhov swung his MiG back toward the continuing air battle. The three surviving Americans were weaving in and out of a larger mass of seven or eight Russian planes, barely avoiding the overwhelming numbers. If they could finish off these three quickly, Glushko couldn't protest too loudly. Wiping out a full American Tomcat squadron would give Terekhov too much credit for the air wing commander to quibble.

He had one missile left. If the second American wave really was fitted out for a strike mission he could fight them with guns alone . . . and if they weren't, if they were carrying full air-to-air loads, one missile more or less wouldn't make any difference.

Terekhov picked out the lucky Tomcat by the slapdash flying style of its pilot and turned to line up on him. One last attack, and the trap would be complete.

0948 hours Zulu (0948 hours Zone)
Viking 704
Northeast of the Faeroe Islands

"Viking Seven-oh-four, this is Camelot." Magruder recognized the voice—Owens, the junior air wing officer. He sounded worried. "Seven-oh-four, what's your status out there?"

At Harrison's nod Magruder took the radio mike. "Seven-oh-four, still hunting," he said. "We scratched one sub, but we may be on the trail of another one. What can we do for you, Camelot?"

Owens was slow to reply. "Commander, CAG's been hit," he said at last. "Coyote just reported it. No survivors."

"Goddamn . . ." Though he'd been infuriated by Stramaglia's attitude toward him, angry at the restrictions he'd placed on Magruder's employment, Tombstone had admired CAG. He couldn't believe the Old Man had bought it out there.

Then it hit him. With Stramaglia dead, *Jefferson* had a new CAG. Commander Matthew Magruder.

"What's the situation, Camelot?" he asked, forcing aside his emotion and trying to sound brisk and businesslike.

"Not good," Owens responded. "Coyote's flight ran into heavy opposition. Most of the Vipers are gone. The Javelins will be in the thick of it in a couple more minutes, and we're still launching the Fighting Hornets, but it's pretty grim. And all hell's breaking loose in Iceland. Keflavik's been hit pretty hard, and the planes that got off before the base went won't be able to make it to an American base. Iceland's refusing permission to let any of our boys land . . . I guess they're afraid the Russians'll hit civilian fields next."

Magruder didn't like the sound of the younger man's voice. Owens was clearly out of his depth, floundering, and *Jefferson* couldn't afford an indecisive CAG in Air Ops now.

"All right, Camelot, I'm getting the picture. I'll head back ASAP. Meantime tell the Javelins to get into that fight if they have to get out and push . . . and get in touch with those stranded Air Force boys and get an update on their status."

Owens sounded better when he replied. "Aye, aye . . . CAG."

"Seven-oh-four, clear." Magruder replaced the mike and turned to Harrison. "Break off the hunt, Commander, and take us back to the *Jeff*."

Harrison looked unhappy. "But what if this contact's another sub?"

"Look, Commander, we don't even know for sure that it *was* a separate contact. I've got to get back to the carrier and try to salvage something from this mess." His thoughts turned to Batman and Malibu, who might already be dead. And Coyote too, who'd reported CAG's death but could still go down before the Hornet squadron arrived on the scene. Despite their clash, he could feel that same gnawing, gut-wrenching emotion he'd felt the time Coyote and his RIO had been lost off North Korea. "Anyway," he went on, trying to ignore the inner turmoil for a few minutes longer. "Anyway, that helo from *Gridley*'s due to get here in a few more minutes. They'll take up the search."

Harrison still looked doubtful, but at last he nodded. "I guess you're the boss now," he admitted. "Okay, crew, keep your ears open anyway. And if you'd be so kind, *CAG,* I'd appreciate it if you'd update *Gridley* and the ASW boys on the *Jeff*."

The Viking banked to port and picked up speed as Magruder reached for the microphone again. He was happy

to have something to do, something to keep him from
having to spend the whole flight back to the carrier thinking
about his friends.

0949 hours Zulu (0949 hours Zone)
Soviet Guided Missile Submarine *Krasniy Ritsary*
Northeast of the Faeroe Islands

His name meant *Red Knight,* and he was a submarine of the
class Westerners referred to as the ''Oscar.'' Captain First
Rank Georgi Naumkin had commanded him for less than
four months, having been selected for the task by Admiral
Khenkin himself after the submarine's previous captain had
been pronounced too closely connected with republican
elements to be trusted with such an important command.

Up until now the war in Norway hadn't required the use
of a sub like the *Krasniy Ritsary*. He was neither one of the
vital boomers, armed with ballistic missiles, nor one of the
far more glamorous attack subs designed to harass enemy
surface ships and submarines. Against Norway's ships
using him would have been like using a sledgehammer on a
mosquito. But with the Americans coming, *Krasniy Ritsary*
could finally come into his own.

He carried twenty-four conventionally armed antiship
cruise missiles, a formidable armament of high-tech weapons like the ones the Americans had used with such
devastating effect in the Persian Gulf a few years before.
Lurking here, near the edge of the exclusion zone, he was
perfectly placed to strike from the depths at any American
ship that came within range.

Right now the SSGN was drifting just over the rugged sea
floor, waiting. Naumkin wasn't the only man aboard whose
eyes were turned upward. If he had been a religious man, he
would have been uttering a prayer that the Americans would
pass on and overlook the sub.

They had followed the savage battle between the American ASW aircraft and the sub's escort, *Komsomolets Tbilsiskiy*. The passive sonars had tracked the attack sub, and the sounds of torps in the water had been audible right through the hull. Everyone aboard knew that the other boat had been destroyed. There was no mistaking the death throes of a crippled submarine.

Then there had been nothing for a long time, nothing but the occasional bursts of sonar activity from the enemy sonobuoys. Now even those had fallen silent.

"They must have proceeded to a new leg of their search pattern, Comrade Captain," Captain Second Rank Vitaly Maleshenko said quietly. "We are surely safe from detection now."

"That will not last once we launch, Vitaly," Naumkin told the executive officer with a frown. "We must be sure we can break contact and escape. Trading *Krasniy Ritsary* for one shot at the Americans is a useless waste."

"But doing nothing would be an even greater waste," the *zampolit,* a rabbit-faced man named Vorontsov, countered.

"True enough," Naumkin admitted reluctantly. He paused. "Very well. Raise the antenna. We will update our situation report and find ourselves a worthwhile target for our missiles. Vitaly, pass the word to missile control to prepare all missiles for firing."

"Sir!"

He turned away as his crew got to work. The next few minutes could cover them all in glory . . . or leave them as dead as their comrades aboard the stricken attack sub.

0949 hours Zulu (0949 hours Zone)
Tomcat 201
Northwest of the Faeroe Islands

"Hang in there, Batman!" Coyote called. "I'm on him!"

He dropped the F-14 behind a Russian MiG that was trying to keep up with Batman's desperate evasive maneuvers and triggered a short burst of 20-mm cannon fire, but he didn't see any immediate damage from his attack. Still, it was enough to rattle the Soviet flyer, who banked his plane right and down in an effort to turn the tables on Coyote.

Grant turned into the enemy attack and tried his guns again, but though his burst stitched across one wing the Russian dropped out of the line of fire, trailing smoke from the damaged wing but still in action. Coyote cursed.

Then the shriek of a radar warning filled his ears, and he cursed louder as he twisted the plane to the left, trying to break the radar lock.

"It's no good!" the RIO yelled. "He's still got us!"

Pulling back on the joystick, Coyote clawed for altitude.

"Missile launch! Missile launch!" John-Boy reported.

"Chaff!" Coyote ordered, cutting power and rolling sideways into a steep dive now. The chaff dispenser chattered twice as the RIO popped a pair of antiradar decoys.

"Watch your six! Watch your six!" That was Sheridan's voice. "You've got a bandit on your tail, Coyote!"

"Missile's still coming," John-Boy added.

"Chaff again!" Coyote snapped, weaving from side to side.

A moment later the missile exploded behind and below the Tomcat. Coyote fought the controls as the shock wave slammed into the plane, but managed to keep it steady.

Then cannon rounds were slamming into the Tomcat's undercarriage, making the F-14 buck like a wild mustang. He jerked the stick hard over, but the Russian pilot kept with him.

"Batman!" he shouted. "Big D! Somebody give me an assist!" Even as he spoke he knew neither one could get there in time.

But then, incredibly, a Sidewinder smashed into the middle of the MiG, breaking the plane in two. Coyote looked around, trying to find the source of the fire. Had the Hornets made it? Where *were* they?

"Tomcat Two-one-one, reporting for duty!" a young, ragged voice called out. It was Powers, late but finally in the battle.

"All right Tyrone!" Batman said. "A kill for the kid!"

"I've got another one," Powers announced. "Come on . . . come on . . . Tone! I've got tone! I'm taking my shot! Fox two! Fox two!"

"John-Boy, you okay back there?" Coyote asked over the ICS.

"Yeah . . . just shook up," the RIO replied. "But my panel looks like a Christmas tree. That sucker really nailed us."

"Coyote . . . hey, man, you look like shit," Batman broke in. "Get the hell clear if you can. We'll hold 'em here."

"Not much point in that," Coyote countered. "If I try to break away you know they'll be all over me. Might as well stick it out here as long as this turkey'll hold together."

He didn't add that none of them had much time left in any event. He didn't have to remind any of them of that.

0950 hours Zulu (0950 hours Zone)
Fulcrum Leader
Northwest of the Faeroe Islands

Terekhov switched his selector switch from missiles to guns. With his last radar-homer expended, he was reduced to the same condition as the surviving Americans. It seemed like these Americans just didn't know when they were beaten. Each time he thought they could do no more, they managed to pull off another surprise. The return of the Tomcat that had fled at the very start of the battle had been completely unexpected . . . and another MiG had been lost as a result. The second American Sidewinder hadn't found its target, luckily, but the kill ratio was still far out of proportion to what the Russians had gained today.

And the clock was ticking. The longer he spent here, the more likely Glushko would be to accuse him of disobedience in not going after the new wave of Americans. Shaking his head, Terekhov knew they couldn't keep up this fighting much longer.

"Comrade Captain! Comrade Captain!" That was Oganov, his voice panicky. "Radar lock! An American plane has radar lock on me!"

"Impossible!" he snapped. Or was it? Nothing the Americans did would surprise him any more.

He glanced at his radar screen and cursed aloud. The American reinforcements were just coming into range for their radar-homing Sparrow missiles. So much for Glushko's conviction that they were strike aircraft armed for an attack on Soyuz.

"All planes, all planes, disengage *now*!" he shouted. "Return to base! Repeat, return to base!"

0951 hours Zulu (0951 hours Zone)
Soviet Guided Missile Submarine *Krasniy Ritsary*
Northeast of the Faeroe Islands

Naumkin leaned against the back of the radioman's chair, looking over his shoulder as he adjusted his receiver with quick, precise movements of his stubby peasant's fingers. With an antenna deployed to the surface, the sub could tap into the transmissions of the An-74 airborne warning and control plane circling far above the North Sea. The information from the plane's sophisticated array of radars would locate every plane and ship in the area.

It was the ideal way to find a target without using his own active sensors. Though he ran the risk of an aerial searcher spotting the antenna while it was on the surface, that was a far slimmer risk than the prospect of using his own radar to seek out the enemy. Active sensors probing the enemy fleet from here would call down the full weight of the American battle group's ASW force on *Krasniy Ritsary,* and Naumkin wasn't prepared to do that yet. Not until it became absolutely necessary.

He straightened up and crossed to the chart table, where Maleshenko was already studying an electronic plot of the An-74 data. The Exec pointed to one coded symbol.

"The American carrier," he said, looking up at Naumkin with a predatory grin. "Well within range . . . an ideal chance, Comrade Captain."

Naumkin studied the chart, stroking his chin absently. He indicated another symbol, between the sub and the carrier but closer to *Krasniy Ritsary*. "What is this one?"

"Frigate," the Exec said. "Oliver Hazard Perry class. An ASW vessel, not a major target. Not compared to the carrier."

"Agreed, Vitaly. But notice the positions. We might slow their reactions somewhat by attacking *both* Americans. If they believe the frigate is the target of the full attack . . ."

"Their carrier defenses might not react in time," Maleshenko finished. "Excellent, Comrade Captain. Excellent!"

"Prepare the attack," Naumkin ordered. "Eight missiles. Six against the carrier, two more against the frigate. Be ready to follow up with another wave . . . or to maneuver if need be."

The Exec began passing the orders, leaving Naumkin to study the map. If *Krasniy Ritsary* actually damaged or destroyed the American aircraft carrier, Admiral Khenkin would know his choice had been a good one. And a captain with such an achievement could expect to go to the very top in the Union's New Order. He savored the thought until Maleshenko returned.

"Ready to launch, Comrade Captain."

He smiled. "Begin the attack."

0952 hours Zulu (0952 hours Zone)
***Gridley* LAMPS Helo Two**
Northeast of the Faeroe Islands

"*Madré de Dios!*" Lieutenant Jimmy Mendez gasped as the sea erupted less than a mile ahead of the SH-60 Seahawk. "What *are* those? Nukes?"

His TACCO, Tom Jennings, shook his head emphatically. "SS-N-19," he said, calm and controlled even in the face of this startling proof that the Russians were launching a major new strike. "Soviet cruise missile. Kind of a cheap version of the Tomahawk." His voice changed as he switched on the radio. "Jericho, Jericho, this is Trumpet. We have visual on Sierra Sierra November One-Niner cruise missiles, inbound your position. Estimate six . . . seven . . . eight

missiles. We are prosecuting the search for the launch platform. Over.''

"Trumpet, Jericho," the ASW officer aboard *Gridley*
replied. "We've got them on our screens. Thanks for the
warning."

"Good luck and Godspeed," Jennings said. "Trumpet
clear. All right, gentlemen, let's find us a submarine!''

0953 hours Zulu (0953 hours Zone)
U.S.S. *Gridley*
East of the Faeroe Islands

Gridley's SPS-49 5 C/D band air-search radar tracked the
flight of Soviet missiles from the moment they broke the
surface, and the Tactical Officer on duty in CIC promptly
sounded the battle stations warning. Crewmen swarmed
through corridors and across the deck in response to the
blaring siren.

The Mark 13 launcher on the forward deck could handle
thirty-six Standard SM-1 medium-range surface-to-air missiles, the frigate's main line of defense against aerial attack.
Ten SAMs streaked skyward in response to orders from
CIC, knocking out five of the eight cruise missiles while
they were still several miles out. But the SS-N-19s were
coming in fast, too fast for a second SAM launch.

As they closed the range, the Phalanx CIWS system took
over. A 20-mm Vulcan Gatling gun mounted near the stern
of the frigate, CIWS—standing for Close-In Weapon System and pronounced Sea-Whiz in the technical jargon of the
Navy—could fire fifty depleted-uranium shells every second, tracking and locking on to its targets automatically
using Pulse-Doppler radar. But the angle of the incoming
missiles wasn't ideal for the Phalanx to intercept the three
remaining targets. Two of them, both targeted on the

Jefferson, passed overhead and into the firing arc, and the Phalanx hummed like an angry buzzsaw.

The last missile, though, struck *Gridley* just above the waterline only a few feet forward of the Mark 13 launcher, the explosion ripping through the hull and setting off secondary blasts in the SAMs remaining in their launch tubes.

Within seconds, U.S.S. *Gridley* was ablaze from midships to bow.

0953 hours Zulu (0953 hours Zone)
Tomcat 201
Northwest of the Faeroe Islands

"The Russkies are running! Hot *damn,* Coyote, they're actually running away! We beat the bastards!"

Coyote Grant couldn't believe Batman's excited shout any more than he could believe the symbols crawling across his radar screen. Yet both told the same story. The Russian MiGs were withdrawing.

The fresh blips on the radar, the Hornets from the first wave of reinforcements, were the real reason for the enemy retreat, of course, but Coyote could understand how Batman felt. Despite the odds, Viper Squadron had stood up to a savage attack and escaped with their lives . . . some of them, at least. Eight men wouldn't be going home, including Stramaglia.

"Lancelot, Lancelot, this is Galahad. Stand down, boys, and let some real birds take over from those turkeys of yours." The voice belonged to Commander Bobby Lee "Tex" Benton, CO of VFA-161, the Javelins. Benton, his broad Texas accent even more pronounced than usual, sounded eager for a fight.

Letting out a long, shuddering sigh, Coyote cut back on

his throttle and turned southeast. "Galahad, Lancelot. Good
to see you, Tex, even if you guys are flying Tinkertoys."
Even after everything they'd been through, he couldn't
resist the chance to needle his counterpart. There was a
long-standing rivalry between the Tomcat and Hornet
squadrons aboard *Jefferson,* focused on the relative merits
of the heavy but sturdy F-14 versus the versatile, lightweight F/A-18.

"Ninety-nine aircraft, ninety-nine aircraft." The voice of
Lieutenant Commander Owens interrupted him with the
general signal directed at all aircraft. "RTB. That's Return
to Base. All aircraft return to base."

"Ah, shit," Benton said. "Guess we don't get to party
with the Russkies after all!"

"Suits me fine," Coyote responded. "Vipers, you heard
the man. Let's go home."

"You think you can make it, Coyote?" Batman asked.

"I'll sure as hell try!" he said. Coyote didn't relish
bailing out this far from the carrier and waiting for a SAR
chopper.

"I'll stick with you, man," Wayne said. "Just to keep an
eye on you."

He started to thank him, then had another thought.
"Thanks anyway, Batman, but that's not your job. My
wingman's supposed to be looking out for me." Powers had
screwed up at the beginning of the fight, but it must have
taken guts to get back into the battle the way he did.
"Tyrone, you copy?"

When Powers answered, his voice was choked with
emotion. "Copy, Two-oh-one. I'm with you."

The joystick was mushy, the Tomcat sluggish, but Coyote
barely noticed. He was still getting used to the idea that he
had lived after all.

0953 hours Zulu (0953 hours Zone)
Soviet Guided Missile Submarine *Krasniy Ritsary*
Northeast of the Faeroe Islands

The hull echoed with the deep, bell-like tolling of sonar pings, so loud that the source had to be close by. Naumkin looked up from the plotting board as the sonar operator reported, unnecessarily, what the captain already knew. "Comrade Captain! Active sonar, bearing one-one-two!"

Naumkin swung around. "Identify!"

"Sonobuoy. American SSQ-53 DIFAR type!" The sonar operator's voice was tense. The man knew what that meant as well as Naumkin did. The DIFAR (Directional Finding and Ranging) sonobuoy was employed by ASW hunters to get an exact fix on a target prior to making an attack.

Krasniy Ritsary had been discovered after all.

"Evasive action!" Naumkin snapped. "Full right rudder, maximum revolutions! Ten degrees down angle on bow planes, and prepare to release decoys!"

"Torpedo in the water," the sonar operator announced. "Two torpedoes!"

The hull rang as the two American torpedoes added their own sonar pings to the cacophony in the water. They rose in pitch and frequency as the torps closed, guided unerringly by reflected sound waves that plainly marked their intended target.

"They will hit us!" the Exec shouted.

"Brace yourselves!" Naumkin added.

The first Mark 46 torpedo struck near the blunt, rounded bow of the submarine. Seconds later the other impacted as well, striking just below the sail and blasting a hole that breached both the outer hydrodynamic hull and the inner pressure hull. Water poured into the control room, flooding it in moments.

Krasniy Ritsary plunged toward the sea floor, never to surface again.

1107 hours Zulu (1107 hours Zone)
Flight deck, U.S.S. *Thomas Jefferson*
South of the Faeroe Islands

Magruder climbed down from the cockpit of the Viking, trying to avoid the looks Harrison and Meade were giving him. The S-3B had been off her station less than five minutes when the missile attack began, and Harrison's ''I-told-you-so'' looks had been making Tombstone feel like a fool ever since.

Gridley had never stood a chance. The frigate was still afloat—barely—but the fire was raging out of control. Rescue helos from *Jefferson* and the rest of the battle group had managed to rescue 120 crewmen, just over half the ship's complement, from the decks and the cold waters around the sinking vessel before the effort had finally been abandoned.

Had the Viking remained on station, keeping up the hunt, the Russian sub would never have dared to fire. Magruder might as well have launched those missiles himself.

And in the end, Harrison had been right to argue that Magruder wouldn't do any good by heading back to the carrier immediately. The air battle had ended with the arrival of the Hornets and the retreat of the Russian squadron. The Viking had been kept in the Marshall stack while the remnants of Viper Squadron landed. Coyote hadn't made it all the way back, but an SAR copter had fished Grant and his RIO out of the Atlantic after he ditched less than a mile from the *Jeff.* So Magruder's efforts hadn't even helped his friends.

The one positive contribution he'd made so far was the

order dispatching one of the KA-6D tankers to rendezvous with the Air Force planes off the Icelandic coast. Luckily Navy and Air Force tanker fittings were compatible, and the fuel he'd sent would keep the survivors flying until they could pick up another tanker and escort on their way to Greenland. But he'd accomplished that much by radio, passing the orders to Owens on the flight back.

It was a poor start as CAG. A frigate destroyed, *Jefferson* put in danger, all because he'd let his impatience with sub-hunting convince him that he was the indispensable man aboard the carrier now.

Matthew Magruder didn't feel indispensable any longer.

A fresh-faced junior grade lieutenant from the admiral's staff met Magruder before he could take three steps across the flight deck. ''Sir,'' the young officer shouted over the roar of a helicopter's rotors—probably one of the SAR choppers returning from the search for *Gridley* survivors. ''Sir, the admiral's compliments and would you please come to the Flag Bridge right away?''

Magruder nodded dully. If Admiral Tarrant wanted to see him for the reason Magruder expected, his tenure as CAG was likely to be the shortest one on record.

1115 hours Zulu (1115 hours Zone)
Flag Bridge, U.S.S. *Thomas Jefferson*
South of the Faeroe Islands

Admiral Douglas Tarrant looked into his half-empty mug, staring at the coffee inside without really seeing it. The past few hours had been shattering, but he fought to keep his features impassive. Things were bad enough now without letting the crew see that their top brass had come close to breaking.

He'd never expected the Russians to launch such a blatant

attack on American forces. His Soviet counterpart, or his bosses in the Kremlin, had raised the stakes a long way over the limit. Tarrant had spent too long learning the rules of the game in the Cold War. This new post-Cold War era wasn't anything like that. Now the Russians were playing for keeps, and none of the conventional wisdom of past confrontations seemed to apply.

In hindsight it was easy to see. Over a decade the new Russian leadership had seen first-hand that hesitation and half-measures were worse than useless. Hesitation had lost them Eastern Europe, had left the abortive coup of '91 in tatters before it ever got off the ground, and had condemned the federal government in Yugoslavia to a long, bitter civil war nobody could win. By contrast, a swift, decisive, ruthless strike had driven Iraq out of Kuwait, and the Russians watching that war from the sidelines had taken the lesson to heart. The fall of Yeltsin's Commonwealth to the reactionaries of the new Union had been the result of the same kind of decisiveness. They had exploited the weaknesses of a disorganized government and a broken economy and brought back Communism where their clumsier Cold Warrior predecessors had failed before.

This had been the same kind of operation. The ambush set for the Tomcat squadron had been bad enough, but on top of that the Russians had dealt very effectively with Keflavik. Following up their initial missile strike, Soviet bombers had made a close-in bombing attack on the American base. Even though most of them had fallen prey to defending Eagles, SAMs, and Phoenix missiles, a few had made it all the way in. And those few had dropped enough five-hundred-pound BETAB retarded antirunway bombs, the Russian equivalent of America's Durandal, to make the airstrips there totally useless for the foreseeable future.

The destruction of Keflavik and the loss of half of Viper Squadron together put *Jefferson*'s battle group in serious danger. The carrier and her consorts were sailing into hazardous waters, with each mile putting them closer to Russian land-based air forces that could overwhelm *Jefferson*'s defenses easily. The Americans would be hard-pressed to survive, much less do anything substantial in support of the embattled defenders. Under those circumstances, was it worth the risk to go on?

But the alternative was turning back, and if they did that the President might as well concede defeat. As long as Europe was staying neutral, Keflavik had been the only possible staging area for American forces flying into Norway. Without it, all support would have to be by sea, and by the time any of the ships preparing off the East Coast could make it to Bergen the fight for Norway would be over. A modern amphibious operation needed a close base of operations for any hope of success, and that was precisely what the United States would face if Bergen fell. Unless Bergen could hold out a few more weeks, the Soviets would soon be sitting pretty in a secure bastion.

Tarrant looked up as a pair of officers entered. One was young Lieutenant Craig, from his own staff. The other man he knew mostly from news reports and magazine stories, though he'd seen him among the CAG staff on the day of the briefing. Commander Magruder had a haunted look. He seemed older than Tarrant had thought, and didn't look much like the reckless hero aviator depicted in the media.

"Magruder. Good." Tarrant gestured for him to join him at the chart table. "Sorry to fetch you up here so soon after you touched down, but this is important."

"I understand, sir," Magruder replied slowly. Close up, the haunted look was even more noticeable. Tarrant couldn't help but wonder if he was as capable as his reputation claimed.

"You know about Captain Stramaglia's death by now, of course," Tarrant went on, studying him carefully. "Losing him was a blow we couldn't afford. He was a good man, and one of the best tacticians I've ever seen in action.''

"Yes, sir." There was no spark of energy in his words or his eyes. It was as if he had died, not Stramaglia.

"You're the next in line in the Air Wing, and you've got the experience to make a good CAG. I don't envy you the job, though. It's a killer under ordinary conditions, and what we've got is a situation that's anything *but* ordinary."

"Sir?" That seemed to get a rise out of him. For a moment Tarrant couldn't help but think that Magruder hadn't expected the advancement. That was silly, of course. As Stramaglia's deputy Magruder was the automatic replacement.

He put the thought out of his mind. Probably young Magruder was still a little bit dazed by everything that had happened. Viper Squadron . . . *Gridley* . . . Stramaglia. It was a lot to take in all at once.

"Your immediate concern is the defense of this ship," Tarrant told him. "Viper Squadron's at half strength, and that's going to put a crimp in our CAP umbrella. Do what you have to, but make sure we're covered. Next time the bombers could be headed our way."

Magruder nodded slowly. "Yes, Admiral."

"I also want ASW tightened. I don't want another *Gridley.*" Magruder seemed about to say something, and Tarrant paused, but the new CAG didn't speak after all. "The real problem, though, is bigger," he went on after a moment. "After what's happened this morning we need to husband our resources. I don't know how we're going to defend the carrier and still project any kind of substantial offensive power, but if we don't come up with something pretty damned quick we might as well call off this whole cruise and go home. So we need some ideas, Magruder. Some way to hit those Russian bastards where it hurts and slow down the offensive against Bergen."

"That's a tall order, sir," Magruder replied, still thought-ful but less distracted than before. "I don't know if there's anything we *can* do."

"That's not what I want to hear, mister," Tarrant snapped. "Stramaglia would have come up with something. I expect you to do the same. Because if you don't, Commander, this war is over."

The new CAG stepped back, looking stricken. "I'll . . . do what I can, Admiral," he said.

Tarrant nodded. "That's what I want. Get on it, Com-mander. Dismissed."

1132 hours Zulu (1132 hours Zone)
Wing commander's office, Soviet Aircraft Carrier *Soyuz*
The Norwegian Sea

Captain First Rank Glushko regarded his subordinate with distaste. "Well, Terekhov, it seems your victory was less than complete."

Terekhov stared at a point on the bulkhead somewhere behind Glushko's head. "My men did all they could, sir," he said stiffly. "Had the Sukhois remained in the battle we could have destroyed the rest of their F-14 squadron and faced the reinforcements as well. But without the Sukhois . . ."

"You intend to put the blame on my decision to defend *Soyuz* then? Is that how your report will read?" He tried to keep from betraying his emotion, though he knew that Terekhov already understood how Glushko felt about him.

Terekhov didn't answer.

"Listen to me, Captain," Glushko went on, dropping his voice. "You think you can ruin me with an accusation like that. I, on the other hand, am in a position to ruin you as well. The operation was based on your plans, and the weakness of the defenses devoted to *Soyuz* was certainly a cause for legitimate concern. Even though the Americans did not attack, it was a possibility that had to be thought of, and your ambush, bold as it was, took no account of the possibility. So I may be censured for my part in this, but I can assure you that I will not crash alone. Do you understand me?''

"Yes, sir," Terekhov replied. His tone was wary.

Glushko smiled. "On the other hand . . . our casualties were not light, but we inflicted much damage on the American fighters. And the bombers carried out their strike on the base in Iceland successfully. This morning's events can be presented as a substantial victory . . . perhaps even a decisive one. But it would not look good for one of us to . . . spoil the image of success through recriminations. It is easy enough to look back on an event and speak of those things which might have been, Terekhov, but it is not always the wisest course."

The younger officer shifted his gaze to Glushko's face. "I do not intend to let you destroy me or the reputation of my men, Comrade Captain. If this is some attempt to keep me from defending myself . . ."

Glushko laughed. "You have a suspicious mind, Sergei Sergeivich. I am proposing that we stop working at cross-purposes. The Americans are our enemies, and to defeat them we should learn to work together, no?''

"If you say so, Comrade Captain," Terekhov responded reluctantly. "But just what do you have in mind, beyond not making any accusations in our reports on the action?"

Leaning back in his chair, Glushko smiled broadly. He hadn't been sure if Terekhov would be willing to sacrifice his self-righteous ideals for the benefits of practical politics, but it had certainly been worth trying. And it seemed the man wasn't quite the idealist he appeared on the surface after all.

"We can be an effective team, Terekhov, if we try. Hard though it is to admit it, I recognize that you have a talent that the *Rodina* needs. A talent that I frankly lack. My skill is in . . . effective human interaction. But I have influence. Several of the political officers in the fleet are well disposed toward me, and that gives me a measure of power that your talent cannot alter. Work *with* me, Sergei Sergeivich, and together the two of us will go far. *Soyuz* and his air wing hold the keys to the success of this campaign, and with those keys we will unlock the door to power in the new Union."

He smiled again, hoping Terekhov would accept it as a sincere expression of warmth. The younger officer would be a useful asset once he was put in harness, and Glushko intended to exploit that asset for all he was worth. They would defeat the Americans and finish the Norwegian campaign, and Glushko would attract the notice of the Kremlin.

As for Terekhov . . . well, ambitious young fighter pilots were always at risk. If Terekhov didn't survive the campaign, there would be many solemn mourners at his funeral. But Captain First Rank Glushko would not be one of them.

1715 hours Zulu (1915 hours Zone)
The Kremlin
Moscow, RSFSR

Vladimir Nikolaivich Vorobyev studied the summary of Admiral Khenkin's report with a smile of cold satisfaction. Thanks to the initiative of Soviet Naval Aviation, it seemed that the American carrier's air wing had suffered a major defeat while entering the Norwegian Sea. Coupled with the success at Keflavik, that opened a window of opportunity in Norway. For the next few days Western intervention would be next to impossible.

Now was the time to act.

"Korotich!" he said, pressing a key on the intercom box on his crowded desk. "My office. Now."

Colonel Boris Ilyavich Korotich was Vorobyev's senior aide, an unimaginative but loyal officer who excelled at carrying out his master's wishes. He appeared at the door promptly, wearing the characteristic frown that suggested he was afraid he had forgotten some crucial detail but at the same time refused to accept any suggestion that he had failed. Korotich set far harder standards for himself than any of his superiors. It was one reason he made such an efficient aide.

"Yes, Comrade General?"

"Korotich, what is the current situation in Norway? The Bergen offensive specifically." Vorobyev knew it well enough, but he wanted to hear the words aloud. It helped him focus on the strategic problem to hear someone else present the data.

The aide's frown deepened as he summoned the information from his excellent, orderly memory. "Very little progress so far, sir. The 45th is stalled in the mountains. A comparatively small force of partisans can delay the advance significantly."

"And there has been no further progress in suppressing their SAM defenses?"

"The diversion of aerial resources to North Star has slowed the operation, sir. However, the most recent report indicates that the air base at Orland has been cleared and can be put back into operation. This will allow the deployment of additional tactical air support, which in turn should speed up the hunt for the enemy SAM emplacements."

The Norwegians had been clever in their use of surface-to-air missiles. A nearly impenetrable curtain of SAM fire had derailed the air strikes that should have opened the way for the occupation of Bergen. Finding the SAM batteries was a job on the same order as the American "Scud hunts" during their war with Iraq. But with the *Rodina*'s full aerial resources brought to bear those defenses would soon be neutralized.

"I want the efforts redoubled, Korotich. Continual strikes into that area, until those SAMs are out of action. Even if you have to burn up half the planes in the theater doing it."

"Yes, Comrade General."

"I want the path cleared for an airborne landing near the coast in two days, Korotich. By this time Saturday I want a full regiment on the ground within the Norwegian defensive perimeter." His finger stabbed at the map spread out on his desk, indicating the region where *Soyuz* aircraft had previously reported success in reducing Norwegian defenses. "Here . . . at Brekke."

Korotich examined the map and nodded solemnly. "*Da* . . . Brekke. That will distract the RNA forces defending the line between the Sognefjorden and the road junction at Gol. A sound plan, Comrade General."

"They will do more than distract, Boris Ilyavich. At the same time you relay those orders, you will also order all amphibious forces and naval infantry to assemble. Within twenty-four hours after Brekke is secured from the air, we will pour every man we can transport by sea into that position. They will be less than a hundred kilometers from Bergen, and squarely across the line of retreat for the Norwegians around the Sognefjord. That will produce the breakthrough we need."

Korotich nodded again. "It will be difficult to assemble some of the forces, Comrade General, but I think the bulk of them can be en route in time."

Vorobyev gave him a cold smile. "Tell any officer who does not think he can have his men moving in time that he will answer to me. In person . . . and in full."

Now was the time to strike. Now, while the Americans

were reeling from their defeat, the new Soviet Union would reclaim its proper place in the world. Norway would break, and the rest of Scandinavia after it. Then Europe would face the full weight of Russian's military securely placed in a flanking position that rendered useless its traditional defensive lines in Germany.

All it would take was one final push, and the humiliations of a decade would vanish forever.

1145 hours Zulu (1145 hours Zone)
Air Wing Intelligence office, U.S.S. *Thomas Jefferson*
In the Southern Norwegian Sea

"So what you're telling me is that we can predict what they're going to do, but we can't do a hell of a lot about it." Tombstone Magruder massaged his forehead with both hands. He had been awake most of the night going over every aspect of the military situation, but all he had to show for his work was a pile of file folders on his desk and a headache ten times worse than any he'd ever suffered from G-forces in a fighter cockpit.

"I can't speak for what we can do, sir," Lieutenant Commander Arthur Lee replied. "But yes, we'll see what they're up to. Satellite recon will be able to monitor the bastards, and I'm confident we can sort out any decoy operations."

Since the fighting the day before, *Jefferson* had continued on course into the Norwegian Sea, but cautiously, carefully. ASW forces had flushed six more subs in that time, with two more confirmed kills and the others either knocked out or driven off. Magruder's involvement in the submarine-hunting had been peripheral at best, but each reported contact had brought back thoughts of *Gridley*'s destruction.

No number of successes could erase that first disastrous failure.

Through the night hours Commander Lee had been working with Aiken's OZ division to analyze every scrap of available intelligence data. Satellite recon images had been tracking some major Russian activity overnight, and now Lee was prepared to make solid preparations concerning enemy activity in Scandinavia.

The most noticeable development was the increased naval activity along the coast. Photographs taken by an orbiting KEYHOLE spy satellite had tracked nearly fifty ships gathering Trondheim. Some were clearly warships, centered around the powerful helicopter cruiser *Kiev*. But the majority had been identified as troop carriers, ranging from two Ivan Rogov-class LSDs to a mixed bag of smaller LSTs and several freighters plainly pressed from civilian into military service. Lee had cited numerous technical points to support his contention that they were fully loaded, and that suggested that they were beginning a new campaign now that they had neutralized Keflavik and given the *Jefferson* battle group a bloody nose.

The possibility gained credence when taken in conjunction with activity reported around Murmansk, where elite Soviet paratroopers had been kept in reserve practically since the start of the conflict. Now they seemed to be getting ready to move out. Lee couldn't predict where they would strike, but it was his opinion that the Soviets at this point had few options left.

"The Norwegians are dug in tight and ready for damn near anything that comes in on the ground," Lee had said at one point. "They're fighting the kind of war they were always supposed to fight, holding a few key passes against Russian columns that can't push them back without unacceptable casualties. If they keep following the same basic strategy they've been using the Russians'll try an end run starting near the coast. Drop a major *desantniki* force near a usable port, then funnel in all the amphibious troops they can manage. All of a sudden the RNA's got a whole corps inside their lines and driving on Bergen, and that's all she wrote.''

"If it's that predictable, will they really try it this time?" Magruder had asked, still not entirely comfortable with the ins and outs of ground strategy and tactics.

"No guarantees, of course," Lee had replied. "They could make maybe two other moves. One would be a major drop right behind the lines somewhere near the center of the Bergen defensive perimeter, with the idea of creating a large hole in the line that the armor could exploit. Problem with that is that Norway's still an easy place for a defender. They run the risk of achieving nothing more than a short advance before getting bogged down all over again.''

"And the other option?" Magruder had pressed.

"Use the naval force as a decoy, then drop the paratroops behind the end of the line opposite Oslo. They've built up a pretty fair contingent around the capital, and a determined drive on that side supported by *desant* troops could lead to a nice little penetration.''

"But you don't think that's what they'll try?"

"Not really. First off, that's the longest overland route to Bergen they've got, and again they're up against the defensive advantage. Number two, all their logistical support down there would have to come in by air. They've got air superiority now and they could have air supremacy in a few more days, but a determined offensive by the RNAF or even a spell of nasty weather could cut those troops off with virtually no supplies. They're already at risk keeping Oslo fully supplied. I really don't think they'd want to risk the whole offensive on something like that.'' He had grinned. "Don't forget, the Soviets've had experience seeing what kind of havoc a determined partisan with a hand-held Stinger can play with a well-planned op. Afghanistan's going to haunt them the way Vietnam did our boys until the Gulf War came along.''

It all made good sense, and Magruder was willing to rely on Lee's expert opinion. In addition to his Intelligence experience, the man had a genuine flair for strategy. He seemed able to pick out the advantages and disadvantages of just about anything the Russians chose to do. But in the end, Tombstone didn't see that any of it would be much help.

He stopped rubbing his throbbing forehead and looked at the map again. ''All right, we can spot their airdrops as they happen. The satellite coverage gives us that much. If they do what you expect, then this amphibious force will start moving in to support the parachute troops within a few hours. Assuming we can sort through whatever diversions they mount, we'll be able to predict where they're heading and probably their ETA. Right?''

Lee nodded. ''Almost certainly. They'll stay bunched up so the escorts can cover them from subs and missile attacks. Don't forget, the Norwegians still have some of their navy left. But they wouldn't be much good in a head-on fight with the Soviets.''

''Okay. That's the good news then. The bad news is their air power. They already have a damned strong contingent of fighters and bombers from Frontal Aviation out there, and you say they're about to reactivate Orland with more squadrons of MiGs and Sukhois.''

''It's already in service on a limited scale, Commander,'' Lee corrected. ''By tomorrow they'll be flying six or eight squadrons out of there.''

Magruder rubbed his chin. ''And, of course, we've got their naval air to contend with. Not just as extra cover for their operations ashore, but as a direct threat to us as well. I don't like these odds, Art.''

Lee shrugged. ''I can't do much about them, sir. I deal in facts. This is what we've got to work with.''

"How reliable is our coordination with the Norwegians? Can we get any help from them at all?"

"They're pretty hard-pressed, Commander," Lee said slowly. "You know they'll be doing everything they can, but I expect their resources will be stretched to the limit by what they're already up against." He paused, studying the map with a thoughtful expression. "One thing we might do is encourage them to mount a strong raid toward Oslo, though."

"How would that help?"

"Well, it would probably take every extra plane they've got, and it might not cause a whole lot of damage, but as sensitive as the air supply pipeline has to be right now, I'd say we'd draw a lot of their Frontal Aviation units away from the navy. That would also probably block them if they'd planned on an end run out of Oslo."

"Hmph." Magruder was still frowning. "Narrows the odds some, but not enough. I've got one and a half interceptor squadrons, two Hornet squadrons I can use as fighters or bombers but not both at the same time, and one squadron of Intruders that are bombers only. With that we have to make a dent in their attack force and still cover the *Jeff*." Suddenly overwhelmed with fatigue, he looked away. "Hell, I don't know the answer. I don't think CAG could've covered all these bases."

The damnable thing was that it was almost possible. If he was willing to take some risks, he could probably put together an attack that would have a shot at crippling the enemy amphib forces, but if he made one wrong step the results would make the loss of the *Gridley* look like a minor lapse in judgment. There were just too many variables . . . and Magruder wasn't sure he could face the tough decisions that would have to be made.

If he attacked and failed, a lot of good pilots could follow Stramaglia and the others . . . and the *Jeff* herself could come under attack again. Thousands of American lives were potentially at risk.

And if he did nothing, it would be thousands of Norwegians who might die, and at the end of that road lay the ultimate victory of the Russian war in Scandinavia, with all the potential for future trouble that carried with it.

As a squadron commander, back in North Korea, Magruder had first been forced to face up to his responsibility for the life-and-death decisions that went with command. He could still remember the torment of losing Coyote when his plane went down in that first dogfight off of Wonsan. It was a lesson every leader of men learned sooner or later.

But time and rank didn't make that lesson any less painful. As a squadron commander he'd been directly responsible for twenty or thirty lives at best, though often his own personal actions had reached far beyond that immediate circle. Now he was responsible for hundreds of lives directly, and the fate of many more could also be affected by his decisions.

"Look, Art," he said at last. "We can't do anything else for now. Why don't you pack it in and get some sleep. We'll get together and go over whatever OZ gets in later on. Okay?"

Lee looked at him with a worried expression. "You going to be all right, Commander?" he asked. "Seems like all this is hitting you pretty hard."

"I know what I'm supposed to do, Art," Magruder said slowly. "I just have to find out if I've still got the guts to do it or not. And it's something I can only work out on my own."

As Lee left, Magruder's thoughts went back to North Korea. Back then issues of right and wrong, action or inaction, had all seemed so clear-cut. Now they didn't seem so easy to resolve.

Yet that was exactly what he had to do.

1308 hours Zulu (1308 hours Zone)
Sick Bay, U.S.S. *Thomas Jefferson*
In the southern Norwegian Sea

Fatigue and numbing cold . . . gray skies and an angry
gray sea . . . those were Coyote's world. A part of him
thought he was trapped in a dream, in the old familiar
nightmare, but another part insisted that it was all too real.

The water had been icy, sucking the warmth right out of
him as he struggled into the life raft and fought to control
his panic. He needed a cool head to stay alive, a cool head
and his survival training.

Coyote remembered cradling his RIO to him, seeing the
striped helmet hanging at an impossible angle, knowing that
the man was dead yet unwilling to accept it. But
no . . . John-Boy had helped him into the raft out there in
the rolling waters of the Atlantic, had helped him later when
he couldn't get his hands to work to attach the harness so
that the SAR copter could hoist him aboard.

Two dreams, then . . . that was it. His RIO had died in
the waters off North Korea, but John-Boy had lived through
it to help him when he needed it. Through the fog of a
half-dream other memories played against one another. The
harness cutting into him as the SAR copter lifted him
aboard . . . the mustard-colored uniforms of the Oriental
soldiers dragging him onto the deck of the North Korean
patrol craft . . . One dream blended with another until
Coyote no longer knew which was which.

He remembered the prison camp, the brutal guards, the
beating. They had finished with him and marched him into
the yard outside, and there they had prepared him for
execution. Julie . . . he'd held on to thoughts of Julie, and
with her picture in his mind he'd accepted the idea of death,

but when the guards pulled their triggers the only sound had been the *snicking* of bolts on empty chambers. A mock execution, designed to break him down . . .

Coyote came fully awake with a start, disoriented, confused, soaked with sweat. It took a long moment to get his bearings, to realize he was still in Sick Bay, safe after being fished out of the Atlantic following the ordeal of the battle with the overpowering Russian forces.

"Hey, Coyote, you okay?" John-Boy asked from the next bed, sitting up and looking concerned.

"Yeah . . . yeah, I'm okay," Grant replied, knowing he sounded anything but convincing. "Just . . . a bad dream."

He shuddered and turned over, unwilling to face John-Boy, but equally unwilling to go back to sleep. He had dreamed much the same dream every night for six months after the end of the Wonsan fighting. He'd spent a long time getting over Korea before finally driving himself to return to the carrier and face his fears, and in the skies over the Indian Ocean he'd proven that he still had the old edge. The dreams had come back from time to time, but over the months they had finally faded away.

Now he was dreaming again. When his Tomcat had finally given up the ghost he and John-Boy had punched out, close enough to the carrier to make a recovery fairly easy. Still, the same chill waters that had dragged Jolly Greene to his death after the crash on the flight deck had nearly claimed Coyote as well, and would have had it not been for John-Boy's help. This time help had been close at hand, but the parallels with Korea were still vivid.

Someday his luck would run out. He would fly out on a mission and never make it back. Like Greene . . . or Baird . . . or Stramaglia.

In that camp in Korea Coyote had thought he'd made his peace with death. After the mock execution, he had truly believed that he was ready to die, and that had made it easier to endure everything that had followed. But he had been given a second life, one that included not just Julie but a new daughter and the chance to start with a clean slate.

Yet he'd come back to this life, and some day it would take him for its own. He would lose everything . . . and the two people he cared about most would have to go on without him. He wasn't just playing with his own life, but with theirs.

That thought hurt worst of all.

"Coyote?" He rolled over again. It was Tombstone, looking haggard and drawn with a uniform that looked like it had been slept in. "They say you check out fine, Coyote. You'll be flying again in no time."

"Yeah?" He couldn't muster any enthusiasm.

Magruder took a step toward him and stopped. "Hey, look, man, I wish I'd been out there with you guys. Maybe if CAG had let me go up there things would've been different."

"Sure," Grant said. "You'd be dead and he'd be alive. Hell of a trade, huh?"

After their confrontation outside CAG's office Coyote had cooled down enough to realize that Magruder hadn't deliberately turned his back on him, but the gulf between them was still there. Even as tired as Tombstone plainly was, Coyote could see that same wistfulness in his friend's eyes. Magruder wanted to recapture something in the past, something he'd lost . . . the same thing Coyote still had but would gladly have given up in exchange for the chance to live in peace with his family. That gap between the two men could only get wider the way things were going now.

Tombstone forced a feeble smile and broke the long, awkward silence. "Hey, look, the least you can do is try to bribe me to give you a good efficiency report. I mean, what's the good of being best buddy to your new CAG if you don't use it, huh?''

"Damn it, Stoney, leave me alone!" Coyote exploded. "Just leave me the hell alone!"

Magruder took a step back, as if recoiling from a blow, and his face grew hard. "I would if I could," he said harshly. "I'm sorry you seem to think I've suddenly become the enemy or something. I never wanted that." He paused. "I came down here because I needed you. I was thinking about Korea, and I realized how much our friendship always meant to me, how it helped keep me sane sometimes. But even if I can't have your friendship anymore, I still need *you*. We're up against it, Will, and I need help sorting out what to tell the admiral."

"I can't help you with that," Grant said quietly. He wanted to say something more, to try to explain or apologize, whatever it would take to get past the empty look in Tombstone's eyes.

But Magruder didn't give him the chance. "That dogfight yesterday . . . it was a good trap, but it didn't work. The Russians screwed up and didn't finish you guys off when they probably could have. I want to know why. If we end up going up against them again, I need to be able to make them screw up again and give us a chance to win. Without some kind of edge we'll never pull it off."

"What do you want from me?" Coyote asked. "We fought, we got our asses kicked, the cavalry showed up. That's all I know."

"Come on, Will. You were up there in that dogfight. In command, for all intents and purposes. I wasn't there, and all I've got to go on are the reports from the Hawkeye and a few vague ideas. Why did the Russians pull those planes out?"

He shrugged, unable or unwilling to come to grips with the question himself. "Ask Batman. Or Ears."

"God damn it, Will, I'm asking *you*! It's your instincts I need. Your nose for tactics. The Hawkeye report makes it look like they pulled those planes out because our Hornets were forming up over *Jeff*. Was that it? Were they screening their carrier, or did they just think they didn't need the overkill to take you guys out? Come on, you must have had some kind of feel for how they were doing. If they were screening their carrier, that means there's at least one bastard out there who can be bluffed into pulling in his horns on cue. But if it was just a miscalculation of how much strength they needed up there . . ."

Grant sat up slowly, frowning, forcing himself to relive the dogfight. "They were doing pretty good," he said. "They frightened off Tyrone and nailed Trapper. Then the Sukhois bugged out . . ." He hesitated. "But we'd been doing okay ourselves. If I'd been in charge I wouldn't have sent off a third of my planes then. Not unless I had to."

Magruder looked animated for the first time since he had appeared. "You don't think it was just a mistake then?"

"Hell, no," Coyote answered, trying to muster a smile but failing. "Whoever was in charge up there knew what the hell he was doing. No doubt about it. That bright boy wouldn't just let go of a whole squadron unless some bigger boy made him. And the only reason I can see for that would be to cover their carrier."

"That's what I wanted to hear," Magruder said. "Thanks, Will . . . and, uh . . . I'm sorry. But I needed to know, and you're still the one whose judgment I know I can trust."

"I wish I could," Coyote muttered. But Magruder was gone, leaving him alone with bitter thoughts.

1430 hours Zulu (1430 hours Zone)
Admiral's quarters, U.S.S. *Thomas Jefferson*
In the southern Norwegian Sea

"It still doesn't sound good, Commander," Tarrant said
heavily. Across the table, Magruder seemed to slump. The
man was plainly dead on his feet, and even though he
looked freshly shaven and was dressed in a crisp new
uniform, it was obvious he'd been up all night.

That made his report that much more disturbing. Tarrant
knew Magruder had done his best, but he just didn't have
enough of a safety margin in his calculations to convince the
admiral that they could do any good.

It was frustrating. Magruder and his Intelligence Officer
had some good ideas for pinning down a large chunk of the
Soviet air arm to allow an Alpha Strike to get through, but
the carrier's slender resources just wouldn't support it. After
all, the only way to draw off the Soviet air carrier involved
a convincing diversion against the carrier itself, so that
meant spreading American resources among at least three
different missions.

"If we could just deal with Orland," Magruder was
muttering darkly. "We might manage it then . . ."

Tarrant shook his head. "That's easy enough, Commander. I don't even need your planes to take out Orland.
No, the real problem is getting enough of a strike in on both
the carrier and the landing ships without leaving us so
vulnerable that we can't hold out. We can't count on hitting
them with surface-launched missiles, because Red Banner
Northern Fleet's got enough missile defenses to handle
whatever we throw their way. Our only real hope of getting
to either target is to get in close with manned aircraft that
have a shot at evading their ship-mounted SAMs. But if we

keep a squadron to cover the battle group I just don't see enough planes left to cover two strike forces *and* carry enough Harpoons and bombs to do any damage.''

Magruder was nodding slowly. ''That's what I was afraid of, Admiral. If we just had a few more planes . . . Tomcats to cover the *Jeff*, one squadron of Hornets to bomb the troopships, one to ride cover . . .''

''And you end up sending the Intruders in on *Soyuz* without an escort. It's suicide.'' Tarrant shook his head. ''No, unless you can come up with another squadron by magic, we're stumped. I think our only choice now is to steer toward Iceland, make it look like we're trying to skirt their fleet and get in behind them or something. Maybe that'll draw off *Soyuz* and enough of Red Banner Northern Fleet to give the Norwegians a shot at doing something themselves.'' He sighed. ''It was a good effort, Commander. Don't blame yourself over circumstances beyond your control.''

''Yes, sir,'' Magruder said dully.

''If we're going to head any further north I'll want the ASW patrols increased. We'll be moving out of the SOSUS net soon and I want the sub threat covered. That means more work for your Vikings, but—''

''Vikings?'' There was a gleam in Magruder's eyes. ''Hold on a minute, Admiral. There's one idea we didn't explore . . .''

0759 hours Zulu (0759 hours Zone)
CVIC, U.S.S. *Thomas Jefferson*
In the Norwegian Sea

The folding chairs in CVIC had been taken down this morning, replaced instead by television cameras and a team of technicians from the OE Division. Admiral Tarrant watched them checking over their equipment one last time as he waited to one side of the lectern for the closed-circuit broadcast to begin.

The director, a first class petty officer, stepped forward and started the countdown. "Ten seconds, people," he said, pausing and glancing at his stopwatch. "And five . . . and four . . . and three . . ." Then he stepped back and pointed at Master Chief Petty Officer Mike Weston, *Jefferson*'s grizzled Command Master Chief. As Chief of the Boat, Weston was a crucial link between officers and enlisted men. He hosted a daily program of announcements and general information . . . but today he was giving it up so that Tarrant could make his own announcement.

"It's 0800 hours," Weston began. "And time for this morning's edition of *Attention on Deck*. Today, instead of the usual announcements, we'll be hearing from The Man himself, Admiral Tarrant." He paused, stepping back from the podium. "The admiral . . ."

Tarrant stepped forward and looked toward the camera. His prepared speech began to scroll across the teleprompter.

"Most of you know by now that the situation here in the Norwegian Sea has turned serious in the last few days," he said without preamble. "Two days ago the Soviet Union launched a major attack on the U.S. airbase at Keflavik, Iceland, and when *Jefferson* fighters attempted to intercept the attackers they were ambushed by Russian planes. The fighting on Thursday was a major escalation in hostilities, and proves beyond a doubt that the Soviets are willing to go to any lengths, even outright war with the United States, to pursue their Scandinavian invasion."

He paused. Words were hardly adequate in this situation. American lives had been lost, and it was a dead certainty that more would die in the days ahead. A discussion of global strategy and politics couldn't convey the realities of war, the danger that each new incident would lead inevitably to the ultimate horror of a nuclear exchange. He felt he had to give these men some idea of what they faced, but listening to the bald words he wondered if anything he could say would prepare them for what was to come.

"Our orders, confirmed overnight by the President himself, are to support the Free Norwegian forces around Bergen until other U.S. forces can be deployed there. I can't pretend this task will be an easy one. This battle group is up against the full strength of the Soviet Union's Red Banner Northern Fleet, a powerful force of ships and planes backed by ground-based air and lurking attack subs. The odds against us are steep, and before my discussion with the President I was forced to consider the possibility of withdrawing from these waters on my own discretion in order to protect the lives entrusted to my command.

"But retreating in the face of Soviet aggression now would expose our allies in Norway to certain defeat, and the successful consolidation of Russian control over Scandinavia would destabilize all of Europe. As long as there is any chance that we can make a difference in this conflict I intend for Carrier Battle Group 14 to remain in the Norwegian Sea and make every effort to hamper the enemy advance. It is absolutely essential that we do everything we can in support of the President's policy of defending Norway from aggression.''

If the President had only reacted faster, Tarrant thought bitterly, *things might not be so bad now.* The President's so-called policy had been forced on him by events, and even now, judging by what Tarrant had heard in his voice, Connally wasn't eager to pursue this confrontation. But that decision wasn't his to make anymore. The Russian attack on Keflavik made continued hesitation impossible.

Magruder was going ahead with plans for an Alpha Strike, and after his talk with the President Tarrant had dispatched orders committing the battle group's two attack subs, *Galveston* and *Bangor,* to action. There would be no turning back, not this time.

''We *will* carry out this policy,'' he continued out loud. ''It will call for maximum effort from every man in this battle group. The Air Wing staff is even now putting together a detailed plan of operations which we will put into effect against the Soviets as soon as conditions are ripe. This could come tomorrow, or it might not happen for weeks. We have no way of being certain when the best time for a counterstrike against them will present itself. Therefore we must be prepared to act on short notice, and that will require intensive preparations on the part of all of us. I want to emphasize that each of you, no matter what your rating or your job, has a vital role to play in this operation, in the very life of this ship and this battle group. There are no unimportant jobs, and I need each and every one of you to give me a hundred and ten percent in the days ahead. Together we can show the Russians that they cannot drive

America from the world's oceans. Together we will show them once and for all that no power on Earth can suffice to ruin the proud name of *Jefferson*." He paused and looked straight into the camera. "Thank you all . . . and God keep you."

1215 hours Zulu (1215 hours Zone)
Vulture's Row, U.S.S. *Thomas Jefferson*
In the Norwegian Sea

Willis E. Grant leaned against the rail and looked out across *Jefferson*'s flight deck, shivering a little despite the warm afternoon sun.

He had been discharged from Sick Bay two hours earlier, along with John-Boy. Doctor Chapman had been reluctant to release them at first, but with the Air Wing needing every man they could muster he had eventually given in. Coyote was glad to be out of the ward, but in a way he wished Chapman had been less inclined to give in to pressure from the admiral to certify his patients as ready for a full return to duty.

If the Medical Department had kept him out of the coming fight, Coyote would have loudly protested . . . but something inside him would have welcomed the excuse not to go back up there again. Now he had to make a choice on his own, and it wasn't a choice he relished.

Down on the flight deck a Tomcat was roaring off the number-two catapult. He recognized the markings identifying it as one of the War Eagles, VF-97, the carrier's second F-14 squadron. The tail number was 101, but he knew that Commander Alex Caton, the squadron's CO, was in the squadron's offices hard at work on his contribution to the plan of battle for the Alpha Strike Magruder was organizing. The activity on the deck showed just how intense the preparations for action had become. From his vantage point above Pri-Fly Coyote could see work crews in their colored jerseys swarming over a line of parked aircraft, Hornets and Intruders for the most part. Further down the flight deck more handlers were servicing all ten of the S-3B Vikings from the King Fishers. It was odd to see the whole sub-hunting squadron on deck at the same time. The carrier's helos would be doing extra duty looking for Soviet submarines until the Vikings returned to duty again.

The thought of helicopters made Coyote glance off the port side of the carrier, where the Ready SAR helo was keeping station. It sparked unpleasant memories.

He turned away and watched the dance on the deck again. An EA-6B Prowler was coming in on final approach. Built on the Intruder's versatile frame, the Prowler was an Electronic Warfare aircraft designed to jam Russian radar and communications signals. The scuttlebutt Coyote had heard below decks maintained that the five Prowlers from the VAQ-143 Sharks had been doing rotating flight duty since early the night before, doing their best to make Russian lives miserable.

It was an all-out effort, just as the admiral had indicated in his closed-circuit TV speech. He still didn't know any details of the plan Magruder was putting together, but he knew any fight with the Soviets would be a desperate one. And after the last fight, Coyote wasn't sure he could face another one.

He thought back to the night Magruder had come aboard. *She must love you bugging out for sea duty again so quick,* Tombstone had said. And he had made a flip reply. *You know Julie. No complaints there.* He had always looked at it from his own selfish point of view, never seen what Julie must have gone through each time he let his love for blue skies and thundering jets lure him back to duty.

Magruder had lost Pamela Drake over the same stubbornness. Pamela had been strong-willed and forceful, willing to fight for her side. Julie wasn't made of the same stuff, so she had let Coyote leave her time and again.

His latest brush with death had reminded him of what he'd almost lost. He had almost given up flying after Wonsan, but that had been an instinctive reaction to the whole situation he'd been through in Korea. In the long run he hadn't changed his viewpoint that much. This time it was different. This time, Grant knew, he could finally say for sure that his family meant more to him than anything else. He couldn't keep playing the daredevil flyer when each time he went up he might never make it home to his wife and daughter.

His hands gripped the rail more tightly. That left him with a tough decision to make right now. Any aviator could turn in his wings any time, just walk away from duty if it got to be too much, if he thought he had lost the edge. There was nothing to stop Willis E. Grant from doing the same right now . . . nothing except his own sense of duty.

It's your instincts I need. Your nose for tactics. Magruder had turned to his experience when he needed help. And although Admiral Tarrant had been talking to everyone, his words had hit home too. *Each of you has a vital role to play.*

Batman Wayne was more than capable of taking over command of the squadron . . . but Coyote couldn't just turn his back on his men now. Viper Squadron was down to half its original strength, and they needed every pilot they could muster. He *couldn't* leave them in the lurch now, on the eve of their most difficult test. Even if it ended in disaster, he had to go up with the others.

He turned from the rail and headed for the ladder, his mind made up. When he got home—if he got home—he would find out what Julie wanted. He would give up flying, even give up the Navy, if she asked him to. But in the meantime, he couldn't let his shipmates down.

Lieutenant Roger Bannon raised a hand to knock on the door, then hesitated. He had screwed up his courage to come to see Commander Magruder, but now that he was here he found it hard to go ahead with his plan.

He couldn't keep postponing this movement. Bannon gritted his teeth and rapped softly on the door.

"Come!" Magruder's voice called out, sounding distracted.

The commander was sitting at Stramaglia's old desk, pouring over an open file folder that matched ten more stacked beside his elbow. It was plain that Magruder hadn't taken any time to clear away his predecessor's personal effects. A mug on the desk still held a pair of Stramaglia's notorious cigars, and there was a picture hanging on the bulkhead beside the door of Stramaglia and his teenaged son at an air show Stateside. It was hard to believe Stramaglia was really dead. It looked like Magruder was just keeping his chair warm until CAG turned up again.

But he was dead, and now Magruder was in charge. The commander looked tired. If he had managed more than six hours sleep in the last forty-eight it didn't show. He had thrown himself into his new job with a single-minded determination, but the talk in the other offices of the Air Wing hinted that he would burn himself out if he kept pushing himself at this pace. Looking at him now, Bannon was forced to agree.

Magruder held up a hand as Bannon came in and said, "Wait a moment." He never even looked up from the folder. Bannon waited, hoping his resolve wouldn't wilt in the meantime.

Finally Magruder put the folder aside and looked at him.
"Oh . . . Bannon. Didn't know it was your shift yet. Did
you bring the report from Lieutenant Lowe?" Lowe was the
chief of S-6 Division, responsible for Aviation Supply.

"Uh, no, sir," Bannon replied. "I'm still on my own
time, sir. I . . . needed to see you about a personal
matter."

Magruder frowned. "I don't have a whole lot of time,
Bannon," he said. "Make it quick."

"Y-yes, sir." Bannon hesitated again, reluctant to go on
despite Magruder's admonition. "Ah . . . well, sir, the
fact is, I've been thinking about what I should do. The way
you told me to the other day."

Magruder looked blank for a moment, then seemed to
remember the conversation that had started on the hangar
deck. "If you'd rather not stay stuck on the staff, I can
probably put you in a slot as Assistant LSO for the Death
Dealers. That'll free up Jeffries to fly. Talk to Owens to take
care of it." He reached for another folder.

"Uh . . . that's not it, sir," Bannon said.

The commander's frown deepened. "Look, Bannon, I
don't need this. I've got maintenance men giving me a
dozen reasons why they can't get enough planes in the air to
make this strike work, and about twenty different variable
plans to put together before we get word the Russians are
moving. So spit out whatever it is you want and then get the
hell out of here!"

"Yessir!" he responded automatically. There was nothing left now but to take the final plunge. "Commander, I
want you to restore me to flight status. I want to fly the
strike when it goes in."

Magruder leaned back in his chair and studied him
through narrowed eyes. The scrutiny made Bannon feel
uncomfortable, and he had to fight to keep from fidgeting.
"Are you sure, Lieutenant?" The tone suggested that
Magruder was anything *but* sure of Bannon's competence.

"Yes, sir," he said again. "I've given it a lot of thought." It had kept him awake nights, until he'd finally managed to talk out his problems with one of *Jefferson*'s chaplains. Lieutenant Commander Stocker hadn't said much, but in the course of the talk Bannon had come to realize that he couldn't just give up. Nothing he could do would ever bring Commander Greene back, but Bannon owed it to Greene, and to himself, to try again. He needed the chance to prove himself once and for all . . . or die trying.

Magruder kept studying him for a long moment, and Bannon shifted uneasily. "I can do the job, Commander," he said. "I know I can."

"You sound sure of yourself," Magruder said quietly. His hand absently picked one of Stramaglia's cigars out of the mug. He toyed with it for a second without even seeming aware of what he was doing. Then he went on. "But I wonder if you're that confident on the inside."

He started to make a glib reply, then hesitated. "No sir," he admitted at last. "I'm not. But it's something I have to do. Please don't refuse this, Commander. It's important."

There was another long silence. Then Magruder nodded suddenly. "All right, Bannon," he said. "Lord knows we need every pilot we can get for this. Keeping the strike ready to launch is going to be hard on everybody, and the more spare officers I've got on tap the better prepared we'll be." He pointed the cigar straight at Bannon's chest, a gesture that reminded him of the old CAG. "Just don't screw this up, Bannon. If you can't pull your weight, don't drag the rest of your buddies down. You understand me?"

"Yes, sir."

"Tell Owens you're back on the roster and report to your CO. Dismissed."

Bannon's mind was a battlefield of conflicting emotions as he left the office. He knew he had made the right decision, the *only* decision . . . but Magruder's words had reinforced his own doubts and fears. If he lost it up there, would he end up killing another of his shipmates?

2318 hours Zulu (2318 hours Zone)
CAG office, O–3 Deck, U.S.S. *Thomas Jefferson*
In the Norwegian Sea

Tombstone Magruder leaned back in his chair and looked up at the overhead, rubbing his eyes. He had snatched a few hours' fitful sleep, but now he was back at his desk grappling with the details of the proposed Alpha Strike.

As a squadron CO he'd faced his share of paperwork, but somehow the magnitude of the burden of running a full air wing had never hit him until he had to do it himself. In the movies, the carrier pilots just climbed into their cockpits and went off to do battle with the enemy. But in real life, there was a lot going on behind the scenes to make that possible. CAG had to work out battle plans with the admiral, with Captain Brandt, and with each individual squadron commander. He had to coordinate activities with the Air Boss and S-6 Division and half a dozen other individuals and groups, and any one of them could throw a monkey wrench into a complex plan. He'd learned *that* lesson after Maintenance had written up down gripes on two Hornets and thrown his entire carefully prepared launch schedule out the window.

He was beginning to understand something that had puzzled him. It was no wonder Stramaglia had been so eager to go up with Coyote on that last mission. CAG had always been an aviator before all else, and it must have been galling to be chained to this desk trying to coordinate the activities of the entire air wing without going crazy. It made those hated days in Magruder's Pentagon assignment look like a quiet vacation.

But it was finally starting to come together. From the moment Admiral Tarrant had changed his mind and decided to proceed with the mission, the Air Wing staff had plunged into the preparations with a dedication that made Magruder proud to be a part of it all. If and when the Intelligence types spotted the opening they needed, CVW-20 would be ready for it. It would still be dicey trying to strike a blow against the Russians with their overwhelming air power, but at least now they could do something. At least *Jefferson* wouldn't be slinking away with her tail between her legs, defeated. It was a chance, no more, but a chance was all anyone could ask in a situation like this.

In the meeting with Tarrant the day before, after Magruder explained his new idea for evening the odds, the admiral had given Magruder the credit for that chance. *I would never have thought of the S-3s for this,* Tarrant had said. *Back in my day they weren't fitted for this kind of op. If we win this, it'll be because of you and your sleight of hand, Commander.* Flattering words for someone who had been thrust into the CAG slot without warning and without adequate preparation.

He hadn't protested at the time, but Magruder knew that the credit for any success they earned now should still go to Joseph Stramaglia. He had been fine-tuning the Air Wing long before Magruder had arrived, and it was his staff—Lee and Owens and others—who were performing miracles to organize the operation. And Stramaglia had insisted on broadening Magruder's own experience when Tombstone had wanted nothing more than a chance to cling to the past in the cockpit of a Tomcat. That more than anything else was what had earned *Jefferson* her chance at striking back.

A knock on his door brought Magruder out of his reverie. At his call it opened to admit Lieutenant Commander Owens, his young, eager features little changed by the hard work he'd been putting in all day. The young officer had developed an overprotective attitude toward his new superior, and seemed unduly worried at the pace Magruder was trying to maintain, but he was a rock when it came to the administrative details. If Owens had been a little better used to taking responsibility and making tough decisions, he would have made a better CAG than Magruder.

Not that the tough decisions came any more easily to Magruder. It had taken every ounce of self-control to contemplate the possible results of the Alpha Strike without breaking down entirely. When young Bannon had requested the chance to go back on the roster, it had required a real effort to keep from giving in to his urge to keep the kid out of combat for his own good. And Coyote's decision to return to duty had been even harder on him, despite their strained relations. Too many friends were at risk in this whole operation, and Magruder had to live with the knowledge that it had been his crazy idea, in Tarrant's eager hands, which had put them all on a collision course with battle.

"Sir . . ." Owens began breathlessly. "Sir, it's going down. OZ has been tapping into real-time satellite data, and it looks like they're on the move out of Murmansk."

That made him sit up straight. It was the moment they'd been waiting for, when the Soviets finally committed themselves. The next few hours would tell them where the Russians were going and whether or not *Jefferson* had a hope of intervening.

They were as ready now as they would ever be. Magruder could only hope and pray that they were ready enough for what lay ahead.

CHAPTER 22
Sunday, 15 June 1997

CVIC was crowded, more crowded than the briefing Tombstone had attended with Stramaglia the day after he'd arrived aboard. Was it really less than a week ago?

That briefing had been for ship commanders and other senior officers of the battle group, and it had mostly dealt in generalities. Tonight, by contrast, only *Jefferson* officers were in attendance, most of them squadron COs and XOs from the Air Wing. And tonight's session was focusing on concrete plans to deal with the unfolding situation on the Norwegian coast.

Magruder had never been much of a public speaker, but Tarrant had turned the bulk of the meeting over to him so that he could explain the attack plan, code-named Operation Ragnarok, step by step. Watching the reactions of the men who would be executing the operation, Tombstone had started worrying all over again. It was clear that most of them were dubious about the strike. But it was too late now for changes. He had done the best he could in putting together the plan. It was up to these men to take the ball and run with it.

"That wraps up the highlights of the mission profile," he said as his presentation was winding down. "There are more details in your folders. Familiarize yourself with the operation and then pass on the info to your squadrons."

He paused and looked around the room again. Admiral Tarrant and his staff were near the front, along with Brandt and his Exec. Their expressions were somber, but receptive enough. Commander Monroe, the Air Boss, seemed cheerful enough, a study in contrasts with the officers representing other parts of the carrier's Air Department. Getting the percentage of aircraft rated FMC—Fully Mission Capable—to a level that would support Ragnarok's tough requirements had taken everything from cajoling to threats to bribes, and most of those officers were less than happy with the pressure Magruder had been bringing to bear ever since the admiral had authorized the strike.

But it was the squadron commanders and their executive officers who counted most. Commander Quinn of VA-89 looked especially grim. In *Jefferson*'s last cruise two full squadrons of Intruders had been deployed on the carrier, but budget cutting had reduced CVW-20 back to the old mid-Eighties organization of one attack squadron. They would be regretting that change in the hours ahead.

The skippers and execs from the two Hornet squadrons formed a tight-knit group. They looked reasonably happy with their roles in the coming mission, taking their cue perhaps from Bobby Lee Benton of the Javelins. His opposite number in VFA-173, the Fighting Hornets, was a craggy-faced lump of a man, Commander Henry "Bigfoot" Henderson, and while Henderson wasn't as flashy and charismatic as Benton he had a reputation for steady reliability. He'd need it, given the part of the mission Magruder had assigned him to.

Magruder cleared his throat before continuing. "Now for some updates we didn't have time to include in the formal briefing material," he said. "Starting just before midnight Zulu time last night, the Russians launched the paradrop we've been expecting. Actually it was a series of drops, but satellite recon has discounted most of their operations as decoy deployments to distract the defense. The main enemy landing area is around the port town of Brekke, about halfway up the Sognefjord and maybe eighty kilometers as the MiG flies from Bergen. That conforms with the best estimates Intelligence made originally when we were mapping out our strategy. The location doesn't change the basic mission profile at all."

Magruder looked down at the lectern, checking the hastily scrawled notes he'd made of Lee's latest findings. "The Russians have also launched a general offensive all along the line to pin the Royal Norwegian Army while they bring in their amphibious troops to support the Brekke paradrop. Our last contact with General Lindstrom brought word that he had only enough reserves to contain what was on the ground already. He doesn't think they have much hope of holding against a larger force with the resources he's got on hand. So if those transports get through Bergen will fall. That's all there is to it."

Commander Harrison held up a hand. "What about the Norwegian air force? Where are they while we're sticking our necks into the noose?" Harrison hadn't liked any aspect of Magruder's plan, and he wasn't making any effort to hide his feelings.

"Every bird Lindstrom can spare is starting on cyclic ops on the southeastern end of the front," Magruder told him. "This was at our suggestion. By mounting a serious threat to the Russians in Oslo, we're hoping to draw off a large chunk of their air force until our strike is finished. We're also hoping this will encourage the Russians to believe that we've fallen for some of their decoy operations down in that neighborhood. We *want* those transports to keep moving toward Brekke. It's the one chance we have to nail them."

Harrison looked unhappy. "You won't sucker all of them that way, Commander," he said.

"No, we won't. But in conjunction with the other phases of Ragnarok we should be able to neutralize most of them." He glanced at his watch. "*Galveston* and *Bangor* should be starting their end of the process pretty soon now. It's going to take a lot of little pieces fitting together."

"I've got a question, Stoney," Batman said. He and Coyote were sitting side by side near the back of the room. "Looks to me like you're counting pretty heavy on getting some of our planes in using nothing but low altitude, jamming, and a couple of Hail Marys. I thought those new AEW planes of theirs were supposed to be almost as good as the Hawkeyes."

"Yeah." Magruder frowned. It was probably the weakest part of Ragnarok, but with his resources already stretched to the limit he didn't see any way to deal with the Russian An-74 that was sure to be monitoring the battlefield from a secure location far from the front lines. "Yeah, that about sums it up. If anybody has any ideas, toss them in."

Coyote looked up, his eyes meeting Magruder's across the long room. "There's something we could do. But it means thinning down the carrier defenses a little bit."

That made Magruder frown again. Then he shrugged. "Like I said, let's hear it." He didn't like any suggestion of leaving *Jefferson* exposed to the enemy . . . but on the other hand, in a gambler's last throw like this one, it might just be worth the risk if they could increase the chances of the rest of the plan falling into place.

2108 hours Zulu (2108 hours Zone)
Control room, U.S.S. *Galveston*
Fifty miles Northwest of Trondheim, Norway

Commander Mark Colby stretched his long legs under the chart table and listened to the low voices of the men manning *Galveston*'s control room stations. He was tall for a submariner, and was developing a perpetual stoop from the cramped conditions he had to endure as part of the Silent Service.

Sometimes Colby thought he had been born into the wrong era. He would have felt at home commanding one of the old-time frigates in the age of Jones or Preble, pacing the quarterdeck and feeling the wind on his cheek as his command maneuvered under full sail to close the range with her quarry and unleash the fury of her broadside.

But there wasn't room to pace the confines of an attack sub's control room, so Colby had to be content with sitting still and listening to terse reports and his Exec's crisp, precise orders.

Still, *Galveston* had one thing in common with the frigates of Colby's idle daydreams. When she had closed to the appropriate range, she could let loose a devastating broadside of her own.

In this case, the broadside would take the form of six Tomahawk TLAM missiles, each carrying a warhead more with more sheer destructive power than a whole fleet of vessels from the days of wooden ships and iron men. The Tomahawk cruise missile had proven itself in the Gulf War, forming a powerful part of the initial bombardment that had opened the air war against Iraq. While tonight's attack would be nothing near the scope of that assault, flights of the deadly missiles from *Galveston* and her sister ship

Bangor would surely disrupt their target and cause plenty of damage to keep the Russians occupied while Admiral Tarrant launched the main attack of Operation Ragnarok.

When the orders had first come in from the admiral, tight-beamed and bounced off a passing satellite to reduce the chance the subs would be detected, Colby had been disappointed that *Galveston*'s role was essentially diversionary. She carried cruise missiles for antiship attacks as well as the TLAMs, after all. But on careful consideration he had finally decided the admiral was right. The Soviets possessed both ASW and antiair abilities that would have sharply curtailed a sub-launched attack. *Galveston* wouldn't have been able to get in close enough to launch a short-range sneak attack, but a missile launch from longer range would have run into the antimissile defenses of the Soviet ships escorting the critical troop transports. *Galveston* just didn't have enough missiles to saturate those defenses . . . the whole carrier battle group probably couldn't have done that, even with the missile capacity of the Aegis cruiser.

In a situation like this, even the smart weapons of modern high-tech warfare couldn't match the smartest weapon of them all—the pilot in the cockpit of an attack airplane. That was the weapon best suited for penetrating the enemy defenses in this conflict.

Lieutenant Commander Richard Damien looked across the chart table at him. "Time, Skipper," he said. "All tubes loaded and ready."

"What about our friends?" Colby asked.

Damien frowned. "Still at the edge of detection range. I think we can outrun them if we have to."

For several hours they'd been dodging a Russian squadron working up and down the Norwegian coast, apparently searching close in to shore for submarine activity. No doubt the Norwegian navy had been giving the Soviets headaches by slipping some of their small conventionally powered coastal subs in behind the Russian fleet to play havoc with supply ships. If Colby had been free to choose the time for the launch, he would have waited to see if the Soviets moved further off, but the admiral's timetable was tight. "Fire all," he said softly.

"Fire all! Fire all!" Damien called, and the bridge talker took up the chant and relayed the message to the weapons officer. Seconds later the submarine shuddered as the Tomahawk missiles left her torpedo tubes in quick succession.

"Come to course two-one-five," Colby went on. "Make her depth two hundred feet, and go to maximum revs."

As *Galveston* started her turn, the missiles broke the surface above her, and leapt skyward with their rocket motors lighting up the long, dim twilight of the north. On-board guidance systems kicked in, unfolding electronic maps of their targets and aligning the hurtling missiles toward their destinations. The missiles skimmed in low over the water.

At the air base at Orland, klaxons sounded the alarm as radar picked up the incoming missiles, and Soviet troops poured from their barracks buildings to take up their defense stations. One SAM battery managed to get off a pair of missiles despite the surprise, and these accounted for one of the six incoming Tomahawks. But the remaining five came on, arcing gracefully toward the base. Their impact turned the quiet Norwegian landscape into a scene from Hell.

The first to hit tore into a tank farm on the edge of the base, raising a pillar of flame that outshone the sun. The explosion broke windows for miles around and echoed off the mountains like summer thunder, reverberating over the embattled installation. Another missile hit close by the base control tower, while the other three fell on a hangar and a pair of runways. The Russians running for their stations scattered under the rain of destruction.

A few seconds later the six missiles launched from *Bangor* slammed into Orland, completing the devastation.

Orland burned.

2120 hours Zulu (2120 hours Zone)
Control room, U.S.S. *Bangor*
Northwest of Trondheim, Norway

"Conn, sonar. Reading a target, bearing one-seven-nine degrees, closing."

Commander Jason Wolfe rubbed the bridge of his nose and looked across the plotting table at his Executive Officer. "Looks like they're on to us, Tom," he said. "Let's hope all they've got is second-line crap."

"Better not count on it, Skipper," Lieutenant Commander Tom Guzman replied. His shrug was eloquent. "Nobody ever won a war on wishes."

The Exec made good sense, of course, but his bland comment still irritated Wolfe. The Russian ships had doubled back unexpectedly just as *Bangor* had launched her flight of Tomahawks. Now they knew the American sub was nearby, and the hunt was on.

"Helm!" he snapped. "Make your heading three-five-four. Ahead slow. Diving Officer, fifteen degrees down angle on the planes. Make your depth two-zero-zero."

"Aye, aye, sir," men responded crisply from around the control room.

"Conn, sonar," Lieutenant Wells, the Sonar Officer, sounded worried even over the tannoy.

Wolfe picked up the handset. "What've you got, Lieutenant?"

"Captain, we've got IDs on their lead ships. They've got

at least two Krivak II ASW frigates up there, and a Kresta II backing them up. We've definitely spotted the *Kronstadt,* but we're not sure about the others yet. Not exactly the best reception committee, sir.''

"Yeah.'' Wolfe licked lips gone suddenly dry. "Keep me informed as you get more—''

Before he could say anything further the hull seemed to shake with multiple sonar pings, a noise like a jangling of mismatched church bells.

"Christ, Skipper!'' Wells swore. "They've gone active!''

Wolfe slammed down the handset without answering. "Give us flank speed!'' he shouted.

The pings continued in an almost steady stream. The Soviets were hammering at the depths with everything they had. At this range, they were surely picking up *Bangor* clearly.

"More active sonars ahead, sir!'' This shout came from the Sonarman Second Class manning the control room's sonar repeater. "Looks like they're dropping sonobuoys ahead of us!'' There was a pause. "Fish in the water! Torp! Torp! Torp!''

"Ready countermeasures,'' Wolfe snapped. He snatched up the handset again. "Sonar, conn. Talk to me, Wells!''

"Torpedo bearing zero-three-two, range three thousand, speed four-eight knots, closing. It's pinging us!''

"Helm, come to zero-three-two,'' Wolfe ordered. That was the risky way to deal with torps, turn into them and pray you could dodge your way past.

"Range twenty-five hundred, closing,'' Wells reported. Then, all too soon, "Range two thousand, closing.''

"Decoy! Fire a decoy!'' There wasn't much else they could do.

"Range fifteen hundred . . . fourteen hundred . . . thirteen hundred . . .'' The chant was a litany of doom.

Wolfe licked his lips again. He'd never really believed he'd face a situation like this, a real combat scenario. But it was happening. In the next few seconds *Bangor* and her crew of 134 officers and enlisted men would live or die according to the decisions he made.

"One thousand . . . nine hundred . . . eight hundred."

"Take her down, Mr. Kyle," Wolfe ordered. "Helm, come to three-five-five. Engine room, crank up the revs as far as they'll go. Let off some more countermeasures as she turns. Go!"

It was as if he could feel *Bangor* twisting and turning in the water trying to escape the deadly torpedo. Wolfe grabbed a stanchion as the sub angled down and tilted sharply to port. He thought he heard Guzman saying a prayer under his breath, and wanted to add one of his own.

The sound of the torpedo's screw as it raced past the *Bangor* was loud, louder even than the continued sonar pinging from the Soviet ships above. "Yes!" someone shouted as the torp passed them by, the propeller noise fading away.

"Change in aspect," Wells reported over the tannoy. "It's turning . . . turning . . . I think it's locking onto the noisemakers . . ."

The sub was leveling now, and Wolfe thought about breathing a sigh of relief. But it was too soon for that.

Shock waves slammed into the stern of the boat, shaking *Bangor*. Wolfe gripped the stanchion for balance, but Guzman wasn't so lucky. The Exec staggered sideways and barely stayed upright. "One torp down," he said, looking pale. Before he could go on he was interrupted.

"Torp in the water! Torp! Bearing zero-one-three!" the control room sonarman said breathlessly. There was a pause. "Two . . . three . . . Three torps, same bearing! Goddamn! These bastards mean business!"

Jason Wolfe closed his eyes. This time he did pray.

"Twenty meters," the diving officer announced. "And eighteen . . . fifteen . . ."

"More torps! More torps! Bearing two-one-six! Closing!"

This time the torpedoes did not miss.

The first one smashed squarely into the submarine's bow, shattering the radar and sonar housings and flooding the forward torpedo room. Emergency klaxons blared warning, sailors scrambled for safety behind watertight doors, and the sub's Diving Officer struggled to maintain trim.

In the midst of the desperate fight for survival the second torpedo struck home amidships, just below the sail. Water flooded the control room, sweeping Lieutenant Commander Tomas Guzman against a bulkhead with enough force to cave in his skull. Somehow Wolfe managed to stay on his feet through the torrent, but in the end it didn't matter.

By the time the third torp hit, *Bangor* was already on her way to the bottom. Her shattered hulk settled in the cold, shallow waters.

2338 hours Zulu (2338 hours Zone)
Tomcat 204, Odin Flight
Five miles south of U.S.S. *Thomas Jefferson*

Batman Wayne checked his instruments anxiously for what must have been the tenth time since his Tomcat had topped off its tanks from an orbiting Texaco. This was the part of an Alpha Strike that always frayed most at his nerves. It wasn't the battle, or even the approach to battle, that got to him, but the long wait for the diverse elements of the attacking forces to get aloft and assemble.

He was eager to get on with it, but at that same time he recognized that this time out they were facing a top-of-the-line opponent. Viper Squadron had been mauled by the Russians last time, and any desire to even the score was counterbalanced by the knowledge that none of them might be as lucky the second time around as they'd been the day CAG bought it.

"Two-oh-four, Two-oh-three," Coyote's voice said over the radio. Grant was flying Tomcat 203, since his regular plane was now at the bottom of the Atlantic. "Double-check your Phoenixes, Batman."

"Roger," he acknowledged. Coyote was obviously worried. The Phoenix missiles would be critical to Viper Squadron's mission, but it wouldn't help to check them again now. They weren't in a position to ask a red shirt to take care of a problem.

Then he chuckled. Grant's request wasn't that much different from Batman's constant double-checking of his own instruments.

He hadn't really expected Coyote to fly this one. He should have stayed in Sick Bay. But Batman was glad he'd decided to fly. Thanks to Coyote the Vipers weren't going to be relegated to BARCAP after all. Instead they had a key role to play in the attack. And anyway, Wayne told himself, it was bad enough to face the biggest Alpha Strike of his career without being saddled with a squadron CO's extra duties as well.

At least they were both better off than Tombstone. Magruder had put in long hours ever since CAG's death, and he was still stuck on board the carrier coordinating the operation from CIC. Knowing Tombstone, Batman knew he'd be fretting, wishing he was in a Tomcat flying alongside the Vipers. This would be a tough mission, and Batman would have been happier himself if Tombstone had come along.

"What do you think, Mal?" Batman asked over the ICS. "Think we can pull this one off?"

"If we can't, nobody can, compadre," Malibu answered, sounding cheerful enough.

"Odin Flight, Odin Flight," Magruder's voice broke in. "This is Asgard. Operation Ragnarok, go for Phase One. Repeat, go for Phase One."

"That's us!" Batman said. His hand closed around the throttles and advanced them into zone-one afterburner. Banking sharply, he steered the Tomcat north.

Behind him, twenty-four more planes followed, the first wave of the attack that would determine if Bergen stood or fell.

2345 hours Zulu (2345 hours Zone)
Flag Plot, Soviet Aircraft Carrier *Soyuz*
In the Norwegian Sea

"Yes, Admiral, I am certain. The AEW aircraft has counted a minimum of twenty-five enemy planes heading directly for *Soyuz*. There can be no doubt this time."

Admiral Khenkin listened to Glushko's anxious voice and studied the tracking data being relayed from the An-74 to his own plotting board. This time Glushko didn't seem to be exaggerating. "Very well, Glushko. Get as many planes off the deck as possible to assist in the defense."

"You know that the MiG squadron on deck has been arming for ground-support operations, Admiral," Glushko pointed out. "They will not be useful for dogfighting."

"Get them off the deck anyway," Khenkin snapped. He had studied the disastrous mistakes of the Japanese carriers in the Great Patriotic War, caught all too often with planes on deck loaded with ordnance when American air strikes hit. He wouldn't allow that to happen today.

"Yes, Admiral," Glushko said. "But that still leaves us weakened against the enemy attack. I request permission to recall Escort Mission Osa." That was Sergei Sergeivich Terekhov's MiG squadron, currently sharing escort duties over the invasion fleet hugging the Norwegian coast, about three hundred kilometers to the east.

Khenkin bit his lip, thinking. Glushko had foolishly allowed an imaginary threat to the carrier to distract an entire squadron during the last fight with the Americans, and though neither Glushko nor Terekhov had raised the point, Khenkin knew the victory had been less than complete as a result. But this time was different. This time the American target was clear. And they could guard against additional American attacks easily enough. *Soyuz* was closer to the invasion fleet than the Americans, and her jets could make it back to the fleet any time a threat materialized.

It was odd, he thought idly, that the Americans had chosen to launch their strike on the carrier rather than trying to interfere with the transports. Had they been taken in by the *maskirovka* then? It certainly appeared that the Norwegians believed the token paratroop landings southeast of Bergen were the real threat. Perhaps the Americans agreed, and discounted the risk of a landing.

Or maybe they saw an attack on the Soviet carrier as somehow symbolic. They could do little enough damage in any event except by the greatest possible good fortune. Striking out at Red Banner Northern Fleet's flagship might be perceived as a dramatic gesture demonstrating American courage or determination in the wake of the defeats they had already suffered.

"All right, Glusko," he said at last. "Recall Escort Mission Osa, but wait until the Americans are thoroughly committed. Understood?"

''Yes, Admiral,'' Glushko responded.

Khenkin looked at the plotting board again and smiled. As long as the Americans were ignoring the transports, they were only compounding their earlier mistakes.

CHAPTER 23
Monday, 16 June 1997

0004 hours Zulu (0004 hours Zone)
Fulcrum Leader, Escort Mission *Osa*
Off Bremenger Island, Norway

Sergei Sergeivich Terekhov scanned the waters below, his heart swelling with pride at the sight of the ships of the invasion force keeping tight formation as they rounded Cape Bremenger on the last leg of the journey south. Soon the landings would be accomplished, and the drive on Bergen would begin. Then this war would be over, and the new Soviet Union could take its place again as a superpower, able to dictate terms to a weak-willed world and restore her broken economy and political structure once and for all.

All it would take was one more success, and after the defeat of the Americans in Iceland and in the ambush over the Norwegian Sea this last success would be easy enough to obtain.

The Russians had kept an eye on the progress of the American carrier, of course, tracking the ships and planes from the An-74 AEW plane over the *Soyuz* battle group. The Americans had hung about at the fringe of the exclusion zone for three days, seemingly unable to depart and unwilling to advance. Terekhov had advocated launching a strike on the battle group early on, but orders from Moscow had required *Soyuz* to concentrate on preparing the battlefield south of the Sognefjord instead. When the Americans had started trying to jam Soviet radar and radio signals, there had been some concern, but the jamming effort had been clumsy at best. As long as the An-74 stayed on the job, there was little danger of an American surprise attack even if they were in any shape to launch one.

So one squadron of fighters at a time shared the duty of combat air patrol over the invasion fleet with a squadron of land-based MiGs out of Orland, while another of the carrier's squadrons remained on standby to protect *Soyuz,* just in case. The other two were currently on the flight deck, where busy technicians were prepping them for action to support the landings in the morning. All four had been brought up to full strength the day before by replacements out of Murmansk and Archangel.

"*Osa, Osa,* this is *Gnyezdo.*" Glushko's voice snapped him out of his reverie. "You are ordered to return here at once. Repeat, return at once."

What was the air wing commander playing at this time? Terekhov keyed in his transmitter and gave a curt reply. "*Gnyezdo, Osa.* Request clarification."

"American aircraft have been detected approaching *Soyuz.* ETA now three minutes. Your squadron is needed to reinforce the defense. The admiral has ordered it. Comply immediately."

Terekhov cursed under his breath. He wasn't sure if he hoped this was another of Glushko's paranoid delusions or not. If it wasn't, the Americans would regret falling in with Terekhov's squadron a second time. "Acknowledged, *Gnyezdo.* On our way."

Terekhov shifted uneasily in his seat and changed frequencies to report to the other escort commander. Just when everything had looked so right . . .

0006 hours Zulu (0006 hours Zone)
Tomcat 203, Odin Flight
Over the Norwegian Sea

"They're painting us six ways from Sunday, Skipper. They've got so much radar coverage out there we're likely to end up looking like a microwave dinner."

Coyote smiled under his mask at John-Boy's hyperbole, but he knew how the RIO felt. Flying exposed like this, clearly in view for the entire approach to the target, went against every instinct he had. The fact that the Prowler accompanying the attack was deliberately keeping its jamming selective and largely ineffective was no comfort either. He hoped they would be able to switch over to a more useful mode when the time came for action.

"Don't sweat it, John-Boy. But keep your eye on that scope. If they start shooting, I want to know about it."

"Trust me, Skipper, you'll know. They'll know back on the *Jeff*. Maybe back in Washington if I scream loud enough and the wind's right."

"Odin Leader, this is Asgard." That was Magruder calling. He sounded tense. Was he still reacting to the pressures on him because of his new position, or was he worried over the fate of the Vipers? Coyote suspected that he'd been unhappy at the thought of sending his old squadron into the killing ground understrength, but it was the only division of responsibility that made sense. The special operation Coyote had proposed wouldn't take a full Tomcat squadron . . . but BARCAP over the *Jefferson* absolutely demanded one. That made the choice for this phase of the operation inevitable. "Status?"

Coyote's reply was curt. "Unchanged." He paused, then continued. "Still nothing from the bad guys. Looks like they've pulled in their horns and plan to defend right over their battle group.''

"Makes sense," Magruder said. "The closer in you get, the more of a target you make for ship-launched SAMs. As long as they're confident of taking out anything you throw at them from long range, they're sitting pretty."

"Yeah." Grant didn't find the words encouraging. He hesitated before going on. "Look, Stoney . . . I let a lot of petty shit make me crazy. If I don't come back . . ."

"You'll be back, Coyote," Magruder interrupted. "You're indestructible."

"If I don't come back, just know I still think you're the best. And I think you're going to make a pretty good CAG someday too."

Magruder didn't respond for a long moment, and when he did his tone had changed. "Tango Six-fiver just spotted a squadron heading your way from the invasion fleet," he said. "Time to turn out the lights out there, Coyote. Phase Two . . . Execute."

Coyote changed radio channels. "All Odins, all Odins, this is Odin Leader. Phase Two."

"Roger that," Batman replied, and the rest of the diminished squadron, four more planes, followed suit. Coyote pulled back on his joystick and rammed his throttles forward. The Tomcats surged skyward, climbing high above the rest of the strike force and leaving them far behind.

0009 hours Zulu (0009 hours Zone)
CIC Air Ops module, U.S.S. *Thomas Jefferson*
In the Norwegian Sea

"Loki Leader, this is Asgard," Magruder said, striving for the kind of calm Stramaglia had always been able to muster. "Phase Two commences now. Start the symphony and launch your attack."

He could hardly contain his nervousness, his impatience. Magruder had never realized how hard it would be to have to sit out the fighting back in Air Ops, surrounded by constant reminders of the situation facing the men in the air but without the means to take direct action. It was a frustrating experience.

Of course, he might have gone up with one of those squadrons. Stramaglia had given in to the urge. At least he had gone out fighting.

But his new responsibilities as CAG held Magruder back. His job was now the coordination of multiple efforts, not only each of the components of the Alpha Strike but also of the Tomcats flying BARCAP over the battle group and the helos conducting ASW searches. Just as a modern general couldn't indulge in leading infantry charges in the field anymore, so he had moved beyond the realm where he could take part in an air battle in good conscience. It was too easy when you were up there to lose track of everything but your own immediate problems. Losing *Gridley* because of his impatience to deal with a different crisis altogether had shown him that much.

For now, he knew, he had to be in CIC. But knowing that simple fact didn't make the decision to stay put any easier.

"Asgard, Loki Leader," Bigfoot Henderson replied. "Acknowledged. We're going in."

0010 hours Zulu (0010 hours Zone)
Air Ops, Soviet Aircraft Carrier *Soyuz*
In the Norwegian Sea

"Captain! Enemy radar jamming has just intensified. It is as if they suddenly flipped a switch and turned up their power tenfold."

Glushko crossed to the radar technician and peered over

his shoulder at the screen, which was fuzzy with streaks and static. "Compensate!" he growled.

"Captain, I cannot," the technician protested. "Perhaps the feed from the An-74 will be better, but the equipment I have here—"

"Then patch in to the AEW," Glushko shouted. "Do it! Before they start their attack run!" They needed effective radars to track the American attack. He hoped the SAM batteries in the fleet wouldn't be too seriously hampered by this sudden change in the enemy jamming technique. If it turned out that the surface ships would not be able to bring their firepower to bear, his decision to let the Americans come all the way in would turn out to be a disaster.

The image on the main plotting board jumped and danced, then suddenly became clearer. The An-74, looking down on the battleground, was in a better position to penetrate the American jamming.

Glushko studied the board for a moment, then pointed to a pattern of dots that had broken away from the other American aircraft. "What are these?" he demanded.

An aide peered at the symbols. "American interceptors. F-14 type." He paused, looking uncertain. "They are gaining altitude and heading north, away from us." Sudden understanding flooded over his features. "Heading for the AEW plane, Comrade Captain! They carry the American Phoenix missile. The An-74 will be in their range in a matter of seconds!"

"Warn the AEW plane!" he barked. "And order our CAP to engage them. Now!"

"But that will uncover the ships, Comrade Captain."

"Do it!"

0012 hours Zulu (0012 hours Zone)
Tomcat 204, Odin Flight
Over the Norwegian Sea

"We've got company coming, Batman. Sukhois . . . looks like a whole squadron!"

"Watch them," Wayne ordered. "Two-oh-three, this is Two-oh-four. You copy, Coyote?"

"Read you. You see our new friends?"

"That's affirmative, Coyote. How you want to handle these guys?"

"Tyrone and I will stay on the target. You take the rest and keep those guys off our backs."

"Roger that, Coyote," Batman told him. "Heads up, gang. Follow me!"

He stood the Tomcat on its wing in a tight turn, banking right and shedding altitude fast. Three more F-14s followed.

"Go to Sparrows," Coyote ordered. "Save your Phoenixes until we nail the target."

"Roger," Batman said. He thumbed his selector switch to choose the medium-range radar-homing missiles. The targeting diamond bracketed a tiny dot on his HUD display and flashed red. "I'm locked on . . . taking the shot. Fox one! Fox one!"

The Sparrow roared off its launch rail.

0012 hours Zulu (0012 hours Zone)
Tomcat 204, Odin Flight
Over the Norwegian Sea

"Lock. I've got target lock. Go for it, Coyote!"

His finger tightened on the firing stud and the Phoenix spouted flame and leapt from the Tomcat's wing. At a range of ninety miles, the Antonov An-74 AEW aircraft, code-named Madcap in NATO parlance, was beyond the reach of most air-to-air missiles, but still well within the reach of Phoenix. The oversized missiles rode a semi-active radar beam to the target, switching to an active beam in the terminal approach.

Seconds passed slowly, with John-Boy reciting the distance between missile and target in the same tone he might have used to read off baseball scores.

"Twelve miles, closing . . . ten . . . eight . . . five and still closing . . . Bingo! That's a hit, by God! You nailed him, Coyote!"

"All *right*!" Grant said. The exhilaration of battle had taken hold, and suddenly there was nothing left but the Tomcat and the fight raging below them. "Tyrone, let's get into the game. Follow my lead!"

0015 hours Zulu (0015 hours Zone)
CIC Air Ops module, U.S.S. *Thomas Jefferson*
In the Norwegian Sea

"It's a hit! The Madcap's been hit!"

A cheer went up from the controllers in the Air Ops module, and Magruder found himself joining in. Coyote had managed it just as he'd promised in the briefing. Now, with their AEW plane out of action and the heavy jamming from the Prowlers, the Russians would find their command and communications seriously disrupted. And that was precisely what the American plan required to be successful.

He grasped a microphone. "Thor, Thor, this is Asgard. Commence Phase Three. Repeating, commence Phase three. Acknowledge, please."

Benton, the flamboyant Texan Hornet pilot, replied promptly, "Asgard, this is Thor, and we're on our way! Just let us at 'em!"

Magruder put the mike aside with a faint smile. All the pieces were in motion now. As long as the Hornets and Intruders of the strike group designated Loki could hold the Russians' attention for another half hour, the attack just might work out as planned.

0015 hours Zulu (0015 hours Zone)
Intruder 507, Loki Flight
Over the Norwegian Sea

"Break off, Banshee. Break off!"

Bannon cursed and obeyed the order from Commander Ralph Quinn, turning away from the Soviet battle group but keeping the Intruder right down on the deck. Ever since they had entered Harpoon range, the aircraft of Loki Flight had been skirmishing with their Russian opponents. The Hornets, armed for air-to-air operations, had seen their fair share of the action. Each time another plane rose from the Soviet carrier's deck, one of Henderson's Fighting Hornets would swoop in to engage, spreading a trail of chaff and flairs in their wakes and dodging SAM fire from the ships.

But the Intruders, so far, had spent all their time setting up attack runs that they weren't allowed to press home. It was all part of the original plan, of course, to harass the Soviets by continually threatening to attack. If they ever actually released their Harpoon missiles, the Intruders would pose no further threat, and that could undo the whole plan to draw the enemy planes away from the critical target to the east.

Knowing it was part of the plan didn't make it any easier to keep breaking off, though. Since most of the Sukhois on BARCAP had been sent after Viper Squadron, the Soviets were open to a quick stroke now. It was just possible that they might actually inflict damage on the Russian carrier, and turn the diversion into a genuine triumph.

His Bombardier/Navigator, seated beside him, was looking at Bannon with an unhappy expression. "C'mon,
Banshee," Lieutenant (j.g.) Scott Gordon protested. "Ease
up a little. You don't have to make it look so damned
realistic!"

"You want to end up on the wrong end of one of their
SAMs, Gordo?" he shot back. "You just sit and think nice
thoughts. I'll do the flying, thank you very much!"

Maybe if he'd taken that attitude with Jolly Greene right
from the start the accident might not have happened. He
should never have let the man in the B/N position rattle him,
no matter how big a hero he was or how important his
position aboard *Jefferson* had been. There was only room
for one pilot in an attack plane.

"Okay, Death Dealers, circle back for another run,"
Quinn ordered. "Let's see if we can get close enough this
time to smell the borscht!"

Smiling for the first time in days, Banshee Bannon swung
his Intruder into formation and started plotting his next run.

0015 hours Zulu (0015 hours Zone)
Tomcat 203, Odin Flight
Over the Norwegian Sea

"Talk to me, John-Boy," Coyote said. "Find me a play-
mate."

"Bearing zero-four-two," the RIO replied laconically.
"He's closing fast."

Coyote banked right and thumbed his selector switch to
the Sparrow setting. The targeting reticule flashed almost
immediately, and he opened fire. "Fox one! Fox one!"

The missile lanced toward the target, but veered off
suddenly and dropped toward the ocean below. The AIM-7
Sparrow was probably the least reliable weapon in the naval

aviator's arsenal, which was one reason why they were generally unloaded earlier in a dogfight. Their weight was another factor, since a Tomcat without Sparrows slung under the wings performed slightly better in tight maneuvers. That didn't count today, though. He still had a Phoenix, and those were a lot bulkier and heavier than a Sparrow.

"Coyote! Watch your six!" John-Boy warned.

He twisted to look over his shoulder and saw the Sukhoi dropping into place behind his tail. "Damn," he swore, throwing the Tomcat into a sharp turn. His adversary clung to him, and Coyote swore again.

"Tyrone! Tyrone! Get this bastard off me!"

The threat alert screamed a warning as the enemy targeting radar locked on.

0016 hours Zulu (0016 hours Zone)
Tomcat 211, Odin Flight
Over the Norwegian Sea

"On my way!" Powers said, wrenching his joystick forward and to the left with a violent motion. He had let himself get distracted by a pair of Sukhois weaving a complex pattern around Sheridan's Tomcat, and he wasn't in the best position to save his wingman.

"Whoa, there, Tyrone!" Ears Cavanaugh protested. "Pass the Dramamine, for God's sake!"

Powers ignored him as the Tomcat dropped like a stone toward the dueling planes. He rammed the throttles full forward and rolled to the right. The acceleration pressed him back into his seat, blurring his vision.

The two planes flashed on either side of the cockpit as he plunged between them.

0016 hours Zulu (0016 hours Zone)
Tomcat 203, Odin Flight
Over the Norwegian Sea

''Good God!'' Coyote exclaimed. ''What the hell was that, Tyrone?''

The other Tomcat had flashed past almost faster than Coyote could react, right through the gap between pursued and pursuer. The sudden appearance of Tyrone's plane must have startled the Russian pilot even more. The Sukhoi rolled left, losing its radar lock as he tried to dodge the crazy American.

Coyote banked sharply, trying to turn and line up a quick shot on the enemy plane. But by the time he finished the maneuver the Sukhoi was already chasing new prey.

It was Powers.

The Tomcat juked and weaved like a mad thing, but the Soviet pilot matched Powers move for move. ''I can't shake him! I can't shake him!'' the young lieutenant was shouting.

Coyote switched to Sidewinders and accelerated. It seemed to take forever to get the tone in his earphones that announced a lock-on. Finally he heard it, and his finger tightened convulsively. ''Fox two! Fox two!'' he called. ''Hang in there, kid. You can—''

At that moment a missile jumped from the Russian's wing. Tomcat and Sukhoi exploded at almost the same instant.

"Khrahneetyehly, Khrahneetyehly, this is *Osa. Guardian,* this is Wasp. Do you copy?" Terekhov bit off a curse. What was happening? The An-74 wasn't responding to his calls, and radio communications in general were suffering from heavy jamming.

"Osa, Gnyezdo." Glushko was hard to make out against the interference. *"Guardian* is out of action. The Americans shot it down. What is your ETA?"

Terekhov didn't respond. Pieces of a puzzle were falling into place. The Americans had launched their attack without taking even the most basic precautions against detection, flying with their Electronic Warfare aircraft hardly functioning and not even taking advantage of radar distortion at low altitudes. They had *wanted* their approach to be detected.

And now they no longer wanted the Soviets to track them. Otherwise why waste time pursuing the An-74 when there were many more valuable targets available? And their jamming was suddenly more efficient.

An observant American would have noted Glushko's caution in covering *Soyuz* from attack. Would the enemy feint toward the carrier as a prelude to striking the amphibious force?

"Wasp, Wasp, this is Nest," Glushko said urgently. "Wasp, what is your ETA? The American bombers are not pressing their attack yet, and we can crush them if you can just get here and join the fighting."

The American bombers were not pressing their attack . . .

"Wasp Flight, this is Wasp Leader," Terekhov said

crisply. "The attack on *Soyuz* is a fake. The real attack will be against the invasion fleet. We will return there."

Banking sharply, Terekhov set his new course. The diversion had very nearly worked. But he still had time to get back and join the land-based planes in defending the transports.

Glushko would demand his head for this disobedience, but that didn't matter any more. Terekhov knew right from wrong, knew what he had to do to save the campaign in the face of the American trickery.

0019 hours Zulu (0019 hours Zone)
CIC Air Ops module, U.S.S. *Thomas Jefferson*
In the Norwegian Sea

"No doubt about it, Commander," Owens said glumly, pointing to the plotting board. "Those Russkie bastards have turned around. They didn't take the bait after all."

Magruder stared at the flashing symbols, a sinking feeling taking hold of his guts. This had always been possible, of course. But the Russians had seemed to fall for the trap. This sudden change of course could only mean that some Russian squadron leader was showing an unaccustomed amount of individual initiative. He should have expected something like that after seeing the reports on the well-conceived operation that had nearly wiped out the Vipers. There was at least one Russian out there who was too smart to be taken in.

It was down to a simple matter of mathematics. Strike Group Thor, heading for the invasion fleet, was slow, too slow. The MiGs had double their effective speed, and a lot less distance to travel to get back into position over their transports. And the planes in Thor wouldn't be able to make much of a showing against determined opposition. True, the

Hornets carried some air-to-air weaponry. The plan had called for each to release a Harpoon before closing in to deal with the reduced escorting aircraft. But they would be hard-pressed to outfight two full squadrons, both dedicated entirely to air-to-air operations. And the other planes in Thor had never been designed with dogfighting in mind.

There were no options left. They had to call off the attack, or watch twenty American planes go down in defeat to no good purpose.

With one daring move, that unknown Russian pilot had just saved his fleet and condemned the Americans to stand by and watch helplessly as Bergen fell and freedom was extinguished in Norway.

CHAPTER 24
Monday, 16 June 1997

0020 hours Zulu (0020 hours Zone)
CIC Air Ops module, U.S.S. *Thomas Jefferson*
In the Norwegian Sea

Magruder reached for the microphone, feeling dead inside.
They had come so close . . .

"Asgard, Asgard, this is Odin," Coyote's voice boomed
from the speaker. "The Sukhois are on the run! I think
they've had enough. Request instructions, over."

Tombstone swallowed and studied the plotting board again.
There was still a chance to stop those Russians . . . but only
if the Vipers could get to them in time. If only he had gone up
with them. He knew that he and Batman could have done it,
just like at Wonsan and in the last wild fight of the Indian
Ocean intervention . . .

He shook his head. He didn't have to be up there. Coyote
and Batman were two of the best, and the rest of the Vipers
were as good as he had been three years back. It was time
he realized that the torch had been passed on.

Magruder's fingers closed around the mike and he spoke
with sudden animation and urgency. "Odin, this is Asgard.
New orders. Proceed toward Target Thor, repeat Target
Thor. Use any means available to support Thor Strike
against enemy aircraft. Do you copy, Odin?"

"Odin copies," Coyote came back, sounding cool and calm, more like his old self than he'd been for a long time now. "We're on our way, Stoney!"

He bit his lip, deep in thought. It was an unplanned diversion of the Tomcats, and that could play havoc with the logistical side of the operation. The Vipers were as fast as the enemy MiGs, so they should be able to close the range before Thor Group arrived on the scene. But by the time they finished those F-14s would be flying on fumes. He would have to send a Texaco to rendezvous with them.

There was something else he could do too to turn up the pressure on the enemy. If they wouldn't respond to a threat, perhaps they would react better to something stronger. He raised the microphone again, and now he was smiling.

0021 hours Zulu (0021 hours Zone)
Intruder 507, Loki Flight
Over the Norwegian Sea

"All Lokis, all Lokis, stand by for new orders."

Bannon cocked his head as Magruder's voice came from the radio. Was *Jefferson* ordering a recall already? It was early for that, according to the mission timetable . . . unless something had gone seriously wrong.

"Loki Flight, primary target is now designated active. Repeat, active. Commence attack runs."

The words sent a thrill through Bannon. This was what he had been waiting for! He felt his grip on the yoke tightening. "You heard the man, Gordo. Time to send them a little something to remember us by!"

Quinn formed them up into two waves of four Intruders each, with the Hornets thrown out ahead in case any more interceptors tried to block the attack. Bannon was part of the second wave, holding back from the battle until the first four planes had taken their shot at the Soviet carrier.

"Tighten up your formation," he heard Quinn order as the Intruders dipped low over the ocean and started their run. "Watch those SAMs . . ."

"They've got a lock on me!" another pilot shouted.

"Climb! Climb! Drop some chaff and climb!"

The radio crackled once. Then Quinn announced somberly, "They got Hoops." That would be Lieutenant Commander Jack "Hoops" Wilson.

"Firing," another voice announced calmly. Seconds passed. "Shit! Defensive fire's too damned heavy!"

Then Quinn again, sounding disgusted. "Second wave, take your shots. We didn't even scratch 'em."

Bannon pushed the throttles ahead and swooped down, ready to start his attack.

0023 hours Zulu (0023 hours Zone)
Tomcat 203, Odin Flight
Over the Norwegian Sea

"Range?" Coyote demanded.

"One hundred fifty miles," John-Boy replied. "Still closing . . . one-thirty now."

Coyote flipped the selector switch to the Phoenix setting. "All right, Vipers, let's get some value for the taxpayers' dollars. Make every one count."

"Don't I always?" Batman interjected. Somebody else, probably Malibu, was chuckling.

"Minds on the job, boys," Coyote admonished. "Batman, you'll just have to pretend."

"One hundred ten miles," John-Boy announced. That was the maximum range of a Phoenix, but Coyote didn't want any slipups.

There were just four of them left, Coyote and Batman, and Sheridan and Lieutenant Joe Travers, running name

"Shorty." The other Tomcat had gone down during the brief struggle with the Sukhois, about the same time as Powers. Seven Phoenixes—all the reduced squadron had left—wouldn't account for all of the defenders by any means, but they would surely disrupt the Russians. And the Vipers still had a few Sidewinders and Sparrows ready for when they closed the range.

"Ninety-five miles, Coyote. I've got one in my sights."

He held his fire a few second longer, then hit the stud. "Fox three! Fox three!" The Phoenix dropped from its hard-point and ignited, driving across the darkening twilit sky.

The others joined the cry in chorus. "Fox three!"

0024 hours Zulu (0024 hours Zone)
Intruder 507, Loki Flight
Over the Norwegian Sea

Bannon squinted into the dim sky, picking out the shape of the lead Intruder up ahead. Hacker Hackenberg was flying her, having traded his LSO job for the pilot's seat tonight. The thought brought an unpleasant reminder of things best forgotten. The last time he'd spoken directly to Hacker, it had been over the radio, ending in shouts of "Wave off!"

Now Hackenberg's voice was tightly controlled. "Firing now," he said. One of the two Harpoons slung under his wings ignited and sped into the distance. A moment later a flash lit up the sky. "No good," Hacker said. "They're knocking everything down when we fire from out here. I'm getting closer . . . if I have to ram it right down their throats."

"Don't be an idiot, Lieutenant," Quinn broke in. "You won't have a chance dodging that crap. It's like the night sky over Baghdad in there!"

"We didn't lose that much over Baghdad!" Hacker said. His Intruder surged forward, jinking back and forth to dodge missile and cannon fire erupting from the decks of an Udaloy-class DDG.

Bannon let the range open. Hackenberg was right, they would never get a missile in past all those defenses unless they could close the range and let go at the last possible moment. But it took guts to drive in past all that SAM and Triple-A fire. He wasn't sure he was up to that. Not yet . . .

"Ready . . . ready . . ." a voice chanted. Bannon thought it must be Hacker's Bombardier/Navigator, but he wasn't sure.

"She's coming up!" Hackenberg shouted. "Coming up fast! This is it—"

Another flash, farther off this time, lit the sky like a flare. It was right on the line Hackenberg had taken.

"I'm hit!" Hacker said, as if to confirm his thoughts. "I'm hit. Can't hold her . . ."

Then came the brightest explosion of all.

0025 hours Zulu (0025 hours Zone)
Air Ops, Soviet Aircraft Carrier *Soyuz*
In the Norwegian Sea

The impact made Glushko stagger. "We've been hit!" someone shouted. Smoke was billowing from a bank of radar screens, acrid, tangy. Glushko bent over, coughing.

"Fucking Yankee rammed us," someone said, hacking on the smoke. "Crashed right on the flight deck."

The Air Operations center was buried deep in the shelter of the island, but even here they weren't safe from collateral damage from the fiery impact. The ventilator fans whirred, but they weren't adequate for the job.

Eyes tearing, Glushko pushed open the watertight hatch and staggered into the corridor outside. He was still coughing, and his lungs felt like they were on fire. Fresh air . . . he had to get some fresh air.

A tiny voice of conscience protested that he should stay at his post, help fight the fire. If the admiral found out he had deserted Air Ops, his career would be over.

Gasping, wheezing, he started up the nearest ladder. Glushko was past caring about career or duty anymore.

0026 hours Zulu (0026 hours Zone)
Intruder 507, Loki Flight
Over the Norwegian Sea

Even this far out, Bannon could see the flames rising from *Soyuz* where Hackenberg had plowed his Intruder into her flight deck. It brought back his own crash in a flood of images and memories, but Bannon clenched his teeth and denied them all.

Hacker had shown the way . . . and his sacrifice was sure to distract some of the defenders for a few moments at least. Now was the time to follow up that explosion with a missile attack that would compound the damage to the Russian carrier.

"Get ready, Gordo," he warned. "We're going in."

"We're what?" The B/N looked incredulous. "Didn't you see what just happened, man?"

"We're going in," he repeated. "Hold on!"

The Intruder plunged into the maelstrom.

Time seemed to move in slow motion as they weaved through the defensive fire, skimming almost at wavetop height. After his first protest Gordon was quiet, his face set in a grim frown of concentration as he prepared to hit the release button.

The Intruder seemed to stagger as something exploded just ahead, but Bannon fought her, kept the ungainly bomber on course. *We can make it,* he told himself. *We can make it . . .*

And for a disconcerting instant he thought he heard Jolly Green answering him. *You can do it, kid. Take her in . . . make me proud . . .*

"Firing!" Gordon shouted, triggering one of the Harpoons.

"Give 'em both barrels, Gordo!" Bannon urged, trying to hold the Intruder steady.

The second Harpoon followed smoothly in the trail of the first, and Bannon banked left, climbing, climbing . . .

"Radar lock! They've got lock!" Gordon's voice rose an octave. "Evasive—"

The SAM struck them amidships, and Intruder 507 vanished in a ball of raw heat and light.

0028 hours Zulu (0028 hours Zone)
Flight deck, Soviet Aircraft Carrier *Soyuz*
In the Norwegian Sea

With an effort Glushko threw open the hatch and emerged into the dim twilight of the deck, gulping down clean air. He leaned against the hatch frame, still coughing a little. Finally he straightened, chest heaving, and looked up.

The first Harpoon smashed into the side of the island directly above him. He never saw the second missile. Captain First Rank Fyodor Arturovich Glushko was already dead.

0030 hours Zulu (0030 hours Zone)
Fulcrum Leader, Escort Mission *Osa*
Near Cape Bremanger, Norway

Even over the static, Terekhov could hear the confusion that surrounded the hits on the carrier. It was plain that *Soyuz* had come under genuine attack this time. And he had turned his back on him in the crisis.

Sergei Sergeivich Terekhov raged inwardly. The Americans had caught him neatly between two equal threats, and tonight they had been the ones to earn the victory. Even his gesture in returning to the invasion fleet had gone wrong. He knew that now with the same certainty that he knew it would be almost impossible to evade the incoming wave of American AIM-54 missiles. They were the most dangerous weapon in the enemy arsenal, hard to evade, harder to stop, and though he went through all the motions Terekhov knew it would be useless in the long run.

Seconds before impact he pulled the ejection lever. The canopy blew clear, and a second later he had the sensation of having his seat slam upward into his spine.

Terekhov was well clear, his parachute deploying, when the Phoenix hit his MiG. In the end, it seemed, the Americans had retained the edge, in technology and in strategy. The *Rodina* could claim to be a superpower, but with inferior men and machines, that claim would continue to be a hollow one.

The Tomcats from Viper Squadron had already broken up the defending squadrons, first with long-range Phoenix missiles, then with shorter-range weapons, before Thor Group reached their target. Their attack had plainly rattled the Soviets, who put up no more than a token defense before fleeing northeast.

The Hornets made the first attack run, launching a wave of Harpoons toward the Soviet escorts. Lacking the central control of the American Aegis system, without an AEW aircraft to sort through threats, and hampered by jamming from the Prowler accompanying Thor Flight, the Russian ships were hard-pressed to defend themselves, much less extend their protection to the ill-assorted fleet of transports in their care.

That was the moment Commander Max Harrison had been waiting for. All ten S-3Bs had been pressed into service as attack planes under Magruder's plan. Harrison had opposed it from the start. A Viking was a sub-hunter, not a poor man's Intruder, and he hadn't believed it possible to open up the enemy defenses far enough for the slow, ill-armed Vikings to actually challenge the Soviet Red Banner Fleet.

But it fell into place as Magruder had predicted, and by the time the twenty Harpoons were on their way it was almost an anticlimax. The Vikings turned for home, but behind them rippling flashes of light marked the end of the Soviet amphibious force . . . and perhaps of Russian hopes for completing the conquest of Norway.

0105 hours Zulu (0105 hours Zone)
Flag Plot, Soviet Aircraft Carrier *Soyuz*
In the Norwegian Sea

Admiral Khenkin slumped in his seat, overwhelmed by the reports streaming in from all sides. *Soyuz* was on fire, with half her complement of aircraft destroyed or fled and most of the rest trapped useless on deck or in her hangars. The ship's captain had requested permission to turn him about and withdraw to the north, farther from the Americans, in case they planned to rearm and launch a follow-up strike.

And the invasion ships were scattered or destroyed. There would be no hope of supporting the paratroops at Brekke now, no hope of the quick breakthrough that would carry the Soviets to victory. The only good news in any of it was the recovery of some of the pilots lost off Cape Bremanger. Fortunately the captain of the *Kiev* had deployed helicopters to carry out search and rescue as soon as he had seen the air battle develop.

Young Terekhov was one of the survivors. Now that the incompetent Glushko was dead, Khenkin thought, there was no better officer in the air wing to take his place than Terekhov, though he lacked the seniority for such a position. Terekhov's ideas made up for his junior rank, though. If he had been in charge from the start, perhaps the Americans would never have found the opening they exploited.

Khenkin picked up an intercom handset. "Captain," he began reluctantly. "Khenkin. *Da.* Order the fleet to steer north. All ships will rendezvous around North Cape. And inform me when you have repairs in hand."

He set down the handset again and let out a sigh. It had been a costly defeat, and it might be costlier still for him once the Kremlin started seeking a scapegoat. But the war was not over yet, and if he remained in command he would not underestimate the Americans again.

0115 hours Zulu (0115 hours Zone)
CIC Air Ops module, U.S.S. *Thomas Jefferson*
In the Norwegian Sea

They were cheering in CIC again, this time in response to word passed from the Hawkeye that enemy ships had been detected turning north. The Soviets were in retreat . . . at least for the moment.

Commander Matthew Magruder sagged back in his chair, physically and emotionally drained. Now that the crisis was over, he wanted nothing more than a chance to seek out his quarters and sleep for a week or two.

But that wouldn't be possible yet, of course. The strike forces were only now beginning to return to *Jefferson*. They would need to be debriefed, and their planes would have to be checked over by the technical people in the Air Department. Combat Air Patrols would have to be organized, and perhaps a Tomcat carrying a TARPS pod would have to be sent to confirm the initial estimates of the damage to the Soviet fleet. Until the Russians had withdrawn further it would be necessary to maintain a high state of readiness, just in case they were still able to lash out against the American battle group.

And there would be the butcher's bill to deal with too. Some good men had died out there, including Bannon and the unfortunate Lieutenant Powers. Commander Henderson of the Fighting Hornets had been lost while keeping a pair of Sukhois from breaking through to the Intruders during their final attack run, and there were sure to be others Magruder hadn't heard about yet. They would have to rebuild the CVW-20 with reinforcements from the States before they could put up a fight again.

Yes, there was a lot to be done before he could rest. In some ways victory was harder to deal with than defeat. So much to do, so many details.

"CAG?" For a moment Tombstone didn't realize that the question was directed at him. He turned slowly to face Lieutenant Commander Owens. "CAG, the *Hopkins* is reporting a sonar contact about fifty kilometers west of us. They've got one helo down for repairs, and they're asking if we can loan them some support so they can prosecute the contact. What do you want me to tell them?"

As he straightened up to check the plotting board and see what assets he had available to support the frigate, Magruder allowed himself a smile. Once they had their planes on deck and the Maintenance boys had worked their arcane magic, maybe he could put together an Alpha Strike to help the Norwegians clean up the pocket around Brekke. Even with its reduced numbers, CVW-20 could still make a difference.

Tombstone was in the middle of giving Owens his orders when a sudden realization hit him, and he broke off and started to laugh. The Deputy CAG looked at Magruder like he was crazy, and Tombstone didn't know if Owens would understand the joke.

The fact was, he was actually looking forward to settling in to his new job. Hard as these past days had been, he'd carried it off. Maybe someday, he thought with another smile, he would be a real CAG, not just a substitute. And perhaps somewhere, in the Valhalla where Tomcat pilots gathered after the last shoot-down, Stinger Stramaglia would look down at Tombstone Magruder and be proud.

General Vladimir Nikolaivich Vorobyev watched as the
jackals gathered, and under a stony visage he had to fight
hard to keep from smiling. They were so predictable, these
politicians. Doctorov, the KGB plotter, was licking his
figurative lips as he contemplated the chance of eliminating
Vorobyev from the inner circle, while Comrade President
Ubarov vacillated between relief over the military's failure
and fear for what the future might bring. So very predictable . . . and so foolish to think that the wounded lion
could not hold off such a band of jackals.

"Obviously we must rethink our entire strategy," Foreign Minister Boltin was saying. "The West may yet be
inclined to let the whole question of war slide if we move
quickly to evacuate Norway and Finland. They did not
interfere in Iraqi affairs once they had achieved their stated
goal of liberating Kuwait, and the peace movement is still
strong. But delay would give them time to rally against us."

"We must not be stampeded in this," Doctorov countered. "Our esteemed colleague here has allowed his
vaunted military to set back our plans, but with a redirection
of leadership resources we may yet be able to salvage
something from this debacle." He favored Vorobyev with
an oily smile. "Don't you agree, Comrade General?"

Vorobyev matched his smile, enjoying the uncertainty
that spread across his face as the KGB man realized that the
crisis in Scandinavia hadn't shaken Vorobyev's composure.
"Yes, Comrade Doctorov, new leadership may well be
needed, and at the very highest levels. To retrieve our
position and carry through Rurik's Hammer successfully,

all elements of the national leadership must be working smoothly together, and not wasting time pursuing short-sighted political goals.''

He looked toward the double doors where Korotich was standing, the patient aide. Vorobyev gave a curt nod. Then Korotich threw open the doors.

The soldiers who filed into the room were elite Guardsmen, handpicked by Vorobyev for this assignment long before the developments in Scandinavia had taken their unexpected turn. His men had been well-briefed, and took up their positions ringing the conference room with smooth efficiency.

"On the other hand," Vorobyev continued calmly. "On the other hand, it may be no replacements at all need be made, once all are aware of the need for absolute military authority. I am sure all of you will be glad to cooperate in this effort?"

No one answered for long moments. Then Ubarov nodded. "Of course, Comrade General, of course. You are correct. We must have unity of purpose."

"If the general has plans to redeem our situation in Norway, I am sure we are all eager to hear them," Boltin added. The other politicians chimed in with their own platitudes.

All but Doctorov. He sat still, his eyes on Vorobyev. At last he nodded his head slowly, a gesture which was as much one of respect as it was of submission.

"Now we can get down to business, Comrades," Vorobyev said, his smile growing broader. "Let us see what we may do to turn this setback to our advantage."

EPILOGUE
Tuesday, 17 June 1997

Tombstone Magruder took down the picture of Stramaglia and his son and put it into the box he'd been using to clear out the dead man's belongings. It was the first time since CAG's death that he'd had any time at all to take care of personal effects, and now that Admiral Tarrant had confirmed that Magruder was staying on as CAG, it was time to bury the ghosts once and for all and put his own stamp on the Air Wing.

It didn't promise to be an easy job, filling Stramaglia's shoes permanently. The Soviet fleet had withdrawn with a damaged carrier, a pair of destroyers limping from lucky hits by attacking Hornets, and a few battered troopships that had survived their Harpoon strikes, but the damage actually inflicted on their force had been minor. Magruder's plan had called for concentrating on the transports, but the corollary to that was the basic fact that the striking power of the Soviet fleet was undiminished. It was doubtful that the Soviets would mount another flanking naval landing, but they could still dominate the Norwegian Sea anytime they wanted.

Their land-based and long-range air units were intact too, and that posed a second potent threat to *Jefferson* and her battle group. By creating multiple distractions, the Americans had managed to even out the inequities once, but they couldn't count on doing it again. And the cost of the Americans' success had been almost prohibitive. *Galveston* had eluded pursuit and reported in, but *Bangor* had been lost in the strike against Orland, and that was a Pyrrhic victory at best. And the RNAF planes lost in the demonstration against Oslo would be sorely missed when the stalled campaign lurched back into action.

That would come soon enough. The Norwegians were concentrating reserves to eliminate the airhead at Brekke, but the rest of the Soviet forces were in the same positions as before the Alpha Strike, still poised to drive on Bergen. It might not be a blitzkrieg, but eventually sheer weight of numbers would overpower Lindstrom's army.

Indeed, the defeat of the flanking movement had spurred new efforts by the Soviet military. In the morning intelligence report, Commander Lee had pointed to several signs that fresh forces, land, sea, and air, were mustering in the Baltic, and there was more activity around Murmansk as well. Plainly one lost battle was not going to deter them from continuing their campaign of conquest, and as long as it went on the *Thomas Jefferson* was liable to be at the center of the action.

But the news wasn't all discouraging. Good things had come of the Battle of Cape Bremanger too. Bare hours after the Soviet defeat, Britain's Labour Party had lost a vote of No Confidence in Parliament and resigned. Until elections were held, the Conservatives had been asked to form a caretaker government that would take a harder line against the Soviets under an experienced and uncompromising Prime Minister who could be counted on to support America's interests. Though it would take time to organize the new British government, military forces were already preparing to join in the effort to support Free Norway.

And there was an American Task Force on the way as well. Now that Lindstrom's hold on Bergen had been shored up for a while longer, America had a focal point for arms, men, and other assistance to pour into the embattled country. *Jefferson* still faced the Russian threat by herself for now, but soon she would not be alone any more.

Yes, the cost had been high. *Gridley* and *Bangor* lost . . . Powers and Bannon and Trapper Martin and the other pilots who had died fighting in *Jefferson*'s private, remote little war. And Stramaglia. But they had all died making sure that the Russians would not turn Norway into another occupied Kuwait. Now all that remained was to turn the respite they had won into final victory.

He turned back toward the desk and noticed the mug with Stramaglia's cigars there. Magruder picked it up, but stopped before putting it into the box. Stramaglia's cigars had been the stuff of legend at Top Gun and afterward. Like the man himself, somehow bigger than life.

Back at Miramar Magruder had once made the mistake of protesting that the mock fights weren't fair. Even though Top Gun used aggressor aircraft that matched their Soviet counterparts, the teachers didn't fly using Russian tactics or doctrine. It had been bad enough questioning Top Gun policy, but on top of that Magruder had made the mistake of voicing his opinion in front of Stramaglia, who had promptly scheduled an extra exercise for the day in which the instructors did adhere to Soviet fighter tactics . . . and still beat the students handily. "Doctrine's only as bad as the pilots who are following it," Stramaglia had said afterward, stabbing at Tombstone's chest with the inevitable unlit cigar. "If you get yourself beat playing by the rules, how do you expect to do when the enemy decides not to play fair?"

After the desperate fighting off of the Norwegian coast, Magruder thought he finally understood just what his old teacher had been driving at.

Smiling, he put the mug and the cigars back on the desk. They could be a reminder to everyone who saw them to always expect the unexpected . . . and to never play by the rules.